CW01497684

RHYTHM
&
RHYME

WYNTER WILD 3

Sara Creasy

Content warnings

The Wynter Wild series as a whole includes or refers to:

alcoholism
animal death
child abuse, neglect, death
domestic violence
drug use
incest
mental health issues (anxiety, grief, self-harm)
profanity
religious trauma
sexual abuse
sexual activity and references
suicide
violence

Rhythm and Rhyme
by Sara Creasy
www.saracreasy.com
© 2019, 2024 Sara Creasy

ISBN: 978-1-0898-4389-4

All rights reserved. No part of this book may be reproduced or transmitted in any form without prior permission in writing from the publisher, except as permitted under US copyright law.
For permissions contact: saracreasy@gmail.com

The characters and events in this book are fictitious and any resemblance to real persons, living or dead, is purely coincidental.

Cover image by Midjourney. Cover design by S. Creasy.

Dedication

For Donna
and the guy on the train

Family tree

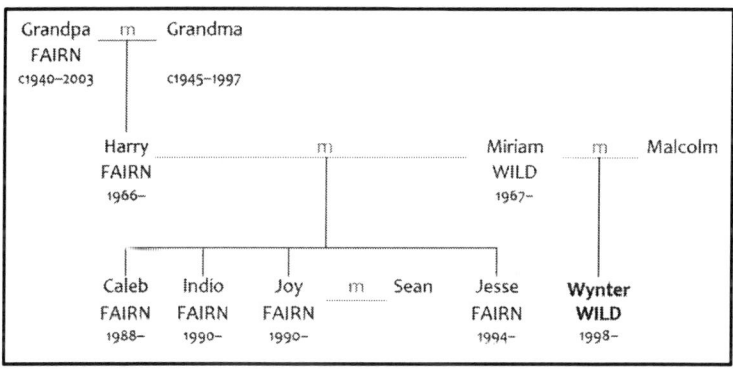

Wynter's family tree at the start of this book.

The Wynter Wild Series

The Fairn Boys Series

Sign up

to my newsletter for updates and a free story:
saracreasy.com

Song lyrics

This edition includes song lyrics. Wondering what the songs sound like? Visit the playlist on YouTube: saracreasy.com/WWsongs

Maps

To help orientate yourself in Wynter's world, visit my website for maps showing the places mentioned in the books: saracreasy.com/WWmaps

Sentimental

Jesse poured a tall glass of cran-apple juice at the breakfast bar.

"You feel nauseated because your blood sugar was up last night, and now it's crashed," he explained as Wynter took a seat. "I'm gonna buy a whole roast chicken today and boil up its bones to make real broth. Next week, when you're eating normally again, we'll practice our chef skills and make something different every night."

Wynter stifled a yawn and pulled her robe tightly around her frail body. "We need to learn to make lasagne for Caleb."

"And stir-fry pork. *Anything* pork, really."

Talking about food was not helping with Wynter's nausea. She'd had nothing but water for eight days, other than a few sport drinks and a little juice last night.

Caleb came into the kitchen in his dark blue Coastie work uniform. She'd hoped he would stay home with her for even one day. That was an unfair expectation – Jesse was here, after all. While Wynter's life was about to change dramatically, with a new foster home on the horizon and high school starting in September, Caleb had the same commitments as always and a mortgage to pay.

He threw her a concerned look as he made coffee. She returned it with a tentative smile, unsure of his mood.

"Jesse," he said, "put your drum stool in the bath. Wynter, you need to sit when you take a shower – just for a couple days. I don't want you falling in there."

Jesse balked. "That's not gonna do it any good, getting it wet."

Caleb was unmoved. "Put a garbage bag over it."

"I don't feel dizzy anymore," Wynter said as Jesse launched into another protest at the same time. "I'll be okay in the shower. I don't think—"

"Guys." Caleb silenced them with a word and a look. "Jesse, you can deal with the food. That's fine, you've read up on it, so you're in charge of health. I'm in charge of safety. Go fetch the stool."

Jesse left to obey.

"They're sending a nurse at eleven to check up on you," Caleb told Wynter. "It'll be someone different, someone local."

"I'm alright now. I'm drinking the juice and I'm gonna eat today."

He leaned on the counter, opposite where Wynter sat. "Can I talk about this with you? You won't put your hands over your ears again?"

Wynter drew a breath and nodded for him to continue.

"You need to promise me you'll never do that again."

One last flash of stubbornness made her test him. "Or what?"

"I'm not giving you an ultimatum, Wynter. I just need to hear it."

"I don't have any *plans* to do it again," she said truthfully.

He raised an eyebrow, waiting for what he'd asked for.

"I promise I won't do it again."

"Or anything like it?"

"Or anything like it."

He closed his hands over hers and smiled. He looked so tired. "Thank you. Now, you concentrate on getting stronger. Bea's coming over when she finishes work."

"I thought Bea doesn't like me."

"Of course she likes you."

"I heard her say I was stroppy. I had to look it up."

"Uh-huh." He looked confused. "Honestly, I don't remember her saying that. What does it mean?"

"It means *difficult*. That day I burned the dinner and said something that made Natalie walk out on Jesse, and then Bea left early, too."

"That was months ago, hun. Bea likes everyone."

Jesse talked the nurse's ear off, assuring her that he had Wynter's recuperation under scientific control. The nurse weighed her and made a list of what she'd eaten, and told Jesse to keep writing it all down.

Wynter was glad when she'd gone. She fetched her laptop and notebooks and brought them into the dining room, where Jesse was studying the chess game he and Caleb were in the middle of.

"Why were you so jumpy around her?" he said. "She's here to help you."

"I hate it when strangers come into the house. Will you stay when Bea comes over?"

"Bea's not a stranger."

"I don't really know her."

"Here's your chance to get to know her better. I'll be at the grocery store and I have four other things to do before that."

Wynter slumped in her chair. Carrying the laptop that short distance through the house was enough to make her arms ache. "How do you tell if someone likes you?"

"She likes you just fine."

"But how do you tell? I'm not good at telling. I gave up trying to figure out if the girls at school liked me. Hunter acted as if he liked me, but he sure didn't respect me and he said mean things behind my back to make his friends laugh. I still don't know if Rosa ever liked me or just thought I was an interesting case study."

"You're never gonna see your *former* foster mother or any of those kids again, so it doesn't matter."

"That doesn't help me, Jesse. I always knew *you* liked me, and Caleb and Indio, so I started to think siblings like each other, but plenty of kids at school have siblings they loathe."

Jesse sat beside her, tapping his pen against the table top, looking at her like he was expecting more.

"What?" she said.

"You left someone out."

She sucked on her lower lip. "I don't know if Joy likes me. Where is she? She left the courthouse after the hearing without talking to me."

"She's still on that retreat. When she gets back, we'll see if she's interested in... y'know, any of us. Did Caleb give you that picture yet?"

"What picture?"

"The photo from the file of stuff she gave him at the courthouse."

"A photo... of me?"

"Yes, a baby photo."

"There aren't any photos of me." *None.* None at all from her entire childhood at the ashram.

"Don't know why he hasn't shown you," Jesse muttered. "It's part of Joy's affidavit about your birth."

"Show me."

Jesse hesitated. "It's in there." He indicated the filing cabinet next to the buffet. "All our important paperwork is in there. How about *you* fetch it, so I don't get in trouble for showing it to you. The key's in the vase."

"Why would you get in trouble?" Wynter asked as she retrieved the key from the ceramic vase on the mantelpiece.

"I don't know. Just seems odd he hasn't shown you."

The folder from Joy was at the front of the filing cabinet, and the first thing inside the folder was a small rectangular photograph of a baby — a close-up of the head and shoulders, a fuzz of hair, pink lips, blotchy skin, closed eyes, and a tiny fist pressed to the cheek. On the strip across the bottom, Wynter's name and birthdate were written in fading ink, in childish handwriting.

She took the picture over to Jesse. "I never saw anyone at the ashram with a camera."

"This is from an instant camera. That's why it has the white border and backing sheet. It's meant to be a square. Joy said she cut herself out of the picture, years ago." He pointed out the edge of a child's hand in the lower corner. Joy would've been seven when the picture was taken.

Wynter examined the baby, trying to form a connection with it. At the ashram she often felt like she didn't exist, that no one cared or even really saw her. But here was proof she was real, a human being who started life as a tiny person with a name and a birthday and a big sister.

"What am I supposed to do with it?"

"Whatever you want."

"I guess it belongs in the file."

Jesse gave her an exasperated look. "Seriously? No, Wyn, you put it in an album. You scan it to make sure we always have a copy. That's the *only* photo of you before January of this year. It's important."

"Since when did you become sentimental?"

"Give it to me. I'll keep it," he snapped, holding out his hand.

"Why would you want a baby photo of me?"

"Because I was supposed to be there. Or you were supposed to be here. There should be a thousand photos of you and me, together, as babies and as children, and there never will be. Maybe, when it comes to you, I *am* sentimental. Okay with you?"

She mouthed *Okay*, taken aback by his tone. He recovered quickly, and took another look before tucking the photo into one of the books on the table.

"You were cute, as babies go," he said with a shrug.

"Not as cute as you were."

"True. True."

Beatrice arrived with Jilly, and Jesse left on his dirt bike to run his errands and buy the roast chicken he'd been talking about all morning. Wynter watched, fascinated, as Bea unpacked the bags she'd brought with her. A toddler seemed to need an awful lot of *stuff* for a two-hour visit — one huge bag of toys, another huge bag of clothes and blankets and bottles and snacks, and a third smaller bag that unfolded into a change mat, with pockets for diapers and wipes and powder and cream.

"Jilly's second birthday party is this Saturday," Bea said, helping her little girl stack colored cubes into a tower. "Would you like to come along with Caleb?"

"Okay. Thank you." Maybe Bea liked her, after all.

When Bea went to make herself coffee in the kitchen, Wynter attempted to play with Jilly. Bea often used a silly voice to talk to her, which Wynter couldn't do. She talked to Jilly in a regular voice about the cubes and showed her how to make a repeating pattern of colors. Jilly watched her attentively with those big brown eyes and Wynter let her have a go. When she did it wrong, Wynter dismantled the tower to start again. Jilly shrieked and started crying.

Wynter sat back on her heels. Bea dashed out of the kitchen, coffee filter in hand.

"What happened?"

"I didn't hit her."

That made Bea look at her like she *had* hit her. She went to console Jilly.

"I was showing her how to do it properly."

"It's a toy, Wynter. There's no proper way."

"The tub says, *How many patterns can you make?* I was showing her a pattern." Wynter wished Jesse was home. He'd back her up on this, for sure.

"Never mind. I expect she's a bit cranky because she's hungry. Jesse told me to make sure you finish that vegetable juice this hour. Why don't you do that, and I'll get Jilly a snack."

Bea took Jilly into the kitchen and balanced her on her hip while she finished making coffee, sliced an apple, hulled three strawberries, spread butter onto bread and cut them into fingers — all with only one hand. Wynter was good with a knife and could've done what Bea just did, baby and all. The rest of motherhood — the silly talk, the toys, and knowing whether your child was hungry or just being *stroppy* — she wasn't sure about that.

And what did you do when your child misbehaved? Wynter knew several ways to deal with misbehaving children. She couldn't imagine Bea doing any of them.

Bea clipped a special little chair to the countertop, strapped Jilly in, and gave her the food in a plastic dish.

"What do you do when she's naughty?" Wynter said.

"She's not even two. She can't really be naughty. She doesn't understand."

"What about when she's older?"

"What do you mean?"

"Say, when she's older, she steals food from the kitchen. Something she wasn't allowed to eat. What would you do?"

Bea looked uncomfortable. "Are you asking me about punishments?"

"Yes. I don't know what a normal punishment would be."

"If you'd like to talk about something that happened to you, Wynter, I'm here to listen. Caleb told me you might want to talk—"

"He meant we should talk about boys and sex, or makeup or periods or shopping."

"Of course. But, anything at all. I'll try to help."

"It would help if you'd tell me what the punishment would be if Jilly stole food she wasn't supposed to have. Would you not give her any dinner?"

"That would depend on exactly what... on what she..." Bea frowned and put her hand on Jilly's back, as if Jilly needed comforting — which she didn't. Jilly was perfectly happy with her strawberries.

"Would you stop feeding her for a while?" Wynter said. "How many meals should she skip?"

Bea looked like she was going to cry. Wynter wasn't sure what to do.

"You told me we could talk about anything at all," Wynter said, to break the horrible silence.

"I don't like these questions. I would never do anything to hurt Jilly."

"Then how will she learn what's right and wrong?"

"There are other ways to teach a child. I would never—"

The front door clicked open and Bea startled. Jesse came into the kitchen with his backpack. He looked from Bea to Wynter and stopped in his tracks.

"What's going on?"

"Nothing," Bea said, with an awkward little twist of her shoulders.

"Jeth! Jeth!" Jilly said.

Jesse put the backpack of groceries on the counter and ruffled Jilly's hair. He studied them each in turn. "Wyn, did you finish that juice?"

"Yes."

"Bea, you brought strawberries! Can I steal a few?"

"I don't know, Jess. Stealing food is wrong." Bea's voice had a strange wobble to it. "I might have to punish you."

He chuckled, then stopped himself, realizing he'd lost half the joke somewhere. Wynter had no idea how to fix things.

"Okay..." Jesse threw his hands up. "Ladies, I don't know what I just walked into, but I'm gonna carve up this bird. We can make chicken salad when it's cold, although I don't think you can handle mayo yet, Wyn, so we'll do that tomorrow. We'll boil the bones for soup tonight. I've never made chicken soup from scratch. Supposed to be good for the soul."

"You don't believe in souls," Wynter said, because it was the most obvious thing to say.

"Sure I do. I just define the word differently."

Wynter thought that was cheating. She didn't want to put Jesse on the spot in front of Bea, so she stayed silent.

"Cayrub?" Jilly said.

"Not today," Bea told her daughter.

Bea looked like she wanted to leave *now*. Wynter tried to think of some questions about boys and sex she could ask her. The truth was, she'd rather talk to Jesse about that. Perhaps makeup? That had to be a safe subject, but she didn't care to know anything about makeup. If she tried wearing it, Caleb wouldn't like it and Jesse would laugh at her.

Jesse gave her the chicken legs and wings to clean the bones with a fork. Handling the greasy meat made her feel sick again. She kept at it. Jesse and Bea talked over her head. Bea explained her parents' complicated vacation plans, which were surely of no interest to Jesse, and he skillfully segued into convincing her to watch *Futurama*. They made jokes at Caleb's expense — which Wynter would never have thought to do. Clearly, Bea liked Jesse, and so did Jilly. He had no trouble making that little girl giggle. If Caleb and Bea married, Bea and Jilly would fit in nicely with this family — this family *before* Wynter had come along.

Wynter scraped at a chicken bone and thought about Caleb in his suit at the courthouse, and what the wedding photos would look like. Jilly would wear a frilly pink dress with a sash, her sparse hair tied into bunches. She'd grow up with an amazing dad who had decided to love her, a mother who didn't punish her for stealing food, one uncle to teach her about dinosaurs and supernovas and video games, and another to teach her music and drawing.

Picture-perfect. Wynter was happy for them. She couldn't figure out where to put herself in the picture.

"Wyn, that's enough," Jesse said, taking the fork out of her hand.

She dropped the clean bone in the soup pot. Jesse looked like he wanted to ask her a dozen questions. He covered the bones with water and put the pot on the stove.

Bea took Jilly outside to play.

"I don't understand her," Wynter said. "I don't understand being a parent."

"You don't need to, not yet."

"How do you know if you're doing it right?"

"I guess you don't. There's no rule book."

"Caleb has rules."

Jesse sighed. "Yeah. I think that started as an emergency measure. Good parents instill good behavior into you from a young age — mostly by example, I guess. We didn't really have that. When Caleb took over from our dad, he had to make it clear so we knew where we stood. He was just a kid himself. He laid down the law to keep control of us, so he could handle everything else that needed to be done."

"If he didn't hit you, how did he make you do what he wanted?"

"You know how he is. He's always been like that. And it didn't work so well on Indio. Still worked a hundred times better than anything Harry tried."

"Do you think Jilly will just do what Bea tells her, as she gets older?"

"I doubt it. Bea doesn't have Caleb's mojo."

"I asked her how she would punish Jilly, and she got upset. I think she thinks I would hurt Jilly."

Jesse put down the knife he was using to cut up the chicken meat. "We all know they hurt you at the ashram in Arizona, Wyn. Maybe you have a screwed-up idea of how kids should be treated. Maybe that's why she's uncomfortable talking about it." His voice turned hard with frustration. "If you would *tell* us, maybe we could... adjust your worldview."

"You just cried for a week because I chose to hurt *myself*, and it was for a good reason. You don't want to hear how someone else hurt me for no reason at all."

"Can you give me a chance, please? You were so thin when you showed up on our doorstep. They punished you by not feeding you, right? I know that happened."

"Parents do that here on the outside, too. I've heard kids at school say they were sent to bed without dinner."

"One meal, sure. How many meals did you skip?"

"Sometimes it was a day or two. One time it was longer."

"How do you stop a kid from eating for *days*?"

"You lock her in a room."

Jesse went pale. She *knew* that would happen and now she was angry with him for making her talk. She was angry enough to make him cry.

"The worst part wasn't the hunger. The worst part was the fear they'd forgotten about her in that locked room. And when they did those other things, the worst part wasn't the pain, it was the fear they'd forgotten she would break if they didn't stop."

It didn't feel good, making Jesse cry.

Boxed In

"This is ludicrous," Caleb said.

He and Wynter stood together inside the doorway of the toy store, stunned. Spread before them were endless aisles and carousels stacked with unidentifiable boxes and round-eyed plush toys. Wynter followed his gaze upward to a huge cartoon car model suspended from the ceiling.

"Is that something you can buy?" she asked.

"I think it's a promotion for those tiny toy cars."

"Why would they make a huge car to sell tiny cars?"

He shrugged, squinting at the ropes and hooks. "Sure hope whoever hung that knew what they were doing." It was right over the busy checkout counters.

"Where should we start?" Wynter said. "This is my first time inside a toy store."

"Same here."

"I don't know what Jilly wants."

"She's two. She doesn't know, either. We'll figure it out together."

"What did you get her?"

"Bea said she wrapped something from me. I don't know what."

Wynter was aghast. "How can you give a gift and not know what it is?"

"I don't do gifts. Hence our problems here today."

It was Saturday, and Wynter had been eating normally again for three days — small portions, a bit of everything, five times a day — so, Caleb told her she could come with him to Jilly's birthday party. Although she tired at unpredictable moments, the purple rings under her eyes had faded and her cheeks had some color. She was acting like herself again. He, on the other hand, still felt traumatized over what she'd felt driven to do to herself.

They wandered around aimlessly, confused and overwhelmed. Caleb asked an assistant where they could find something for a two-year-old, and the guy directed them to the baby aisles. On the way there, Caleb picked a teddy bear off the shelf.

"Here you go."

Wynter shuddered and shook her head. "Bea says Jilly is creative. We could get some crayons, maybe?"

"Okay. Keep in mind all parents say their kids are creative."

As they searched for crayons, Wynter gave him a sidelong look and said, "Jesse showed me that baby pic from Joy."

"I see," he said warily.

"He seemed to think it was important. You never showed it to me."

"I've had other things on my mind this past week-and-a-half, hun." *Other things* being her hunger strike.

"Still, the last few days when I've been home, you could've—"

"I was going to show you." Caleb stopped in front of the art supplies and studied the bottom shelf, unable to meet her eye. Which was ridiculous. This was Wynter, who trusted him completely. He didn't trust *himself*, didn't trust his own judgment when it came to talking about her past when *she* wouldn't talk about it. "I wasn't sure how you'd react," he said truthfully.

"I think Jesse wasn't sure, either. He still showed me."

"Well, Jesse... Jesse likes to put it all out there and then sit back with a big tub of popcorn."

Her expression showed she had no idea what he meant.

"I reacted just fine, by the way," she said reassuringly. "It's just any old baby. Might not even be me — who would know?"

"She told me someone at the ashram sent it to her. Is that her handwriting on it?"

"Yes, when she was younger," Wynter conceded.

"It's you, hun. I'm no expert on babies but it looks like Indio's baby pics, and even a bit like Jesse."

"Not like you?"

"Hmm, be thankful you didn't look like me. I was so serious and grumpy as a baby."

"Nothing at all like you are now, then."

He checked her for signs of sarcasm. She looked up at him, straight in the eye, and managed to hold it three seconds before giggling. He put his arm around her and she turned against him for a proper hug, first one in what seemed like ages.

They explored their crayon options. Crayons, it turned out, were not as simple as they'd been in his day. They came in all shapes and sizes, round or triangular or pebble-shaped "for little hands", metallic and glitter, erasable and scented. Some came with coloring books. Some came in complete "artist" kits with felt tip pens and pastels and stencils and stickers. They stared at the display, dumbfounded.

"She probably already has crayons," Wynter said, and they moved on.

They passed a rack of drink bottles — hundreds of the brightly colored things with names on them. Wynter loved them. They searched in vain for *Jilly*.

"They don't even have Joy or Jesse," Wynter said. "Aren't those common names?"

"Maybe not for today's two-year-olds."

Wynter looked through the bottles again. "Yours is the only name from our family they have."

"Yeah, you're never gonna find Wynter or Indio on anything personalized, I'm afraid."

"Buy this." She pushed a green-and-blue *Caleb* bottle against his chest. "I read you're supposed to drink eight glasses of water a day, although Jesse says there's no scientific evidence for it. Still, he says water is brain food. You can keep it on your desk at work."

"I could. I'm not going to," he said with a laugh, putting the bottle back. "Let's hurry or we'll be late for the party."

"This!" Wynter stopped suddenly and took a big box down. "Look, you push these gears into the base, in any design you like, and when you turn the handle it makes them all move."

"Very educational."

"Jesse asked to put his name on the gift, once he's approved it, and this is exactly what he'd choose." Jesse had been unable to get out of his shift at the mini-golf. "Is it age-appropriate?"

They puzzled over the box for a minute, finally figuring out the "18m+" in the corner meant it was suitable. Wynter snapped a photo of the box and sent it to Jesse.

> Buy an extra one for me!

"Is he serious?" she asked Caleb, showing the message.

"Probably. We're not buying two. What else do we need? Gift wrap?"

"And tape, a rosette, and a gift tag."

"You sure about all that?"

She grinned. "I know these things because I occasionally watch TV. Also, a gift bag and tissue paper and that shiny ribbon you curl with scissors."

"Let's restrict ourselves to the bare essentials."

He watched her choose a square of gift wrap from the enormous selection available. A wave of sadness hit him. While Jesse lamented all the things he wouldn't be able to teach her because she'd be once again living in someone else's house soon, Caleb was sorry he wouldn't be able to simply observe her as she absorbed all these new experiences. She would learn a thousand new things a day, tiny insignificant things he'd never know about.

She wrapped the gift on her lap as he drove to Renton. He complimented her on doing a good job.

"You think so? I never wrapped a gift with sticky tape before."

"You've discovered a new talent today."

"Gift wrapping is a talent?"

"Sure. You're good with your hands. Meticulous and neat."

"Maybe all those bracelets I braided, all those mandalas I wove, prepared me for this moment," she joked.

Caleb was glad she could occasionally speak lightly about her past, however obtusely. Meanwhile, since the day he'd met her and seen the bones sticking out of her shoulders, he'd agonized over the unspecified abuse they all knew she'd suffered, and which she refused to divulge.

Bea's parents' house and garden overflowed with guests. He'd been here two evenings already this past week, helping with the complex and frankly bizarre preparations. Half a dozen toddlers, parents, neighbors, relatives with food allergies, banners and loot bags and fruit skewers, balloons and a bouncy castle... It was out of control. And all the while, her parents fussed over him like... well, like their son-in-law. Jilly's father had been a manipulative jerk, by all accounts, so anyone would've been an improvement for their daughter. Bea's parents had latched on to him in a way he should've welcomed because he loved Bea and because he had no decent parents of his own.

This morning, her dad waylaid him in the kitchen to talk politics. Through the doorway, Wynter sat in the corner with a couple of the young mothers. She answered their questions shyly, discomfort radiating off her.

Caleb excused himself and went to rescue her.

"You want something to drink?" he said, crouching by her chair. Jilly saw him and ran over, throwing herself on him as she always did when he went low.

"Oh, so cute," one of the mothers said. "She just loves you."

Caleb saw wedding bells in the woman's eyes, as with Bea's parents. There was not-so-subtle pressure from every direction, even from himself. Yet he felt further from marriage than he had last Christmas when Bea had wanted to move in with him, or in February when he'd almost popped the question, thinking Wynter was leaving.

Caleb took Wynter outside to the food table, to give her a break from the women.

"Hasn't he done a lovely job with the streamers?" Bea said, seeing them picking at the sandwiches. "Everyone's saying it looks amazing.

Wynter, my cousin's organizing the children's games. Do you think you could help?"

Wynter gave Caleb a dubious look. He responded with an encouraging smile, and she left.

"Can we talk for a minute?" Bea took his hand and they went around the back of the bouncy castle, out of sight of the guests. "You've been looking a bit shell-shocked, and it's breaking my heart. You know how sorry I am about the custody decision. I know how much it meant to Wynter."

"And to me."

"I didn't want to confuse the issue before. Now she won't be living with you after all, maybe we could talk again about moving in together?" She clasped both hands around his, her smile belying the uncertainty in her tone. "This seems like the perfect time. A fresh start for everyone."

He ached to hear her dismiss Wynter as an inconvenience. He'd imagined Bea becoming the sister Wynter didn't have, the sister Joy should've been. The truth was Bea had her own vision for the future and Wynter was a far smaller part of it than he'd hoped. For the first eight months of their relationship, Caleb had devoted himself to her. For the last eight months of it, his attention had been divided and Bea was still adjusting.

"What about Jesse?" he managed to say.

"He's how old now? Twenty? Shouldn't he move into dorms for his sophomore year? I thought that was the plan."

"He's nineteen. And no, we hadn't planned on him leaving home. It's cheap and convenient for him to live with me. I intend to get a foster parent license, Bea. I told you that. Wynter will come live with me eventually."

Bea drew back her hands. In less than a minute she was going to be crying. "Who puts a sibling before the person they're in love with?"

"You've always put Jilly first, and that's how it should be."

"That's different. She's *my child*."

Caleb didn't say the obvious, because if Bea couldn't see it she certainly wouldn't accept being told. Wynter had been *his* since the day he took her frozen hands in his and she gave her name, Wild, the same as his mother's.

"She needs me." That was all he could think of to say. "For now, and for a while longer, she needs me."

"That's not fair to me."

"I know. I'm sorry."

"It's just that I love you, and Jilly loves you, and everything was perfect. Everything was on track until... And now I'm so scared we won't be together for years."

"We *are* together. What do you mean?"

"I mean *alone* together. If you go ahead with this foster parent idea... That's almost three more years before you're all mine. I can't even imagine waiting that long."

"Wynter has to be my priority."

"And I'm not?"

"You both are, that's what I meant to say. I can take care of both of you, and Jilly too, and Jesse for as long as necessary."

"I don't want to share you." The tears welled up.

He rubbed her arm. "Bea, not here. Don't get upset today. We can talk about this later."

"What is there to talk about? What will change tomorrow? My dad found us this perfect little duplex near the base. He says he'll help us with the down payment."

"Jesus, Bea, now you're talking about buying a house together?"

"I thought you were close. Close to making a real commitment. Everything was going so perfectly."

She didn't know how close to the truth she was. A few months ago, he'd been thirty minutes away from asking her...

"Then let's keep it perfect," he said. "Just keep things as they are."

She shook her head, turning away to wipe her face with her sleeve. She walked back to her guests with a forced cheerfulness in her voice as she called encouragement to a small boy trying to hit his teenage brother with a water balloon.

Caleb was in no mood to join the festivities. He slipped out the side gate and sat on the hood of his truck in the driveway. Two cars blocked his exit. No escape. He heard them singing Happy Birthday and gritted his teeth over a memory from Jesse's sixth birthday party, where Harry had gotten drunk and sung that tune with a bottle in his hand, spilling beer on the cake so they couldn't eat it. That must've been one of the last family birthdays they'd made the effort to celebrate.

Wynter came out and walked over to the truck, concerned to see him sulking. He *never* sulked. What was the matter with him?

"Did you want to go home?" she said.

"No, hun, we can stay a bit. Unless you're ready to go."

"I'm ready. Why were you fighting?"

"We were discussing, not fighting. Bea's a little further along in our relationship than I am."

"Do you love her?"

"Very much." His chest was so tight, it hurt to say the words.

"If you married her, I could be like an older sister to Jilly."

He didn't want to tell her Bea didn't want her to live with them. "You could. You'd be great."

"I think I'd rather be a big sister than a mom. I'd be terrible at being a mother."

"God, Wynter, that's not true. Why would you say that?"

"I don't know what mothers are supposed to do."

"There's a house full of them right there. Go observe, take notes on a napkin."

"It's the responsibility part of it. I could be a sister — babysit her, walk her to school, take her shopping. But if I had a baby of my own, it'd be all my responsibility, all the time." She glanced at the house with a wistful look. "Babies just love their mothers, don't they? They don't know how *not* to. What if I didn't love it back? What if it wasn't enough for me, and I decided the responsibility wasn't worth it?"

"You're not like our mother, hun."

"I might be. I think my mother piece is missing. I don't even know how to play with Jilly. I made her cry, by mistake. I didn't know how to help those kids play their silly games. I don't know those games." Her voice quivered with panic.

Bea came out on the porch. "Cake, guys?" She was in a snit, and gave him and Wynter a disapproving look. Caleb wanted to get home. This was the wrong time and place to sort things out with Bea.

"We need to go," he called back. "Can you find out whose cars these are? I'm boxed in."

Bea gave a tight nod and went back into the house.

"Are you two gonna be okay?" Wynter said.

"Of course."

Maybe not.

A Good Start

Despite all the sibling drama, Indio was on a high. A natural high, for once. He'd had one hell of a fantastic summer touring the country with dedicated musicians. With the after-tour parties done, he still had a month of freedom before the new semester at Portland State. And he had a healthy bank balance — healthy by his standards, anyway.

On Monday, he drove home to return the Caprice, which he'd borrowed to catch up with his bandmates after his detour to visit Wynter during her... what should they call it? Her *protest*.

Only Jesse was home, concocting a pungent marinade for the lunch menu. Caleb was working and Wynter had gone with someone from Social Services to meet her new foster parents.

"*Potential* foster parents," Jesse said, carrying his tray of chicken outside to the grill. "That's what her caseworker called them. They don't have to take her. They're in *Enumclaw*. That's as far south as you can go and still be in King County."

"It's a lot closer than before. What is *this*?" Indio picked a hunk of pale, gnarled... *something*... off the tray.

"That's ginger root."

"You're kidding. This is what ginger looks like?"

"Yeah, I freaked out, too. I always thought ginger was, y'know, gingerbread. Never thought about where it came from. Ugliest edible item in the world. It's going in my lemon ginger chicken and it's gonna be delicious. Caleb's miserable, by the way." Jesse drew breath and opened up the grill. "He and Bea are falling apart. Don't mention it in front of Wynter. She knows something's up and she's gonna blame herself."

"What is up, exactly?"

"He came home from Jilly's party the other day looking like he'd been to a funeral. I don't think they're gonna make it — and the thing is, it *is* because of Wynter. It's not her fault, but she's the reason. Caleb is always gonna put Wynter first. Maybe it shouldn't be that way, but it is."

"She won't need him forever."

"How long, though? How long until she's ready for the world? Sometimes she seems... ancient, somehow, but she's not. She's so far behind and she needs protection."

"I think you're overstating—"

"She doesn't know how to *be* with anyone. She says the wrong thing and they think she's weird."

"She's not weird."

"I know that! But *people* think she's weird. Last week she's asking Bea how long you should starve a child if she steals food. That's not normal. That scares people." Jesse grabbed the wire brush and scrubbed the grill with twice the necessary vigor. "I mean, she did study the suffragettes last semester, so maybe that's where she got the idea for the hunger strike. But then she tells me they locked her up. They starved her. They—" He stopped and cleared his throat. He resumed scrubbing. "They hurt her. They did terrible things. I think she spent her childhood scared all the time she was going to disappear or die. Why won't she tell us? I want to drive to that hellhole in the desert and scream at them until someone tells me what they did to her."

"That place has been turned into a fancy retreat for rich housewives, hasn't it? No one there knows what happened."

"What do we do, then? How do we help her?"

"She doesn't need help with the past, Jess. What's important to her is where she's going to live and how often she gets to see you and whether Joy will show up. In a short while, it'll be a nightmare of high school dramas, SATs, dating, and crushing on your friends."

Jesse stopped again to take that last bit in. "God, that *will* be a nightmare."

"You two better get the Code sorted out. You don't get to date her friends, either, by the way."

"Her friends are fifteen."

"In a more general sense, it could be an issue down the track."

"We don't need more girl trouble in this house." Jesse scowled. "All those times Caleb talked to us about how to treat a girl — he's the only one who actually does it right. I keep trying. Unlike you, I start with good intentions. I try to be accommodating about different belief systems or whatever. And then two weeks down the track they blindside me by mentioning astrology or ghosts or alien abduction and I *can't* respect that. The girl I was seeing before you went on tour? She was amazing. She asked *me* out. She fools me for a month before I find Erich von fucking Däniken on her nightstand. I can't deal with someone whose brain works like that."

"Pretty sure there are plenty of girls out there with rational brains."

"Yeah, found one of those, too, and she wouldn't sleep with me. Wasn't even a religious thing. She had to hear *I love you* first."

"If you were that desperate, you could've just said it."

"No way." Jesse studied him a moment. "Have *you* ever said it, just to get laid?"

"No. Never said it at all, and I sure as hell will never be the first to say it."

"That's so depressing. And cynical. I think I'll restrict myself to only taking relationship advice from my other brother."

Indio stretched his lips into a sarcastic grin. "That's probably for the best."

Jesse settled into a seat. "So you have to tell me, was there something going on with you and Charity Thorne on that tour?"

"I don't *have* to tell you."

"Uh-huh. That answers my question. Is she as screwed up as I predicted?"

"Not really. Just making the most of being outside her daddy's line of sight. It was less awesome than you imagine. I went along with it for reasons that had nothing to do with her."

"Such as?"

Indio was pretty sure Jesse knew nothing about what happened with their father's girlfriend all those years ago, that woman with the same accent and charm as Charity, and he wasn't going to mention it now.

"C'mon, bro, how else am I gonna learn from your mistakes?" Jesse prompted.

"You'll never make my mistakes."

"I think Wynter might. Something about her is a lot like you. Can't quite put my finger on it."

Her self-destructive protests, perhaps? But that wasn't fair to her. Wynter had a genuine, if misguided, excuse to protest. Indio had no excuse at all for the things he'd done. And he couldn't bear to think Jesse might be right. He'd tried to work out his demons with Charity. What might Wynter do to work out hers?

Jesse meticulously fixed Wynter's lunch, monitoring what she ate like he was her personal trainer. Indio counted down the seconds until she'd had enough.

"They have a girl my age," Wynter said, brushing away Jesse's hand when he tried to place an extra piece of chicken on her plate. "She's a junior, actually, so she's two years ahead of me at school. And they have two little boys."

"Enumclaw's only forty miles from here," Jesse said brightly. "I'm gonna drive up at least twice a week and help with your homework. Assuming they let me."

"We asked about visits and they seem pretty lax about it. The parents, I mean. They're sort of quiet and calm. I guess that's a good thing." Wynter pushed her food around the plate while Jesse pretended not to watch how much went into her mouth. "I wanted to be closer to Seattle. Am I that hard to place?"

"Pretty soon you'll be placed with Caleb. Just hang in there," Jesse said. "When are you leaving?"

"They already said they'd take me, so it'll be soon. Before school starts. I wanted to go to *your* school, Jesse. You were gonna show me around."

"I will, when you're living here."

She set her jaw at his patient responses, and Indio felt for his little brother. Really, what else could he say?

"How long are you staying?" she asked Indio.

"Until Thursday, if Jesse lets me crash on his floor. Then it's back to gigging this weekend."

"With Blunderbelly? Jesse, can we go see him?"

"They're not all-ages, baby," Indio said. "Turk lined up some local venues around Portland over the next month. When I'm back at college you'll be able to come."

"She can't leave the state," Jesse reminded him.

Wynter sat back, deflated. "If I'm not living here by Christmas, I'm gonna—" She bit her lip. "I'm gonna..."

"Gonna *what?*" Jesse said, a challenge in his voice.

"I'm gonna cancel Christmas!"

"Only I get to cancel Christmas. Which I won't do. I already know what I'm getting you."

Her eyes lit up. "What? Tell me."

"Nope."

"Do I have to get you something?"

"Not if you upstage me. I'm the only Santa in this house. Indio, you coming home for Christmas? Wynter and I plan to cook up a feast."

"Wouldn't miss it."

"What do you guys want to do this afternoon? They don't need me again at the mini-golf until Friday. We could go for a ride."

"My bike's in Portland," Indio said. "You think Caleb will let me ride the Beast?"

"No," Jesse and Wynter said in unison.

"I want to go down to the jamroom for three days," Wynter said.

So they did.

৵৹

"That's your bed. Those two shelves are yours. Those three drawers are yours. The left half of the closet is yours. And the left half of the window sill." Madeline pointed out the features of the bedroom Wynter would be sharing with her. "In the bathroom, the bottom shelf is yours. The teal towels are yours, not the aqua ones."

Wynter sat on her assigned bed to unpack, hoping she'd recognize the difference between teal and aqua.

"The girl before you left a few weeks ago," Madeline said, sitting at the mirror to apply purple lipstick even though her lips were already purple. "It'll be nice to have another girl around."

"What happened to her?"

"She went back to her mom. How about you? When are you going back to your family?"

"Not for a while."

"I'm never going back to mine. Is that a guitar? Do you play?" Madeline grabbed the guitar case and unzipped it. "Oh, this is cool. Will you teach me?"

Two young boys ran past the open door, yelling about zombies.

"That's Aiden and Nathan. They're seven."

"Are they twins?"

"They're not real brothers. They've lived here forever. Debra and Brian love them to death. Don't expect much left over, by the way."

That was okay. Wynter didn't need or want Debra and Brian to love her.

"They're little bastards, always coming in here dropping cookie crumbs and taking my stuff. Don't leave your things lying around. Nathan's mom killed herself and they're gonna adopt him soon."

Wynter blanched at the casual way Madeline spoke about it. She kept her head down and folded her t-shirts into one of her assigned drawers.

This rambling house in Enumclaw was unlike both Caleb's small plain suburban home and Rosa's pristine mansion. Sitting on a large block on a frontage road that separated it from the busy main street, its unkempt yard surrounded by trees gave it a semi-rural feel. Wynter liked the house, and her foster parents were kind enough.

Madeline took some getting used to. She knew a lot about makeup, sex, TV, and shoplifting, and was not shy about sharing her knowledge. Wynter thought half of what she said might not be true — she was careful not to say so. Because Madeline liked to talk so much, she rarely asked questions. Even when she did, she didn't listen to the answers. This suited Wynter, who could make her talk for an hour without drawing breath just by accidentally glancing at the *Vampire Diaries* poster taped to Madeline's assigned wall space as they settled into bed on Wynter's first night.

Madeline turned off the light and switched on a red strip light below the poster, which threw a ghoulish red glow onto the actors' faces.

"I leave this on all night. You let me know if it bugs you." Madeline then relayed the entire plot of the TV show's first four seasons, and finished by asking, "Which one's hotter? C'mon, which one is hotter?"

Wynter studied the two brooding brothers on the poster. There might only be one right answer and she didn't want to give the wrong one so early in the relationship. She figured out a safe answer, pointing to the actress between them.

"She's pretty. Her hair is lovely." The girls in middle school had been obsessed with hair.

"I can do your hair like that. I have a ceramic curler. You can borrow it any time you like, if you teach me to play guitar."

"Okay, deal."

The friendship was off to a good start.

Forever

Five days after Wynter left, Jesse drove up on Sunday to work with her. She was making good progress on the ninth-grade math and science syllabuses, and had done most of the required reading for English. His boast to Rosa about her graduating high school early had become his personal mission in life.

He was glad to get out of the house because Caleb wasn't good to be around right now. And he'd left Jesse with the task of explaining the situation to Wynter.

The house in Enumclaw turned out to be a dilapidated dump, although Wynter didn't seem to notice as she walked him through. Their own home wasn't exactly a palace, but at least it was well maintained and tidy.

"Debra and Brian have gone to church with the boys. Madeline went to the mall, which she's not allowed to do, so I'm supposed to keep that a secret." In her room, she pointed to a poster. "Madeline asked me this morning, when I told her you were coming, which of these two guys you looked the most like."

"Who are they?"

"It's a TV show teenage girls like, so I guess I'm supposed to like it. I said you look like neither, except for having dark hair."

Jesse bounced his hand on top of his head. His free-range curls had gotten out of control over the summer. "I'll get a haircut like the one on the left. Whadda ya think?"

"No! Don't ever cut off your curls. Would Caleb's hair grow like yours, if he let it?"

"Yep. Good luck getting him to throw out his clippers, though. He'll be in the Coast Guard until his hair falls out."

"How can he stay in the military if he fosters me? They don't allow single parents."

"Not strictly true. Now we have Patricia to take care of you if he's deployed, it'll work out. Don't worry about it."

Wynter offered a brave smile. Caleb always got what he wanted — except when he didn't, like three weeks ago at the custody hearing they'd all been counting on.

"By the way," she said, "I told Madeline you were short and dumpy and spotty so she wouldn't want to meet you."

"Thanks, I guess."

"I don't want a repeat of what happened with Stacey in middle school. The other problem is *you* might think Madeline's hot. She's almost seventeen and she has amazing hair."

"Nah, amazing hair does nothing for me."

"Other than your own?" Despite their height difference, she managed to reach up and ruffle his hair like he was three years old before he had time to wriggle away.

They went out the back to work at the picnic bench and enjoy the last of the summer weather.

"So, what's it like, living here? Do you like your foster parents?"

"I don't talk to them much. They sort of let us be, me and Madeline. The little boys are hyperactive and very funny when they're not being very annoying. I don't know how I'll get any study done after school."

"I'll bring over some noise-canceling headphones — those huge ones that block out everything, even when the music's quiet."

"Nothing blocks out Madeline's screeds. She never stops. She keeps me awake at night. Did you bring that old guitar like I asked? You need to take back the Fender. It's gonna get wrecked here."

"I brought it." Jesse sat next to her on the bench, anxious about what he had to tell her.

She was fussing with her pens and books. "I have a new caseworker — Svetlana."

"Svetlana! Now there's a name. Always wanted to meet a Svetlana. It means *shining light*."

Wynter pulled a face. "Really? Her name means *light*?"

Jesse realized his mistake. "Pure coincidence. Don't go looking for a deeper meaning, Wyn. We don't do that. Is she an improvement over Tina?"

"She seems friendlier. She's very young — she only just graduated. Madeline's already plotting ways to make *her* caseworker dump her because she wants Svetlana, too."

Jesse drew in his breath. "Caleb and Bea split up."

Wynter stopped what she was doing. "They can make up, like you and Natalie did that time."

"They're not making up. They both decided it's over. They haven't been good in a while, Wyn. Sort of limping along."

"I thought..." Wynter frowned. "They were supposed to get married."

"That's not gonna happen."

"They have to. He loves her so much. He's always looking at her and smiling. Nothing else makes him smile like that." Her voice was little more than a whisper. "She was here that first morning when I woke up. I thought she'd always be here."

"Yeah, I did too."

"Is Caleb upset?"

"Yes. He'll be okay."

Jesse trusted this was true. Having been through Caleb's past breakups, he also knew this one was different.

"He sent me four texts yesterday," Wynter said. "Why didn't he tell me about this?"

"Well, he wanted to be sure about it first. They've been trying to sort things out for a few days, and last night they decided to end it. Caleb thought it'd be better if I told you in person, as I'm here anyway, rather than him doing it over the phone."

She was shaking her head, pressing her hand into her sternum, that signal he'd seen before that she was too overwhelmed to draw breath.

"It's okay, Wyn. Sometimes this happens. Nobody's fault. We'll all be sad for a while, especially him, and then it'll pass."

"Why... why would you spend all that time with someone... and throw it away?" she stammered.

"I guess that's a risk you take when you start a relationship." Jesse felt out of his depth. He'd never gotten far enough along with his steady stream of girlfriends to think about them in a long-term way.

"I don't know *anyone* who stayed together. Even Rosa. She was supposed to know all about fixing people, fixing relationships, and she was divorced. She couldn't fix herself." Wynter gulped on a sob. "Joy left her husband in Arizona. You told me your dad's had a new girlfriend every year for fifteen years. Our mother had two husbands. I don't understand. When is love forever?"

"Family loves forever."

"But that's not true! Joy is forgetting how to love me. I sent her loads of pictures of the house and my new bedroom and she sent one smiley face. You almost never see Harry. Our mother left five children. Does she love us? Did she ever love us?"

Jesse swallowed the lump in his throat. Those words were so tough to hear. "I don't know what to tell you." He recalled something Indio had told him, not too long ago. "There's something wrong with them, not us. There's nothing wrong with us."

"What if she's made it so we can't love forever?"

"What do you mean?"

"Mothers are supposed to love their children. That's what helps children grow up and learn to love someone else, isn't it? If she didn't love us, maybe we can't love, can't marry someone and love forever." Her breath came out in great sobs as she struggled to breathe. "And now it's happened to Caleb."

He shouldn't have said anything. This was Caleb's job. Why did Caleb make him do it?

"I think you're wrong," he said, grasping her hand. "I think we will find people to love and marry, and we'll love our children, and we'll be okay. But even if we don't, you know we love you. Me, Caleb, Indio — we love you, and you love us, and that's forever."

Jesse did his best to help Wynter concentrate through the morning. The foster parents came back and introduced themselves. They seemed reasonable and sensible, if preoccupied, and clearly adored the younger boys. They would have to do, until Caleb got his way.

Madeline returned half an hour later. From the discussion he overheard in the house, Jesse gathered she'd intended to return before the parents got home so they wouldn't know she'd been to the mall. They expressed their disappointment and told her not to do it again. That was what passed for discipline in this house, apparently.

Madeline came outside and sat with them, to Wynter's annoyance. Madeline did indeed have great hair — auburn waves that bounced on her shoulders when she tossed her head, which she did a lot.

"You're right, he doesn't look like Stefan or Damon," Madeline said, like he wasn't there. "He looks a lot like Ryan, my boyfriend when I was twelve. I wasn't allowed to see him," she added, "because he was nineteen."

"Jesus Christ!" Jesse said, though he'd intended to ignore her.

Wynter said nothing at all, still upset from the earlier news. She kept her head bent over her math problems.

"I was mature for my age," Madeline said, pleased by his reaction. Her pancake makeup and too-tight clothes were doing her no favors. What had gone on in her past to make her want to present herself like that? On her arms was the evidence she was a cutter, another reason to feel sorry for her. Jesse was too focused on Wynter today to feel much of anything for a stranger.

"We've got a lot of work to get through," he said.

Madeline didn't take the hint. "Why on earth are you doing school work before the semester starts?"

"In our family, education is important. Wynter wants to get ahead."

"Who's your family, then?"

"Me and Wynter and our two older brothers. And another sister," he added, for Wynter's sake.

"Are your parents dead?"

"No."

"So, do they not want you, or are they not allowed to have you?"

"Well, I'm an adult and so are the others, so it doesn't matter."

"I'm gonna age out of the system in a bit over a year."

"That's too bad. Hope it works out for you."

"What about you, Wynter? What's gonna happen to you?"

Jesse waited for Wynter to answer, wondering what she'd already told Madeline. When she said nothing, he answered for her.

"Our oldest brother will foster her in a few months, when he gets licensed."

"Huh, I bet he won't."

"He will."

"My best friend's mom was gonna foster me last year. That would've been awesome. But she backed out. They always back out."

Jesse put his hand on Wynter's, to reassure her just in case she had the slightest doubt. "Caleb won't back out. Wynter is the most important person in the world to him."

"That's why they broke up, isn't it," Wynter said quietly.

Jesse put his arm around her and had nothing to say, because she was right. Eventually, Madeline lost interest and went away.

Jesse suggested they call Caleb. They went to the far corner of the yard for privacy and she sat on the grass and listened to Caleb tell her he was going to be okay, just like Jesse had already done.

She held it together until the call ended, and then cried for real. Jesse had never seen her cry and it hurt him more than he could've imagined, not only seeing her pain but feeling his own inadequacy because he didn't know what to do about it. No one had ever comforted him as a child and he'd never wanted it. He was sure Wynter *had* wanted comfort as a child, and hadn't gotten it, and still wanted it now. So he put his arms around her and shushed her, which had little effect, and let her wipe her face on his sleeve.

Afterward, he found her foster mom and explained what had happened. Debra was sympathetic but unsure quite what to say, and distracted by the boys. Didn't matter. He wanted them to know what was going on, but knew Wynter wouldn't want their sympathy.

Back home, when he told Caleb that Wynter had cried in his arms for an hour, Caleb put his head in his hands.

"Have you ever seen her cry before?" Jesse asked.

"No. And I never want to be the reason for it."

"You're not the reason. She has much larger concerns — the end of love, the end of hope."

"Are you *trying* to make me feel worse?"

"I'm just saying it's a good thing. It's normal. Anyone should cry over that."

Closely Supervised

Indio turned into the driveway of an oddly shaped cottage with crumbling stucco and broken gutters — the kind of place he dreamed of owning one day, a place he could fix up. No way was he going to live in a box and call it home. Home was something you created with your hands and your heart. Whoever owned this house had a different idea of home. It wasn't a box, nor was it a place anyone had lovingly created or cared for.

Two young boys roamed around the front, playing in the dirt with an assortment of action figures. They stared wide-eyed as Indio walked down the long driveway. Halfway there, as Wynter was coming out of the house to greet him, he felt something tugging the hem of his t-shirt — one of the boys had snuck up behind him.

"Nathan says you're Thor, from the movie. Prove it! Where's your hammer? Are you from Asgard?"

"Sorry, buddy. I'm from Montana."

The kid pulled a face and wandered off. A teenaged girl leaned in the doorway.

"Spoilsport," Wynter said, hugging him. "Jesse would've gone along with it. That's Madeline. She likes college guys and vampires."

Indio acknowledged the girl as she sidled out of the house. His attention returned to Wynter. "You ready to go?"

"You have to meet Svetlana first. Social worker rules."

Ah, because he was supposed to be *closely supervised* around his sister. Now Wynter had a new social worker, he'd hoped they could get past that.

"Is she gonna let us go out somewhere?"

"Don't know." She touched his arm to make him pause as he took a step toward the house. "So, there's a chance she might be a sort of fan of yours."

"A Blunderbelly fan?"

"Well—"

Wynter cut herself off because a young woman was coming out of the house. Blonde and quite pretty with a squarish face and heavily made-up eyes. She wore jeans and boots and a floaty top that altogether screamed, *I'm not your typical fuddy-duddy social worker. I'm hip! I'm cool with the kids!*

And she was a fan of his? Was Wynter trying to tell him Svetlana was a groupie? Had he... slept with her?

"Good morning, I'm Svetlana Verenich." She was all business, with a breezy undertone that signaled nervousness.

As he shook her hand, he wracked his brain for the name, the face, the slight European accent. Would it help or hinder his case if they'd hooked up at some point?

"Indio," he introduced himself. "I'm taking Wynter out for lunch, and maybe a drive."

"It's Indio's birthday," Wynter said, with a hint of desperation. She was practically wringing her hands.

"Oh, happy birthday."

"It was actually last Wednesday," Wynter added, because she wasn't one to let even an irrelevant inaccuracy stand. "Indio! Guess what?" she said brightly, like she'd only just remembered something. "Svetlana is a big fan of Wages and Gifts."

Indio felt weak with relief. Okay, he had definitely not slept with any person associated with Wages and Gifts, other than the headline act the band had been supporting. He gave Svetlana his most charming smile.

"Awesome. Did you catch us in Seattle last month?"

"Wynter only just introduced me to them," Svetlana said, coy now.

"I found out she loves Christian rock music," Wynter explained, "so I told her all about Wages and Gifts."

"Been listening to them ever since," Svetlana said.

"Sorry to say that's not me on their albums," Indio said, aware that Madeline was coming casually up the driveway to join them. "I was just filling in for their guitarist on tour."

"You never told me he's in a band," Madeline said, nudging Wynter so hard she stumbled against Indio. "I met your brother, Jesse," she told Indio, like he might not be aware of his own brother's name. "What a total bore."

"He's an acquired taste," Indio conceded.

Madeline liked that. Liked being noticed and included like an adult, instead of dismissed. She had that sixteen-going-on-twenty-five vibe that set off alarm bells in Indio's head.

Then she said, "Are *you* an acquired taste?" and licked her lips, her gaze bouncing straight to his groin and back again. Forget the alarm bells. This was DEFCON 1.

Svetlana, who actually *was* twenty-five or thereabouts, pretended not to hear and Indio took the same attitude.

"Let's go over the ground rules," Svetlana said.

Ground rules. Indio's stomach dropped. Svetlana might be hip and cool and a fan of the band he toured with, but she was also newly qualified with bosses to impress.

She continued, "Wynter's previous caseworker left a note permitting supervised visits with you. So, here I am."

Wynter glared at Indio as though he was supposed to fix things.

"Is that discretionary?" Indio said.

"It's Tina Campbell's recommendation from—"

"So, it's discretionary."

"I guess so."

Indio felt he could get her where he wanted her on this issue. It would take some work. "Let's head out for lunch," he suggested. "I passed a Mexican place a couple blocks back."

"Oh, I love Mexican!" Madeline said, deliberately mistaking his invitation as including her. "I'll just let Brian know I'm leaving, because I'm sort of half grounded right now." She raised a plucked eyebrow at Wynter, who shrugged assent.

"That's kind of you to include her, Wynter," Svetlana said when Madeline had gone back inside. "Well done." From her patronizing tone, it looked like she'd been told to nurture and encourage Wynter's social development.

"I'm trying to make friends with her, so I should be nice, right?" Wynter didn't look happy about being nice.

Indio didn't fuss about it because he knew exactly what Brian was going to say. Sure enough, Madeline returned a minute later with a pout.

"He says no. What a bitch. Are you a registered sex offender or something?"

"Or something," Indio muttered cryptically. He tapped Wynter's shoulder. "Let's go."

Svetlana went inside to fetch her purse, Madeline trooping after her.

As he and Wynter went out the gate, she noticed the car. "Whose is this?"

"Turk's. We're not allowed to eat in it or park it on the street."

"But you *have* parked it on the street."

"Downtown, I mean. At least, I assume that's what he meant."

"Why did you ask Svetlana along? I don't want her here."

"No choice. We'll make the best of it. I think we'll be able to shake her off, don't worry."

Svetlana joined them and Indio drove to the Mexican place. Wynter had only had Mexican once before and he persuaded her to try new items off the menu.

"We'll get ice cream later," he said. "How's the new school?"

"It's only been three days, so I'm still lost. It's *huge* and kinda rough. Strange being the youngest all of a sudden, after being the oldest. I think everyone else in ninth grade feels the same. Some of them don't know each other, or don't know anyone, so I don't feel too different. The school is all about sport, and they don't care about music at all."

Indio segued into asking Svetlana about her college days at Saint Martin's and showed careful interest in the pictures of her Dalmatian puppy. Half an hour later she went to pay for the meal, saying it was a business expense. Indio was, for once, in a position to pay without blinking. Still, he wasn't going to offer.

"What d'you want to do next?" he asked Wynter as Svetlana came back to the table. "We could explore downtown, or drive out to one of the State parks. There's a lavender farm twenty minutes away."

"I should get going," Svetlana said. "I have another client to visit."

"Sure, I'll drop you at your car," Indio said, like it had been the plan all along.

He sensed Wynter holding her breath all the way back. Svetlana gave the two of them a final glance as she got out, an unspoken acknowledgment that she shouldn't be leaving but that *of course* everything would be fine.

Wynter climbed into the front seat and Indio drove off as soon as her seat belt clicked.

"So, where to?" he said.

Her mood was practically euphoric compared to one minute earlier. "What do *you* want to do? It's your birthday."

"We could do one of the local hikes. There's a day hike up a little mountain just south of here."

"Let's do it." She was watching him closely as he drove. "What did you think of Svetlana?"

"She seems a little unsure of herself. By-the-book to make up for a lack of experience."

"You managed to work around her. No *close supervision* today."

"She was looking for a reason to give me the seal of approval. Makes her life easier."

"She *likes* you." Wynter leaned on the word meaningfully.

"Because I liked her puppy."

"I laid the groundwork. Having a rockstar for a brother was a pain in middle school. Now I see it's gonna come in all sorts of handy."

"I swear, it was the puppy. Always fuss over a girl's pets — or pictures of them. I learned that when I was seven years old."

"Did you have a girlfriend when you were seven?"

"Esmeralda Grey. Her dad and Harry worked together at the state prison and somehow I ended up at her place for a playdate, the first boy she'd ever had over, so she declared herself my girlfriend. I was fine with it cuz she had a Nintendo 64. She was crazy about her goldfish, Silver. I pretended to like Silver so she'd keep asking me over. Live fish freak me out, by the way. I hated that thing."

"Why was its name Silver, if it was gold?"

"It was a silver goldfish."

"How is that a thing? Jesse would make me look it up." She checked her phone. "I'm still waiting for him to... oh, here it is. Today's day in history for me to study."

"You're exempt when you're with me." They exchanged a grin. "What did he send?"

"In 1936 the last known Tasmanian Tiger died," she read from her email. "It was a stripy sort of dog, two feet tall at the shoulder, native to Australia."

"Like a dingo?"

"It was a marsupial, which means it had a pouch for its babies. Scientists are trying to clone it back into existence. Jesse says that's unethical because they'd have to live in zoos." She pressed the phone into her lap, staring out the window, and sighed. "It's an awful thing, though, isn't it? That something alive and unique just stopped existing. His name was Benjamin."

Indio wasn't sure how these little instructional sessions were supposed to go. "Do we now have an ethical discussion about animals in captivity, or cloning, or...?"

She threw him a quick smile, a reassurance that ethics were off the table, and returned to studying her phone. "He says today is the birthdate of the first Queen Elizabeth, almost five hundred years ago. He sent some links about her but warns me against clicking them because royalty is an *abomination*. And Keith Moon *self-destructed* today in 1978. Those are Jesse's words."

"You know who Keith Moon was?"

"The Who. How could I not know, with a drummer for a brother?"

"Look up the album *Who's Next* on your phone, and together we'll struggle through an insightful commentary on the drumming."

"Jesse says I have to listen to three specific tracks from... *Live at Leeds*," she read from her phone.

"That puts you in a tough spot, huh?" Indio teased. "Whose advice you gonna take?"

"No contest. I'll take yours."

"Because I'm sitting right here?"

"Jesse is remaking me with history and science. Remaking me with music is your job."

Her tone was light but it twisted a knife in Indio's gut.

"Oh, baby..." he breathed, "you don't need to be remade. Least of all by me or Jesse."

"Who, then?"

Indio was in no mood to get philosophical on his birthday. As he braked for lights, he took Wynter's phone and found another of The Who's songs. He tapped *play*, handed back the phone with a quirk of his eyebrow, but without further explanation, and they listened to *Who Are You?* She knew the song and they harmonized all the way to Mount Peak.

Falling

The walk was short but steep. Indio set a slow pace, mindful that one month ago Wynter had been too weak to even stand up. The temperature must be hitting eighty degrees, although it was cooler on the thickly forested trail. At the top, they walked off the path a few yards into the undergrowth and sat cross-legged together in a small clearing to rest with bottled water and chocolate.

"I have a gift for you," she said shyly, retrieving her phone from her tiny backpack. "It's a joint effort, all three of us. I already sent it to Joy — it's her birthday, too, after all. I'm sending you a link. You have to check it out."

"Now?"

"Yes!"

He followed the link on his own phone — it took him to a music sharing site. In her bag she also had two pairs of earbuds and a splitter borrowed from Jesse. They plugged in to listen at the same time.

They'd made him a song. He grinned at her when he realized, sharing her excitement. Then he lay back and closed his eyes to really listen. Half the lyrics were his own — he'd given them to her a while back, not needing them himself. Someone had written more, and Wynter sang them. He loved her voice. She had a husky emotional tone in her lower range, and on the higher notes the tone was brighter but still had a rich undertone. The song's tempo was up-beat, the feeling wistful and hopeful. Not the sort of stuff he usually wrote. He loved every note.

"Again." He knew she wouldn't mind him listening to it twice before reacting.

They listened through again.

"I wrote that bass line for Caleb," she said as soon as it ended. "I had to talk him into it."

"It's beautiful. All of it. I'm touched."

"I can tell."

She was on her stomach, propped up on her elbows looking down at him. Jesus, he must look choked up or something. He *felt* choked up.

"When did you record this?"

"After you left Seattle at the end of August. We had two days before I moved here. Jesse mixed it. He did four mixes — took him all night — and then we voted on the best one. Actually, I just chose the best."

"Who wrote the rest of the lyrics?"

"Jesse. That's how it ended up being called *Rate of Change*. He wouldn't let me write anything — said it would be too obscure."

"Your lyrics aren't obscure. Jeez, no one writes more obscurely than Jesse. I love it. Thank you." He lifted his head to kiss her cheek. "Guess what? I'm picking up a new guitar from Frankie next time I'm in Seattle."

Her eyes lit up. "Another one?"

"C'mon, you can never have too many guitars."

"Are you replacing the Les Paul that Jesse sold?"

"No, that'll have to wait. It's an Ibanez Talman from the mid-nineties. Awesome vintage tone, pale blue with three lipstick pickups. Small neck, real comfortable to play. You'll like it."

"What's a lipstick pickup?"

"Looks like a tube of lipstick. In fact, originally, they *were* lipstick tubes, back in the 'fifties and 'sixties. Single-coil. The tone's got some bite. Sounds great with distortion, too."

"Will you play it on stage?"

"The pastel finish might wreck my rock n' roll reputation. I'll leave it in Seattle so you can play it." Wynter had been at the forefront of his mind when he'd bought the guitar in the first place, of course.

"I want to learn all about your guitars. About all guitars."

"Would Jesse approve?"

"In between his scheduled lessons, he does tell me to follow my own interests. So, this is my interest." She pulled out her earbuds and fidgeted with them for a moment. "Why d'you think Brian wouldn't let Madeline come with us to eat?"

"I'm glad she didn't come. We didn't need her tagging along." He could see that answer didn't satisfy her. "He's responsible for her — he can't let her go out with a complete stranger."

"D'you think he knows about... about what you did when you were seventeen?"

"Dunno what he's been told about that, or about the other arrests. Jesse told you about those, yeah?"

She nodded. He hated that she knew — and at the same time, because she hadn't judged him, it was a huge relief.

"Do you ever get to put that time in juvie behind you?"

"I have. It's everyone else who has a problem."

"Caleb?"

He sighed. "Caleb knows teenagers make mistakes. Now I think about it, I don't think he's ever brought it up since it happened. He had plenty to say about the rest of it. I'm not a teenager anymore."

"Will you tell me what you did that day?"

"You already know. I beat up a boy at school."

"But how did it happen?"

"If I tell you, will you tell me something?"

She was instantly wary. "Like what?"

"I have a million questions for you. I'm happy to *never* ask them, I truly am. I don't need to know anything more than you want to tell me. But I am curious."

For a long moment she said nothing, chewing her lip as she pulled at blades of grass under her fingers. Then, "I don't think I want to play this game."

He backed off. "Okay. That's okay. I'll tell you my sordid tale anyway."

She rested her cheek on her arms to listen.

"So, Lewis Shanck was in tenth grade. He was short and skinny but somehow he was a bully. I don't know where his power came from — he could make kids do anything, even kids two years older. He got them to do his dirty work so he rarely got into trouble himself. I was a junior and much bigger than him. I figured him out — a lot of the older kids figured him out, but it was none of our business. One day, I broke up a fight between one of his henchmen and a friend of mine, and after that Lewis was out to get me. He set it all up — a gang of his friends waiting for me after school."

Wynter's eyes widened. "Were they gonna kill you?"

"I don't think they had much of a plan. I heard about it but I wasn't gonna be intimidated. See, this is the part where I should've walked away, just called Harry to come fetch me, or told a teacher. But I went out to confront Lewis. Turns out his friends weren't that eager for a fight, after all. I ignored them anyway and went straight for him. I figured, if I knock him to the ground, humiliate him, he'll lose his power in the eyes of the other kids. I did knock him down. Then the anger took over and I kept punching." He winced at the memory. "I was so fed up. The entire school was fed up, and I was the one at that moment with the opportunity to do something about it. I broke his ribs, smashed his nose..."

He glanced at her, to make sure she wasn't completely disgusted with him yet.

"I got charged with felony assault in the county juvenile court and they sent me to JR. That's juvenile rehabilitation, about fifteen miles east of Seattle. Caleb was deployed at the time and out of the loop.

Harry was useless about the whole thing, of course. He absolved himself of responsibility for me. And for Jesse, too, I think, even though Jesse was never in that sort of trouble."

"What was juvie like?"

"More or less like school with therapy sessions. I buckled down and behaved myself, but I was angry about being there. That was supposed to be the best summer of my life. My buddy lined up a job for me at his dad's auto shop. He'd give me use of a car on weekends and the car itself, as payment, if I lasted the three months. I was dating Frances Feeney and she was teaching me to play classical guitar. Then... one bad decision and it all vanished. No job, no car, no classical guitar lessons."

"No Frances Feeny?"

"No Frances Feeny. I don't blame her."

"Were you angry all the time when you were seventeen?"

"What d'you mean?"

"You don't seem angry all the time now."

"What am I, then?"

She held his gaze from twelve inches away, assessing him carefully. "Sort of lost, I think. Falling."

Falling... until that day in January when he'd held Jenny in his arms. Jenny could've been his solid ground, yet he'd been unable to tell her the truth even while she was reaching out to him. And now he'd told Wynter the truth and already he felt just a little more stable.

"So," she persisted, "were you angry all the time back then?"

"Not *all* the time."

"What made you so angry on that day?"

"I don't remember." He stared into the overhead web of tree branches for a long moment. "I do remember. That morning, I found Jesse leaning over the basin in the bathroom, spitting out blood. He'd followed Harry to the car to ask for a few bucks so he could buy a cymbal from a kid at school. Harry had promised him that money on payday. He went back on his word, of course, and Jesse asked one too many times. I should've..."

Indio spanned a hand over his eyes as the old anger surged again, the anger that lifted him up, that stopped him falling but left him without a safe foothold.

"I was sleeping in, like I always did. Knew nothing about it until Harry had already gone to work. Jesse cleaned himself up and headed off to school on his bike, and I headed off to high school in the other direction. I was so mad at myself for not protecting him. Went through the entire day in a blur, and Lewis Shanck tipped me over. Maybe..." He hesitated, unused to this feeling of vulnerability as he opened up. "Maybe when I was punching him, I was really punching Harry."

"I think," Wynter said, "you were really punching Caleb."

He gave her a sharp look.

"If Caleb hadn't gone away," she said, "he could've protected Jesse. Or he could've thrown Harry out years earlier and saved you both."

"I was *glad* when Caleb left. I don't blame him for choosing that career."

"You blame him for something."

Indio closed his eyes briefly. "He does remind me of Lewis. They both have this power to control others, to hold them in thrall."

"But Caleb uses his powers for good."

"I didn't see it that way. While I was living through it, my first instinct was to resist whatever he told me to do. Always."

"Hmm. Whenever I think about doing the wrong thing, in the back of my mind I feel his disappointment. It makes me reconsider. I know I still screw up a lot, but I do think twice. Don't you feel that, too?"

Indio sneered. "I don't need him weighing in. My own conscience works just fine." The constant spiral of shame and guilt surely proved that. At her troubled look, he added, "I don't *like* disappointing him. That's not it. I screwed up in Ohio, I know that. Now I'll graduate a year late, costing him a shitload more money. And he wants me to move back to Seattle when I'm done, and I'm not going to, so there's more guilt waiting down the track."

"What's wrong with Seattle?"

He put his hands behind his head. "Nothing, baby. I can't live in the same city as him. I just can't."

"Won't you do it for me and Jesse?"

"Not even for you and Jesse. Which means *more* guilt for disappointing you."

"I once said I wanted to play music on stage with you all, and you said I would. You have to move to Seattle so that when I move home as well we can have a band."

"We'll play together, I promise. But not in a band. Not as a long-term thing."

"I think we will. I'll make it happen."

He chuckled as he glanced over. "Give it your best shot."

The confident way she held his gaze made him wonder what she was plotting.

The gaze wavered. She said, "My turn. I want to tell you something."

A Different World

Wynter chewed her lip, already having second thoughts about going through with it.

Indio's turn to hold his breath, scared to break the spell.

Finally she said, "If I did tell you something you're so curious about, would you tell Caleb?"

"He has that *no secrets* rule..."

"He told me this was a privacy issue. The stuff in my head, in my past, it's not a secret. It's my own private business until I want to share."

Indio shrugged in agreement, and then the compulsion to cast his older brother in a less favorable light kicked in. "He only said that to give you a way out, so you wouldn't feel pressured. He'd give anything to get inside your head and pull all those *privacy issues* out into the open."

"I don't want him to think differently of me."

She'd once told him that talking about the past would hurt Caleb. Now, suddenly, he recognized a different fear.

"Have you done something you're ashamed of? Because if you have, I know all about that, believe me."

"A bit ashamed. Mostly I'm *scared* of it."

Indio turned on to his side to face her, tucking his bent arm under his head. "I understand that. I didn't know I could hurt someone that badly. I've always been scared I could do it again, if I was angry enough."

"You did do it again."

That guy in Eugene — yeah, he'd done it again.

"I'm never gonna feel badly about *that*. I'm not ashamed of it." He touched her hand. "Tell me."

She drew breath, hesitated, started again, stopped. He willed her to speak.

She shook her head in frustration. "I'm trying to say the words..."

"I know."

"There are things I only half remember. I don't want to tell it wrong. When I try to bring the pictures back, everything gets misty and then vanishes like it was a dream. But something... there's something that's very clear because it happened so many times. I remember doing it, and I remember how it felt. I wasn't angry like you were. I don't know why I did it."

"Did someone tell you to do it?" She nodded miserably. Indio cupped his hand around her face. "That's not your fault, baby. You were just a kid."

"But I knew it was wrong. I did it to them. They did it to me. Why didn't everyone just *stop* "

He withdrew his hand and waited until she was ready to continue.

"The teachers made us sit on them, on the kids they were beating. We sat on their arms and legs to hold them down on the floor. *I did that.*"

Indio forced himself not to react as her pain and shame clutched at his heart.

"What if someone told me to hurt someone again," she whispered, "and I did what they said?"

"It won't happen again. That was a different world with different rules. I know you wouldn't hurt anyone."

"I'm hurting you right now. I can see it."

"That's not the same thing—"

"I just want the dark pieces to go away. They're not written in a police report like yours. I should be able to sink them under the water forever. And that piece was nothing, except that I feel so bad about it. The other pieces are worse."

Her sudden candor chilled him. What she'd told him only scratched the surface.

"Okay, listen to me," he said. "If you bring those pieces to the surface, it might hurt me — that's true. It's hard for me to hear that you were hurt or manipulated. But you have to know this: I'll be okay. I'll get through it. I promise I won't run away from it."

"I can't. I can't do it."

"It'll get easier. The further you get from that place, the more time that passes, the easier it'll get." She looked ready to panic. "I won't ask you for more. When you're ready, okay? Tomorrow or next week or next year, or when you're old and gray — you can tell me when you're ready."

She nodded, still unsure. She drew a deep breath and exhaled slowly, controlling it.

"God, I wish I could be like Jesse," he said, "and just say something funny to make you smile again."

She gave a tremulous smile anyway, and sat up. "Let's visit that lavender farm. Joy loves lavender. I'll mail her something."

They drove out to the farm, in the foothills of Tiger Mountain. The season was drawing to a close but some plants were still in bloom. The glorious weather, pretty scenery, and perfumed air didn't uplift Wynter's mood as Indio had hoped, as she'd no doubt hoped after their earlier strange, intense conversation.

She walked through lavender fields beside him with her arms folded across her body, like she regretted coming. His own thoughts were clogged with the awful things she'd told him, leaving no room for his own feelings on what she'd suffered.

"Did Jesse tell you he has a baby picture of me?" she said.

"He sent me a scan of it, a while back. He seemed to think you didn't like it."

"Well, it's a baby. I'm not good with babies. Just ask Bea." They winced in unison, because there was no longer a Bea to ask.

Indio fished out his phone, tempting fate, and found the photo to see if she'd talk about it. "You look lost in thought, with your finger on your chin like that."

"Does it look like you?"

"Why d'you ask?"

"Caleb said it does, and he said I looked like you when you were about ten. I was just wondering if you agreed."

"I'm not good with babies, either, to be honest. It just kinda looks like a cute baby to me."

"Yeah..." Wynter stopped walking, took the phone from him, and stared at the photo. "Why don't I feel anything when I look at this?"

"What did you expect to feel?"

"I don't know. This is the only picture of me in almost sixteen years. When Caleb showed me your family photo albums, I felt something. I love those photos. I love watching you all grow up, and seeing the things you did and the places you lived. I feel connected to your family. My family. But I don't feel any connection to this photo of me."

He struggled to think of something useful to say as they headed for the gift store. "Maybe because it's all there is. There's no sequence of photos as you got older, each year looking more and more like someone you recognize. Baby photos are sort of generic, I guess."

"I wish Joy hadn't cut herself out of it. She was seven, so I'd recognize her even if I'd never seen your family photos, and then the baby would feel more like me." They entered the store and Wynter picked up a little sachet of dried lavender. "Joy gave me one of these. She put it under my pillow when I was sick." She sniffed it and turned pale. She put it back and grabbed some soap and a bottle of lotion from the shelf. "I'll get these for her."

It was clear she needed to get out of there fast. Indio offered to pay but she had some money of her own.

"Time to get you home," he said as they walked back to the car.

"It's not home," she said in rebuke, softened with a smile. Her expression clouded. "Are you gonna tell Caleb what I told you?"

"You could tell him yourself." He leaned on the roof of the car, blocking her from opening the door. "If he knows this, he'll wonder about the rest. He's the one person on the planet I think *should* know the rest. I told you before, you can trust him. But it's up to you. I won't tell him without your permission."

"Sometimes I try to tell him something. The words don't come out." She touched her throat. "The words just stop."

"Do you want me to tell him?"

She nodded mutely.

"Do you want to be there when I tell him?"

"How?" Her voice was at the point of breaking. "We're almost never all in the same room."

"We will be — at Christmas. Maybe Thanksgiving, if I can get away."

"That's ages away. I might change my mind by then."

"Okay, I'll call him right now and put him on speaker."

"He'll be at the dojo. And I can't do this over the phone."

"Then tell me what to do, baby."

She stood there fretting. At last she said, "I guess just do it when I'm not there. I think he'll be okay."

"Don't worry about *him* being okay."

"It's news to him. It's not news to me."

"It was news to me and I survived."

"That's because..." She thought for a moment, getting her words in line. "There's something about you that's the same as me. Something more accepting. Caleb's not like that. He'll want to *fix* it."

"I'll do my best to set him straight."

He opened the door for her and went around to get in the other side. His focus drifted to the glove compartment, an involuntary reaction, and he made a decision.

"I brought something to show you," he said. "Didn't know whether I should. I think I will."

He leaned over to open the glove compartment and handed her several sheets of cartridge paper. She gasped when she realized what they were.

"Your sketches. Your *confiscated* sketches."

"Some of them." He'd left behind the fantasy sketches of his ninth-grade crushes — he wasn't about to risk Svetlana's wrath by showing his little sister so-called *borderline pornography*.

Wynter looked through the other sketches on the drive back to Debra and Brian's. She spent several minutes on each, rather than rushing ahead to satisfy her curiosity. She'd once accused him of not wanting anyone to see inside. Well, he could let her see inside his fifteen-year-old self. He was ready for that if what she said was true, if some part of him was the same as her.

"This is my favorite," she said at last, as they pulled up in front of the house. She moved to the top of the pile the picture of a child cowering under an onslaught of formless shapes. "Is he six years old?"

"Six, seven, eight... The years I thought she was coming back."

"This is me, then, at ten or eleven. I don't remember when I stopped hoping. I guess it was a gradual thing. I didn't exist for anyone else in that place, and eventually I didn't exist for her, either. These shapes—" Her fingers traced the forms. "—they surrounded me, choked me, in the spaces she was supposed to be." She gave him a weak smile. "I never thought of it this way before. Never imagined what it *looked* like. This is exactly what it *felt* like."

According to Jesse, Caleb had assumed the sketches were about growing up with Harry. That had been tough, but Indio was fairly sure his relationship with his father would've been rocky whether or not Miriam had left. Their mother's absence had changed them all. It had changed him, formed him, and destroyed him. He would spend a lifetime rebuilding.

"Do you still feel that way?" he managed.

"She was one of the dark pieces I pushed down long before I left the ashram. But there must've been some hope left because I took the bait, twice. I wanted her back, to fill these spaces. But now I have you and Caleb and Jesse. And Joy. I hope I have Joy." A frown flickered across her brow. "You still feel this way."

"Yeah, sometimes."

"I wish we were enough for you, like you are for me."

He didn't know how to respond. After so many years, it was hard to fathom there might be another person in this world who unconditionally accepted him at his most vulnerable, and who trusted him never to judge when she opened up to him.

One problem—

He was pretty sure that person wasn't supposed to be his sister.

"Did you have a good birthday?" she said, letting him off the hook yet again.

"A really good one."

Today, you were enough for me.

❧

Indio drove back to Portland before calling Caleb that evening, sitting in the car in the parking lot of his apartment.

Caleb wanted to know how he'd gotten Wynter to talk.

"I guess you could say we swapped stories."

"Did she tell you what she was beaten with, or why?"

"No. I didn't want to interrogate her. Her concern was the guilt because she participated in it. Didn't Jesse say she mentioned six of the best? That implies a cane." He pressed his thumb and fingers against his burning eyes as the full impact hit him.

"How could anyone hurt her? Was she *nobody* to them?" Caleb muttered.

"Yeah, I think she was nobody to them. They did worse, too. She wouldn't tell me, but there's worse. Things she can't fully remember, things that surface in dreams."

"Don't let it eat you up, Indio. It's a good sign, that she told you even this much. We have to be strong for her. And we have to do something. We have to report it, get an investigation started."

"To what end? There are no kids there anymore, right? No more classrooms like that. Wynter wants to put it behind her. And this is the tip of the iceberg. If she goes through an interrogation, if she's forced to tell more, if she has to go on the witness stand and look those witches in the eye – how does that help her?"

"What more do you think there is?"

"Aside from the physical abuse, this shows she was terrorized and manipulated. And betrayed by Joy, who didn't do a damn thing about it until the end."

"I think it's fair to say Joy was manipulated as well. She was six years old when she went in."

"I'm not blaming Joy. I'm saying, from Wynter's point of view, she was betrayed by the one person who could've saved her. And Wynter doesn't blame her, either. Wynter's okay. She's somehow figured out a way to be okay through all of this. She told me you'd want to fix it, and that's where your mind immediately went."

"Someone should pay."

"It can't be fixed. It can't be undone."

RATE OF CHANGE

The world spins faster every day
I can't keep up, can't find my way
Life is a fundamental force
That's pushing me beyond the source

The algorithms of society
Are way beyond my capacity
To comprehend, to understand
To keep the formulas on hand

In the quantum flux of my mind
I try to calculate, try to find
The answer to this age-old question
What is the rate of change in this dimen-
    sion?

The world spins faster every day
I can't keep up, can't find my way
Life! a fundamental force
That's pushing me beyond the source

I won't give up, I'm switching gears
Equations are just souvenirs
Of my place in space and time
In this rate of change paradigm

The pace of life is exponential
The curve is steep, it's radical
And I'm just trying to stay on my feet

In the quantum flux of my mind
I try to calculate, try to find
The answer to this age-old question
What is the rate of change in this dimen-
    sion?

The world spins faster every day
I can't keep up, can't find my way
Life is a fundamental force
That's pushing me beyond the source

Wondering what the songs sound like?
Visit the playlist on YouTube:
saracreasy.com/WWsongs

Third Eye

Wynter sat in Joy's living room with the Light pressing down on her.

She hadn't been in many houses — from the outside, this one in Magnolia, a few streets back from the water, seemed fairly typical. Inside, everywhere were signs of the life she'd left behind. Lecture materials on the coffee table, a meditation altar in the corner, crystals over the doorway. Even the bead curtain in the hallway and the incense in the bathroom reminded her of the Light.

Caleb had finally managed to pin Joy down for a visit, suggesting they go to her house where she was more comfortable, and that the two sisters spend a couple of hours alone, which they hadn't done since leaving Arizona. He'd brought Wynter over on the Beast and left her there.

Joy returned from the kitchen with tea for them both, and sat on a floor cushion. She looked happier than the last time Wynter had seen her, five weeks ago at the courthouse. The Light was making her happy. She had that placid, pleasant demeanor that Wynter remembered from the ashram when things were going well.

"This is so nice, just the two of us," Joy said.

"Caleb thought maybe he intimidated you."

"Yes, he can be a bit intimidating. All of them. I feel their judgment."

Joy was right, they did judge her, so Wynter didn't defend them. Judgment was not allowed in the Light.

"Tell me all about your new school.".

"It's okay, I guess. They don't have a music program. I wanted to be in another band, but the older kids don't want a ninth-grader. I signed up for singing lessons."

"Wonderful. Are you writing songs?"

"Yes. On my weekend visits we've been recording demos in the jamroom. Jesse has this mixing software and we're both learning to use it. You should come sing with us."

"Oh, I can't sing that sort of music."

Wynter didn't attempt to persuade her. She'd realized months ago there was nothing about her life that might tempt Joy to participate in it.

"And you have a new foster sister?"

It seemed strange to call Madeline a *sister*, but what did Wynter know about sisters?

"I'm learning a lot from her. Different stuff than from Jesse, of course. She tries to hog Jesse's time when he drives down to tutor me even though she pretends not to like him. Actually, I think he would help her if she wanted it but she never does any homework. Jesse's teaching me to speed read and to summarize. My reading speed has gone from three hundred to five hundred words per..."

Joy's attention was already wandering. Wynter struggled to think of something to engage her. Her eyes fell on a fat Buddha on the mantelpiece. It must belong to Joy's housemate, the dark-haired woman in a sunhat working out in the yard. The Light claimed people could keep the beliefs they brought with them, yet eventually everything was discarded for the Light's own teachings — which, according to Jesse, were themselves a mish-mash of various world religions, New Age ramblings, and pagan beliefs. In any case, the Buddha statue wouldn't last long. This particular one had a glittering third-eye bead on its forehead that saw right through Wynter into the dark doubts of her soul.

She shivered.

"You remember that teddy bear I had?" she asked Joy, tearing her gaze away from the statue. That bear had had the same glittering fake eyes that hid a dark soul of his own.

"A teddy bear?"

"His name was Deedee. What happened to him?"

Joy's serenity faltered. "I don't remember every toy you ever had, Wynter."

"I didn't have any toys. I just had Deedee."

"I really don't remember."

Why was she lying?

Pointless to persist. Joy was closing up, and Wynter didn't want that. She wanted Joy to rejoin the family.

"You could go visit Caleb and Jesse any time, even if I'm not there," Wynter said. "Jesse would take you out. He takes me out with his friends to the movies and different kinds of restaurants — well, the cheap ones — and to all-ages gigs."

"His friends don't care you're four years younger?"

"No, because he doesn't care. I mean, he leaves me behind sometimes if he's gonna be out all night. Do you have friends? Who lives here with you?"

"Her name is Rain. She's from Port Douglas in Australia, and she's studying to become a healer."

"I knew some Australians at the ashram."

"You mean that boy you thought you'd found?" Joy scoffed. "You remember the four Celestial Signs, don't you? If you try earnestly to do something, and the universe stops you in your tracks, it's a sign you're on the wrong path. The universe always gives you what you want, if you're on the right path."

"I once told Jesse about the Celestial Signs. He said it was circular reasoning."

"Well, Jesse has a different way of looking at things." Joy spoke evenly but Wynter noted the flutter of annoyance under the surface.

"His way makes sense to me."

"It's such a shame you've forgotten everything you were taught."

"I haven't forgotten it. I've rejected most of it, and the rest I never believed in the first place. I used to have arguments all the time with Roman. Xay thought it was all rubbish. Roman was trying to understand it, trying to make sense of it."

Joy had gone pale. "Xay?"

"Roman's friend. They were as close as brothers. They lived in the same buildings as you for over a year—"

"Yes, yes, I know who Xay was," Joy said impatiently.

At the ashram, Wynter wasn't supposed to talk to the older kids and the adults on the other side of the fence, so she'd never told Joy she knew Xay. But they were on the outside now. Those rules didn't apply.

"Do you know where he went?" Wynter asked. "He and his mother left the Light more than a year ago, and then Roman ran away too. I want to know if they found each other."

"Why are you concerned with those boys? You didn't even know them."

"Xay was my friend."

"Goodness, how can that be? He lived on the farm. When did you ever see him?"

"I used to sneak out at night." *That* was a big secret she'd never have dreamed of telling Joy when they lived at the ashram. "There was a hole in the fence, and I'd go to an old storage shed in the corner of the compound where he and Roman hung out sometimes. They let me listen to their radio. They played cards. They had these little wind-up animals and robots that they'd set against each other in an arena."

Joy was horrified. "What are you talking about? You knew Xay well?"

"Yes. He's the reason I knew about rock music when I left. He knew all about it because in Australia, in Byron Bay where he grew up, they were allowed to live in the world while their mothers were involved in the Light... Where are you going?"

Joy was jamming her feet into her sandals, her fingers fumbling with the straps as she cast hasty looks out the kitchen window where Rain was collecting her gardening tools together.

"Come with me. We're going for a walk."

"But Caleb's coming back to collect me at—"

"Just a short walk." She hurried to the door and practically threw Wynter's shoes at her. "Hurry!"

Wynter slipped on her shoes and followed Joy outside. Joy gave Rain a wave and said they wouldn't be long. They walked down the quiet, curved streets, with Wynter struggling to keep up with her sister's long strides. Joy's arms were wrapped around herself, her hands clutching her shoulders, her gaze straight ahead, and she didn't speak for a long time. They turned left, toward the water, and walked for several minutes in silence. Wynter sensed Joy's agitation rising with every step.

"When we left the ashram," Joy said at last, her pace not slowing, "I told you not to talk about anything that happened there. And you promised you wouldn't. Have you kept your word?"

Wynter didn't know what to say. She'd told Indio just one little thing last week, and he'd told Caleb, though Caleb hadn't mentioned it this weekend. And they knew about Roman, that she'd run away in February in an attempt to meet him.

What else? She'd told Jesse — accidentally or otherwise — all kinds of things she was taught in the Light. She'd let Jesse make fun of those beliefs. She'd let him show her why they weren't true...

Joy stopped and grabbed Wynter by both shoulders. Her eyes were red-rimmed from staring too long without blinking. "Have you told our brothers about Xay?" she hissed.

"No. I never did," Wynter said in a thready voice, her heart pounding. Joy's tone, that pent-up frustration on the edge of boiling over, took Wynter back to the ashram in an instant, back to fear and danger and imminent pain.

"Are you sure?"

"It's true. I didn't want them to know. He was..." How to explain it? "He was something I wanted to keep for myself."

Joy exhaled sharply, and some of her anger dissipated. She walked on, and Wynter rushed to keep up.

"They should never have come to Arizona," Joy said in a clipped voice that sounded so much like Momma. "Miriam and Ember, Xay's mom, had a history. I didn't know about it until right before they left. I'll tell you about it, Wynter, so you'll understand why you must put Xay out of your mind, and why you mustn't tell our brothers about him."

"What have they got to do with this?"

"Ember is the reason Harry and Miriam got divorced."

Wynter couldn't grasp it. She'd had no clue Ember had a connection to their family.

"When I was very little in Montana," Joy said, "when Harry and Miriam first got involved in the Light, they left me, Indio, and Caleb with our grandparents and went on a long retreat in San Diego. Ember was studying in California — I'm not sure exactly where. She was on the same retreat."

Joy stopped abruptly at the top of a narrow path leading to the beach, and stared over the top of Wynter's head as she kept talking.

"Harry had an affair with her. Miriam found out about it. Even though she was heavily pregnant with Jesse at the time, Miriam forgave him. It wasn't until a few months later, when she heard Ember was pregnant, that she threw Harry out of the house. Ember had the baby and took him back to Australia."

Joy's words tumbled around in Wynter's head. San Diego. Affair. Ember's baby.

Harry's baby.

Batteries

Wynter hardly dared to speak, but she had to know. "Xay... is Harry's son? He told me he didn't know who his father was."

"He didn't know. And I knew nothing, either." Joy grabbed Wynter's hand to lead her down the path. "I didn't know he was my half-brother until they made him leave. Our brothers don't know about him. Harry... he wanted nothing to do with that woman or her son because he just wanted Miriam back. And as you can imagine, Miriam wanted to wipe them from existence."

The path opened onto a rocky beach. Wynter stumbled as a vast expanse of water came into view, and beyond that the Olympic Mountains. As they walked closer to the shore, she grew dizzy. While Joy faced the water, hugging herself again, Wynter had to turn her back to it.

"Ember brought Xay to the ashram a few years ago because she wanted to get more involved in the Light," Joy said. "For the year they lived there, only a couple of leaders knew the history. They didn't tell me. Xay didn't know, either. And then Miriam found out, all the way from Thailand, that Ember and Xay were living there. She was furious. She had them sent away."

Wynter didn't care *why* they were sent away. What did that matter now? Surely there was something far more important to consider...

"How can you keep this from Caleb and Indio and Jesse? They should know they have another brother."

"Harry would've told them, if he wanted them to know. Think about it, Wynter. Why would they, why would *I*, want anything to do with the woman who wrecked our parents' marriage, who broke our mother's heart? After I found out the truth, I was glad Ember and Xay were sent away. Every person that woman touched was infected by her unbalanced, deceptive energy. And now you're telling me you spent time with Xay, in secret? No wonder you were so closed off to the Light. It makes me wonder what could've been."

"Xay was the only person who was always nice to me. *He* wasn't unbalanced or deceptive."

"It's not his fault, or yours. But Ember was wrong to come to Arizona, to rake up the past, and she only got away with it because Miriam wasn't there anymore."

"It's not fair to keep this from them."

"What if they resent Harry for it? What if it wrecks whatever's left of that relationship?"

"They never resented anyone when they found out about *me*."

"That's different," Joy snapped. "Momma married someone else and had you. There was no deception or betrayal." She reached for Wynter's hand again, squeezing it painfully. "You won't tell, Wynter. Promise me you won't tell. It's not your decision to set their lives on a new path. It's Harry's business."

No secrets was Caleb's rule, in Caleb's house. This was Joy's secret. Harry's secret, really, and what right did Wynter have to throw Harry's past in his sons' faces?

Wynter nodded numbly. "Okay, I promise."

Joy stroked Wynter's arm, a gentle touch this time. "I always wondered why you were so resistant to the Light. That last year or so was the worst. The leaders were convinced you would never find the right path. I was so scared for you. I lay awake at night wondering what was wrong with you. The universe wants to help, but we bring these terrible things on ourselves. Xay was a test — you should've obeyed the rules and stayed on your side of the fence. You failed the test but there are always second chances. Will you meditate with me for a while?"

Joy made her sit on the damp rocks and went through a lengthy visualization. Wynter wasn't meditating or letting in the Light, although she didn't let Joy know. She was thinking about Xay, after trying not to for so long. Remembering the first time she saw him, with Roman, through the chain-link fence. Those clear blue-green eyes and messy sun-bleached hair, the scowl on his face because he resented being dragged across the globe to the barren desert. His strange accent.

Hey, can you get us some batteries?

For their radio.

And now every moment she'd shared with him was colored in a new way. Those times she felt abandoned and thought she belonged to no one, a part of her brothers had been with her, for the short time she'd known Xay, because he shared their blood.

She and Joy walked back to Joy's house, arriving just as Caleb did. He asked Wynter to wait outside with the motorcycle while he talked to Joy for a few minutes. He was being sent overseas on Monday to teach a two-week course, and had arranged for Wynter to come to Seattle next weekend — but Joy had to be there as the "supervising adult".

Joy had assured them she'd come. Apparently, Caleb felt the need to remind her one last time.

Caleb came out looking upset. Of all the moods she'd seen her brothers in, Caleb in turmoil was the worst. Had Joy backed out of the weekend? He said nothing as he checked Wynter's helmet and strapped on his own.

When they arrived home, she took off her helmet and, when she didn't immediately dismount, he looked over his shoulder.

"Why did you talk to Joy just now?" she asked.

Caleb hung his helmet on the handlebar. "I asked her about what you told Indio last week, about the teachers beating you. I wanted to know what she knew."

"Did she say I deserved it?"

"Pretty much." He was facing forward so she couldn't see his expression. "She told me what she told him a while back — that the kids were hard to control. She said there was some hitting or slapping sometimes. She saw a cane in someone's office but it was only a threat, she said. She denied anyone was held down."

Wynter sat hugging the helmet against her stomach, staring at the back of her brother's head. She knew Indio believed her, but what if he'd explained it wrong to Caleb? And if Caleb didn't believe her, what was the point in talking about any of it? Why did he always say *You can trust me, you can tell me anything*, if he thought she would lie?

She *did* trust Caleb. Joy had told her not to talk about the Light, but Joy's power over her was diminishing. She'd give it one more try.

"They did hit and slap, and they were always screaming. They would bang our heads together until you saw spots. Maybe you were arguing or maybe you were just talking to someone and making too much noise. They hit you around the head with books. I saw someone knock a little boy out like that. They caned your hands if you messed up in the warehouse, or your bottom or legs or..."

She swallowed hard, dragging in a new breath. It was a bit easier to talk like this, to his back instead of his face.

"I don't remember a week when *someone* wasn't punished or locked up. You never knew if you were next and you were so glad when they picked someone else. And then, if that kid cried afterward, you laughed at them for being weak even though you knew your turn was coming. And when they got something worse, you just didn't talk about it at all."

After a moment he said, "Who did this?"

"The women assigned to the classroom, the teachers. They were rotated in and out. They never got enough sleep because they still had to do their other work and go to the temple meetings. They didn't want to be there. After a while they became bad-tempered and they'd copy the others. They started out nice but it was like a disease."

"Did you ever get *something worse?*"

"Yes," Wynter whispered.

"Can you tell me?"

Wynter felt that familiar lump in her throat that stopped her words every time the dark pieces started to rise. Just once, she'd overcome that fear and talked to Indio, somehow knowing it wouldn't change him.

"Not today."

Caleb's shoulders sagged as he exhaled. And this was why she couldn't tell him — because she couldn't bear to see him bend under the weight of it. And Jesse wouldn't only bend, he'd break.

Caleb said, "Was Joy... was she ever assigned to the classroom?"

"A few times. She wasn't too bad, Caleb, not as bad as some of the others."

Wynter was shaking now, so afraid he didn't believe her. To him, Joy was quiet and fragile. It was hard to believe she'd throw a book at someone's head or drag them by the hair into a closet. Caleb lived in a world where teachers weren't allowed to touch students, even in kindness. Why should he believe her?

"Joy wants to forget all about that, like I do," she said. "She likes the Light but in the end she didn't like the ashram, what it had become. She's got her own dark pieces there. So whatever happened, it's over and it doesn't matter now. It's okay if you don't believe me. It really is."

It wasn't, though.

"Hop off," Caleb said.

Wynter got off the bike and put the helmet on the seat. Caleb swung his leg over and drew her close.

"Of course I believe you. I know you want to put it behind you, but don't ever think I won't believe you."

He hugged her tightly, comforting them both.

"I'm so sorry these things happened to you." His voice was muffled against her shoulder. "I'm sorry you were scared all the time. I'd do anything to change it. I'd do anything to have been there for you."

Someone *had* been there for her, for a while anyway. Wynter was still processing what Joy had told her.

Xay was there for me. I think he's your brother. I want you to meet him...

Then a picture came to mind of what Caleb's life would've been like if his father had never met Ember, if Xay never existed, if *she* never existed because Harry and Miriam stayed together. Caleb would've grown up in Montana with his brothers and Joy and both his parents, without the weight of the world on his shoulders. He and Indio would be close like brothers are supposed to be. They'd have a band and Joy would be the one singing with them. He'd have fallen in love with someone else, not Bea, someone he could give his full attention to, and he wouldn't now have a broken heart.

She trusted Caleb to love her. She didn't trust him not to resent Xay for being the reason that perfect life fell apart. And what if she told him, and he didn't even care? What if he felt nothing? Somehow that was even worse — that Xay might be nothing more to him than Harry's forgotten mistake.

She'd made a promise. Caleb thought promises and commitments were important. He wouldn't want her to break her promise to Joy. So the problem really solved itself.

She clung to him, knowing he had no clue about her line of thought. She said, "Thank you for believing me."

"Go get your things together. We'll head back to Deb and Brian's."

She went to pack, and it was a long time before she heard him come into the house after her, to find the car keys.

The Box

"I'm fine with Caleb bossing me around," Jesse said, parking the truck on the wide, perfectly flat driveway of a large house in Shelton, behind four other vehicles. "I'm not gonna stand for Indio doing it. He's not bad, as brothers go. He taught me stuff. Gives me advice on girls and music and porn. But this, today, this is way out of line."

Wynter, in the passenger seat, sucked in her cheeks to stop from giggling.

"Laugh all you want," he said. "We got two solid days of him being in charge. See how you like it once he gets started."

"I'm not laughing. And Joy's in charge."

"She's nominally in charge."

"What does that mean?"

"It means she's the *nominated* supervising adult. In reality Indio's gonna take over because Joy's... Well, she does not have a commanding presence, if you know what I mean. Would *you* do what she says?"

An expression halfway between a wince and a frown crossed Wynter's face, and Jesse regretted his question. She looked away, out the side window.

"What a weird house," she said.

"Ugly as sin."

"I agree. I also like it, somehow."

The asymmetrical A-frame house stood amid an untended clearing in the woods surrounding a lake. It was covered in cream-colored siding, *vertical*, just to be different, with black downpipes and window frames. A mismatched pale wood deck ran underneath the steeply angled roof overhang, and on the deck was Indio's Moto Guzzi.

"Doesn't *look* wrecked," Wynter mused. "Didn't you say he must've wrecked his bike?"

The bike was indeed in perfect shape.

"Maybe he fried the engine or something, taking girls for joy rides around the lake last night. If not, he better have a damn good reason for ordering me seventy miles out of my way to collect him."

All they knew was that Indio had ridden up from Portland for a party the night before. Had he secured the use of a car, he could've picked up Wynter from Enumclaw this morning, on his way to Seattle for her weekend visit. Instead, Jesse had to drive down to fetch her. Which was fine. It was only fifty minutes and he made the trip twice a week already to help with her homework and to eat Debra's pot roasts. But a few minutes before he left, Indio had called instructing him to drive the Silverado, not the Caprice, and to pick him up as well. He wanted to put his bike in the truck bed, which Jesse assumed meant he'd wrecked it.

Two girls and a guy came out of the house, saying goodbye to someone inside, and got into a Honda on the driveway. The guy flicked his hand at Jesse to indicate he should back out of the way although there was plenty of room, in Jesse's estimation.

"Even total strangers boss me around," he grumbled. "What's with that?"

He backed up a couple of feet and the Honda departed.

"Was this a huge sleepover, d'you think?" Wynter said as they walked up to the front door. A few people were visible through the windows.

"This is what the aftermath of a college party looks like, Wyn. People stay over because friends don't let friends drive drunk. Actually, looks like it was a pretty sedate party. No empty liquor bottles on the porch, no one's underwear on the roof, no cop cars in sight."

A stunning woman answered the door. Jesse had never met a model before, and she must surely be a model. Six feet tall, makeup-free soft olive skin and artfully styled tresses of long dark hair, legs going on forever. Breasts, waist, hips, all shaped exactly as they should be—

"Is Indio here?" Wynter said, but she was glaring at Jesse because Jesse was gawping.

"Wynter! And you must be Jesse!" The woman gave Wynter a quick hug, and Jesse a rather longer one. Her hair smelled divine. "Come on inside. It's a bit chaotic at the moment. I'm not sure where he is..."

The entryway opened onto a huge room with a cathedral ceiling and a stone fireplace and chimney in the middle of the floor. Kind of retro, but impressive nonetheless. Half the room was set up as a sitting room, the other half an open space with a piano, bookcases, and a wall of windows overlooking the backyard and the lake beyond. Wynter actually turned a circle on the spot, admiring it all.

What on earth was Indio doing at a party for gazillionaires?

People sat in the living room talking and eating toast and corn chips, and others wandered around, some still in their PJs or half-dressed.

"It's not my house," the woman said, almost apologetically. "It's my cousin's house. I'm just staying for the week. Flying back to Ohio tomorrow. Now, where *is* he? I've got the little fellas lined up for you. Just need to go through a few things..."

Jesse exchanged a look with Wynter — *No idea what she's talking about.* He got an awful sinking feeling in his stomach. Had she mistaken them for someone else? But she'd called them by name.

"He's probably in my room," the woman said, leading the way down a corridor.

But of course. When a gorgeous girl was involved, Indio was bound to be in her room.

"Are you Indio's... uh, girlfriend?" Wynter blurted out. Clearly she was having the same trouble figuring things out as Jesse was.

The woman threw a laugh over her shoulder before opening a door. She poked her head inside. "Not in here. Let's try the den. I just know he can't resist those guitars. Down we go."

Jesse took a brief look of his own into the room, clearly a guest room — sparsely furnished, a queen bed with rumpled-possibly-post-coital bedding, a near-empty bookcase, and various color-coordinated decor items.

The den, it turned out, was an enormous basement with an orange-and-brown patterned carpet from the 'seventies, and packed with old couches, a pool table, a jukebox, rugs and lamps, and guitars hanging on the wall. There was another fireplace, too. The room was dimly lit and someone was rolled up in a sleeping bag on one of the couches — not Indio, but a skinny young guy with a bushy beard. He was snoring. Blankets and pillows were scattered around where others must have bunked down for the night.

The woman went to knock on one of several doors. Jesse nudged Wynter. "This basement is bigger than our entire house. I hate rich people."

Indio emerged from the room — a bathroom — and squeezed the woman's arm like he was thanking her for the privilege of using the facilities. He wore his usual faded jeans and t-shirt, and his hair was damp, towel-dried, tangled. He had a three-day growth on his jaw, purple stains under his eyes, and his t-shirt wasn't the cleanest.

"How come he's so fucking sexy when he looks like crap?" Jesse muttered.

Wynter was trying not to giggle again.

Indio came over without so much as a *Thanks for picking me up*, gave Wynter a side-hug in greeting and said, "I've got a little job for you. You guys met Lia?"

Jesse knew that name. "Whoa, you're Turk's sister?" Turk was Indio's roommate, best friend, and founding member of Blunderbelly.

Lia sidled over to Indio's other side and took it upon herself to hook his damp locks behind his ears. "I'll see you upstairs, okay?"

She left. Indio proceeded to upturn pillows and jackets until he found his sneakers, and sat to pull them on.

Jesse figured it out. "Dude, I'm sorry, you slept down here on the couch?"

"Where did you think I slept?" Indio didn't wait for an answer. "Joy didn't come with you? Is she at the house?"

"Yep. She arrived bright and early, so I got out of there ASAP. I figured if I hung around talking for any length of time, I'd probably say the wrong thing and scare her off. This place is amazing." They headed upstairs. "Thought at first I'd walked onto a porn set."

Behind him, Wynter asked, "What's that?"

"Uh, all you need to know is that it requires a tacky mansion."

"Is this mansion tacky?"

"The decor could use an update." Time to change the subject. Indio had stopped at the guest room door. "So, what are we doing here?"

Indio reached around him, took Wynter's hand, and directed her into the bedroom. Jesse followed them in. On the bed was a large cardboard box. The box was mewling. Lia sat beside it. She beckoned Wynter over by crooking her finger.

"My cousin's neighbor's cat produced a little surprise a few weeks ago," Lia said as Wynter cautiously approached. "I agreed to help her find homes for them on the condition she neutered her cat. Would you like to choose one for Turk and Indio?"

Jesse's jaw dropped. "Whoa, you're getting a kitten?" Indio had sent him miles out of his way for *kittens*?

"*Turk* is getting a kitten," Indio growled. "Nothing to do with me."

"I was going to drop one off when I visited Portland," Lia said, "before I fly home next week. But Indio decided to come to my party after all. Then he tells me he'll strap the box to his bike. Obviously that would scare the kitten to death."

Wynter, who had lifted a flap of the box, yanked back her hand. "Do they scare easily?"

"No, it's fine."

Lia reached in and took out a dark gray fluffy kitten. It hung over her palm, rear legs dangling. Jesse felt a distinct fluttering in his stomach — a totally normal and unavoidable reaction. Humans were preprogrammed to turn gooey at the sight of wide-eyed balls of fluff. Even Indio, whose mood was off because he wasn't a morning person, quirked his lip.

Wynter, who didn't even like teddy bears, glared at it.

"Take it," Lia prompted her.

"I might squash it."

"You won't squash it."

Wynter cupped her hands, and Lia placed the kitten into them before removing another identical one from the box and holding it out for Indio. Making a show of being reluctant, he hunkered down next to the bed and took it.

"Just the two left, both boys," Lia said. "Eight weeks old today. What d'you think, Wynter? Choose one, and the other's going to my cousin's colleague at the tennis club."

"They're identical," Jesse said, unimpressed with this *little job* Indio had set up for Wynter. "Just stick them in a hat and pick one at random."

Wynter was examining the kitten in her hands like she was checking an apple for spots. "They're not identical. This one is licking my finger, and that one is exploring."

"Choose the curious one." Jesse plopped down to take the kitten off Indio's arm, where it was trying to climb up onto his shoulder. "Curiosity is a sign of intelligence."

"This one is curious about what my finger tastes like," Wynter pointed out, sitting on the bed and placing her kitten on Indio's arm, perhaps to see if it would crawl upward as the other one had. "If they're brothers, you shouldn't separate them."

Lia said, "Turk only wants the one, so..."

"He needs to take them both. You already took them from their mother. You can't take them from each other."

Jesse exchanged a look with Indio. Wynter might not have fallen in love with the kittens, but she sure was concerned with their emotional welfare.

"You're anthropomorphizing," Jesse said.

Wynter punished him with a scowl, annoyed by the long word she didn't understand and didn't want to ask about in front of a stranger.

"No rush," Lia said.

"There is, actually," Jesse said. "Our sister's waiting back in Seattle. We got a big weekend planned, and if she leaves, which could happen cuz she's kind of unpredictable, then Wynter can't stay because Caleb's gone to Guam, I'm a poor influence, and Indio's not an upstanding member of society." He was pretty sure he wasn't giving anything away there. Surely Lia knew enough about her brother's best buddy to know all about that.

"I have chosen," Wynter announced. "Indio, take them both. Lia's cousin's colleague at the tennis club will have to find another kitten."

Lia suppressed a grin at Wynter's determination. "That's okay, actually. He won't mind. You should definitely take them both," she told

Indio, enjoying his discomfort. "Turk won't mind, either. He's a total softie. Here you go."

She pulled an old towel out of a tote bag, along with a tub of kibble. Wynter arranged the towel in the box and gathered up the kittens, like it was all decided.

"Congratulations on becoming a kitty-daddy." Jesse slapped Indio on the back as he secured the box flaps. "One cat, two cats, what's the difference, really?"

"I dunno, two cats cost twice as much to keep?" Indio muttered.

"They've had their first shots, so they'll need boosters in three, six, and nine weeks," Lia explained.

"Send Turk a schedule."

"And you need to... that is, Turk needs to get them castrated at four months or I'll castrate *him*."

Jesse Won't

Indio thumbed Jesse out the door in a gesture that was altogether too much like something Caleb would do. Jesse lifted the box and Wynter took the kibble. Outside, Lia lingered on the deck, grabbing Indio's arm before he could escape.

"If I'd known you were going to take both of them off my hands," she said in a low voice that Jesse nevertheless overheard, "I'd have tried a little harder last night to get you into my bed, as a thank you."

Indio gave her a peck on the cheek, faking a stern look. She called goodbye and went inside. Jesse put the box on the back seat and went to help Indio wheel the bike up the ramp into the truck bed.

Wynter, sitting with the kittens, put her head out the window. "We should cut a hole in the side or something."

"Cats like small dark spaces," Jesse said.

"They're crying."

"I think that's just regular kitty noises. Bro, how are you gonna get those critters back to Portland?"

"I'll buy a pet carrier, and Turk will pay me back. One of those specially designed backpacks."

Wynter wasn't happy about it. "Lia said that would scare them to death."

"She didn't mean *literally*—"

"Jesse will drive you and your bike back to Portland tomorrow."

"Uh, Jesse won't," Jesse said.

"You drive down to Portland all the time to see Blunderbelly."

"Not on a Sunday. I have a date, and my classes start this week." He handed Indio the tie-downs from the tool box. "So, what's with Lia? You never told me she was quite so..." He gestured meaningfully at the house.

"You never asked," Indio said.

"I'm sure I did. I'm sure I always ask about your buddies' sisters as soon as I learn of their existence. You turned her down last night?"

Indio shook his head in annoyance as he tightened the straps around the bike. "I hardly know her. I met her about three times in Ohio."

"Girls you hardly know are your *thing*."

Indio whipped the keys out of Jesse's back pocket and took the driver's seat, adding nothing more to the discussion.

"Guess what," Jesse said as they set off. "Word's getting out that Caleb's on the market again. He's had two ex-girlfriends and two hopefuls calling, 'just to chat'." He air-quoted the words, grinning over his shoulder at Wynter. "Hey, we should set him up with Lia."

"Doesn't that violate the Code?" Wynter said.

"How do *you* know about the Code?"

"Madeline told me, now we're friends, that she's not going to flirt with you anymore because of the Code."

"Good to hear. Tell her I have a girlfriend. Although, Madeline seems like the type who tries twice as hard when the guy's taken. Strictly speaking, in Lia's case, the Code applies to Indio, not his brothers."

"Do you have a girlfriend?"

"More or less. Met her at the robotics club fundraiser. She just transferred from Central so I showed her around campus and we've had four dates. Four dates is a girlfriend, right?" He waited for Indio's pithy putdown and got nothing.

"Is that the college we walked around in Ellensburg?" Wynter said.

"Uh-huh. She's gonna major in psychology."

"If she likes human brains, why was she interested in robotics?"

"She wasn't. She bought a doughnut from our stand and I persuaded her to pay another dollar to drive my robot around an obstacle course for three minutes." Fiorella was a spoilt princess, which Jesse didn't normally go for, and nor did he plan on calling her by her requested nickname, Fifi. But he couldn't resist her fascination for that robot. "She had fun handling my gearshift," he added, with a smirk at Indio. "So, back to Lia. Is she a model?"

"She's a post-grad student at Ohio State," Indio said patiently. "As it happens, she has also done catalogues and promotional stuff—"

"Aha! She *is* a model."

"—handing out free ice cream at monster truck shows."

"In shortie shorts and a crop-top. Nice."

"You're pathetic."

"What's she studying?"

"Final year of veterinary science."

"Is she gonna be a vet, or a vet's assistant?"

"An actual vet, Jesse. She's smart. Seriously, ask her to play Scrabble if you need empirical evidence."

"I will absolutely do that. Turn this vehicle around immediately."

Indio was looking more annoyed by the second, which was of course the point.

"Can't believe you turned her down," Jesse mused. "What's wrong with you? Did something awkward happen in Ohio, one of those three times you met her?"

"No."

"When your answer comes back real quick like that, it kinda sounds untruthful."

"What if the kittens can't breathe?" Wynter said, putting a stop to Jesse's probing. "Can I take them out of the box?"

"As long as you keep them under control," Indio said.

Wynter opened the box and gingerly placed the kittens in her lap, putting her hands around them in a vague sort of barrier. Jesse twisted around to study her for a minute. Dammit, she *was* going to fall in love with Indio's kittens.

He reached over to thump Indio's arm before slumping in his seat. "You did this just to win points, didn't you. Brother of the Year Award. Well done."

From the back, Wynter said, "Are you jealous?"

"Yes! Yes, Wyn, I am jealous! Lia said she was gonna drop a kitten off when she drives to Portland next week. But no, he rides all the way to Shelton to party with people he doesn't even know except for the hottest smartest girl on the planet, who he's not allowed to sleep with, just so you can meet the kittens. He thinks a weekend with kittens, and a guitar with lipstick pickups, and a rhyming dictionary, make him the superior sibling. I call you almost every day. I drive down to Enumclaw twice a week. I'm teaching you a thousand new things to help you fit in and survive, and to improve the wiring of your stimulus-deprived brain." He drummed his forehead with his fist to make his point. Indio chuckled at the display, the dickwad. "I'm teaching you skills for life! And I gave you a cuddly bacterium as long as your arm and *without* a creepy teddy bear face."

"It's not a contest," Wynter muttered.

"That's what I told him!" Indio cried.

"Also, Jesse, you said *who* when I think you meant *whom*."

Jesse groaned and kept quiet for the rest of the trip, while Indio cemented his number one position by getting Wynter to talk about the songs she was writing, the music she was listening to, and the utter lack of opportunity at her new high school to put together another band.

"Let's take bets on whether Joy's still here," Jesse said, feeling mean, as they turned into the driveway.

Wynter clearly didn't appreciate him making light of it. With Caleb overseas, this Seattle visit depended entirely on Joy's cooperation.

Joy was sitting on the porch, reading from a book and making notes. She looked up briefly as the truck stopped and Indio yanked on the parking brake.

"I'll roll my bike down and leave it out here," Indio said. "Put the truck in the garage."

Indio got out to deal with the bike before Jesse had time to grouch about being bossed around again. He slid over to the driver's seat.

"You haven't told me today's day in history," Wynter said, making it obvious she was trying to improve his mood. "Did you prepare something?"

"Of course. We'll read *The Hobbit*, which was published today in 1937. I loved that book when I was six."

"I'm not six."

"I'm doing you a favor, Wyn. Indio's gonna make you read *The Lord of the Rings* trilogy eventually, and this is the prequel."

"Indio would never *make* me read anything."

That was probably true. In fact, Jesse couldn't imagine Indio making her *do* anything, unlike Caleb enforcing his rules and Jesse controlling her education.

"Also today, around one hundred fifty years ago, H.G. Wells was born. He was a futurist, which means he predicted stuff about the future, and he was a science fiction writer, which means he made up stuff about the future."

"We watched his movie!"

"We watched the 1960 *Time Machine* movie, yes." Jesse spoke distractedly because Joy was making her way over to the truck — hopefully to talk to Indio. He didn't want to talk to her.

"Did they make other movies of his books?" Wynter asked.

"Yes, but I thought we'd explore the social implications of the 1938 radio broadcast of *The War of the Worlds* as a fake newscast, which freaked people out for real. Orson Welles the actor, no relation, was accused of abdicating responsibility for the alleged—"

Joy tapped on his window and he reluctantly wound it down.

"Where's your herbal tea? I can't seem to find it."

"No one in this household drinks that crap," Jesse said. "We have robust English Breakfast tea. We have fair trade coffee, milk, beer, and a liter or two of hard liquor."

Joy was a model of serenity today. "I'll walk down to the store and buy some. Wynter, what would you like?" She peered past him to Wynter in the back seat. "Hibiscus? Lemon balm?"

"Wynter doesn't drink—"

"Hibiscus is fine," Wynter said quickly, to shut both of them up.

"Indio can take you to the store on his bike," Jesse said.

"I'll walk."

Joy waited at the window, watching Indio untie the motorcycle.

"Jesse, can you use shorter words sometimes?" Wynter said, taking up where they left off. "I don't know what *abdicated* means."

"I will not use shorter words. I'll make you a dictionary on a shared file so we can both add to it, and we'll learn from each other. As an incentive... You know what that word means?"

"Yes, Jesse." She reached out and flicked his ear.

"Ouch!" What the hell was this? Indio was acting like Caleb, and now she was acting like Indio, and everyone was ganging up on him. He decided to ignore it because, after all, she was being playful and he should encourage that, on principle. "As an incentive, I'll give you ten dollars for every word *you* add that I didn't previously know what it meant."

Joy gave him a disapproving look. "Wynter, you shouldn't accept money in that way."

"What's the correct way to accept money?" Jesse fired back. "An honest day's work? In which case, the Light owes Wynter about seven years' back pay, right? Or was that work not honest?"

Joy's serene expression returned. "The ashram didn't function that way."

Jesse turned away from her. "Ground rules, Wyn. You can't go looking for words. It has to be something you come across in your daily life, at school or in an article you read. Just warning you that I used to read the dictionary for fun. Also, I'm capping the payment at ten dollars a week, averaged over the year." He pulled a face as he reconsidered. "Wow, five hundred twenty dollars. That's a lot of money. Not that I think you can find fifty-two words I don't know."

"I don't want your money, Jesse," Wynter said, uncomfortable that Joy was upset, or whatever it was that Joy was. Hard to tell. Most of the time, as far as Jesse could tell, Joy wasn't all there.

"How about one dollar per word?" he said.

"Sure."

"You're a terrible negotiator." The bike was down. Jesse handed Wynter the roller door key from the dash. "Hop out and open up, will you?"

"Debra and Brian have a remote control for their garage door."

"Great! Call them up and ask them to press the little button for me."

"Will that work?" Wynter thought about it for a moment as Jesse watched her, stunned, and very much regretting making fun of her credulity. "I don't think that'll work, will it?"

"You shouldn't tease her like that," Joy said after Wynter had gotten out of the car. Nice to know Joy, at least, was still acting like Joy.

"She doesn't mind."

"She doesn't understand how the world works."

"Do you?"

"Not really."

"I think it's you who doesn't like being teased. It'll help her to develop a bullshit detector."

His conscience niggled him, though, as he watched Wynter struggling to lift the roller door until Indio went to help. He was doing what Indio used to do to him, seeing how far he could be tricked or persuaded. It had made him, from a young age, wary of Indio's authority on any subject. The last thing Jesse wanted was for Wynter to doubt his knowledge or intelligence.

"We're going down to the jamroom later," he told Joy. "Wynter says you sing. You could join us."

"I'll be happy to listen in," Joy said, disinterestedly. Then she added, like she *was* interested, "Caleb used to pick out tunes on the piano at Grandma and Grandpa's house. Whatever happened to that piano?"

"It's at Harry's place in Everett. Caleb had lessons from about fourth grade. I gotta say, he wasn't a good fit for the piano. We used to turn up the radio to drown him out when he practiced scales. He was okay on guitar. There's this 'seventies song, *Hit Me With Your Rhythm Stick*. That song practically taught Caleb how to play bass."

"I've never heard of it. It sounds horrible."

"That's nothing. Same guy did another one called *Sex and Drugs and Rock and Roll*." He enunciated the words carefully. "Very cool riff. Indio will be happy to play it for you."

Joy gave him a long-suffering smile, which Jesse returned sweetly before rolling up the window in her face. He drove into the garage.

And crashed straight into his dirt bike, which he'd stupidly left parked in the middle of the space. In the rear view mirror, he saw Wynter clap her hands over her mouth.

Then she called out, in case he hadn't noticed, "You wrecked your bike!"

The Wrong Idea

Wynter carried the box of kittens out the back and sat with them on the patio until Joy joined her. Joy had not contacted her all week, since telling her about Xay. She was acting now like nothing unusual had happened, asking about school, fussing over the kittens.

"Is there anything else we need from the store?" Joy asked Jesse when he appeared.

"Dunno. You're in charge."

"Jesse," Indio said, coming up behind him. "Get in the kitchen and make a list to last us the weekend."

Jesse glared at Joy like it was her fault for making Indio boss him around, but he went inside without a fuss. Wynter wanted this weekend to be perfect, yet nothing about it seemed right. If Caleb were here, things would run smoothly. Instead, Jesse was being openly hostile to Joy *and* Indio, Indio was making some kind of statement with the kittens, and she and Joy were holding this huge secret from their brothers while having nothing to say to each other. She didn't want to ask questions about Joy's life because everything in Joy's life revolved around the Light. She pointedly did not look at the notebook Joy was reading while idly stroking a kitten in her lap, because she knew it was Light mantras or lecture notes.

Indio fetched a beer and squatted to pet a kitten with nothing to say, either.

"Could I possibly have cash to pay for this?" Joy said, looking over the list Jesse brought out.

Indio handed her some money from his wallet and offered to drive her to the store. She reiterated the desire to walk by herself, and he didn't try to persuade her otherwise. She left.

Indio settled on the lounge chair with his beer. "So, what's the plan?"

"We'll go on a family outing," Jesse said. "And this evening we have a movie to watch, as suggested by this day in history—"

"Can we give that a rest?" Indio grumbled.

"Thirty-two years ago," Jesse said ignoring him, "Sandra Day O'Connor became the first female Supreme Court justice. For a conservative, she wasn't too bad. I think the world should be run by middle-aged women."

"Sounds like something someone with mommy issues would say," Indio said.

Jesse punched Indio in the solar plexus, right where he'd taught Wynter it was the most painful. Beer spilled all over Indio's face and chest. Indio was grinning and didn't retaliate, so he must think he deserved it.

"Lastly, two birthdays," Jesse continued. "The first is totally random — Emma Watkins, the first girl Wiggle."

"*Wiggle?*" Indio and Wynter said in unison.

"You don't know the Wiggles, bro? Marcus's kid brother was crazy about them when he was six. Which, I gotta say, is way too old to be into the Wiggles. We'll track down some Wiggles to watch, Wyn. We could all learn a lot, musically. They have a dinosaur and a pirate and a—"

"You know a hell of a lot too much about preschool entertainment," Indio cut in, sounding both surprised and uninterested.

"And they're Aussie. *Mate,* we'll practice our Australian accents and Wynter can adjudicate which is better."

Wynter's heart stuttered. "How... how would I know which is better?"

"You said your friend Roman was Australian, right? I bet he knows about the Wiggles."

"Let's do the other birthday," she said. She couldn't bear the idea of spending her weekend listening to her brothers — or a dinosaur or a pirate — speaking in Aussie accents. Not with Joy's presence reminding her she wasn't allowed to talk about Xay.

Jesse looked like he was going to insist. Something in her expression stopped him and he caved. "Bill Murray, an actor, so we'll watch *Ghostbusters.*"

"Nope, we'll watch *Groundhog Day*," Indio said.

"*Ghostbusters* is funnier."

"Yes, it is. It's also stupid."

Jesse's lips thinned. He turned to Wynter. "You decide."

"I don't know anything about either of those movies."

Indio said, "*Ghostbusters* is stupid, and *Groundhog Day* is touching and clever. We'll watch *Groundhog Day.*"

"Wyn," Jesse said, "you have to overrule him."

Wynter had a brief mental image of Xay sitting here, joking around with his brothers. Would he get along with Indio and Jesse as well as they got along with each other? Xay was easy going and sensitive like

Indio, but in her mind's eye she saw them staring at each other in silence. *Glaring* at each other. No, it was Jesse he'd click with first.

She pushed the image aside and played along with her brothers' little spat. "Do I have the power to overrule Indio?"

"Won't know till you try, baby," Indio said.

"Hmm." She assessed him, and they exchanged half-smiles. "I don't think I will."

"Goddammit!" Jesse yelled. "Kittens don't mean he gets to win *everything*."

"You told me he's in charge. I'm sure Caleb would say I can't overrule the person in charge."

"Y'know what? We'll watch the next movie on our 'sixties sci-fi list instead," Jesse said. "*Fantastic Voyage*, where they shrink a submarine and crew to microscopic size and inject it into a guy's bloodstream to perform a medical procedure. We'll critique the movie based on its biological accuracy. It'll be educational. Indio, you're not invited. Wyn, what are you *doing?*"

Wynter had distracted herself by gently holding down the kittens on their backs to tickle their stomachs.

"See? This one likes the tickling and bats at my hand. But *this* one..." She hovered her fingers over its stomach. "This one does a starfish. Why do they behave differently? Shouldn't they both be doing whatever's best for their survival?"

Jesse got on the ground with her. "It's called genetic variation. The starfish thing can't be good for survival — exposing his belly like that. The other one must've gotten all the good genes. Was this the curious one? Damn, they both look the same."

"Survival of the fittest has nothing to do with it," Indio said. "They're domestic animals, bred to leech off of humans. The difference in behavior is called *personality*."

Wynter had never considered animals to have personalities. "You have to name them according to their different personalities," she told Indio.

"That's Turk's job. Nothing to do with me."

"You could suggest something creative or poetic."

"Cat A and Cat B."

"Are you kidding me?" Jesse said.

"Are you overruling me?" Indio mocked him.

Wynter tried not to roll her eyes. She'd never met Turk. Hopefully he'd do the right thing.

"I love them," she said.

Indio grinned slyly at Jesse, who exploded into a tirade.

"You don't love the kittens! How can you love them? You haven't even cuddled them. Joy paid them more attention than you. You're doing experiments on them! Which I love, by the way, because it's what I'd do. But you don't love them!"

Wynter was bewildered by his overreaction. "I do love them," she said quietly. "I want the best for them, which according to Caleb means I love them. I wanted air holes in their box. I want them to have meaningful names. I want to understand their needs. Do they need toys?"

Indio pulled a gas station receipt out of his back pocket, scrunched it up, and dropped it on the ground. Cat A pounced on it.

"Kittens need cuddles!" Jesse was still hyped up on jealousy, or whatever it was. "Their mothers lick them all the time."

"I'm not gonna lick—"

"You have to hold them and stroke them."

"You know I don't like cute furry things."

Jesse snorted. "You don't *like* them, but you *love* them?"

"I don't like their cuteness. I love them for their personalities, and because they need me. They need *something* from me. From us."

"I'll get you a paintbrush to stroke them with," Indio drawled, entirely unconcerned by Jesse's outburst. "It'll feel just like momma cat's tongue."

"She doesn't need a paintbrush. Jesus, Wynter, when a human being sees a kitten, that human has an innate desire to stroke it. Why can't you do that?"

"Maybe I'm not human!" she shot back, piling the kittens into her lap. She turned to Indio. "And don't use that name." Tears pricked her eyes and her throat tightened.

Indio narrowed his eyes at her, his expression sobering.

Jesse's anger evaporated. "What name?" He looked between them, trying to figure it out. "*Momma?*"

"That's for our mother," Wynter whispered. "Not theirs."

"Knock-knock?"

They turned as one to look across the patio, where Svetlana stood in the frame of the sliding door.

"I did ring the bell but no one came, and your front door was open."

Wynter's stomach sank, leaving a sickening feeling down to her bones after the adrenaline surge from yelling at Jesse. It wasn't his fault. She was trying not to think about Xay, which only made it impossible not to think about him, and about Joy's secret and whether or not she was even supposed to be keeping it...

"We weren't fighting," she said, in case Svetlana got the wrong impression about her home life. Her voice came out wobbly and breathless. "We were discussing kittens."

Indio surreptitiously slid his beer under the chair. "Can we help you?" he said, very politely.

"I just dropped by to check how things are going." Svetlana accepted the kitten that Jesse plucked from Wynter's lap and thrust into her hands. She'd met Jesse once before, when he visited Enumclaw. "So cute! What's her name?"

"*His* name is Cat A," Jesse said. "Is that right, Indio? Or did I mix them up already?"

Indio hauled himself to his feet and assumed a casually authoritative stance, imitating Caleb, except that she couldn't imagine Caleb wearing a grubby shirt soaked in beer. "Joy just went to the store. She'll be back any minute."

"Oh, good. I'll wait for her, if you don't mind."

Of course they all minded very much, but Joy was *nominally* the supervising adult for the weekend and Svetlana needed proof she was actually present to supervise. Wynter felt guilty for no good reason.

Svetlana handed the kitten back. "May I take a quick walk through the house?" Presumably no answer other than *yes* was acceptable.

"Go ahead, take your time," Indio said jovially. He didn't sound like himself.

Svetlana went into the kitchen. They heard her opening the refrigerator and pantry doors. She walked through to the back of the house.

"I'm praying you don't have illicit substances on the premises," Indio told Jesse.

"It's not illegal in the state of Washington."

"It has to be locked up," Wynter put in.

Indio gritted his teeth. "Do you have any recently legalized *for adults over the age of twenty-one* substances on the premises, Mister Nineteen Years Old?"

"Not one gram," Jesse conceded, tucking the kitten into his arm. "I even hid my papers and lighter."

"Do you have a key for this credenza?" Svetlana called from inside.

"What's a credenza?" Jesse muttered.

"*Credenza* means liquor cabinet," Wynter said. "That's what Caleb calls it." She took the other kitten and they went inside. "And you owe me a dollar."

Svetlana was indeed examining the contents of the liquor cabinet in the dining room. "This liquor needs to be locked up."

"I'm not going to drink it."

"Is there a key?"

Jesse gave Wynter his kitten and squatted in front of the credenza. The bottles and glasses clinked as he felt around inside, to no avail. "Caleb got this from a flea market. I don't think it has a key."

"It has a lock," Svetlana said, as if that fact would make the key appear from thin air.

"Well, it doesn't have a key." Jesse straightened, barely hiding his annoyance. "I guess he got what he paid for."

"Is there somewhere you can lock up the liquor?"

"We could put it in the gun safe in Caleb's bedroom," Indio said. "Jesse, d'you know the combination?"

"It's our street number and zip code."

Svetlana threw up her hands. "I can't accept that it's locked up if you've just told Wynter the combination. Is there a gun in that safe?"

"It's a *gun* safe," Jesse said.

"I'm not going to drink any alcohol or touch a gun!" Wynter exclaimed, feeling the situation slip away, wishing desperately that Caleb were here.

Svetlana turned an expectant look on Indio, awaiting an answer to her question.

"Caleb has a handgun."

"You need to change that safe combination, right away. I can't allow a child to remain in a house where she has access to firearms."

"Changing the combination," Indio said, "would mean I value your rules and regulations more than my life when Caleb finds out. And I don't."

Svetlana's eyes hardened against his as she decided how to proceed. Last time they met, they'd gotten along fine. What went wrong? Then again, Wynter's previous caseworker Tina would've made a scene by now, throwing around the weight of her authority. Svetlana was at least trying to keep things pleasant.

"Is there anywhere else in the house you can lock up the alcohol?" Svetlana said.

"We could put it in the metal closet in the garage," Indio suggested, "with the shotgun."

"And that closet has a key?"

"Jesse, find the key."

Jesse went through to the garage, stiff with irritation. Svetlana followed, telling Wynter to stay put, and the three of them moved the alcohol, and the Glock from the gun safe, into the garage closet. Wynter sat in silence in the living room, patting the kittens in her lap as they nuzzled each other sleepily, until the ridiculous ritual was done.

Svetlana checked the time on her phone. "When did you say Joy was coming back?" Wynter had the awful suspicion she thought they were lying about Joy being at the store.

"I'll ride in that direction and find her," Indio said, going into the kitchen where he'd left his helmet and gloves on the counter.

"I can't stay much longer," she called after him.

"I'll be quick," he barked. Now he sounded as pissed off as Jesse. Only two weeks ago he and Svetlana had been chatting like old friends.

"Wynter, my most important job is to ensure you have a safe visit," Svetlana said, "so we need to go through the rules. If Joy isn't here, then Indio will have to leave right away and you won't be able to stay overnight."

"Joy only went to the store."

"I hope that's true. She is the adult supervisor in this house." Svetlana flicked a look at Indio, unable to help herself. He stood behind the couch, pulling on his gloves, his expression blank. "When she comes back, I'll let her know I'd like Indio out of the house by ten."

Indio yanked on his helmet.

"Please leave him alone," Wynter said, her heart in her throat.

"He has a string of convictions. I only found out the extent of it yesterday." So, that explained the change in her attitude. "He can't be left in charge of—"

Wynter stood and yelled, "Leave him alone!"

The kittens fell from her lap onto the floor with tiny yowls of protest. Wynter reached for them in dismay as they tumbled over each other and skittered across the floor. While she and Jesse chased them down, she heard the bike ride off. She pushed Svetlana away when she tried to help.

"Are they hurt? Did I hurt them?" Wynter could hardly speak.

"They're fine." Jesse calmed the scrabbling balls of fluff. To Svetlana he said, quietly, "You have the wrong idea about him. You don't know him. And you know nothing at all about our family."

"I'm putting the welfare of your sister first. You all need to work with me. I've got departmental regulations to consider. This visit was organized on the condition that your sister would be here. That's why I'm being extra cautious. That's why—"

The front door clicked open and Joy walked in with her grocery bags.

"Ah!" Svetlana looked even more relieved than Wynter felt as she followed Joy into the kitchen to introduce herself and reel off a list of instructions, apparently on the assumption Joy understood or cared about any part of it.

Wynter sat at the breakfast bar to wait for Indio to come back.

Svetlana ended her marathon lecture by placing the key from the garage closet in Joy's hand as she left, warning her to guard it. Finally, she was gone.

"What am I supposed to do with this?" Joy said, bewildered by the entire episode.

Jesse took the key and tossed it on top of the microwave where a collection of receipts, rubber bands, pens, and old batteries had accumulated.

"Did you see Indio on his bike?" Wynter asked. "Where is he?"

"He found me just a few doors down, on my way back. He said he was going to ride around the block a few times."

"He's cooling down," Jesse said. "Let's eat." He yanked open a pack of flatbread so aggressively that Joy flinched. "And then we'll look up the etymology of the word *credenza*."

Indigo

Indio came back halfway through lunch and demanded the key when he realized Joy had no interest in the rules. Wynter didn't see where he put it. Indio hated rules, especially pointless ones, so it was odd seeing him obeying Svetlana's instructions.

Wynter put together a chicken wrap for him and he joined them at the dining room table.

"Jesse wants you to check his bike," she told Indio. "He ran over it earlier."

"The bike's fine," Jesse said, annoyed she'd mentioned it.

"Some bits fell off. It might not be safe to ride."

"I'll take a look later," Indio said.

He was subdued, angry under the surface. And Jesse was restless, like he knew something bad was going to happen. Joy — she knew exactly what Joy was doing in her mind. Joy had drawn rays of Light around herself, which meant nothing negative in the physical world could touch her.

"Where are we going out?" Wynter said, hoping to raise spirits. "We can leave the kittens alone for a while, can't we?"

"We'll go to the Pacific Science Center, like we talked about," Jesse said.

"Or we could find somewhere that won't cost us fifty bucks," Indio said. He had his elbows on the table and his phone in his hand, both of which violated Caleb's house rules regarding table manners. Wynter thought better of commenting on it. "The Olympic Sculpture Park is free."

Jesse dropped his head in his hand. "*Art.*"

"It has giant sculptures, to make up for not seeing dinosaurs," Indio told Wynter. "The topography of the entire park is a sculpture, actually. I haven't been there in years. You can see the mountains to the west. We'll head out after dinner and watch the sunset over Elliott Bay."

Wynter liked the sound of it. She waited for Jesse to object.

"Fine," Jesse said. "Let's play downstairs until five. We can take the Link to the park, walk around for an hour, watch the setting sun because I've *never* seen a sunset before, and come back for our movie."

"Where are you going to sleep tonight?" Wynter asked Indio.

"You can have Caleb's room," Joy told him. "There's no need for me to stay. I'll take a bus back to Magnolia after we've visited that park. It's right near there."

"You're not allowed to leave!" Wynter's voice rose in frustration. "And Indio isn't allowed to stay. You can't break the rules just because Caleb isn't here, or I won't be allowed to visit again."

"I'll sleep on the patio," Indio said. "That's technically not *in* the house, right? And Joy, you're staying overnight. That's what you agreed to."

Joy went pale and stiff with anger. In the Light, negative emotions like anger weren't allowed. Joy was going to have to let it go, let those rays of Light take it away, instead of letting it out, and she wasn't good at that.

Joy directed her ire at Indio. With bile in her tone, she said, "Why do you care what I do, all of a sudden? You never cared what I did when we were kids. You completely ignored me, most of the time. All you ever wanted to do was play with Caleb. Remember the seesaw a neighbor gave us on our fifth birthday? You never once played on it with me." Wynter hunched in her seat as Joy worked herself up like she used to at the ashram, but only when no one else was around. "You refused to get on it. You said, *Seesaws are for babies.* I wanted to try it but you wouldn't get on, not even once. Just to spite me!"

Jesse was staring at Joy like she'd sprouted an extra head. Wynter clutched her hands together under the table, her entire body heating as adrenaline surged. There was nothing you could do when Joy got like this.

"I don't remember any seesaw," was all Indio said, entirely unaffected by Joy's tone.

"We had to leave it behind when we moved to Bozeman. How could you not remember it? It was metal, with flaking blue paint and red plastic seats. I put Jesse on it but he didn't weigh enough, and anyway he couldn't hold on. He'd only just started to walk. I kept trying with him, and he kept falling off." Her face was distorted, her voice an anguished bleating. "I kept trying and he was screaming and hitting me. He wouldn't shut up. I put my hand over his mouth and he bit me, right through the skin with his tiny teeth. That seesaw was supposed to be for you and me. Something we could do together. We were supposed to be together. You were supposed to come with us!"

Indio frowned, taken aback. "Come with you where?"

"To the ashram!"

"I wasn't asked."

"Momma asked you. We could've lived there together, the three of us, and then Wynter."

Jesse didn't look too happy about being excluded.

"That didn't happen," Indio said. "She never asked me."

"You should've come. You don't belong in this world. Look at all the trouble you've been in. You can't function out here in darkness."

Now Indio was the one who needed to let the Light take it away. He rapped his knuckles on the table as he said, loud and firm and barely in control, "She. Never. Asked. Me."

"I was standing right there! You shot her with a water pistol and made her angry. I didn't want to leave you behind but *you made her not want you.*"

Wynter looked from one twin to the other as they glared across the table at each other. Wynter had been where Indio was right now, on the receiving end of Joy's painful anger, the words that stung like a lash. And Joy never apologized for her words, never. So you knew that's how she really felt. You knew it was true.

Indio drew a deep breath, sat back, stood up. "I'm outta here."

Wynter felt like she'd been punched in the gut. "No-no-no-no!" she cried after him. "Please don't go!"

He slammed the door behind him.

Indio walked half a mile north, to the playfield where he and Caleb used to play basketball with their friends after school. It wouldn't be dark for another hour or so, and the place was full of teenagers as well as families and kids on the equipment. He turned west and walked for another fifteen minutes, to a neighborhood in Beacon Hill he hadn't visited in years.

You made her not want you.

Rationally, he knew he wasn't supposed to blame his six-year-old self for the crap others had done to him. Hard not to when his twin sister threw it in his face, though he didn't remember her being there and now she was claiming he'd wronged her, too. He already held enough shame to see him through this lifetime. He didn't need Joy adding more.

He found himself in front of a large brick house in a dead-end street. His blood was already buzzing. At some point during the walk he'd counted the cash in his wallet. He had thirteen dollars, which shouldn't be enough to set anyone's blood buzzing. It was the anticipation, the sense memory from all the way back to his mid-teens doing that to his body.

A skinny guy in his forties opened the door.

"Is Danny here?"

"Danny?" The guy tilted his head and looked at Indio with pink eyes propped open by god-knows-what. His flannel shirt was open to reveal a caved-in chest strewn with half-hearted tattoos. "You mean Dan?"

"Sure."

"Does he know you?"

"Yeah, from high school."

A crooked grin split the guy's face, revealing missing teeth and black gums. "Indigo, right? The guitar player."

He offered a hand, and Indio shook it, a cold sickness settling in his stomach. He recognized him now — recognized the voice, not the skeletal splotchy face and sagging eyes. This was Danny, and he wasn't in his forties. He was twenty-three.

"Didn't you get kicked out of school?" Danny said. "Heard you went to Ohio."

"I'm just visiting." He found he couldn't ask for what he wanted. And why bother? Danny knew damn well why he was here. He prolonged the small talk. "How's your mom?"

"She's up in her room. Doesn't get out much. They chopped off her leg. Diabetes!" Danny seemed to think it was hilarious. "Come on up and say hi. She'll remember you."

She'd probably remember his name correctly, too. Danny's mom had always been kind to him when he was fifteen or sixteen.

"Can't hang around."

"Alrighty then." Danny assessed him, head to toe. "What can I do for you?"

"I have thirteen bucks."

Danny screwed up his face at the paltry sum. "Coupla points of Molly?"

"A joint will do."

"Aw, we can do better than that." Danny stood aside, inviting him in.

Indio kept his feet rooted to the doormat. The air wafting out of the house stank of cat urine and stale smoke. Rap music churned from the dark recesses, and someone was loping back and forth in the shadows of the hallway. Indio had eaten meals in this house with Danny's middle-class parents. He and Danny would score weed from the neighbor three doors down and smoke it behind the shed in the manicured backyard. By the time Danny was a senior and his dad had left, he was selling baggies to his friends. He dropped out of school and his nice suburban house became the place to go for whatever you wanted.

Indio's anticipation had evaporated. He wanted to run.

Danny got a sly, pissed-off look. "Come inside, ya boring fuck. You can have what you like for free if you stay and party. Play us a tune or two. Gus is here, with his lovely cousin from Omaha. *Hillary!*" he yelled over his shoulder. "Get out here and meet my old buddy, Indigo!" He leered at Indio. "She's cold as ice, but she's off her face tonight. I predict you'll get lucky. You look like freakin' Kurt Cobain with that hair. She'll love it. You remember Gus, don't you?"

Indio had no idea who Gus was.

"Just the joint, thanks."

Danny scowled and disappeared into the darkness. Indio staggered against the doorway, breathing deep. All he got was a lungful of revolting smells and a wave of distorted memories from the worst of his years in Ohio. It all went straight to his stomach and made him want to hurl.

He walked away. Ten yards down the street, he was running. Quite aside from his physical reaction, he didn't trust Danny to give him anything he'd feel safe taking.

He called Jesse, surprised to find him still at home. They hadn't gone downtown after all, which was Indio's fault. They were watching their movie. Jesse directed him to an address two streets from home, a cute cottage with pale blue siding and gingerbread trim. Once Indio mentioned Jesse's name to the delightful elderly lady in gray braids and bobby socks, she invited him into her cozy living room, which looked like a textile factory had exploded all over the furniture. Amid the plaid cushions and flowery throws and rainbow hand-knitted sweaters she found a tiny set of balance scales with bronze weights and sold him precisely two grams of weed for his thirteen dollars, "plus an extra sprinkle for love." She threw in a hard candy and a funny story about her long-dead parrot named Pythagoras.

As she showed him out, she said, "You'll remind Jesse he promised to mow my lawn, won't you? I love a wild lawn, but the neighbors are giving me those disapproving looks."

"I'll tell him, Mrs Castiglioni."

"I'll make him my key lime pie."

The sun was setting by the time Indio got home. The sunset they were supposed to be viewing across Elliot Bay with the Olympic Mountains a backdrop.

Blue Eyes

When Indio got home, Jesse and Wynter were pitching a tent, presumably for him. He'd planned to sleep on the couch — his earlier comment about the patio had been a joke. Apparently, his younger siblings were following those Social Services rules after all. He hunkered down beside the kittens' box, which someone had brought out and left under the table, and fed them kibble by hand.

"You gonna help?" Jesse said. "We wanted to get this done before it's completely dark."

Indio made himself useful by untangling a guy rope. No way had Caleb left the rope in this state. Jesse must've been the last one to pack it away.

"Where's Joy?"

"She turned in. Didn't like the movie. It's an awesome movie. I'd forgotten how great it is, given its age. You're learning lots, right, Wyn?"

Wynter bashed at a tent peg with a mallet. "Yes, Jesse."

Indio was hyper-aware of the fact she'd pleaded with him not to leave and he'd slammed the door. On her. Now, she looked up to give him a shy smile, which he returned, and that brief gesture left him feeling like they'd just had an hour-long conversation in which apologies were given and reassurances exchanged, and everything was okay again. He realized, in that moment, she would forgive him anything. The satisfaction of discovering her absolute trust in him should have put an immense responsibility on his shoulders, which was how Jesse described it, yet that weight was light as a feather.

Wynter went to sit cross-legged on the patio, drawing a blanket around her shoulders, to play with her phone. When Indio joined her, she said, "I'm looking up *credenza*. It's the most interesting word I've ever researched."

She showed him her screen, which for some reason had an article about medieval food-tasters. He reclined on the lounge chair, fished out the kittens, gave her one, and plonked the other on his stomach.

She continued, "I've discovered that when you learn something new, you have to learn ten more things in order to understand the first, and each of those needs another ten things. It keeps branching out, getting more and more complex like a fractal. I'll never learn it all."

"You only have to follow the branches that interest you."

"And the ones on the test."

He grinned to acknowledge the reality of that.

"It's not just the facts, though," she said. "I'm still trying to figure out friendships and families. I wanted everything to be perfect this weekend."

"Perfect never happens."

"At the ashram, everyone was striving for perfection. The perfect path to God. The perfect spiritual experience. Even the perfect emotional reaction to any event. Nothing was perfect for me. I didn't expect it to be. Now, I keep expecting, hoping, that soon everything will be perfect. We need Caleb here, or things fall apart."

"Nothing fell apart. And you can't fix things that happened before you were even born."

"What Joy said... What's the perfect emotional reaction to that? If you'd gone with them, I'd have known you my whole life. But it would've been a life in the Light. And Jesse wouldn't even remember you."

"Let's ask Jesse if that idea bothers him," Indio said lightly. He shouldn't be joking about it, not when Wynter was showing him a peek beneath her layers of bewildered naïvety, and simmering fear, and memorized facts and figures, to the person inside — the person she was supposed to have been all along.

"He knows he'd be a completely different person," she said. "Who would I have been if Miriam... if Momma never left? If I was born into this family and we all grew up with a mother? I'd know about making friends. I'd know how to pet a kitten like a human."

"Don't take that to heart. Jesse doesn't know what he's talking about sometimes."

She was, in fact, stroking her kitten's head. Its reaction of pure pleasure, instead of encouraging her to continue, made her pull back her hand. She put the kitten on his stomach and it curled up next to its brother.

"Momma tricked you," Wynter said, crossing her arms on the edge of the chair as she watched the kittens. "She didn't tell you it was forever. She should've taken you, or not taken you. She was supposed to know what to do but she put it all on you, a little boy. Somehow she's done the same to me. She decided Joy wasn't allowed to live with her, for no good reason. It's become my fault and now Joy will never forgive me."

"Do you need Joy's forgiveness?"

"I need her to be part of our family."

"I don't think that's what *she* needs."

Wynter's face fell and he wished he hadn't said it.

"Maybe she does belong in the Light," he said. "Maybe she's hardwired so it makes sense to her. Jesse thinks anyone can be retrained to reject what he calls irrational beliefs but I think he's wrong. People are born the way they're born, needing different things, finding meaning in different things. It's part of their personality. A few years ago, Caleb had this girlfriend who was devoted to the Catholic church. Everything about it enraptured her, and fortunately for her she was born into a Catholic family. It made no goddamn sense to us. Harry tries a different church every year but he still hasn't found the one he's wired for, if it even exists. And ever since he could talk, Jesse sees nothing but physics. That's how he's hardwired."

"But they can't all be right — which means, billions of people are hardwired to believe things that aren't true."

Indio shrugged. "Being human is messy. And truth isn't what Jesse thinks it is. What he calls irrational, I might call... poetic. It's no less valuable in the grand scheme of being human."

She took that in. Then, "Is Joy hardwired not to need us?"

Indio scratched a purring kitten behind its ears, making its neck arch in ecstasy. "I don't know. There's no happy ending, no matter how much you want it. No perfect family. No perfect weekend. But we'll be okay."

She sighed, at least partially convinced, and propped her chin on her fist to look at him. "Where did you go just now?"

"For a walk."

She waited, knowing there was more. He stared right back into her flecked hazel eyes, the mirror image of his own.

"I went out to score," he admitted. "That means I bought weed." In case she didn't understand the word.

Her mouth twisted. "I don't think you're supposed to tell your little sister that."

"I'll never lie to you, baby. You see through me, anyway."

"Not really. I don't know anything about you."

"After I bled out my soul for you, on my birthday?" He clapped his hand to his heart. "That hurts."

"Did you ever lie to Jesse?"

"Ask me if I ever lied to Caleb. That's an easier one."

"I already know. I want to know if you ever lied to Jesse."

Indio's chest tightened. He breathed through it, looking up to where Jesse was opening and brushing off the ground sheet. "I used to, all the time. I used to tell him Momma was coming back. For my seventh birthday. For Christmas. For his fourth birthday, his fifth. Trying to convince myself, I think. Caleb always told the truth and simply said he didn't know."

"Why did you want drugs tonight?"

"Cuz I'm in a bad mood."

"How can you be in a bad mood? You have kittens on your stomach."

He chuckled and stroked his fingers through her hair.

"We *will* be okay," she said. "When Caleb gets back, he'll get his foster license. He already filled out the forms and applied for the courses. I'll be home forever by Thanksgiving. That's my goal."

A ridiculously optimistic goal. Jesse had told Indio nothing was likely to be finalized until the New Year. For now, he kept quiet about it. Was that the same as lying?

"I need to dig out a sleeping bag."

He left Wynter to settle the kittens in their box and went inside. On the way to his room, he found Joy in the hallway, clutching the bathroom door, ghost-white.

What now?

"Are you ill?"

"Yes. It's this house. This house is making me ill. And that room. I hate that room."

"Caleb's room?"

"I can't sleep in there."

"You can sleep in the tent with me." He was being a dick, making fun of her. "You were just complaining how I didn't spend time with you."

Joy gave him a withering look and went outside to the patio. He followed, in case she found someone else to yell at.

"I need to go home."

Jesse, tapping in tent pegs, ignored the announcement.

Wynter, sitting backward on a bench at the table, looked up from her phone, startled. "To Arizona?"

"Don't be stupid. They won't let me set foot on that property until I've finished my atonement."

"Thought you did that already?" Indio said.

"There's, like, seven steps," Wynter muttered.

"You're not going home," Indio said. "You don't want to face Caleb if you screw things up this weekend. C'mon, sit for a while."

He managed to get her to the table, where she sat stiffly next to Wynter. He cracked open a fresh beer and resumed his position on the comfy lounge chair. Jesse was *pulling up* tent pegs now, repositioning them according to the principles of engineering or something.

"By the way, I'm not sleeping in a fucking tent!" Indio called across the lawn. The beer buzz was making him both annoyed at Jesse's perfectionism *and* numb to Joy's discomfort. He didn't actually mind sleeping in tents, but not when a perfectly decent couch inside an insulated building was an option.

"Aw, come on, this is gonna be cozy," Jesse called back. "I'll sleep out here with you. I'll bring Mr Tubbs."

"Who's Mr Tubbs?" Wynter asked.

"A flea-bitten rabbit he slept with when he was a kid," Indio explained. "D'you remember Mr Tubbs, Joy?"

"No," Joy said with a quick, tight smile.

"Huh. Maybe that was after your time."

"What about Deedee?" Jesse asked her, coming over to fetch a couple more tent pegs.

Joy flinched. "Who?"

"Wyn said she had a teddy called Deedee. I was just wondering what was so awful about Deedee that it put her off cute furry things for life." Jesse stood waiting for a response, looming over Joy, surely realizing he was being intimidating.

"Why would you tell them about Deedee?" Joy said, like Wynter had done something terrible.

"Why shouldn't I? Deedee's not a *secret*." The way she leaned on the word, and the way Joy's mouth drew into a thin line, made it clear there were other secrets between the girls that Wynter was perhaps tired of keeping. "I wanted to know what happened to him."

Joy said, in a strange flat voice, "I'll tell you what happened to Deedee. We put him away. We put him in a box, and we put the box away."

"Okay, that's fine." Wynter shrugged, faking nonchalance. "I just wanted to know. I never liked him anyway."

"How could you not like a teddy bear?" Joy's anger bubbled up again. "What child doesn't like a teddy bear?"

Indio tensed in anticipation, because at some point he may need to step in and defend Wynter. Not that Wynter didn't know how to deal with Joy, surely. They'd known each other fifteen years.

"He was *fake!*" Wynter said. "He wasn't real."

"Of course he wasn't real. What a stupid thing to say!"

"Hey!" Indio snapped, a warning directed at Joy that made Wynter recoil.

"There was something wrong with his eyes," Wynter said. "His tiny black eyes."

"Stop talking about Deedee!" Joy yelled, slamming her fists on the table. Written on her face was a bizarre mix of anger and terror and hatred that chilled Indio's blood. He'd seen that look a hundred times on his father's face.

Jesse, who had walked off to resume his work, stopped and turned. He'd heard that *tone* a hundred times in their father's voice. And they both knew what came next. Instinct told Indio to jump up, now, and end this. But he did nothing.

Joy wasn't like Harry, was she?

"I wanted him to have blue eyes," Wynter said, tempting fate, but she was angry, too. "I wanted him to be real."

"Stop it!" Joy's arms shot out and her hands closed around Wynter's throat. She shook her. "Shut up! Shut up!"

Indio was out of his chair in a flash. Not in time. Wynter twisted her body, trying to dislodge her sister, then slid under the table to escape. But Joy hadn't let go and she was dragged under as well.

Indio darted to the table as Jesse ran across the lawn with a wordless cry. No way to get under there except the way the girls had gone, because both ends were blocked by support bars. Indio went belly-down on the bench seat, reached in and grabbed one of Joy's wrists. They struggled together, with Wynter a rag doll in Joy's grip, until he managed to grab her other wrist as well, trying to force her arms apart. Damn, she was stronger than she looked and his movement was hampered by the cramped space and a diagonal strut.

Jesse had scrabbled onto the opposite bench, behind Wynter. He managed to get his hands over Joy's, found her thumbs, and bent them back until with a howl she released her hold, very suddenly, and Wynter's face bounced against a table leg.

Indio dragged Joy out through the space between the seat and table top, not caring if he was hurting her. Perhaps twenty seconds had passed since Joy first laid her hands on Wynter. Those twenty seconds changed everything. Indio's red-hot anger and a visceral need to get her as far away as possible from Wynter made him manhandle her across the patio even though she was barely resisting. As he pushed her inside, he saw Jesse had slipped under the table to check on Wynter, who hadn't made a sound.

Indio thrust Joy down the hallway, hard enough to make her stumble. "Get your stuff and get out!"

That was what she'd wanted anyway, wasn't it?

He stood in the doorway of Caleb's room as Joy gathered together her purse and clothes.

"You'll have to give me money for a taxi," she said shakily, not look-ing up. She seemed as shocked as him and Jesse at what she'd done. Was that merely because there had been witnesses this time?

He had no cash, thanks to Mrs Castiglioni. He found Joy's phone on the nightstand, tossed it at her. "Call a friend. Do it, now."

While she called someone and meekly asked to be picked up, he jammed her stuff into her bag, whatever was lying around. This had been Harry's room when they all lived here, a cesspit of unwashed laun-dry and empty beer cans, forever fogged up with cigarette smoke. He hated this room, too.

He shoved the packed bag into her arms and marched her out the front, ignoring the sidelong glances that were meant to scare him away. He waited with her on the street.

After a long silence, when his blood pressure was finally sinking back to normal, he said, "This is great, huh? Just you and me, spending time together."

Joy's eyes were closed and her lips moved silently.

"I know you're frustrated and upset," he said. "I don't care why you did that and I don't even blame you. Here's what I blame you for. You were in that place with Wynter almost fifteen years and at some point you became aware they were hurting her. Your own sister. *Our* sister." His voice rose, though he was trying to contain it. "You knew what they were doing and you did nothing. Judging by tonight's outburst, and her reaction, I'll bet you were part of it. *You* hurt her."

Joy started to cry. She put her face in her hands and sobbed, her shoulders heaving. "I'm so sorry. I'm so sorry."

She wasn't the first girl to turn on the waterworks. It had no effect on him.

"I hardly remember you, and I'm glad," Indio said. "I'm glad I don't remember your ponies' names or your favorite Disney princess or your fucking seesaw, because it makes it easy for me to say this — I'll never forgive you. All the years you didn't protect her when you could've done something, *anything*. Caleb will give you a world of second chances, so have fun with that. But I'm through with you."

A car pulled up. Indio opened the door. He spared her one second of compassion as she climbed in. Then he thought about the bruises that must be coming up on Wynter's face and neck and he slammed the door without another word. He watched the car drive down the street and around the corner, into darkness.

Did he have any right to hate her for what she'd done? He'd punched a fifteen-year-old out of misdirected frustration, after all.

No, what angered him was that unlike him, Joy would suffer no con-sequences beyond her own short-lived remorse, if that was even genuine. In the Light she was surrounded by people who'd make her feel okay about herself, who'd set her back on the right path. No sin in the Light, Jesse once told him. No guilt, no blame.

No requirement or even desire to retain meaningful relationships with her family, either. Indio's consequence had been fifteen weeks in juvie where Harry was *required* to visit him every Saturday, to sit and glare, sometimes to berate, occasionally to yell until a staff member intervened. Jesse wasn't allowed to visit and had spent much of the summer at his friend Marcus's house, having a normal life for once. Caleb was overseas, contacting the place every damn week to see if Indio had put him on his call list yet. Indio never did. Already had Harry in one ear. Didn't need Caleb in the other.

Caleb was right there in his ear now. Telling him to fix things.

Still standing on the curb, in the dark, he texted Joy.

> They can't know anything went wrong here. They can't think Caleb's home is unsafe. So, we had a great time. You stayed the night. Wynter hurt herself when she tripped on the patio.

God, what was he doing? All their lives, he and his brothers had done this — covered it up. And now he was doing it again. Jesse would hate him for it.

He blinked to clear his vision as he watched the screen, wondering if she'd respond.

> I understand

> Text Debra tomorrow. Tell her you're taking Wynter to the science museum.

> I can't go to the science museum. I have to work. I have a class.

> Tell Debra that's what you're doing

> I don't give a fuck how you spend your day

From behind him, a thumping sound began inside the garage, a regular, muted beat.

The roller door was closed, so Indio ran into the house. Jesse was moving quickly from the kitchen, through the living room, following the sound as well. Indio got to the back door first and opened it. Jesse tried to push past him. Indio held him back. Wynter was thrashing Caleb's wooden bokken against the punching bag, her entire body arcing as she delivered the two-handed blows.

Indio kept a restraining hand on Jesse's shoulder. Wynter glanced up, saw them there, and hit the next few strokes harder than ever. The sword cracked and splintered and broke apart near the hilt. The blade flew across the garage and hit the dirt bike.

Wynter froze, still holding the handle of the sword with its stubby splintered end.

Jesse crossed the garage and deftly extracted it from her hand. "Feel better?" he said warily.

She fell to her knees and Jesse stepped back, unsure what to do.

"Ice pack?" Indio said.

"I already gave her one." Jesse looked around until he found it, discarded on the floor.

Indio drew Wynter against him and sat with her, leaning back against the wall. He wiped off the ice pack on his already filthy shirt and held it to her swollen cheekbone. Jesse sat opposite, eyes ablaze. Indio had fetched many an ice pack for his younger brother, in this house and the one before. Jesse would shut himself in his room to lick his wounds, turning his back on the smallest offer of comfort.

Wynter didn't resist, thank god, because all three of them needed the simple comfort right now of sitting quietly together. Indio pressed his lips to her temple, the unbruised one, desperate to let her know how sorry he was for failing to protect her in that single moment of time, as Joy lunged for her, when it mattered the most. A few months ago he'd grappled with Harry, a grown man, to keep him off of Jesse. Today he'd failed to stop a one-hundred-twenty-pound girl hurting Wynter.

"Has Joy done that before?" Jesse asked.

Wynter turned her face against Indio's chest, very still, all the fight gone.

Jesse persisted. "Has she been violent with you before?"

"I asked Joy about it just now," Indio said, to save Wynter from answering. "She didn't deny it."

"The Light poisoned her," Wynter whispered. "It's not her fault."

Deep Thoughts

Jesse exited the laundry and went up the hall to Wynter's door. Indio was in her room with her, sitting on the bed, talking quietly as he arranged the ice pack between her cheek and the pillow. The kittens scuffled in their box in the corner. Jesse shoved his lighter and grinder and papers, which he'd just retrieved from the lint filter of the dryer, into his back pocket, and leaned in the doorway.

"We'll go to the science museum tomorrow," Indio was telling her, pulling up the covers. "Jesse can drive you back to Enumclaw after. We're gonna sit out on the patio awhile. You okay in the house by yourself?"

"Yes. This room is safe." She grabbed his wrist as he stood, holding him there. "I don't want Caleb to know. What if he never lets Joy come over again?"

Jesse figured Indio would be perfectly fine with that outcome. As would he.

"We'll talk about it in the morning," Indio said.

Jesse went out the back, pausing at the couch to rummage through Indio's jacket pockets for Mrs Castiglioni's buds.

"How on earth did you find her?" Indio said, coming out a minute later to throw himself on the lounge chair. He turned on some music, not too loud – Zeppelin's second album, which they both loved though it wasn't Jesse's idea of stoner music. He let that slide.

Jesse was at the bench, dividing the weed into quarters. The elephant in the room was not to be mentioned, apparently. Jesse went along with it. "She found me. I used to skateboard down her street. It's got the perfect incline."

"So, she's a drug pusher. On underage kids, no less."

"She refuses to sell me anything. I mow her lawn and she feeds me toasted cheese sandwiches and key lime pie."

"Mowing's overdue, by the way."

Jesse acknowledged that and began rolling a joint. He had become determined, months ago, to perfect this particular life skill, and had even been praised for it. Not by Indio, who watched him impatiently now, tapping his fingers on the chair arm, his mind obviously playing over the events of the evening.

Events that were not to be mentioned.

There was another event Jesse had been unable to mention — to Wynter, this time. They'd been alone in the car this morning for over an hour and he'd not said one word about the awful things she told Indio a week earlier. He'd visited her on Wednesday, too, and said nothing. He *was* jealous of Indio today, but not over that — after all, he was the one who'd predicted she'd open up to Indio first. Indio had warned him to "let her be," to not push for more. So they played a weird game of pretense, where she knew he knew but they were both pretending he didn't know.

Jesse twisted off the joint, gave it to Indio, and started on the next.

"About time." Indio examined it, his lip curling.

"Any complaints?" It was a beautiful joint.

"Let's see how it burns," his brother said noncommittally, and fired it up. Indio wasn't the one breaking the law here. He had no reason to be a dick.

No reason except for Joy.

"What a fucked up day," Jesse said. "We never even played. I'm writing a new song we could've tried out."

"Give it a rest. You're not a songwriter."

"I write songs. *Ergo*, I am a songwriter."

"You write... thoughts."

"I have deep thoughts. And I can rhyme them without a rhyming dictionary." Wow, he was still upset about that dictionary. And the kittens, of course. How was he supposed to compete with kittens? "I mean, does anyone actually use a rhyming dictionary? Real songwriters?"

"Yup." Indio exhaled a lungful of smoke and gave the joint a suspicious look.

"Takes the artistry out of it," Jesse said prolonging the moment before the truth about Mrs Castiglioni's weed became unavoidable. "It's cheating."

"It's a tool. You think Vermeer painted *The Milkmaid* without understanding the color wheel?"

"What's *The Milkmaid* got to do with anything?"

"It's just an example of a classic painting using a reduced palette of contrasting colors. You know the one? That's the first thing they make you do, in art class — make a color wheel. It's not cheating. It's a tool like any other."

"Why d'you like that painting?"

"Never said I liked it."

"But why do you?"

Indio narrowed his eyes, sucked on the joint, and said with a sneer, "It's comforting."

"Comforting? Uh-oh..." Jesse slapped his forehead. "I'm having another deep thought. Milk... comfort... Something to do with a maternal substitute? Were you breastfed?"

"Pretty sure we all were."

"But with twins, though — that's gotta be tricky. How does that even work?"

"Two babies, two teats. Doofus."

"How d'you hold two screaming babies in position at once, though? I'll bet she stuck a bottle in your mouth and breastfed Joy. Scarred you for life. God, that explains everything. And you accused *me* of having mommy issues."

He was joking. It was all a joke. But Indio fell into silence, not wanting to talk about Joy, even baby Joy. Jesse was itching to talk about it. About what they were going to tell Caleb and what he might do...

"What the fuck is this shit?" Indio exclaimed after another deep draw. The way he glared at the joint should've made it shrivel up and die.

Jesse sealed the second joint, which was even more perfectly formed than the first. Time to come clean. "Mrs Castiglioni's daughter in Buckley grows it. They're not on speaking terms cuz the daughter is a Mormon. She lets the grandson deliver it twice a month for Mrs C's arthritis."

"Wait, a *Mormon* who grows pot? They don't even do caffeine."

"You're missing the point," Jesse said. "It's a medicinal strain. Guaranteed not to get you high."

"Fuck! Why'd you send me there?"

"She always has some left over—"

"I don't have arthritis."

"Well, I didn't want you visiting your old haunts. I wanted you to come home."

"You little shit." He chuckled, though. "I will never trust you again."

"Should we just chuck it out?"

"No! It's better than nothing. I feel slightly relaxed, so maybe it's doing something after all."

"Probably the placebo effect."

"Good enough."

They finished it and lit another. Jesse sat on the ground to stay within easy reach of it.

"*Did* Mom ask you to go with them?" When Indio said nothing, he persisted with, "D'you wish you'd gone?"

Indio was staring across the yard, his gaze unfocused. "Only so I could've done the job Joy failed to do — protect Wynter."

"If you had gone, though... I can't even imagine growing up without you. You taught me to read."

"You taught yourself to read."

"Don't downplay your influence. You taught me to *love* reading. You took me with you to play Halo with your friends. Made me feel important. You taught me how to ride a bike, how to do an ollie on my skateboard."

"My skateboard."

"Speaking of which, you gave me all those awesome hand-me-downs — the skateboard and pads, your MP3 player, your Chucks. Caleb never had cool stuff like that. He was always so *straight*. I always knew you had my back, and unlike Caleb I knew you wouldn't make it a teaching moment. You'd just head out there and avenge me. Or take the blame, like the time I broke the—"

"It's okay, you can stop now."

"I want you to understand the effect you had on my life, and on who I became. If you'd gone with them, I wouldn't even remember you existed. And then, suppose you showed up now, like Joy did. I'd have a completely different impression of you."

"What's that supposed to mean?"

"Solely under Caleb's influence, I'd be a lot more straight-laced than I am now. I might not *approve* of you and your fucked-up life and fucked-up music. I'd wear V-neck sweaters. I'd listen to Willie Nelson for fun. I'd be in the Army, playing a snare on a sling in a military marching band."

"Nothing wrong with that. Playing in a marching band? That's an enviable skill."

They both snickered.

"Sure doesn't feel like a placebo," Indio said. He remembered something, sitting up to extract a candy from his pocket. "What's this she gave me?"

"That's just a barley sugar."

"Then why did she wink? Thought she was trying to tell me it was something special."

"It's not, I promise." Jesse gave the candy another look. "But just in case, don't give it to Wyn."

Indio reclined again. "Y'know, without me around to absorb the brunt of his frustrations, maybe you'd have rebelled. Maybe you'd be the one in juvie. And I'd be a mantra-spouting hippie guru living off the grid, growing my own weed and shrooms, with pet chickens and a harem of luscious long-haired women, every one of 'em devoted to me and to tantric sex."

"Chickens devoted to tantric sex?"

They snickered again. Wow, that Mormon lady must be messing with her strains. A very gentle high, but a high nonetheless. Should he warn

Mrs Castiglioni? Did Mrs Castiglioni already know?

Jesse waffled on. "Half of that describes how your life turned out anyway. And the other half is where you're heading—"

He stopped at what sounded like the distant ring of the doorbell. Come to think of it, he'd also heard it a minute ago, and ignored it as part of the music. Now someone was rapping on the door, and Indio heard it, too. They exchanged looks, neither one wanting to get up to answer a midnight caller. They heard Wynter moving around inside the house.

Then she slid open the back door, her face a milky bluish-white oval in the moonlight, with that huge purple-and-red stain around her right eye.

"I think there's another social worker out the front."

It took Jesse a few seconds to process the information.

A social worker.

Wynter had a black eye.

Joy was gone.

And they were smoking weed.

"Twice in one day?" Jesse croaked. "We living in a police state now?"

Indio looked stunned. It seemed to take a colossal mental effort to kick himself into action, to finally get up and drag Jesse off his butt, too. They sidled into the house, none of them knowing what to do.

"I peeked through the dining room window," Wynter hissed. "She looks exactly like a social worker. It's dark out there but she looks kind of like Tina. Not Tina, but Tina's type." She glanced at Jesse. "She looks like a type one."

Uh-oh. Type ones were the worst.

"Maybe she'll leave if she thinks there's no one home?" Wynter was shaking with fear — and no wonder. The domestic abuse, the lack of a supervising adult, the weed...

Speaking of which, Jesse still had a joint between his fingers. He dashed into the kitchen to get rid of it.

"We have to open the door," Indio said, pushing his hand through his hair before circling an arm around Wynter's shoulders. "You're supposed to be here. If we pretend like no one's home, we'll only have to explain ourselves tomorrow." He sucked in his lips, considering the situation. "Any idea what our rights are?" he asked Jesse. "Do we have to let her all the way in?"

"Uh, Wynter's in their care. They can do what they like."

The woman rapped on the door again, startling them all. Wynter squirmed out of Indio's embrace and hid behind him, like that would make any kind of difference to how this played out.

"They'll never let me visit again!" she moaned, one hand covering her bruise.

Jesse crept down the hallway and through the dining room arch. He drew back the drape an inch to sneak a look of his own.

"Go back to bed," Indio was telling Wynter, as calmly as he could given the pall of sheer terror in the air. "Pull up the quilt over your head and pretend to be—"

"Fuck!" Jesse jumped back in shock because the woman had chosen that precise moment to peer in through the same window, coming face-to-face with him. *Game over.*

Indio gave him a murderous look.

"Hello?" The woman tapped the window. "Jesse?"

"It *is* a social worker!" Wynter squeaked. "How else would she know your name?"

"It's Kathryn Hayes, Jesse," the woman called softly through the door crack. "I need to talk to you."

Jesse ran the name through his mental contacts list. Nope, he did not know any Kathryn Hayes. Confounded, he shook his head at Indio who was glued to the spot a few feet away.

The woman tried again. "It's Mrs Hayes. Bea's mother."

Of course. Relief flooded over Jesse as he recalled the name, not that he'd ever met Bea's mother. He saw Indio relax, too, drawing Wynter forward to put his arm around her again.

"Okay. Okay." Jesse wiped his clammy hands on his jeans and unlocked the door. "We're good. It's nothing bad," he muttered to himself.

It must be bad, though. Bea's mother, who had never come to the house before, could only be here now because something had happened to Bea. Or to Jilly. Something terrible, because why else would she visit at midnight? Why was she here at all? Bea wasn't part of Caleb's life anymore. Didn't make sense.

"I'm sorry, I know it's late," Kathryn said once the door was open. She looked past Jesse. "Wynter, I didn't think you'd be here. You remember me, don't you? We met briefly at Jilly's party."

"I didn't recognize you," Wynter admitted, keeping the bruised part of her face pressed against Indio's chest. "You had curly hair and a dress."

Kathryn self-consciously touched her hair, which was piled up in a big knot on her head. "And you must be Indio? Can we sit?"

Jesse didn't move. Couldn't move. All he could do was look at Indio, who was similarly transfixed, but with a terrible realization dawning in his eyes.

Indio spoke the unthinkable aloud. "Did something happen to Caleb?"

The Rest of Our Lives

"There's been an accident," Kathryn said.

From the corner of his eye, Jesse saw Wynter stagger against Indio. Feeling his knees waver, he locked them and tried to concentrate on what Kathryn was saying. She was making soothing motions with her hands...

"Caleb is okay. He will be okay. There was a fire in the engine room. Some equipment collapsed on him. He has fractured ribs and burns to his leg, and he suffered smoke inhalation. But he's stable. They're flying him from Guam to Cairns for treatment."

She gave a professional reassuring smile. She was a nurse, Jesse recalled, experienced in relaying bad news to families. She awaited their reactions. The house was silent except for distant music coming from the patio. Jesse should be asking questions. His brain was blank. He couldn't think of one thing to say.

No, *Indio* should be asking questions. He was the oldest. He needed to take charge.

"Beatrice was still listed as Caleb's next of kin," Kathryn said into the silence. "That's why they called her. And she... she asked me to bring you the news. We thought someone should do it in person. Tomorrow I'll call the base and have them update you directly, until Caleb is able to call you himself." She looked from Jesse to Indio, and back again. "Whose name should I give as the main point of contact?"

"Me," Indio said, stepping up at last. "I'll give you my number."

Kathryn handed over her phone and Indio released Wynter to tap in his number. Wynter slunk back against the wall, keeping her face turned away. Jesse felt bitterly sorry for her, that she had to be concerned with hiding the evidence of an irrelevant domestic violence incident at a time like this.

While Indio asked the questions you were supposed to ask, Jesse led Wynter to her room. He sat with her on the bed to wait, curling an arm around her waist to support her. Her arm did the same, to support him.

The front door closed as Kathryn left.

"When can we visit him?" Wynter said when Indio appeared in the doorway. "Where's Cairns?"

"Australia," Indio said, matter-of-factly. "No one's gonna be flying to Australia."

"If they couldn't treat him in Guam and didn't fly him home to the States, that sounds like it's kinda serious," Jesse said.

"But she said he was okay!" Wynter cried, her voice breaking. "I thought he was *teaching* in Guam. Why was he in an engine room? Why was there a fire?"

"Calm down!" Jesse yelled. Why the hell was he yelling? He scrubbed nervously at his hair. "He'll be fine. He's always fine."

"He's in intensive care, awaiting surgery." Indio's voice was flat but calm. "Let's get some sleep and we'll find out more in the morning."

"Cairns is literally on the other side of the world."

Wynter, sitting on the edge of Jesse's bed, watched him roll over with a moan and slowly open his eyes as she twirled a globe around its axis. She'd retrieved it from the top of his bookcase.

"House rule number... something..." Jesse muttered. "No entering someone else's room without permission."

"It's number nine."

"How... how could you possibly know that?"

"You told me. And number nineteen is *Knock before entering.*"

"You're keeping track?"

"We should combine those two rules into one. They basically overlap."

"The numbers don't mean anything, Wyn."

Wynter pondered the vastness of the Pacific Ocean. She tapped a fingertip on the north-eastern coast of Australia.

"See? If you move Cairns all the way around so you can *just* see it here on the left, you can *just* see Seattle up here on the right, across the Pacific Ocean. How many miles is that?"

"They'll fly him back soon. We'll visit him then."

His gaze kept flicking to her cheekbone, to the red splotch there and the purple bruise under her eye where blood had collected. She'd hardly recognized herself in the mirror.

She wrapped her arms around the globe. "I'm terrified, Jesse. We should *do* something."

"There's nothing we can do."

"There are ways to influence the universe."

He sneered. "How? Prayers? Or are you gonna say something about the law of attraction? Don't do it, cuz then I'll have to rant for a good fifteen minutes. At this hour of the morning it'll just give us both a headache."

"I don't know how. That's the truth," she said sharply. "Nothing I tried ever worked."

Jesse rubbed her arm briefly, a sort of apology for the way he'd dismissed her. Her hand found his and they locked fingers.

"I really would like to know how many miles it is," she said.

"The circumference of the Earth is twenty-five thousand miles, so it's something less than half that. Find a tape measure and work it out from the globe by scaling up, or Google it."

"Last time I Googled something about the solar system, I ended up on a site that proved we never landed on the moon because the shadows were wrong."

"The... *what?* Why are you reading conspiracy theory sites?"

"It didn't *say* it was a conspiracy theory site."

"When I rule the world, there's gonna be a law," Jesse grumbled, "which says conspiracy theory sites have to declare themselves as such. Listen, I'm enforcing rule nine and throwing you out now."

He kneed at the small of her back to dislodge her, clutching the sheet to his chest. Wynter had a sudden revelation as to the reason why.

"Are you naked under there?"

"Possibly. Get out."

Wynter left, still cradling the globe, and found Indio in the kitchen with a kitten on his shoulder as he toasted bread.

"Morning!" He sounded far too happy, given the circumstances. Fake happy.

"You told me you'd never lie to me."

"What?"

"Your tone right now is a lie." Wynter took a seat at the breakfast bar and set down the globe.

Indio put the kitten on the counter next to it and smiled grimly at her. "Sorry, baby. Once we find out exactly what's going on, we'll all feel better about it."

"Unless it's bad news."

He gave her a *look* to punish her for being pessimistic, before retrieving four pieces of freshly browned toast and dropping in four more slices of bread. As he got busy finding butter and condiments, Wynter patted the kitten absent-mindedly and watched Indio carefully for signs. Anything at all to signify he was sick with worry like she was, and like Jesse would be when he was properly awake.

"If it takes the rest of our lives," she said, "I'm gonna make you realize what an incredible person Caleb is."

He didn't even acknowledge her comment. Something was horribly wrong.

Jesse sauntered in, wearing sweatpants.

"You take Wynter to the science museum, okay?" Indio told him. "I'll drive to the base and talk to Caleb's executive officer."

"I'd rather go with you," Wynter said as Jesse sat beside her. "So would Jesse. That science museum is for little kids, anyway."

"Jesse *is* a little kid."

Jesse didn't act offended by the remark. He said, "It's educational. It's awesome. It's unsanitary to have a kitten on the table. Where's Cat B?"

"Maybe *this* is Cat B," Wynter said.

"They officially have names," Indio said nonchalantly.

"Proton and Neutron, I presume," Jesse said, "like I suggested."

Indio scowled. "Meet Led and Zeppelin."

Wynter nodded with approval. "Which one is this?"

"Does it matter? They're identical."

"Of course it matters."

"Uh, okay, that's Zep."

She tried not to roll her eyes that he was so obviously unconcerned with such details.

"Did Turk approve those names?" Jesse asked. "Did you even tell him about Proton and Neutron? He's a biochem major, right? He'll love Proton and Neutron."

"Turk is just fine with Led and Zep."

"Indio," Wynter said, "please let us come with you."

"No."

Wynter narrowed her eyes. He *was* hiding something. Which was as good as lying again.

He held her gaze briefly, and caved. "Kathryn texted me half an hour ago. Caleb's developed an infection in the ICU. They have to deal with that before they can even think about flying him home."

"Were you not going to tell us?" Wynter cried.

"Of course I was going to tell you — *after* I get an accurate, up-to-date, first-hand report from his doctors in Australia."

The toast popped.

"Hospitals are the worst places for sick people," Jesse said, staring morosely at the growing pile of toast. "I bet it's a staph infection. Could be a superbug."

"A what?" Wynter whispered.

Indio looked like he wanted to punch Jesse. He slammed a jar of blackberry jelly in front of them. "Shut the fuck up and eat." He threw

Wynter an apologetic look to assure her the cussing wasn't directed at her. "I'll see you guys in a couple hours."

"We're supposed to eat *eight* pieces of toast?" Wynter called after him as he left. Her stomach was in knots. She wasn't going to be able to manage one bite. "We have to stay home and wait for him to come back," she told Jesse.

"Fine. I don't feel like going to the science museum anyway." Jesse nudged Zep's nose out of the butter dish and buttered a piece of toast. The ordinary act seemed to kick up his mood a notch. "This morning we'll create a mini lunar landing scene with Lego astronauts and pebbles. We'll shine a single light source on the model to represent the sun, take some photos, and measure the shadow angles to prove the moon landing was real."

"Are you doubting it was real?"

"I'm concerned *you* might think it wasn't real. So, we'll waste precious hours of our life using science to disprove a stupid conspiracy theory — all because I don't rule the world."

"Yet."

Lullaby

Wynter walked into Debra and Brian's house after school on Thursday and heard Jesse's voice coming from the kitchen. She peered through the doorway. The kitchen table was covered from one end to the other in Nathan and Aiden's racing car track. The boys hovered around Jesse, as they always did, listening to him explain in great detail how the launcher worked. The device was in pieces on the table, because it currently did *not* work. The boys had been whining about it all week.

This wasn't a homework day. Jesse wasn't supposed to be here. He'd driven down on Monday, as usual. He was going to skip visiting for the rest of the week because Wednesday had been his first day of class at the University of Washington, and he had social events every night. Yet, here he was.

Indio had called her every day with news about Caleb, who was no better and no worse. She'd spent the week at school in a daze, unable to concentrate. It wasn't only that Caleb was injured and sick. Jesse convinced her there was nothing they could do about that except trust his doctors. The worst part was that he was so far away. And here in the States, she and her siblings lived in four different houses in three different cities.

Families were supposed to stick together during a time of crisis, weren't they? They were supposed to *be* together.

Wynter touched her cheek. The black eye was fading, the bruises on her neck all but gone. Still, she should fix the makeup before Debra saw her. She'd so far managed to hide it from her foster parents, and none of the kids at school paid her enough attention to notice anything.

Madeline had noticed, of course, ten seconds after Wynter entered their bedroom on Sunday evening.

"If you want to wear makeup, you need to learn how to do it right," she'd said, glancing up from painting her nails black. Then she took a closer look. "Who punched you?"

"Nobody."

Madeline had shrugged and offered to help her use the concealer correctly. With the bruise covered, Wynter was able to put the incident away, push it under with the dark pieces. It was easier than it used to be. She hadn't had to wait a week for comfort, or even a day or an hour. Comfort had been right there in Indio's arms.

As she headed toward her bedroom, she noticed Jesse's backpack and sleeping bag in the hallway. He never stayed the night. Never asked to, and in any case there wasn't anywhere for him to sleep.

"Wynter?" Debra appeared from the kitchen. "Didn't hear you come in. How about some banana bread? Fresh out of the oven."

Debra was being overly attentive. Another warning sign.

"I'll put my things away first," Wynter said stiffly.

In her room, she dumped her school bag, stood before the mirror, and applied a little concealer to the fading bruise with mechanical pats. Her fingertips were numb. She kept forgetting to breathe.

Jesse appeared in the reflection and sat on her bed to watch her finish up. While he'd agreed with her and Indio to lie about what had happened, he hated doing so. Hated that she was covering the bruise "like a battered wife," as he'd put it.

"Today wasn't a planned visit," she managed to say, turning to face him. No hugs or smiles in greeting. She knew what that meant. Things were... worse. And Jesse knew she knew.

"I asked Debra if I could stay a few days. Just through the weekend," he said.

"But you have classes tomorrow."

"I'll skip class." He patted the bed and she went to sit beside him. He clasped her hand.

"Is he dead?" she blurted out.

"God, no. Wynter..." He hugged her close. "If he was dead I'd have told you already." His voice was odd, though. He pulled away, took both her hands this time, and twisted to face her. "So, he's got sepsis. It's not uncommon with things like burns and infections. It means his body is overreacting to the infection. It causes a fever and a drop in blood pressure, which they can treat with drugs. If it gets worse it can lead to organ failure."

No. He was stable. *He had broken ribs. He was going to be okay. And now... organ failure?*

"Have you talked to him?" she choked out.

"No. He's not... he's not really conscious. Indio's in touch with his doctors in Australia."

"When's he coming home?"

"He's in critical condition, so he stays where he is. The other injuries are healing fine. He just has to beat this one thing..."

Jesse started to cry. Wynter pulled him close and they held each other.

"I don't get it," Jesse said between sobs. "He's the healthiest, strongest person I know and his own body turned against him. If he goes into shock, there's a fifty percent chance he'll die."

"He can't die."

"I looked it up." He wiped his face on his sleeve. "Indio told me to tell you everything. I didn't want to. He said, don't lie or you'll just hate us later if... if..."

Wynter hugged him again and they sat like that for a long time, until Madeline's voice echoed through the house. She'd stayed late at school for drama club.

Jesse escaped to the bathroom to wash his face before she saw him. Madeline had been sympathetic to Wynter about Caleb's illness that first day, while playing the big sister role with makeup. Since then she'd shown no interest, and Wynter didn't blame her — Wynter never asked Madeline about her various family dramas, either. They'd barely known each other a month. Madeline might sympathize with a crying Jesse or she might laugh at him. Impossible to know, and Jesse wasn't taking any chances.

"I got thrown out of drama club for giggling during a death scene," Madeline announced, flopping on her bed. "Whose sleeping bag is that out there?"

"Jesse's staying a few days."

"Where?"

"The couch, I guess."

Madeline bolted upright. "We'll have a great time! He likes science fiction, right? We'll stay up all night and watch *True Blood*."

"Tell me the truth, Wyn. My Lego moonscape just wasn't as cool as kittens."

Sitting together on the living room floor, leaning against the couch in the dark, they were finally alone after Madeline gave up on *True Blood* because Jesse had been unable to stop himself with the running commentary on its scientific implausibility.

"I loved our moonscape," Wynter assured him.

"He only brought those kittens to Seattle to prove he's a better brother than I am. Kittens are a slam dunk."

"Well, he failed to prove it because I love all three of you the same."

"We should've gone to the sculpture park in Seattle, like he suggested. He was right. You'd have loved that place. They've got these huge metal waves. Even I get chills walking through it. He understood that. He understood you'd want to *feel* something. Not get a lecture about conspiracy theories and H.G. Wells."

"I love your lectures." Wynter snuggled against him, keen to think and talk about anything else than the awfulness of what lay ahead. "And I'm so glad you're here. It's fifteen minutes to midnight and we didn't do this day in history yet."

"Nothing historic happened today."

"Are you sure?"

"I checked. Absolutely nothing happened."

Jesse's phone rang.

"It's Indio."

Wynter's hand curled into a fist in the fabric of his sweater, to anchor herself to him. Jesse's finger hesitated over the green button, like he was steadying himself. He tapped it and put the call on speaker.

"Hey, bro," Jesse said, attempting a normal voice.

"Hey. Is Wynter with you?"

"I'm here," Wynter said.

"They're telling me Caleb's gone into septic shock."

Wynter felt Jesse exhale and freeze, his arm still tight around her but it wasn't enough to stop her sinking under the water.

Drowning.

Fifty percent chance. Fifty percent.

"He's unconscious," Indio went on, his voice controlled and unemotional. "Uh, low blood pressure, low body temperature, and a severe lung infection. He might have to go onto dialysis if his kidneys shut down. They're finally offering to fly me over there."

"To Australia? That's good, isn't it?" Wynter said, grasping at something. Anything.

"It's not good," Jesse said quietly. "It's in case he doesn't make it."

"I'm not gonna go," Indio said. "I asked Harry to go instead but he's not in a state to make that kind of journey. There's nothing we can do there, anyway. I'll stay here with you guys. I'll ride up tomorrow night and stay the weekend."

"What about your gigs?" Wynter said, her voice strangely normal to match her brothers'. "Caleb would make you play your gigs."

"I'll ride up tomorrow," Indio repeated. "Jesse, can you sort it out with the foster parents?"

None of them pointed out they could meet up in Seattle because... well, they couldn't. Not unless Joy cooperated and agreed to supervise. And Wynter wasn't sure Indio and Jesse ever wanted to see Joy again. One of her brothers must've relayed the news about Caleb, because Joy had sent her a single query about it earlier in the week. After that, nothing.

Indio hung up with assurances he'd call as soon as he had further news.

Wynter and Jesse remained huddled on the floor. No more tears, just breathing through the cold heaviness of dread.

After a while, Jesse said, softly, "Something did happen today." His cheek rested on the top of her head and his breath tickled her scalp. "Forty-four years ago, the Beatles released *Abbey Road*. The first track on side two was *Here Comes the Sun*."

"That's Caleb's song."

"Yeah. Yours and his. Feels like a message from the universe, doesn't it?"

She punched his arm lightly. "No. It feels like a huge coincidence."

"Good girl."

"What does that mean — *side two*?"

She felt his lips smiling. "Vinyl records have two sides. You play one side, flip it over, and play the other."

"I did not know that. Can you flip over a CD?"

"Nope. Completely different technology."

He proceeded to explain the difference between digital and analog in the same soft voice, like a lullaby. At any other time she would've found it interesting. She didn't need to hear about it tonight. But Jesse was so desperately miserable and it helped him to talk, although he did keep losing his train of thought. So, she listened.

With or Without Him

Gloomy weather, glum siblings, hourly texts from Harry demanding updates, and the terrifying prospect of stepping up as head of the family if the worst happened... Indio wasn't having the best Friday night. Two out-of-control cooped-up little boys and a precocious sixteen-year-old girl weren't helping him to relax, either.

"She's not eating again," were the first words out of Jesse's mouth when Indio showed up that afternoon. Wynter hadn't gone to school, although with Jesse around that didn't mean she hadn't been studying.

Indio brushed it off. Wynter could hardly be expected to have an appetite. In between listlessly watching TV and pretending to listen to Jesse as he went through her math, she was looking obsessively at the photos on her phone. Caleb had sent her a message from Guam the day before the accident, a perfectly ordinary message asking about her upcoming visit to Seattle, with a selfie on the beach on his afternoon off. Caleb was smiling, squinting into the sun. She stared at that photo like it would will him back to health.

Debra kept them supplied with drinks and snacks and the occasional word of reassurance as they ploughed through the evening, awaiting news. There was none, which could be seen as a good sign. Debra was letting Indio sleep in the family room with Jesse. He didn't mention Social Services' rules and regulations regarding supervised visitations, and neither did she.

With the wind slamming rain against the windows on Saturday morning, Jesse and Wynter were shut inside with their fears. The little boys were stir-crazy. Indio drew superhero comics for Nathan, and Jesse taught Wynter and Aiden how to make well-engineered paper planes. Madeline changed out of her leggings into a tight black mini-skirt for no plausible reason, and squeezed herself onto the couch next to Indio on the pretext of asking him about the best brand of colored pencils. So much for the Code.

Indio watched his brother and sister going through the motions, one minute distracting themselves, the next indulging their nightmares. While Wynter devised impractical solutions — they could sell the truck and the Beast and *all* buy tickets to Australia, couldn't they? — and Jesse scared himself stupid with medical websites, Indio didn't have the first clue what he was feeling, or what he should be feeling. He only knew he wanted his feelings gone.

This weekend, unfortunately, he was entirely without the means to achieve that.

"Dad promised he'd work on our treehouse," Aiden grumbled over his milk and cookies later in the morning. Indio was in the kitchen fixing the leaky faucet, to escape Madeline.

"We need it finished before the zombies reach our house," Nathan added. "I saw them with my binoculars last night, down Foxtail Street."

"Brian won't be home until Monday," Debra reminded them. "He was working on that treehouse all summer," she told Indio. "Well, thinking about working on it."

Caleb would've taken the information as an opportunity to offer his services. Indio had a little carpentry experience from helping build scenery sets for the drama department on campus in Ohio. That was no reason to get involved. He was fixing a faucet, for chrissake, even after Debra assured him he didn't have to.

He finished the job and went outside in the rain, where Madeline was unlikely to follow, and wandered around the muddy yard, desperate for a drink, just one, or one line, or even a cigarette. He usually only smoked cigarettes as part of a grander plan to get wasted, to calm the jitters beforehand when he was uncertain where the next trip would take him, or to help come down from it after. Today he just needed one little hit of *something* to make it easier to keep himself from thinking.

To the side of the property stood a cluster of trees with the sorry-looking bones of a treehouse platform, made from 2-by-6's set on their edges about eight feet above the ground. He and his brothers had always wanted a treehouse, and Harry had always said he'd build one. Indio felt a surge of unwarranted resentment toward Brian, whom he'd never met, who had promised his boys the same thing and was failing almost as dismally.

May as well take a closer look.

"We need a slide and a pirate ship wheel and a hammock and a chalkboard," Aiden said. "And a rope ladder."

"We don't need any of that. We need a zipline!" Nathan declared. "It's our emergency escape route."

"Of course we need a rope ladder. How are we gonna get in?"

"We'll climb the tree."

"How will we get our supplies up there without a ladder?"

"Zombies can climb rope ladders so we can't have one."

"Zombies can climb trees, too, stupid," Madeline said, rummaging in the refrigerator for a snack.

Aiden and Nathan gave her withering looks, because of course zombies could not climb trees.

"We'll have a retractable rope ladder," Jesse said.

Indio amended the blueprint accordingly. He and the boys, Jesse, and Wynter were gathered around the kitchen table working on the final design. The boys, of course, had been thrilled by his suggestion they build the treehouse. Wynter immediately caught on to the fact that it would be a good distraction and managed to persuade Jesse to participate. It didn't take long for Jesse to immerse himself in the engineering challenges.

"Brian was using planks from an old fence for the floor," Debra said. "The rest of it's in a pile in the shed. I keep threatening to burn it in the fireplace this winter if it's not put to better use before then."

They went to investigate. By the time they'd sorted through the lumber and found the tools they needed, the rain had eased. Brian had a pretty crappy workshop, no surprise given the state of the house. The only power tool was a cordless drill. Indio was going to be sawing planks by hand.

Today's drug of choice: natural endorphins.

While he did that, Jesse and Wynter made a rope ladder using instructions found on the internet — as modified by Jesse because the author was "incompetent". The boys were happy to fetch tools, hold the stepladder steady, and pass up nails as Indio fixed the deck in place. Debra was sent to the hardware store with a long list, and Madeline came outside now and then to observe the progress, never leaving the shelter of the porch.

By suppertime they'd finished nailing down the floor and attaching the railings. They worked into the evening by the light of a few camping lanterns, after the boys went to bed still arguing over the best location for the periscope. Indio and Jesse and Wynter climbed up to fix the roof — a tarp thrown over a line of bungee cord, raised at the four corners with outriggers to create a nine-inch-high continuous window opening.

Around 9PM, Indio's phone buzzed and he spoke briefly with Caleb's doctor in Australia.

Wynter looked at him with tired eyes propped open by anguish as he relayed the news — Caleb's condition had deteriorated, and the next twenty-four hours were crucial.

Jesse was picking disinterestedly at a plate of nachos that Debra had brought out for them. For Wynter, really, who'd eaten nothing but a little soup at lunchtime.

Rain splattered on the tarp. They'd gotten it fixed in place just in time.

Wynter leaned in the corner of the treehouse, somehow still on her feet, staring into the thick foliage surrounding them. She said, "Can we talk about him? We've spent all day not talking about him."

"I'm not gonna talk about him like he's dead," Jesse said bluntly.

"So we'll *avoid* talking about him like he's dead?" Wynter fired back.

Jesse's head popped up, startled by her tone. She was a dark shadow in that far corner, Jesse a huddled ball in another, while Indio sat cross-legged on the floor near the door where he'd been sanding the frame. The three of them were three apices of a triangle, spread across the tiny space that stretched for miles. They'd had a good day, only because they'd kept busy — planning and working and even laughing a little. Now, in the quiet darkness, sleep was unimaginable in the face of an unknown future, and they were each wrapped up in their own anxieties.

Jesse running on empty was never fun to be around. He set down the plate and folded his arms around his bent knees. "So, what did you wanna say, Wyn? I'm all ears."

She pressed her lips together, unwilling to participate when Jesse was acting that way. It was clear she was also trying hard not to cry. Perhaps she didn't want to upset Jesse. By his own admission, her breakdown over Caleb's breakup had left him traumatized.

Indio should intervene somehow. He should step up, take charge, smooth things over. He should act like the head of the family and fix things. He should tell Wynter it was okay to cry. He should indulge her, at the very least, and talk with her about Caleb.

Problem was, he couldn't think of one thing to say. A vision flashed through his mind and stopped his breath — himself, delivering the eulogy. He was the writer of the family, the lyricist, the poet, so they'd look to him for the task. But he'd have to resort to clichés and plati-tudes and fill-in-the-blank internet forms because he couldn't define a single true feeling he held for his older brother. Everything was so messed up and mixed up with childhood resentments and anger, and even then he wasn't sure why. Caleb had done what he had to do, and so had he, and they were incompatible.

"You say something," Wynter demanded, looking down at him from her corner of the triangle.

"Uh, sure." Indio wasn't going to make up something sweet, even for her. "From the time we moved to Seattle, he made my life hell."

"Did you make his life hell?"

Her directness riled him. He dropped his head into his hand and massaged his temples, composing himself.

"I guess I did."

"Dude, you *just* realized that?" Jesse spat out.

"Don't," Wynter said, before Indio could respond. "Don't be like that, both of you. I didn't want to hear bad things about him, or about either of you. I wanted to hear something good. You must have a hundred times more stories than me, because you've known him a hundred times longer."

"Twenty-five," Jesse said.

"What?"

"More like twenty-five times longer, in my case."

Wynter made a sound of annoyance in her throat.

"Okay, I'll play," Jesse said, making the effort this time. "I'm adjusting the rules, though. I'll tell you something nice about Caleb *if* you eat those nachos. You haven't eaten all day."

"But you don't have anything *not*-nice to say about him, so that's no challenge for you. I'll eat the nachos if *Indio* says something nice about Caleb."

"Baby, I don't care whether or not you eat the nachos."

She returned his smile, and even Jesse was grinning.

Her lips trembled, and she said, "If he dies, what happens to me?"

"He's not gonna..." Jesse stopped himself. "I mean, the odds are he's not gonna die."

"You said the odds were fifty-fifty."

"That statistic includes everyone. Old people, and people who were already sick. He's fit and young and healthy, so his odds are much better."

"What about my question, though?"

"We don't need to think about that right now," Indio said.

"Caleb would. He'd have a contingency plan."

"And yet, he doesn't have a contingency plan," Jesse said, feigning surprise. "Unless you count Joy."

"Shut up," Indio said mildly, careful to not disrupt the slight uptick in their collective mood.

"Those are the facts," Jesse persisted. "Wyn, your best chance of getting out of foster care would actually be if Indio and me got married and adopted you. That's the truth."

"We can do that," Indio said. "I'd marry you, Jess."

"Forget it. You're too fucked up for anyone to marry."

"Don't say that! He's not!" Wynter choked out, not quite catching on that they were messing around. She slid down the corner post to crouch on the floor. "You're not. You're not." She sniffed and wiped her eyes, looking from him to Jesse. "We're not, are we?"

"We'll be okay," Indio said.

With or without him, he almost added. But that was unnecessarily cruel. Without Caleb, he and Jesse wouldn't have stood a chance. Without Caleb, did Wynter stand a chance?

Candy Land

"I'm not gonna try anything on. Doesn't mean I can't admire the view. I've thought about it, Wynter, and I've decided *that* one's hotter." Madeline pointed at Indio, who was hammering in a stake for the mailbox at the bottom of the treehouse with Nathan's help.

Jesse was on the porch with the girls, painting a huge *KEEP OUT* sign. Probably should be Indio's job. Jesse and big pots of paint were a disaster waiting to happen. Aiden, who was in silent awe of Indio, had specifically asked Jesse to do it.

"Odd that I'm thinking that way," Madeline went on, "because he looks nothing like a vampire. Sometimes I surprise myself. Jesse, don't worry, you can be my baby daddy because you're cuter, for sure, but he's hotter. Indio!" she called across the lawn. "Maybe I'll check out your band videos after all. Can you teach me to play guitar?"

Indio, who wouldn't have heard the context of her question, ignored her.

"You asked *me* to teach you," Wynter said.

"I love the way he wields that hammer, though. You think he'd pose with me for Snapchat?" Madeline scrutinized Jesse. "So which one of you gave her the bruise? It was him, wasn't it? Always the quiet ones."

"Neither of them," Wynter said, wearily, as if she didn't care whether or not Madeline believed her.

Madeline went ahead and believed her anyway. "Glad I asked, though," she told Jesse, "cuz I was gonna key his bike *and* your car, to cover all the bases."

Jesse was finding Madeline's presence both amusing and irritating. At the very least he could acknowledge those emotions were better than the other ones clamoring for attention in his sleep-deprived, cortisol-drenched brain. And she had, finally, decided to help, offering her talents as a flat-pack furniture wiz. Single-handedly, she was assembling a kid-sized table-and-chair set and she seemed to know exactly what she was doing.

After a restless night and another busy day working outside, they were still waiting to see how those "crucial" twenty-four hours would pan out. Wynter was barely conscious, curled up on a bean bag absentmindedly threading curtains onto a length of plastic-coated clothesline. Debra had whipped up the curtains on her sewing machine after lunch — metallic silver fabric, guaranteed zombie-proof shielding.

Debra called the boys in for bed and brought out a blanket for Wynter, who'd finally fallen asleep there on the porch. Madeline jumped at the chance to help hang the curtains with Indio, climbing the rope ladder she'd sworn she would never touch. She talked his ear off in the confined space as he screwed in hooks. Indio survived, and came down to hold the *KEEP OUT* sign in place so Jesse could hammer it into a tree trunk.

"Damn fine paint job," Indio remarked, dripping disdain. "Innovative mix of upper and lower case lettering. And *four* exclamation points. No way can a zombie ignore this warning."

"Just following instructions." Jesse's new jeans were covered in paint and he was trying not to be pissed about it.

"Zombies can't read, by the way," Madeline called down.

"No shit," Jesse said. "You're gonna make Nathan cry if you tell him that."

"Nathan's got nothing to cry about. Deb and Brian are going to the courthouse next week to finalize his adoption. Then they're going after Aiden's mom."

"Going after?" Jesse queried.

"To make her give up her rights. So they can adopt Aiden."

"Where is his mom?"

"Doing three years at Mission Creek. She got out last year, went right back in. But, y'know, that's the way it goes. My brother's in Highvale right now."

Jesse looked over in time to see Indio flinch — same place he'd been sent at seventeen.

"Lucky S.O.B.," Madeline went on. "Just turned twenty when they sentenced him, but his lawyer kept him out of adult prison. When he gets out next month, we're going to hitchhike to Casper, Wyoming, where we were born." She climbed down the ladder, swinging wildly until Indio went to hold it steady. "Or maybe not. My brother's a huge dickwad. We'll probably kill each other before we get there." She grasped Indio's forearm as a handhold and jumped down the last two feet. "Let's turn on the string lights and play Pictionary on the porch. It's not too cold."

"Pictionary is banned in our family," Jesse said.

"Why?"

He jerked his thumb at Indio. "No fun playing with someone who can actually draw."

"Monopoly, then. Aiden has the Muppets edition. The tokens are super cute."

"I'd rather play Candy Land. I love a good strategy game."

Madeline overlooked his sarcasm and went inside.

"If she comes back with Candy Land," Indio said, "you're on your own with her."

"I'll wake up Wynter. I bet she's never even heard of Candy Land, let alone played it. It'll be a good introduction to board games. She'll be playing Carcassonne by Christmas."

"Let her sleep. I'm gonna hang the zipline. I need to leave in an hour or so."

Jesse noted the deep discomfort in his brother's voice. They needed news — any news — and it was going to be awful if Indio had to return to Portland without having received any. And if it was the worst, the wrong side of that fifty percent, what then?

"What time is it in Australia?" Jesse asked.

"About three in the afternoon, I think." Indio checked his phone, just in case.

Jesse chewed on his lip, willing the phone to ring. Indio watched him with genuine compassion, for once. Jesse would've preferred the usual gruff indifference with a side of sarcasm, because it was embarrassing to be standing there being vulnerable, on the verge of tears...

"Candy Land! Candy Land!" Madeline sang, keeping her voice low because Wynter was asleep. She began setting up the board.

"I guess I'm playing Candy Land," Jesse said. The ridiculous activity might be the only thing to stop him breaking down on the spot.

While Indio drilled and bolted across the yard, holding a flashlight between his teeth, Jesse lost himself in a world of caramel and cookies and gingerbread men.

Wynter slept on.

Jesse didn't hear the phone buzz, but he heard Indio answer it, ten yards away. He hunched over the game board, not even daring to turn around. Indio's voice faded as he walked further away, speaking in monosyllables.

Yes. No. When? Okay.

A hot rush of tears stung Jesse's eyes and he couldn't move. Couldn't even swing his arm a few inches to the right to set down his soda. Madeline turned a card and moved her piece, humming a tune to herself, with no idea of the significance of the call, or the fifty percent odds, or the abyss he and Wynter and maybe even Indio were toppling headlong into...

He was going to fucking cry in front of a sixteen-year-old girl.

A hand closed around his shoulder. Jesse gasped for air and turned to his brother.

"He's out of danger."

Stop

"You can't just hide his medication. That's not ethical."

"I'm not hiding it, Wyn. I'm monitoring it. He could get addicted to this stuff..."

Caleb dragged himself out of sleep and rolled over in bed to ease the pressure on his hip. *Ouch.* Ribs still hurt like a bitch.

His siblings' voices drifted through the open bedroom door.

"So you're gonna let him suffer?"

"Opioid addiction is a thing. A serious thing. I'm giving him exactly what the nurse told me."

"That was the minimum dose. Can't you see he's in pain?"

"He's asleep. He's not in pain."

"Guys... I'm not asleep."

His voice, little more than a croak from his dry throat, brought Jesse and Wynter into the room. Wynter immediately fussed with his water bottle and his pillows. Jesse stood back, scrutinizing him like an incomprehensible piece of modern art.

He pushed away Wynter's hand when she reached for the pillow behind his head for the fourth time.

"Do you need help with your shower?" Wynter said. "The nurse isn't coming until tomorrow."

"Are you offering to help him?" Jesse scoffed. "He's fine."

Wynter ignored that. "You have a physical therapy appointment at eleven, and a check-up right after that." She showed him the calendar she'd made on her last visit, a printed sheet of squares for October with an alarming number of appointments blocked in. Two more sheets were attached behind it for November and December. Caleb had avoided looking too closely at it.

"Why aren't you at school?" he asked her.

"It's Saturday." *Huh.* He'd lost track a few days ago. "Debra drove me here this morning and I'm staying through the long weekend."

The doorbell rang.

"That's Patricia." She went to answer it.

"Why the hell is Patricia here?" Not that he didn't adore Patricia, but he'd spoken to her on the phone only yesterday.

Jesse shrugged. Jesse had been in a perpetually bad mood since Caleb came home. Well, so had Caleb. The two of them didn't have the first idea how to deal with the situation. On top of that was Wynter's suffocating mothering, and now Patricia showing up to witness his humiliation.

He'd rather Harry visited, of all people. He spoke almost daily to his father, which was a new experience for both of them. Harry hadn't set foot in this house since the day Caleb threw him out four years ago.

Bea's mother had been, just the once, while he was still in the hospital in Seattle, and had texted once when he got out. The family had sent flowers — *Best wishes for a speedy recovery, from the Hayes*. Very formal. He and Bea had agreed to a clean break. This was what a clean break felt like. He didn't want Bea to see him in this state, anyway.

But in the moments before he fell asleep at night, he needed her beside him.

"You don't want a fuss, I get that," Patricia said, breezing in with a pile of clean sheets in her arms, "so I won't fuss. I've put some meals in your freezer — one less thing for Jesse to worry about. Out you get, then."

Caleb got up and moved out of her way so she could change the sheets. Thought about asking, in jest, if she wanted to give him a sponge bath, too. He was in fact perfectly capable of taking care of himself. He was on his feet a couple of hours a day, walking with a limp because of his ribs — nothing wrong with his legs, other than the burn scar running up his thigh and over his hip. He tired easily, a lingering effect of the infection on top of drowsiness caused by the painkillers. That was it. He was fine.

Patricia handed him a pillow slip to stuff. "How are Jesse and Wynter?"

"Pains in my butt."

She was unsympathetic. "They need to deal with this in their own way."

"What's to deal with? I'm fine. I will be fine."

"You've never once taken a step back and allowed someone to take care of you." She occupied herself with tucking the sheets, not looking at him, to lessen the severity of her words. "You rescue people. Victims at sea, women, siblings. Now you're being rescued. You need to accept that, just for a while."

"I can't." He threw the pillow on the bed and found another to stuff.

"Caleb—"

"I can't."

Patricia straightened from smoothing the quilt and placed her hand on his arm. "Okay," she said gently, letting him win. She went to put the old sheets in the washer.

Caleb wandered through the house to find food. Wynter had brought him dinner on a tray that first day he came home, a week ago, after scolding Jesse for telling him to get up for it. He'd thanked her and eaten it, and since then made sure he got to the kitchen as soon as he heard food-preparation sounds coming from that direction. Made sure he was seated at the breakfast bar before any food went on any tray.

"Did you take that Percocet in the night?" Jesse asked as soon as Caleb sat.

"I did," Caleb gritted out.

"What time? Did you write it on the chart?"

"Don't remember. No." He gave his brother a warning look that ordinarily would've shut him up.

Jesse sent exactly the same look back at him.

Wynter was at the stove, doing the best she could with pancakes. "Leave him alone, Jesse. You can't expect him to remember what he did in the middle of the night when he's half asleep."

She set a plate on the counter. Her smile warmed his heart. The extra-crispy pancakes did not. Jesse fetched a mug of watery coffee and slid it next to the plate.

"Jesus Christ, both of you, you're killing me."

Wynter's face fell. Okay, bad joke. He held out an arm and she came around the counter for a hug. With his other hand he cut the stack of pancakes in half with a fork. Raw batter oozed out. How the fuck could they be burnt and uncooked at the same time?

He dropped the fork and leaned his head into his hand, stunned by the force of his own sour thoughts.

Patricia came in to say goodbye. He desperately wanted her to notice his "coffee" and offer to make another, so he wouldn't have to offend Jesse by doing it himself. She did notice it, gave him a sympathetic look this time, and did not offer a damn thing. Five minutes ago he'd been pleased when she announced she wasn't going to fuss over him. Now he wished she would.

Jesse was counting out pills into one of those huge seven-day pill boxes meant for old or sick people. Antibiotics, blood pressure meds, anti-inflammatories. No painkillers. Jesse had confiscated those a few days ago, the moment he noticed Caleb taking a second dose within six hours, and now doled them out separately. They were low-dose ones, too. Twenty seconds into Jesse's rant about opioid addiction, Caleb had yelled at him so viciously that Jesse hadn't spoken to him for the rest of the day.

Thank god Wynter hadn't been here to witness that.

"What's this?" Caleb pointed to a new pill among the ones Jesse tipped out for his morning cocktail.

"That's a laxative. You told the nurse the works were clogged up."

Awesome. His bowels were now a discussion topic at breakfast.

"That's a side effect of opioids, by the way," Jesse said. The little fucker was pushing his luck this morning.

Caleb swallowed the pills with a mouthful of lukewarm dishwater, glaring at Jesse over the rim of his mug.

"At your check-up this afternoon," Jesse said, "how about you talk to your doctor about prescribing a non-addictive option?"

"How about you..."

Caleb didn't finish. He'd been about to say something cruel and pointless, which he never did – and to his own brother, no less.

He wasn't in his right mind. Partly it was the pain and the painkillers. Rationally, he knew it was also the trauma his body had experienced. Jesse liked to say body and mind were the same thing – nothing more or less than a cavalcade of complicated chemical reactions. Which meant his mind had experienced trauma, too. Made no sense, because he couldn't remember most of it. Not the accident, not the days in ICU where he apparently almost died, not the flight back to the States. He barely even remembered the first time Wynter and Jesse and Indio visited him at the hospital.

No, he remembered that visit. Wynter climbing on the bed to cuddle up to him, talking softly, her head too heavy on his chest. Jesse reading his charts and examining the machines and telling the long-suffering nurse how to do her job. Indio sitting silently in the corner, then holding on a second too long when they shook hands as he left.

"Would you like toast instead?" Wynter said, bringing him out of his reverie.

Jesse had gone. She was still right there, his arm was still around her. Her head rested on his shoulder and the joint ached from the weight. His joints ached a lot, hence the painkillers. Sepsis ate away at everything. He almost lost his kidneys, they told him. That gentle weight restricted his breathing, too. Hard to fill his lungs, which were still healing from inflammation caused by the chemical fire.

When he didn't immediately answer, she pushed the soggy pancakes aside and said, "I'll make you toast."

She didn't move, and he didn't lower his arm. He held her tighter.

"You need to be kinder to Jesse."

Need to be? Since when did Wynter dictate how he *needed* to act? He didn't trust himself to speak.

"He thought you were going to die," she said. "I mean, I thought you might die, too, but I managed to distract myself. He drowned in his fears. And he's the one who..." She sighed as her fingers traced a small fresh scar on his forearm. "I know you would say, all three of you, that I'd suffer the most if you'd died. It's not true. You're the only stable, caring person he's ever had in his life, the only one he relies on. I have three people like that now, always someone to take care of me no matter what happens. But he has only one."

"Hun, I didn't die," he pointed out, "so none of this matters. In any case, you would all have been fine. People survive worse losses every day."

"We're not *people*, Caleb. We're *us*. And for us, this would've been the worst loss. For one whole week we were terrified. We're still recovering. Those feelings count for something. I think maybe it was the first time Jesse's world fell apart. And you weren't there to fix it."

He was struck by the realization that they'd suffered far worse than him. He hadn't even known the seriousness of his condition until it was over. They were the ones who'd lived through it.

Jesse returned, checking his phone. "You could come with me to the dojo this afternoon," he told Caleb. "Do a few *kata* with me."

"He can't do karate!" Wynter pulled out of Caleb's arms. "He needs to rest."

"He can ease back into it," Jesse retorted. "The doc said gentle exercise is fine."

"He hasn't even walked down the street and back yet."

"Guys." Caleb got up to scrape the pancakes into the trash. "I'll decide what I can and can't do, okay? I'll try some *kata* on the patio tomorrow. The dojo next week, maybe." The thought of his colleagues and students at the dojo seeing him, his limp and his labored breathing, filled him with horror.

"Will you walk down the street with me?" Wynter asked tentatively, scared of being rejected as well.

"Of course, hun. I'll take a shower. Make me that toast, okay?"

The hot water made him feel a thousand times better. He regretted pretty much every word out of his mouth this morning. He was being an ungrateful S.O.B. because of his own insecurities about showing weakness.

He ate the toast and drank a protein shake. He walked down the street with Wynter. She wanted him to sit on a low wall for a few minutes to rest before heading back. He refused. By the time they got back to the house, he was out of breath and every part of him ached.

While she and Jesse studied in the dining room, he went into Jesse's room and opened every drawer, moved every book, felt around every nook and cranny in the top of the closet...

"It's not in here," Jesse said, leaning in the doorway.

"It's been six hours, Jess."

"Well, I wouldn't know, would I, because you didn't write it on the chart during the night."

"It was... 2AM."

"You sure?"

"More or less." This was ridiculous. He was on the lowest dose and he'd never been addicted to anything in his life.

"I'll bring it out for you."

Caleb limped back down the hallway and sank into the couch. Wynter sat with him and turned on the TV, the volume muted. Jesse brought the pill.

"You can drive yourself to your appointments today, right?" Jesse said, standing over him.

"He can't drive," Wynter said.

"Why not? Driving is *gentle exercise*."

"You're driving him," she said.

"Sure, if he can't handle it." There was a challenge in Jesse's voice. "It's only eight minutes down the road, but whatever."

"You're driving him."

"I'm right here," Caleb said wearily. "I would appreciate a lift, Jesse. We'll go to the grocery store after."

"Jesse and me can do that," Wynter said. "You need to come straight back."

Need to, again. He did not appreciate her using that phrase.

"Anyone heard from Joy?" he said, to change the subject.

A look passed between his siblings. What was *that* about?

"I text her every day," Wynter said. "She did a healing ritual for you."

"She did? She came here? Was I asleep?"

"She did it at her house. She shouldn't have, in my opinion. You're supposed to have the person's permission, or at least their implied permission."

"Doesn't bother me."

"Wouldn't you rather she visited you in person than light a candle and ask the universe to heal you?"

"The ritual was to help *her*, Wyn, not him," Jesse said. "To make *her* feel better. That's why people pray for world peace instead of going out and making world peace happen."

"Unless *you're* actually doing something for world peace *right now*, I don't think you have the right to criticize—"

She stopped because Caleb had raised his hand in a clear *STOP* signal.

"I'm going to read in my room for a bit." A euphemism for *taking a nap*, and they all knew it. That walk had tired him out beyond belief. "You guys hold off sniping at each other for thirty seconds, please? Long enough for me to get to my room and shut the door cuz I'm sick of hearing it."

Jesse had the decency to look chastised. Wynter looked miserable. He pulled himself up off the couch, staggering a half-step as his blood pressure dropped suddenly and spots danced before his eyes. He closed them and waited for the blood to make it to his brain, praying he didn't faint.

When he opened his eyes, Jesse had moved forward, just casually, just in case. He looked into his little brother's blue eyes, usually so full of confidence and optimism and curiosity. All he saw was confusion. Jesse was lost.

"D'you need him to help you get down the hall?" Wynter said, asking the question Jesse could not because, like Caleb, he was so deeply in denial.

"Yeah, I think so."

He leaned on Jesse and made his way to his room. The drug had dulled the pain, but he had little strength in his muscles. He felt like an old man. Wynter slipped past them and went ahead to fix the pillows, even though Patricia had made the bed perfectly.

Caleb took a paperback from his nightstand, furthering the pretense he was going to read, and stood there watching Wynter rearrange the stuff on his nightstand, moving the water bottle closer, the lamp further away to make room. She was fidgeting, not knowing what to do.

"Hun, that's fine. Why don't you check the freezer and see what Patricia brought over for dinner? You could make a menu for the weekend, see if there's anything else we need."

She left, relieved to have a task to do.

Jesse stood nervously before him, unable to process the state he was in.

"I should never have signed up."

Jesse blinked in disbelief. "What are you talking about? The Coast Guard was always your dream."

"The Army was my dream, if I'm honest. Just like dad. I picked the Coast Guard because, in the end, I didn't want to be *just like dad*. I should've taken a regular job and stayed home. I should've been here to protect you, every single day. I should've been here for Indio. And by now, Wynter would be living here too."

So unlike him to regret the past knowing he'd always made the best decisions he could, at the time. Jesse wasn't liking it, either. Jesse needed him to be strong and decisive. Jesse did not need to see beneath the surface any more than he needed to expose it. Jesse couldn't even bear to see the cracks.

"Listen," Caleb said, thinking fast how to fix it. "This is just for a week or two. The doc said I'll be good as new in a month, tops, and back at work. We have to grit our teeth and get through it, and I need your help. I need you to drive me to my appointments when you don't have class. Otherwise I'll call an Uber. I need you to let me take it easy sometimes, to take a nap after my so-called gentle exercise. I need you to trust me to control my own pain meds."

Jesse nodded, the confusion clearing a shade. Caleb stepped forward and hugged him. When was the last time he did that? Had he *ever* done that? Jesse patted his shoulder, embarrassed by the display, and wouldn't quite meet his eye when they pulled apart.

"And I need you to learn how to make a drinkable cup of damn coffee."

Anything Goes

Jesse pulled his cloak across his lower face and chased a four-foot-tall werewolf up the driveway. A zombie of similar height poked his head around the door and shrieked. Jesse hissed at them.

"You guys ready to go trick-or-treating?"

"Yes!" Aiden held up a huge plastic pumpkin bucket.

Nathan added, "But we have to wait for the sun to go down."

"Nine minutes, guys. I checked. Who did these awesome decorations?"

"We did! We helped!"

Deb and Brian had made an effort with the house, stringing up orange lights and sticking bats and ghosts in the front windows. The driveway was covered in chalk renditions of spiders and cobwebs.

Jesse hadn't been trick-or-treating in about ten years, and this would be Wynter's first time ever.

"Madeline says you have to come as a vampire, like on TV," Wynter had told him.

Given the high number of vampire TV shows these days, he wasn't sure which one he was supposed to copy. He'd bought a cheap black cloak from the costume store and spruced it up with a black fur shoulder cape. Underneath that he wore a white shirt, and a waistcoat from the one black-tie event Caleb had ever attended a couple of years ago. With his slicked-back hair and plastic fangs and a bit of blood running from the corner of his mouth, he figured the girls would be impressed.

Madeline waltzed into the living room wearing black goth clothing, basically rips and netting held together with threads, and an elaborate black-and-red beaded choker. She'd plastered white makeup all over her face, along with heavy black eyeliner and the requisite dripping blood.

"You don't look scary," she said.

"I'm taking out a couple of first-graders. Figured I'd tone it down."

The foster parents had asked Jesse to chaperone — they trusted him with the children they thought of as their own sons, and he'd become a fixture in the boys' lives, always paying them just enough attention that they thought he was the coolest adult they knew.

Madeline wasn't happy about the kids coming along with them. "Oh, they're not scared of anything. I don't know why they dressed up — they're already monsters."

"Where's Wynter?"

"I just finished her makeup. She's fiddling with her corset."

"Her... what?"

"I lent her some old clothes that don't fit me anymore. You're gonna love it. Wynter!" she screamed over her shoulder. "Jesse's here! He looks like Dracula." To Jesse she said, "You weren't supposed to look like Dracula. Lamest vampire *ever*."

Jesse hissed at her, extending his retractable fangs.

"Oh my god!" Madeline squealed. "That's awesome! How does that work?"

"I don't know. They just do that when I'm hungry."

"You can bite me, any time."

Okay, that had spun out of control pretty fast.

"Uh, do you have a map of the neighborhood?" he said.

"We can go wherever. This entire town is full of evil spirits."

"It is?"

"That's what *Enumclaw* means."

"I'll take your word for it."

"Wynter says you don't have a girlfriend."

"I absolutely do have a girlfriend. Most definitely."

"What's her name?"

"Fifi."

"Is she a poodle?"

"Not to my knowledge. We're going to a Halloween party tomorrow night."

"Will you be wearing that lame outfit again?"

"Yes, because it's awesome."

Madeline sighed, out of small talk. "So, they want us back in one hour with the boys. We could always go out again after."

"Depends on how much candy corn we get. I haven't had candy corn since I was about six but it's my fav..."

His words petered out as Wynter walked in. She wore a tiny low-cut black dress, the top half of which was mostly see-through lace, and a blood red corset laced up under her breasts. She tugged self-consciously at the hem of her skirt.

"Isn't she awesome?" Madeline gushed, circling around Wynter. "Spent more time on her than on me. I did her makeup and hair and picked everything out. She's not a vampire yet. She's, like, a vampire's *victim*. We had so much fun. It was like dressing a doll."

Wynter didn't look like she was having fun. She looked bewildered. She had two puncture wounds in her neck and heavy scarlet smudges under her eyes so they looked like they were bleeding. Her hair was back-combed into a cloud around her face. She wore her own ankle boots, which looked great with jeans but kind of slutty with the micro skirt.

"Um, Wynter, are you allowed to leave the house like that?"

"They don't care," Madeline said.

"I'm supposed to take a photo for Caleb and I think *he* would care."

"What's wrong with it?" Madeline demanded.

Jesse pointed to Wynter's skirt, corset and neckline in turn: "Too short, too sexy, too much cleavage."

"Huh, that's an A-cup, not *cleavage*." Madeline thrust her own assets forward. "*This* is cleavage."

Jesse ignored her. "You look great, Wyn. And it's Halloween, so anything goes, I guess. But..."

He went over and pinched the lacy neckline of her dress between his fingers and thumbs to yank it up an inch. He stood back to admire his work. *Nope.* He took off his cloak and put it around her shoulders, drawing it closed over her chest.

"Just for the official photo, okay?"

He handed his phone to Madeline and she took a shot of the two of them. He took back his cloak and took a shot of the girls, not for Caleb's eyes. Indio would get a chuckle out of it. Debra came in and photographed all five of them, and then Brian appeared with his own fancy camera and took more shots. Madeline was right — they did not seem to care what Wynter was wearing.

"Trick or treat! Trick or treat!" the boys yelled, eager to get going.

"You listen to Jesse," Debra told them. "Stay close and do what he says. Only wrapped candy, remember."

They set out to scour the neighborhood for candy, avoiding Foxtail Street because apparently there was a zombie massacre that way and Aiden was concerned they'd figure out he was faking his undead status. The girls admired the decorations and the costumes of the other kids walking around in small groups going from house to house. Madeline did a pretty good job of explaining to Wynter who Freddy Krueger and Batwoman were. There was a cool pint-sized headless horseman, too.

Jesse took his responsibility toward the boys seriously. He kept them close, held their hands and made them look both ways to cross the street even though there was no traffic. He made them rehearse their "trick or treat" line, as well as "thank you". They listened to him intently and he figured maybe he had a bit of Caleb's mojo.

Then they broke free and ran across the street without looking, grabbed two handfuls of candy at the first house and forgot to say thank you. Madeline was right — they were monsters.

After about the tenth infraction, Wynter caught up with him. "Aren't you gonna tell them to drop and give you twenty?"

"They'll be feeling so sick in an hour. That'll be punishment enough." He took a sidelong glance at her costume. "Are you comfortable in that?"

"No. I don't like wearing someone else's clothes."

"I mean the corset."

"I quite like it, actually. I think it's pretty. But I've read historical novels — it's supposed to be underwear."

"No, that one is definitely intended to be seen. In case I didn't make myself clear earlier, I hope you know Caleb would have a heart attack if he saw you right now."

"I'm not a little girl. In historical times, girls my age were married off."

"That's not the point." He took her hand as they walked. "Next Halloween you'll be at home and we'll do something great. Seriously, though, the hemline's gonna have to be longer to pass muster."

"What does Caleb know about hemlines? He's only raised boys."

"He knows more about girls than you or me. If he was your dad, the hemline would have to be below the knee, so count your blessings."

"I'll have more going on up top next year, too. He'll make me wear a turtleneck." She pointed to a kid across the street wrapped head-to-foot in toilet paper. "Oh, I could go as a mummy and cover up *everything*. I wanted to be home by Thanksgiving. Is that gonna happen?"

"It'll take a bit longer. I'm sorry, Wyn. Caleb has to do these foster parent courses and they only run at certain times. He missed one because of his illness, and the next one was booked out."

"Is he ready to go back to work?"

"After Veteran's Day, on restricted duties, which is pissing him off no end. He's doing great. Last week he went back to teaching at the dojo, and he's been lifting weights with me to build up his strength. He's almost back to his old self."

"His old self... with no Bea."

Jesse nudged her sharply. "He's the catch of the Pacific Northwest. He'll find someone. I love this part of the year — lots of fun stuff coming up. We'll make the most of all your firsts — your first Thanksgiving, your first Christmas, your first New Year. And then you'll have been here a whole year, although it feels like you've been here forever. I can't even remember what it was like before I knew you."

She was lost in thought.

"What's up?"

"If you knew I existed somewhere in the world," she said, "but didn't know how to find me, what would you think?"

"What kind of question is that?"

"Just wondering."

"We knew Joy existed and we just accepted it. We didn't do anything, or think anything. She's Indio's twin and that's supposed to be a special bond. But still we didn't do anything."

"Why not? She's your family."

"I guess because she was tied to Mom, and that made it... too painful. For Caleb and Indio, anyway. And we had our own stuff to deal with."

"So if you knew about me long ago, if I was just another sister in Arizona — a half-sister you'd never even met — you'd have accepted that, too, and done nothing?"

"It's hard to say. Now I know you, I can't imagine doing nothing. But maybe you're right. If we'd heard Mom had another child, maybe it wouldn't have meant much. She was out of our lives."

"Do you think we were supposed to meet?"

"Are you talking about fate? You were brave enough to get on that bus and knock on our door, and not run away at the sight of me, and especially at the sight of Caleb. Don't credit fate when it was you who made it happen."

"It was Joy, really."

"It was both of you."

She stopped suddenly and faced him. "Joy told me a secret and I don't know what to do."

Damn, the secrets in this family were mounting up. "No secrets, remember? Does this have something to do with her attacking you a few weeks ago?"

"No. It's nothing to do with me."

"Then maybe she shouldn't have told you. Anyway, if it's nothing to do with you, why do you need to do anything?"

She didn't answer. She was biting her lip, thinking hard.

He tried again. "Is it about the ashram?"

"Not exactly. Never mind. I have to think it through a bit more."

They set off walking again, and Jesse scanned the kids to make sure he kept Aiden and Nathan within sight. Madeline was lagging, uninterested in supervising when Jesse had essentially volunteered for the job.

"Just tell Caleb," he said. "He'll know what to do."

"I promised I wouldn't."

Jesse made a frustrated sound. "Don't ever agree to keep someone else's secret, Wyn. It's how they get control of you."

"Really?"

"Yes! Any time someone says *I'll tell you something, but you have to keep it a secret* — you have to tell them *no*. You tell them to go ahead and tell you if they want, but you get to decide what to do with the information."

"It's too late. I already promised."

"Well, don't do it again."

Madeline came up from behind, sucking a lollipop. "You guys are so cute, holding hands," she said sarcastically.

"Wynter's still learning how to cross the street." This was actually true — her road sense was terrible, having grown up with no roads.

"I have a big brother." Madeline stopped right in front of them, forcing them to stop, too. "Did I tell you? His name's Zack. He used to come into my room at night and push his hand under my top while he jerked off."

Jesse felt Wynter's hand tighten in his. "Is that a secret?" she said.

"No. Everyone knows. He was sent away for a bit, and my mom's boyfriend did worse."

Madeline raised an eyebrow, awaiting their reaction. Then something else drew her attention. She ran after Nathan and Aiden, yelling at them for eating unwrapped candy.

Wynter turned her face against Jesse's chest. "I didn't want to know that."

"I know. That's awful, what happened to her. But she only told you now, like that, to try and make you feel guilty for having a decent human being for a brother."

"I thought she liked me."

"She's just lashing out." Jesse smoothed down her ridiculous ratted hair. "Don't let it spoil tonight."

"I was teaching her to play guitar. She *asked* me to. She learned three chords and lost interest. Sometimes she sings along when I play."

"Can she sing?"

"She's not bad."

"She had fun dressing you up, right?"

"Loads of fun."

"See, she's trying to be a big sister — she's just not very good at it yet."

Special Dispensation

The Eagle has landed

?

The special dispensation
has been approved

??

All pertinent forms are signed
and stamped in triplicate

???

WE'RE GOING TO PORTLAND
OVERNIGHT FOR INDIO'S GIG!!!

Yesss!

Picking you up in
53 minutes. Go pack!

Please add dispensation, pertinent, and triplicate to our
online dictionary

Look them up later.
ARE YOU PACKED YET?

Indio's apartment complex was rather more impressive from the outside than Wynter had hoped it would be. The sun had set two hours
ago. The well-lit street revealed an iron gate opening onto a paved courtyard, surrounded by a huge red-brick U-shaped building rising four stories high.

"Turk's family pays for the luxury accommodation," Jesse said out the corner of his mouth as he, Wynter, and Caleb passed a young couple exiting the main doors.

"Actually, I pay for at least some of it," Caleb said.

"Okay, I'll clarify. Turk's family pays for it, and Indio rents a room from him with Caleb's money."

Wynter had secretly been hoping Indio lived in a dump. Surely, the worse his situation here, the more likely he'd be to move home when he graduated.

Jesse reached for the elevator button. Caleb swatted his hand away, not quite fast enough.

"It's only two floors," Caleb said scathingly, grabbing Wynter's hand and walking around the corner to the stairs.

"The button's lit up!" Jesse came after them. "It's unethical to call an elevator you're not gonna use."

Wynter didn't mind taking the stairs, but she would rather they'd taken the elevator for Caleb's sake, especially as he was carrying both his bag and her backpack. While he was improving each time she saw him, and he'd been back on duty since Veterans Day, he wasn't himself. Despite claiming he no longer needed painkillers, she saw flashes of pain in his expression now and then. His breathing grew labored if he exerted himself. Jesse continually assured her that his mood swings and depression were normal side effects of a serious illness, and would pass. His belief — and Jesse's — in his infallibility had been shattered and that might take longer to rebuild.

Indio let them in. Wynter gave him the briefest of hugs before slipping away to take a look around. The inside wasn't quite as clean and tidy as the outside, hardly surprising given two men lived here. But it was pretty nice, unfortunately.

"Where are the kittens?" she asked.

"They're well-and-truly cats now." Indio pointed to the balcony off the living room. He told Caleb to put their bags in Turk's room, as Turk was staying with his girlfriend for the night.

Wynter walked past a kitchenette and a small dining table, into the good-sized living room with a couple of deep plush couches piled with colorful pillows. Through the glass doors on the other side of the room were three dried-out plants in huge pots along with two empty window boxes attached to the railing.

She slid open the door, letting in a blast of cold air. "Are those plants supposed to be brown?"

Indio had followed her. "Those are Turk's. He didn't water them, so I guess they died."

"I hope he treats his cats better."

Indio grimaced, slipped outside and plucked one gray cat out of each of the window boxes. Not empty, after all. The bottoms were lined with blankets, too.

"Is this where they live?"

"They live all over the apartment. This is where they hang out."

The cats purred as Indio crushed them against his chest. Indio had been sending her pictures. Still, it was a shock to see how big they'd grown.

Wynter took one of the cats. "Is this Led or Zep?"

Indio made a show of examining his cat before declaring, "No idea."

"Don't pretend you don't know," Wynter said slyly as they brought the cats inside. "Are they getting a special Thanksgiving meal tomorrow?"

"In fact, they are. Turk found some turkey cat food."

"Is it grain-free?" Jesse called from the kitchen, where his head was stuck in the refrigerator. "Cats are obligate carnivores. You gotta buy the good stuff with no fillers."

Indio dropped his cat on the couch. "Turk gets a list of instructions from his sister every other day about these damn cats. How about you add to that list with your advice about the food? He's gonna love you for it."

Jesse swung the refrigerator door closed. "Did *you* follow my instructions and buy groceries for dinner? There's nothing in here. How long do we have?"

"I leave for soundcheck in one hour."

"Awesome! I'll come."

"You can come if you keep quiet about how the drums are sounding." Indio shut down Jesse's next indignant response with a look. "You guys should get to the venue by eight," he told Caleb. He put an arm around Wynter and stole a proper hug. "I'm glad you could make it. That was down to the wire, huh?"

They'd been waiting two days for Svetlana to approve her first out-of-state visit. First official one, anyway. Indio was filling in on short notice for an 'eighties cover band, and it hadn't been hard to persuade Caleb she needed to go to that gig.

Tomorrow, Indio would be coming to Seattle for Thanksgiving and Joy had promised she'd be there, too. No one was more apprehensive about the family get-together than Wynter, knowing Jesse and Indio weren't exactly thrilled about Joy being there. They hadn't told Caleb about how she'd attacked Wynter, and Wynter hadn't told any of them about Joy's secret. For a house with no secrets and lies, suddenly everyone was hiding something.

Everyone but Caleb, whose illness and recuperation had stolen the focus from their other problems for a while.

"We'll have to order take-out," Jesse said, tapping his phone impatiently. "Two pounds of chicken breast and a pre-mixed salad, that's all you had to do. That's all I asked."

"I had classes until five." Indio was unaffected by Jesse's scolding. "I think there's a chocolate cheesecake in the freezer, if that helps."

Jesse gritted his teeth. "I don't like chocolate cheesecake. Cookies and cream. You know this. French vanilla. Strawberry. Not chocolate."

"You like chocolate," Wynter said.

"Not in a cheesecake!" Jesse lifted his finger from his phone screen in a final flourish. "Okay, we're having dumpling soup, California rolls, and pork on skewers. Hope that's okay with everyone."

"What sort of pork?" Indio asked suspiciously.

"No questions. It's Japanese, that's all I know. It'll be here in half an hour and it's forty-eight dollars, cash on delivery." He pointed at Indio to indicate who would be paying.

"I'm not paying forty-eight—"

"We're paying for the feast tomorrow. You can pay today."

"I could've ordered pizza for twenty bucks!"

"You could've bought two pounds of chicken for $6.50. Like I told you."

Wynter glanced at Caleb, who hadn't said a word to mediate the dispute. He was on the couch, flicking through a paperback left on the coffee table, hardly paying attention — which was how she knew he was still recovering his breath from climbing those stairs. The old Caleb was always fully aware of what was going on around him, even if he wasn't participating, even if he was pretending not to listen. This Caleb was drifting. He'd insisted on driving all the way, too. Usually he let Jesse drive, but it was like he needed to prove to himself he could do it.

He needed to rest, and they had a long evening ahead of them.

Her other brothers were still bickering about the cost of dinner.

"I have money," Wynter said, reaching for her purse on the counter.

"Hun, I'll pay for it," Caleb said, snapping back to reality. He took out his wallet, counted out the cash, and handed it to Indio who was standing nearest.

Indio came into the kitchen to find plates and forks. "So, what's on the menu for tomorrow?"

"Wyn and I spent all week planning it," Jesse said. "It's our dry run for Christmas, to knock out the bugs."

"Actually, we may not be at home for Christmas," Caleb said, hauling himself off the couch to help Wynter clear textbooks and folders off the dining room table. "I think we should take a vacation."

Jesse was dubious. "I know you like to rough it, but I'm not camping in December."

"I had something else in mind."

"Aren't we broke?"

"I have friends in high places." Caleb gave a tired smile. "Patricia has that place on Cougar Mountain she used to rent out, about ten minutes up the road from her diner. She'll let us have it for a few nights over Christmas, if I fix some things and get it ready to rent again after the New Year."

Fix some things? Caleb couldn't even climb a few flights of stairs. "Are you strong enough to be fixing things?" Wynter said sharply.

"Minor things," Caleb assured her. "Indio, you'll come, won't you? And I've already mentioned it to Joy."

Indio had opened his mouth to answer. Now he clamped it shut again. Would he opt out of Christmas just because Joy was going to be there? In truth, Wynter would rather Indio come than Joy. She felt safe with Indio. She'd told him things she hadn't even dared think about for months. They'd play music and she'd laugh at him making fun of Jesse. Even the tension between him and Caleb was easier to endure than the awful tension she knew would be there between Indio and Joy — which she'd be witnessing firsthand tomorrow.

"I don't know if she'd want to come," Wynter said. "The Light has all this winter solstice stuff going on during that time."

"Well, she didn't say no," Caleb said.

"Just as long as we're back for New Year's Eve," Jesse said, "cuz I got a killer party to go to."

"With Fiorella?" Wynter asked.

"I broke up with Fiorella. I'm going with Delilah."

"*Another* new girlfriend?"

"We're not dating. She agreed to come to the party with me. So, between now and then there's a good chance she'll become my girlfriend."

"Your dating method sounds so much more complicated than the kids at school make it sound."

"It's in flux, is all I'm saying."

"Can I come?"

"Not this year," Caleb said, before Jesse had time to respond.

"I'd take care of her," Jesse said.

"Not this year." Caleb threw him a severe look. "Hun, you can stay up until midnight with me, if you want. I bet neither of us will make it."

Given Wynter's experience with staying up at all-night prayer meetings, Caleb was probably wrong about her. Given his current condition, he was probably right about himself.

❧

At the venue, Jesse let Caleb and Wynter inside via a back door. This was a real bar with no food service, where neither she or Jesse were supposed to be. He had a pass around his neck that said he was with the band.

"We're not really sneaking in," he said. "The manager is okay with it. Just stay out of public view, Wyn."

He led them into an area at the side of the stage, with steps going up into the wings.

"Can we see Indio before he goes on?"

"Sure, come on through."

Caleb caught Wynter's arm before she could follow Jesse into the dressing room area. "How about you bring him out?"

"These guys are okay."

Caleb sent Jesse off with a flick of his head. A minute later, Jesse returned with Indio. She'd first met Indio after a gig, buzzing with energy. She'd never seen him right before one. He looked the same as always, in ordinary street clothes, but she detected his anticipation, the excitement he usually hid behind a don't-care attitude, tempered by a focused confidence she recognized from their jam sessions at home.

She asked what kind of music he'd be playing.

"Your basic pub rock. Reminds the forty-year-old women in the audience of necking in their boyfriends' cars in high school, so it gets them drunk and dancing. It's all covers. You'll know most of them. I'll bet you can *play* most of them."

His bandmates had started coming out and it was time to go on stage.

"He's different, isn't he?" she told Jesse as they prepared to go up the stairs to watch from the wings.

"Sexier?" Jesse suggested.

"More... intense. More *Indio*. He's Indio squared."

"Indio cubed."

"Indio... um, what's the next one?"

"Indio to the fourth power. That's a quartic equation — very hard to solve."

She would solve Indio. She would figure out how to make him do what she wanted, and bring him home.

Sociopathic

"Do you think Jesse will bring his girlfriend-in-flux to the cabin?" Wynter asked Caleb when they got back to Indio's apartment.

"No, this is just family."

Indio and Jesse had gone out with the band after the gig. Wynter, of course, was not allowed to hang around. In any case, she was as tired as Caleb looked as he rummaged around in Turk's bedroom closet. He found a blanket and a pillow, and took them out to the couch where he planned to sleep. He came back to sit on the bed and remove his shoes. Wynter watched him pull his bag closer and unzip it. His movements were slow rather than decisive, which made him look like someone else.

"Would Bea have come, if you were still with her?"

Caleb stopped digging around for his toothbrush and... just *stopped*.

"No," he said finally. "Family only. Get ready for bed. We'll watch a movie." He found his PJs and toothbrush and went into the bathroom.

Wynter changed and put a second blanket on the couch. Caleb was clearly exhausted and she hated to think he wasn't even going to spend the night in a proper bed.

As soon as she sat on the couch, one of the cats jumped up and stalked over to knead her thighs with his claws. *Ouch!* She pulled the blanket over her legs and lifted the cat on top. He sat contentedly in her lap while his brother eyed them warily from his basket across the room.

"Let's assume you're Zep," she whispered, patting the cat's head.

She shouldn't have mentioned Bea. They hadn't talked about her since the breakup. Caleb's recuperation had taken over their lives, and now, three months later, it was almost like she'd never existed. Sometimes, though, Caleb would fall silent and his gaze would wander off, and Wynter would wonder if he was thinking about her.

"I'm sleeping out here," Wynter announced when Caleb came out of the bathroom. "It'll be fun, like a sleepover." Not that her experience with sleepovers had been any fun.

"You take the bed," he said.

"Nope, I want the couch."

"Okay, I guess I'll take the other couch, then, and Jesse can have the bed."

"You take the bed." She bit her tongue on telling him, *You look like you could use it*, and settled for, "You don't fit on these couches, anyway."

Fortunately, he didn't argue the point. He did seem to think she wanted to watch TV, though. He sat with her, turned it on, and cycled randomly through the channels.

"Where do you usually go on vacation?" she asked.

"Haven't been on a family vacation in years. Harry used to take us all camping, and after I got my license we went without him."

"Can we go camping?"

"Sure, in the summer, or maybe at spring break if you can handle the weather. You'll love it."

"I don't think Jesse loves it."

"I have a *no phones* rule when we're camping. That's the part he doesn't like. Indio likes it, so with luck he'll be in a good mood the whole time, even if he has to share a tent with me." Caleb switched off the TV, leaned forward to place the remote on the coffee table, and then stayed there, elbows on his knees. "You asked about Bea. I wanted to ask if you're doing okay with all that."

"I wanted to ask if you are."

"I miss her. It's getting easier."

"When will you date someone else?"

"Not for a while, hun."

"Do you still love her?"

"I still want the best for her, and always will."

"What went wrong?" She knew the answer, of course. She wanted to see how open he would be.

He didn't speak for several seconds. Then he leaned back and put his arm around her shoulders, and said, "I think, when it works, it's like on a ship. Everyone knows the mission. Everyone has the same goal. Me and Bea... we were sailing in different directions."

Her heart broke for him all over again. She was desperate to figure out how to fix it — not with Bea, of course. With someone else.

She curled up against him, forcing Zep to jump down before he got squashed. "Can you teach me karate? Not the fighting part. The other part."

"The *kata*? Sure, we can do that this weekend. Karate's a good skill for any girl to learn."

"Jesse told me there's a teacher at the dojo who likes you."

"Who? Tien?" Caleb was dumbfounded. "Huh. Is that Jesse's opinion, or did she tell him so?"

"I think it's just his opinion. What's she like?"

"I went to her house once – I mean, not just me. She hosted the owner's birthday party and she cooked Vietnamese. Really good food."

"Is she cute?"

"She's my colleague. I've known her three years and I'm not sensing any... connection. I have no idea if she's single. And I'm not ready to date."

"When you played in bands, did you have groupies?"

This time he tensed and cleared his throat, his gaze fixed on the blank TV. "Oh, hun, I'm not gonna discuss private stuff like that. I'm not Jesse. And for the record, I wasn't Indio, either."

Wynter grinned to herself. "Tell me about your bands, then."

"Well, for the first two years working at the base, up until a few months before you showed up, I guess, I played with a couple of local outfits – very casual. I played guitar for a bluesy band called Lone Reel, and bass for a rock band called Steve and the Stragglers."

"Was Steve the lead singer?"

"Nope, the drummer. He was about sixty years old and played shirtless with a cigarette hanging from his lip. And there was always something going on with my Coast Guard buddies. Just messing around, playing at parties and informal functions. Called ourselves On Guard. We weren't that good and I never took it as seriously as your brothers."

"Would you take it seriously if we all started a band together?" The idea had been on her mind a while, and why not? They were already writing and recording songs. Why not make it official?

"That's not gonna happen," Caleb said. "Even if Indio moved to Seattle, he wouldn't do that."

She pulled away to see his face. "Why not?"

Caleb frowned, a pained expression that told her she shouldn't need to ask the question. "It's great jamming with him, but a band? That's a pretty intense relationship. You have to get along with each other. You have to want to be there."

"Do you fight with him when I'm not there?"

"I don't see him when you're not there. Wish I did." His mouth twisted wistfully in a way that tugged at her heart. "I'll tell you this – since you came along, we're both a bit more relaxed around each other. And Jesse and I have talked about stuff we should've talked about years ago. We used to avoid the difficult stuff and just get on with it. You've done us all a lot of good."

"When am I coming home?"

"My parenting class is in January, and I have interviews and home visits to complete. By then we'll have known each other for more than a year." He squeezed her knee. "It's gonna work out, we just need to be patient. Did you want to watch a movie?"

"No, you should... We should get some sleep."

"I'm fine. It's not even eleven and I predict we can sleep late tomorrow morning because your brothers won't be up early. Hey, I'll teach you to play poker." He indicated a pack of cards on the shelf under the coffee table. "It's one of our Christmas traditions. Won't be fair if you're a complete beginner."

Wynter could see he needed to rest. She'd figured out a while ago that he hated having any physical weakness pointed out. So she went along with it. Caleb shuffled the cards and explained the basic rules, showing her examples of each hand.

"Indio almost always wins, by the way," he warned her.

"Why?"

"His poker face is to act like he doesn't care about the game, so you keep thinking he's not paying attention. But don't be fooled — he plays to win." Caleb dealt the cards. "If only he was as competitive in the game of life."

"He's gonna be okay. He finishes college in March, right? Then he'll move to Seattle and we'll make sure he's okay."

"I don't think he's gonna—"

"He will."

Her determination made Caleb's eyebrow shoot up. "We'll see."

On waking up, Indio automatically checked off the usual two items on his wake-up list.

Where am I?

Am I alone?

He was in his own bed, in his own apartment, and he was alone. Good result. Too many times over the past few years he'd woken up next to a near-stranger because he'd either fallen asleep in her bed by mistake, or failed to politely persuade her to leave his bed.

Not quite alone — Led was coiled under his quilt, a soft heat against his stomach. Zep sat on the nightstand, paws tucked in neatly, staring at Indio. Nothing new there.

The shower was running. Two minutes ticked by. Three. Must be Jesse.

It was definitely too early to be awake, but Indio was going to ride the bike to Seattle today and he needed to work on it first. He dragged himself out of bed, ignoring the cats' pitiable cries for food — feeding them was Turk's job. *Everything* about them was Turk's job.

The apartment was freezing cold. Wynter was fast asleep on one couch, her bare feet poking out the end of the blankets. Jesse had slept on the other couch. Indio touched the back of his hand to Wynter's foot. Also ice cold. His touch made her twitch in her sleep. He draped one of Jesse's blankets over her feet.

The cats followed him out to the balcony where he scooped food into their bowls, shivering in the frigid air. Turk wasn't due back until the afternoon and it was a little unfair to make them wait that long. Led butted his head against Indio's hand, like he always did, and a few bits of kibble shot out of the cup and through the railing to rain down on the pathway below. Zep sat back and waited for Indio to finish.

Caleb was making coffee when he came back inside. Indio sat at the table to wait for it.

"How did she like the gig?" Indio asked, keeping his voice low so as not to wake Wynter.

"She loved it. You're giving her ideas about becoming a rock musician."

"Good." He imagined Caleb wasn't happy with that idea, whereas Indio thought it was a perfect career choice for a talented young woman searching for a way to express herself.

Caleb threw him the expected *look* over his shoulder.

"Is Joy coming to lunch?" Indio mentally crossed his fingers for a negative response.

"Yes." *Shit.* "We're aiming to get back to Seattle by eleven. Okay with you?"

"Just gotta change my brake pads. I'll be there at noon." He could be there by eleven, but pissing Caleb off for stupid reasons was a hard habit to break.

"Fine." Caleb set his jaw because he understood the ritual perfectly well. "Wynter and Jesse have this whole elaborate menu planned. Maybe you could take charge of the fireplace? You're good with that."

Caleb and his roaring fires... Well, it *was* nice to have a fire at this time of year, and Caleb rarely bothered when it was just him and Jesse at home.

Jesse wandered into the kitchen wearing a bathrobe. Turk's bathrobe? That was taking *mi casa, su casa* a little too far.

"We have to start at 11:05 in order to eat at 1:30," he said, yawning. "Joy's driving over." He exchanged a look with Indio, a silent signal that neither of them wanted to see Joy. For Wynter and Caleb's sake they'd play along with the charade that she was a valued member of the family.

"She drives?" Indio said.

"Just got her license. I guess she's borrowing a car." Jesse opened cupboards at random. "D'you have Pop-Tarts?"

"We have bagels, microwave oatmeal, raisin toast, and homemade marmalade."

"Marmalade — like, Paddington Bear marmalade? I have to try that."

"You'll hate it. Bitter." Indio got up to find the jar.

"I'm gonna try it. Did you know that sociopaths like bitter tastes?" Jesse dropped bagel halves in the toaster. "Not that it means I'm a sociopath if it turns out I like marmalade. Just wanna get that on the record. Why do you have marmalade?"

"Turk's sister brought it with her."

Jesse jumped to attention. "Lia's here? Where?" He gave Indio's closed bedroom door a suspicious look.

"Not Lia. His middle sister."

"And her name is?"

"Don't even think about it."

"Okay, I'll just call her Ms Turk when I meet her, shall I?" Jesse mused.

"Klem."

"Is that short for Klementine?"

"Yes."

"And... Klementine is where right now?"

"She and Turk are spending Thanksgiving with Turk's girlfriend's family, because the rest of their family is overseas."

Wynter came to the table wrapped in a blanket, offering a sleepy smile. Zep prowled around her ankles until Jesse leaned down to scratch him.

"Which one is this?" Jesse said.

Indio shrugged.

Jesse looked around at random walls and shelves. "Is there a picture of Klementine in this apartment?"

"Probably."

"Show me."

"No."

Jesse prepared his bagel with a stupid grin on his face. "She sounds like exactly my type."

"You would never survive her."

"Because she's a marmalade-making sociopath?" Jesse indicated the bagel.

"Because she's seven years older than you."

"I *love* older women."

Despite her lack of experience on the subject, Wynter wasn't buying it. "How can you tell she's your type if you haven't met her or even seen a picture?"

"Sometimes you can just tell, Wyn."

"That doesn't sound scientific."

Klem was, in fact and unfortunately for her, exactly Jesse's type — studious without being overly serious, blunt, confident, and a little quirky. Indio's job was therefore to ensure the two never met.

"How come she wasn't at your gig?" Jesse said. "Not a rock music fan?"

"Correct."

"How about jazz?"

Indio had no idea what music Klem liked. "She dislikes all music."

"Awesome! They're the best kind."

Wynter wrinkled her nose. "Why?"

"Cuz if they hate your music," Jesse explained, "it must mean they like you for who you really are. Isn't that right, Indio? Hang on, Indio wouldn't know because every girl he's ever... uh, *met*, loves his music. Or pretends to."

"So, Klementine is like the opposite of a groupie?" Wynter said.

Indio gritted his teeth, waiting for Caleb to shut down the discussion. Caleb was daydreaming or something.

The discussion did shut down, though, because Jesse choked on his bagel. He spat a masticated mouthful into his hand.

"Gross! That's offensive."

"Jesus Christ, Jesse!" Caleb snapped, and Wynter nearly jumped out of her skin. For a moment Caleb looked like he was going to apologize to her. Instead he got up and went to the bedroom to get dressed.

"I thought it'd be like jelly with chewy bits," Jesse said, for some reason finding the need to defend himself as he dropped the gooey mess in the trash. "Since when do Slovenians make marmalade?" he added, like the entire nation had no right. He returned to his seat. "Last time I was here, Turk gave me this rolled walnut pastry thing — told me it was *delightful*. His word. And it was!"

"Marmalade is more of a British thing. Their mom's Scottish," Indio said, covering Wynter's hand with his. Distress radiated from her. She hadn't looked up from her plate.

Jesse noticed, and slumped back in the chair. "He's like that all the time. Drifting off into la-la land. Short fuse. He'll be fine."

"Until it happens again," Wynter said quietly.

"I meant, he'll be fine soon. Takes time for someone to feel like themselves again after sepsis. I've told you that already," Jesse said impatiently. "It's not like he yelled at *you*. I have to live with it 24/7."

"Can something like that stop him getting a foster license?"

"Of course not. He's not sick. If he was still sick, he wouldn't be back at work."

"I don't think he's ready to be fixing up that cabin." She turned a pleading look on Indio. "Can't you make him relax at Christmas instead of working?"

"Baby, I can't make him do anything."

Jesse brushed it off. "He's only fixing a water heater or something. Little jobs, he said."

Caleb came out in sweatpants and a hoodie. "Hun, get dressed. We'll go down to that courtyard out the back and I'll show you the first *kata*."

"It's fucking thirty degrees outside," Jesse exclaimed.

"I don't mind," Wynter said, desperate to rebuild her faith in Caleb. She was already out of her chair, grabbing her bag, pulling out clothes.

"That cold air's no good for your chest," Indio said, because if he didn't say something Caleb was going to kill himself out there.

Wynter looked up in alarm. "So, can we do it inside?"

"There's no room here. We'll go outside," Caleb said.

Indio found himself standing up, exerting authority — a ridiculous notion. "C'mon, man, you gotta teach her to punch first anyway. Do it here."

"I don't want to punch anyone," Wynter said, unnerved by the shifting dynamics. "And I don't want to go outside."

Indio watched Caleb struggle with two unthinkable options — drag her outside and risk exposing his weakness, not to mention a new lung infection, or give in to a younger brother he'd spent a lifetime attempting to dominate.

"Hun, you're just punching air, okay?" Caleb said after a moment, in that gentle voice he only used for Wynter. "We can do it in the corner over there."

She nodded agreement, her relief evident. Indio knew more than to expect even a silent look of gratitude from Caleb, so he went to take his shower while Jesse mooched about the kitchen with a fresh bagel, hiding his own dismay at the morning's weirdness.

Rising Above It

Indio changed his oil and his brake pads and set out for Seattle on his bike an hour behind the others. He had not once been home for Thanksgiving since moving to Ohio for college, nor for Christmas until last year. Holidays with family weren't his idea of fun, and this year's holidays, while unique because they had two extra sisters to share them with, were soured by both Joy's and Harry's recent acts of violence against Wynter and Jesse.

Jesse was all about establishing family traditions. Well, this family had a longstanding tradition of not talking about certain things. That heart-to-heart on the bank of the Cowlitz River last May, after Harry punched Jesse, had been an awkward exception to the rule.

Last night after the gig, when Indio had taken Jesse along to a party, Jesse wanted to talk again — about Joy, this time, and they didn't have the excuse of being stoned. Neither of them was looking forward to seeing Joy again. Given Wynter's desire to include her in the family they had to not only accept it, but not tell Caleb about it.

They did make a pact not to leave the two girls alone together, even for a second. Assuming Joy showed up at all.

A ten-year-old gray Mazda hatchback parked on the street outside the house signaled Joy had, surprisingly, shown up. Indio parked his Moto Guzzi on the porch in case it rained later, and braced himself. The only way he was going to get through this was by not talking to his twin, which would of course only reinforce her opinion that he'd been ignoring her since the day they were born.

"Caleb made pancakes," Wynter said as soon as he walked in the door. "You should eat something. You only had coffee for breakfast and we won't be eating for two hours."

At the breakfast bar was Joy, disinterestedly nibbling a pancake from a fork. Jesse was chopping potatoes and attempting to make small talk with her. Indio took a seat without acknowledging her and rolled a pancake around a couple of pieces of bacon. When he dipped the roll in the pot of syrup, Wynter frowned at him.

"There's a house rule that forbids dipping now?" he said.

"There should be. We don't want crumbs sitting in the syrup and going moldy." She poured a little syrup on his plate instead.

"Sugar is a natural preservative," Jesse pointed out.

"Well, I think Caleb would prefer it if the syrup stayed clean."

"How did your karate lesson go?" Indio said, to deflect any further talk of rules.

"It was fun. Jesse says I can punch his abs for practice. I don't think I will."

"I should think not," Joy said. "Why on earth are you learning karate?"

"Maybe she feels the need to protect herself from random acts of violence," Indio said pointedly, violating his own rule not to talk to her.

Wynter flushed and turned away. He refused to regret his words. Jesse gave him a mild warning look before starting up an intense discussion with Wynter about the schedule for the day. It was stuck on the refrigerator with a turkey magnet. Apparently there were adjustments to be made because the potatoes had been peeled too quickly while the pecan pie was fifteen minutes behind schedule.

"Okay, we *were* gonna pin the tail feather on the turkey between 12:40 and 12:55, during a lull in preparations," Jesse said. "I think we need to move that to later in the afternoon."

"Oh, I can't stay too late, I'm so sorry," Joy said.

"We're playing freakin' pin the tail feather on the turkey?" Indio mumbled through a mouthful of food.

"You're staying for lunch, aren't you?" Wynter asked Joy, ignoring him.

Indio's heart squeezed at the apprehension in her eyes, the fear she was about to be disappointed and discarded yet again. Joy had confirmed she was coming to the cabin for Christmas but Indio knew, he just knew, she'd find a way to back out of that, too.

"Of course, darling. Can I help with anything?"

Jesse set both Wynter and Joy to chopping the rest of the vegetables. Indio went to fetch wood from the shed at the bottom of the yard, remembering Caleb's earlier instructions. Joy's presence sucked the joy from everything. He didn't want her here. He was not going to accept or love her. He'd wear a mask of civility for Wynter's sake.

But not for Caleb's sake.

Caleb was there in the shed, stacking wood into the wheelbarrow. Indio felt a familiar surge of irritation.

"You told *me* to do this."

"Looked like you weren't going to show up for a while."

Well, he *had* delayed leaving as long as possible, but he was here now. Caleb, apparently, had assumed he'd fuck up altogether. But it was a family occasion, so Indio would be nice.

"Pancakes were great. Thanks for that."

"Did Joy eat anything? She looks skinnier than Wynter did almost a year ago."

"She ate one. Didn't look like she enjoyed it. That's our joyless Joy." Caleb scowled at him.

"She's gonna take off after lunch," Indio said. "In fact, I'd place bets on her not lasting past the soup."

Caleb straightened and wiped his hands on his windbreaker. "Give it a rest, Indio. Wynter wants Joy to be part of our lives, so let's make her feel welcome."

"She's not welcome. She flat-out denied anything happened to Wynter in Arizona!" *And she throttled our little sister!* Damn, he wanted to scream that from the rooftops.

"Just... stop. She showed up. She's our sister. And it's Thanksgiving. Since the day Wynter walked into our lives, everything I've done has been for her and that includes trying to keep Joy close. Regardless of her failures, she'll always be family."

"Like Harry? That's what you always said — he's our father, give him a chance, he deserves respect. What about when he's just a no-good violent bastard? What about when she's just a pathetic manipulative loser?"

"I said, *stop*. We'll deal with this later."

"We never deal with it later. Every year we suffer through his drunken self-hating nonsense and his latest idiot girlfriend, and you make us say polite things and show respect. He's not worth it. Family or not, Joy's not worth it. She doesn't want to be part of our lives."

"She deserves another chance."

"She's had a year's worth of chances. You're too fucking noble and hopeful and forgiving. If Miriam walked through that door today, you'd fall at her feet." He was close to yelling now. "You'd forgive sixteen years of indifference and demand me and Jesse offer respect. And Wynter — god, after everything we've found out, and everything we don't know yet — you'd make Wynter give her another chance."

"I wouldn't do that." Caleb's brow furrowed and he spoke calmly, refusing to match Indio's anger. "You and Jesse, I hope you'd show respect. But I would let Wynter do what she wants."

Indio swallowed the lump in his throat. "You're growing soft in your old age."

"Maybe. I made mistakes with you, Indio—"

He flared again. "Mistakes? What the hell...? You're not my parent!"

"I had to be. Someone had to be. I was tough on you, and part of it was in the hope you'd have a better relationship with Harry. We can go back and forth on that forever, but it's done. You don't want Joy here, you don't even like her — fine, I get that. But for Wynter's sake, you need to rise above it."

Indio couldn't rise above it. It was easy enough to avoid Joy, even in that tiny house, because she made herself useful in the kitchen while he built the fire in the dining room and set the table. Jesse angled the TV so they could watch a movie from the kitchen — a ridiculous old sci-fi comedy. He could hear them laughing at it, even Joy.

He was ashamed of the intensity of his feelings toward his twin sister. But those feelings were surely justified. If Joy had stepped up eleven months ago, Wynter wouldn't still be in foster care. If Joy hadn't put a bruise on her face, he might not resent her quite so much.

Caleb came in to mix drinks from the liquor cabinet, saying nothing for several minutes. He held out the finished orange-colored cocktail to Indio.

"Aperitif? It's called a Fabiola."

"That's a terrible name."

They chinked glasses grimly and sipped. Caleb was certainly *rising above* the fight in the woodshed. Good for him.

There was a third drink on the cabinet.

"Is that for Joy?"

"It's for Jesse. He's declared mixed drinks are a new holiday tradition in this family."

"Doing something twice doesn't make it a tradition."

"More than twice. You've skipped four Thanksgivings and three Christmases." Somehow Caleb managed to say it without reproach.

Caleb took the drink to Jesse in the kitchen. It was 12:30 and Joy was making noises about leaving.

"We're going out with Harry for lunch on Christmas Eve," he heard Caleb say. "We do it every year, right before or after Christmas Day. Will you join us?"

"I don't think I could," Joy said. "I've had nothing to do with him."

"Here's your chance to change that."

"I don't want to disparage anyone, Caleb, but I think he would bring negative energy to my life."

From the next room, Indio almost laughed out loud at her phrasing. But she was probably right, for once.

Caleb tried again. "You haven't seen him since you were a child. This is a perfect opportunity. He'd be really touched if you came along. He always asks after you."

"Or I could drive you over to Everett another day," Jesse said. "Just you and me, I mean."

"That's so sweet of you to offer," Joy said blandly.

It *was* sweet of him. Jesse was a sweet kid. And Jesse understood that Joy was intimidated by Caleb, and no doubt thought Indio was negative energy, so he'd found a solution.

Joy went on, "I'm afraid I can't. You know I could never go against Miriam's wishes. She would be horrified if she found out."

What the hell does Miriam have to do with this? Indio bit his lip to stop himself yelling his thoughts as he stabbed at burning logs with a poker.

Jesse and Wynter put food on the table early to encourage Joy to stay a while. They'd made a huge effort, given their fairly limited artistic talents, with homemade placemats woven from paper strips, color-coordinated napkins and candles, and a lopsided corn husk centerpiece with bits of grass sticking out to represent wheat stalks.

Joy made it through the soup and the salad before glancing at the clock on the wall and pushing back her chair.

"That was delicious. You did a great job, Wynter and Jesse. Oh, I brought you a gift." She fetched her bag and produced a little sack. "Homemade cookies, the best kind."

Caleb walked her to the door, and Wynter followed. Caleb reminded her of their cabin vacation and she said she'd drive herself, in the same car she'd borrowed today, and meet them there on Christmas morning. She gave Wynter a hug.

"I love you, Wynter. I'm so proud of you for doing so well."

She left, and Indio didn't care if he never saw her again.

They finished eating, making every attempt to lighten the mood.

"Did you want to play those games I made?" Jesse asked Wynter over the ice cream.

"Indio doesn't want to do that."

"Wasn't asking Indio. I have six games to choose from, if he won't pin on a tail feather. We'll play the alphabet game while we clear up. Okay with you, bro?"

"Depends what the 'alphabet game' is," Indio said noncommittally.

"It's the Thanksgiving version. We each list one thing we're thankful for, starting with A. You start."

"You're kidding me." Had they entered an alternate universe? This was unlike anything Jesse had ever come up with in the past.

"Please play," Wynter said. "Something starting with A. Go on."

"Fine. I'm thankful for the *alphabet* game, because it's gonna be *awesome*."

"Caleb, you're next," Wynter said brightly. "What are you thankful for, starting with B?"

Indio winced at the accidental pun on Caleb's ex's name. Even Wynter got it. She chewed on her lip and looked at Caleb with a mixture of sympathy and hope. Caleb chose to not notice the problem.

"Uh, those *beans* were pretty tasty," he said.

"Wynter, you do C," Jesse said.

"I'm thankful for *Caleb*."

Caleb gave her a side hug with his free arm. In his other hand was a heavy casserole dish that he'd been about to put in the dishwasher. His arm shook with the effort of holding it one-handed.

"And I'm thankful for *dark matter*," Jesse said. "Wyn, you remember what that is? It makes up 85% of the universe."

She was unimpressed. "It has nothing to do with Thanksgiving."

"Sure it does. Without it, the galaxies would fly apart and there would be no Thanksgiving."

"And no Thanksgiving alphabet game," Indio put in. "Okay! Are we done?"

"We're doing the entire alphabet," Jesse said.

"Nope. Not happening. Wynter, you wanna jam?" She was clearly upset about Joy and it was the only thing he could think of guaranteed to make her smile properly.

"Yes! I have some new songs to show you."

"Excellent. Hey, Jess, I'm thankful for Wynter's *excellent* songs. We'll have *fun*. It'll be *great*. I feel *happy* already."

"I'm thankful for *Indio* and for *Jesse*," Wynter said, smiling at him — properly — like they were sharing a joke no one else got.

"You can do K through V," Indio told Jesse, who was tipping out Joy's cookies on the counter, "and then I'll be thankful for *Wynter*."

"Who gets X?" Wynter said.

"*Xenon*, a noble gas, atomic number 36," said Jesse the smartass.

"Also nothing to do with Thanksgiving," Wynter said. "And it's number 54."

"Are you sure?"

"We just did the noble gases in chemistry. Krypton is 36."

"God, you're right." Jesse was genuinely aggrieved. He bit into a cookie. They were covered in seeds and shaped like sunbursts. "*Yum*," he declared. "And there's just Z to go."

"We made those all the time at the ashram," Wynter said. "That's why they're shaped like that. They're Light cookies."

"*Zut alors*. French for *holy crap* or something." Jesse twisted his mouth, unsure if he was supposed to keep eating. "Should we throw them out?"

Wynter nodded. Indio scooped them up and dropped them in the trash.

Everything's Alright

Madeline watched Wynter pack her bag. They were both going home to their respective families for Christmas, although in Madeline's case it was only for a couple of days.

"That's all my mom can manage. She's got a new boyfriend and he's got his new baby staying with him because its mother had a nervous breakdown and went to stay with her mother. High drama. I've got an episode of *Vampire Diaries* and three episodes of *Supernatural* on the DVR that I was going to watch with you over the holidays, and now I have to watch them alone."

Madeline recorded her favorite shows and rewatched them twice, and then went to online forums to endlessly discuss them. To Wynter it seemed like a waste of time when she could be living real life instead. But Madeline's real life wasn't great. Her mom hadn't shown up for two visits in a row, her brother had just gone back to jail — adult jail this time — for selling drugs, and sometimes Madeline sat on her bed and cut perfectly parallel lines across her forearms with a razor blade.

"You could visit me in Seattle," Wynter said, a spontaneous offer that she hadn't checked first with Caleb or with Madeline's caseworker.

Madeline practically bounced on her bed. "Can I come to the cabin with you?"

"Well, no. That's for family only. But maybe over the New Year?"

"Are you going to a party?"

"No, I'm staying up until midnight with Caleb while my other brothers are going to a party."

"Would he let me drink or is he a total square?"

"I don't think he's allowed to let you drink."

"I'll go out with Jesse and Indio, then. Indio will let me drink."

Wynter opened her mouth to deny it, and stopped herself because Madeline was possibly correct.

"You'd have to stay home with us," she said. "We could order pizza and watch your TV shows."

Madeline threw herself back on her pillows with a groan. Wynter struggled to think of a way to persuade her. Madeline could be fun —

she had a mean streak and always made everything slightly sour, but maybe she just needed to feel included. Wynter found it so easy to make her brothers happy. Madeline was hard work.

"Caleb could come fetch you for a couple of nights, and—"

"You know he's never going to foster you, right?" Madeline said slyly. "Why would they let him? You told me he could barely climb a flight of stairs."

"He's a lot better now—"

"He'll have a heart attack or something." Her eyes glinted, like the prospect excited her. "Or he'll get a new girlfriend and forget about you. Cute little kids like Nathan and Aiden? Everyone wants them. They get *adopted*. Girls like us are nobody's priority."

Wynter was Caleb's priority. She had no doubt about that.

"Jesse told me you sometimes say hurtful things only because *you're* hurting," Wynter said, zipping up her backpack.

"What the fuck is the matter with him?" Madeline yelled. Her eyes sparkled with unshed tears. "He doesn't know anything about me!"

"He knows what you've told him. I'm sorry your family hurt you. If you change your mind, you could text me after Christmas and we'll arrange—"

"I won't be here after Christmas. I'll be gone."

"Gone?"

"Gone! Poof!" She fluttered her fingertips to illustrate the point.

"Are you going to kill yourself?"

Madeline barked a laugh. "I'm going to Wyoming, like I told you."

"Are you allowed to?"

"Why are you always so concerned with the rules? Hey, we should run away together. Come with me. My uncle will get us jobs and we'll rent a cute apartment together and throw parties..."

Wynter stopped listening.

She felt truly sorry for Madeline — and that was a new feeling, this sympathy for someone whose life had started out badly like her own. She felt the weight of responsibility to help, and of frustration that the adults in this world hadn't done enough for her. Wynter had help now. Madeline had nothing.

People can only give as much as they're capable of. Indio had told her that, citing Caleb. Wynter wasn't capable of much — a few guitar lessons, a sleepover. What Madeline needed was entirely beyond Wynter's capabilities.

She was glad when Caleb showed up to fetch her. In his street, people had put up decorations.

"Jesse usually does that," Caleb said, "but this year he wanted to wait so you can do it together. He's going to take you to buy a Christmas tree."

A *real* Christmas tree. Jesse had specific ideas about the perfect height, width, branch symmetry and needle density. He and Wynter spent a long time choosing their tree, which he named Annie — after singer Annie Lennox who was born on Christmas Day.

Back home, Jesse pulled out last year's decorations from the garage and sent Wynter to persuade Caleb they needed twenty dollars to buy more. They went to the store and picked out things they liked. Wynter had ten dollars of her own, set aside to buy Jesse a gift. He insisted they spend it on another string of Christmas lights. Then they walked around the neighborhood to look at everyone else's lights. People had blow-up Santas on their lawns and all kinds of lighted candy canes and reindeer.

"Your first Christmas, Wyn. Everything's gonna be perfect." Jesse clutched her hand as they admired their own modest house from the street, with its white icicles hanging from the porch and snowflakes in the windows. "As long as we stick to the schedule."

Early on Christmas Eve, they dragged Caleb to the grocery store to buy the food for their Christmas menu. He complained good-naturedly about half the things on their list, but paid for it all anyway. Indio had arrived from Portland when they got back. While Wynter and Jesse made sugar cookies and apple pie, Indio sat around noodling on a guitar because he'd had a gig the night before and was, he claimed, too tired to move anything but his fingers. Caleb worked outside, checking the pipes and locks in preparation for leaving the house empty while they were at the cabin.

And then Wynter had the house to herself for a few hours while her brothers went to their lunch with Harry. She got everything ready for making the cookie frosting. She was under strict instructions not to actually frost the cookies until Jesse got back. She sat on the floor of the living room with Indio's guitar, playing from memory the fingering exercises she'd heard him working on earlier.

The sound of the doorbell startled her. Caleb had given no instructions about what to do if the doorbell or phone rang. Perhaps someone was visiting to wish them Merry Christmas. It was bound to be someone she didn't know, perhaps a colleague of Caleb's. She didn't want to have to talk to someone she didn't know.

It might be Joy. She stood up nervously as the bell rang a second time, and now someone was knocking as well.

"Wynter?"

It *was* Joy. Wynter opened the door. Joy gave her a fluttery smile. She seemed nervous. Joy was always a bit fidgety, but this was different.

"Darling, are the others in?"

"No. They'll be back in an hour or so, I think."

"Oh, I remember now. They're having lunch with Harry." Joy's tone was fake, like she was pretending to have forgotten. "Let's do something. Let's spend the afternoon together."

"Okay." Wynter stepped aside.

Joy came in, tentatively, like she would dart out at any moment. She followed Wynter to the living room.

"I wanted to tell you," Joy said, perching on the arm of the couch, "just to keep the light between us, I wanted to say you made the right decision by not telling Caleb about that incident. I don't need his judgment. I was overcome by darkness. Do you understand? Surrounded by darkness in this awful house."

"It's not an awful house."

"Bad things happened here. I can't imagine why you want to live here. Don't you feel it? Harry abused our brothers in this house."

Wynter blanched. Jesse had told her, a long time ago, that Harry had a drinking problem and had sometimes hit them. To hear Joy say it so bluntly, to use that word — *abuse* — it made her feel sick.

"How... how do you know?" she stammered.

"I know he's capable of it," Joy went on. "The last time I saw him in Anaconda, do you know what he did? Pulled little Jesse off his seat by the scruff of his neck and whacked his bottom over and over when he wouldn't stop tapping his spoon on the bowl."

"Doesn't that make the ashram an awful place, too? Things happened there—"

"Don't talk about the Light like that. I know it was tough for you sometimes. It was only to get you back on the right path. There are no right paths out here, and Harry was just being a bully. And who stopped him? Momma! She told Caleb to take Jesse to the park for the morning, to let Harry cool down." Joy leaned forward to touch Wynter's hand. "Darling, the darkness out here affects us all. I've atoned, and it won't happen again."

No, it wouldn't happen again because Indio and Jesse would be ready for it next time. And if Joy tried something right now, Wynter knew how to punch back.

Joy's hands twisted in her lap. "There's something I can't get out of my head," she said, staring at a point over Wynter's shoulder. "That teddy bear we gave you when you were four — I don't remember it very well. Can you tell me about it?"

"Why does it matter?"

"I'd just like to know about it."

Was Joy asking in order to discover how much *Wynter* remembered? Why did she want to know?

"I only remember that I didn't like it," Wynter said. "It was like *Invasion of the Body Snatchers*."

"What on earth—?"

"It's an old movie I watched with Jesse, where the people were replaced by aliens with no emotions. Deedee was like a dead thing. You wanted me to love him, but I couldn't."

"Nothing else? Nothing at all?"

"No. What happened to the box you put him in?"

Now it was Joy's turn to go pale. "What box?"

"That's what you told me, that you put him in a box."

"I don't know what you mean." Joy looked around, desperately. "How can you stand living here? Let's go out. Have you eaten?"

Wynter mentally adjusted to Joy's quick change of mood and topic. "I had leftovers. We could go for a walk."

"Wonderful! Yes, let's do that. We'll drive out to Lake Washington."

"I'll get my jacket."

Wynter fetched her jacket from her room, and the door key on the space alien keychain Jesse had given her for Valentine's Day. He'd threatened to buy a her a new keychain for Christmas because the charm was chipped and scratched. She'd told him *no way*.

At the back of her mind was the disappointing notion that Joy might be making an effort today because she didn't intend to come to the cabin tomorrow. Still, the effort was what counted.

Wynter followed Joy outside, closing the door behind her, checking it was locked. A white van was parked on the street, not the car Joy had driven at Thanksgiving. As Wynter walked down the driveway, the side of the van came into view. It had the Light logo on it, and *Seattle Chapter* written underneath. That made sense. Joy didn't have a car, so why not borrow the van?

Someone was in the driver's seat, a middle-aged woman with spiky gray hair.

"Who's that?"

"That's Stella, my good friend. She's been a great help to me. Come along."

Wynter stopped a few feet inside the front gate. She didn't want to get into a van with the Light logo and a stranger.

"I thought it would be just you and me," Wynter said.

"Maybe Stella can drop us off somewhere."

Maybe?

Wynter backed up a couple of steps, her gut clenching. Something wasn't right. She fumbled for her phone and realized she'd left it inside.

"I have to call Caleb and tell him where I am."

"I can do that." Joy took her phone out of her pocket. "Everything's alright, darling."

If everything was truly alright, Joy wouldn't have to tell her so.

Joy wrapped cold, grasping fingers around Wynter's wrist. Her eyes were stark and wild, like those times at the ashram after an all-night Reflections session when she was about to have a breakdown, or what *they* called a breakthrough.

Wynter twisted her hand free and ran back to the house. Her vision narrowed, black around the edges, as she jammed the key in the lock. The door opened and she stumbled into the hallway.

"Wynter, what's the matter?" Joy cried, hurrying after her. "Aren't you coming with me?"

Wynter sank to her knees, light-headed, and made herself fall against the door to close it just as Joy stepped onto the porch.

Did Joy have a key? She couldn't remember. She reached for the handle and pulled herself up to slide the heavy bolt lock across. Then she sat with her head between her knees and waited for the dizziness to pass.

Over the buzzing in her ears, she heard Joy talking some distance away. Someone rapped on the door and she scuttled down the hallway on her hands and knees, not trusting herself to stand.

"Wynter? Wynter? Please, darling, open the door."

The other woman was with her, talking in a low voice, as if instructing Joy on how to talk to her own sister. Then she spoke aloud.

"Wynter, Joy needs to talk to you. It's very important. Come on, don't be silly. Open the door and I'll drive the two of you somewhere to talk." She had a cultured British accent that somehow reminded her of Momma. Not the accent, but the impatient authority.

It made no sense. If Joy wanted to talk, she could talk right here in the house.

The pleading went on for a long time, each of them taking turns. Their sing-song voices became a hypnotic mantra so familiar to Wynter from hour upon hour of prayer meetings and vigils. They started singing. Wynter covered her ears. She had never expected to hear those songs again.

It was hard to judge time when the Light surrounded you. Wynter was exhausted from shaking and sobbing and pushing out the Light so it wouldn't consume her.

She needed help. She could ask God for help, but when had he ever done anything for her?

The floor tiles were cold under her knees. She opened her eyes. These weren't the pitted Spanish terracotta tiles she expected to see. They were cream-colored and smooth. She wasn't at the ashram. She was in Caleb's house.

Caleb would help. The first true thing Joy had told her, when they left the Light, was that Caleb would help.

Somehow she made it to her room. She fumbled around for her phone. It took several tries to get to Caleb's number on the contact list because her fingers wouldn't respond properly. She closed her door and crouched against it, the last line of defense in case Joy somehow got through the front door.

"Hey, hun." The sound of his voice, so normal, gave her a shot of strength.

"When will you be home?" She thought her voice sounded quite normal as well.

Yet he sensed something at once. "What's wrong?"

"When?" she repeated.

"Uh, one hour, probably. Jesus, what's wrong?"

"Okay, one hour." She had no right to take him away from his meal with Harry. She could manage one hour. "I'm okay," she added.

"You sure?"

"Yes."

She rang off and crept out of her room. Her mind went to all the other possible entry points. If the garage roller door wasn't secured, they might get through to the backyard, and then into the house through the sliding door on the patio. She checked it was locked. In the laundry she found the back door to the clothesline unlocked. Another wave of panic hit her. They might've got in there. *So close.* She didn't know how to lock the door. There was no bolt. She didn't have a key for this door. She blinked to clear her eyes and examined the handle. It had a knob in the center, which she turned until it clicked. Her fingers were stiff and clammy with sweat.

She went through every room, checking the windows. She'd rarely been in Jesse's room before, and never in Caleb's. Both beds were a mess, although Caleb had made a haphazard effort to pull up the quilt. She'd been taught to always make her bed neatly, and she always did. Everything about the house was suddenly strange and dangerous.

She could still hear Joy and that woman talking and praying and singing outside the front door.

One hour until her brothers came home. Maybe only fifty-five minutes now. She remembered at the last minute to check the little bathroom next to the basement steps, a tiny room with just a toilet and corner basin. The window was open, although it was set behind a security grille. She wound it closed anyway.

Was there a way in through the basement? She wasn't sure. She went down the stairs and closed the door behind her. She left the light off in case it showed through cracks in the door. This was her favorite place in the entire house, and now it seemed claustrophobic, the air so dead she could hardly breathe. She stepped over the cables taped to the floor, careful not to wake them — she knew where every single one was laid — seeking a safe corner.

She was underground. No other doors, no windows, only a vent that was too small for anyone to get through. She felt silly for thinking there might be a way in. This was surely the safest room in the house. She knew it could be locked from the outside with a key, but not from the inside. Still, it was a good hiding place if they got in. She stumbled around in the dark, careful not to knock the guitars, until she found a chair. She pushed the chair under the door handle like she'd seen Jesse do that one time at Rosa's house.

If they did get in, Joy probably wasn't strong enough to drag her up those steps. The other woman might try. Wynter would go limp.

It's hard to drag a limp body, Jesse told her once. Jesse was full of useful bits of information to help her survive in this world.

Harry was doing okay. He looked fairly smart, his beard was trimmed, and he'd only had three beers. He hadn't brought a woman with him, although eight months had passed since the wedding-that-wasn't. He usually did bring a woman — often as a buffer against his own sons, it seemed to Caleb. No one could get too personal when there was a stranger at the table.

There was one thing they *could* get personal about, this year — Jesse's split lip a few months ago, while Caleb was overseas. No one brought it up. They talked a little about Joy, or rather Caleb answered Harry's questions about Joy, and about his recuperation and return to work. Harry told a couple of funny tales about Lexie, his border collie, that made even Indio crack a smile. He seemed genuinely interested in Jesse's description of a *Scientific American* article about what the Curiosity rover was up to on Mars, asking coherent follow-up questions. Jesse was making a huge effort and Indio was behaving himself.

Wynter's call changed everything.

Something was wrong, something more than mere anxiety at being left alone in the house. Caleb left immediately, telling his brothers he'd be back to pick them up just as soon as he'd checked in on her. He didn't want them to worry. From the looks on their faces he knew they would. But a pleasant meal with Harry was a rare thing, and he didn't want them to cut it short.

He arrived home twenty minutes later. Turning into his street, he saw the van outside the house and the logo on the back. He pulled up slowly behind it and got out. Two women were at his front door — to his surprise, he realized one was Joy. They hadn't heard his truck because they were singing and talking. No, they were pleading. He heard Wynter's name.

He walked quickly around the van. Its ordinariness made it all the more sinister. The cab was empty, the back locked. The rear doors had small windows at the top and he could see the van was empty inside, aside from a few pallets.

He got in his truck and drove around the van and into the driveway. Joy glanced around at the sound of the engine. She and the woman ducked their heads as they spoke to each other. Nothing about this was right. The van, Wynter's call, that older woman with her furtive glances.

Caleb got out of the truck and strode toward them, fueled by carefully controlled anger. The women made an unspoken, mutual decision to leave. They stepped off the porch. They would have to cross his path to reach the gate.

"Get off my property," Caleb told the stranger. "Don't ever come back. Any of you people." He knew how to put authority into his voice without raising it, and the older woman stalked past him without meeting his eye.

Joy froze a few paces away, a deer in headlights. With great effort, Caleb softened his voice.

"What are you doing, Joy? What are you *doing?*"

"I'm trying to help her. One last chance… I just wanted to talk."

Caleb wanted badly to believe her. Joy would no doubt claim she'd always done what she thought was best for Wynter. Trouble was, her perspective was so badly skewed he no longer trusted her with her own sister.

"In the future, you need to call me first. You scared her."

"I'm so sorry."

For a moment he saw her through Indio's eyes, pathetic and self-pitying and somehow malevolent.

"Will we be seeing you tomorrow at the cabin?" he asked.

"I have a session with my mentor tonight for—"

"What does that have to do with anything? Are you coming on vacation with your family?"

"I have some important decisions to make."

He glared at her until she put her head down and walked away. Desperate though he was to get to Wynter, he waited until the van had driven off.

He couldn't get through the door. Wynter had bolted it on the inside. Sensible girl.

He opened the garage roller door, went through to the backyard, and unlocked the patio door. Walking quickly through the house, he called her name, increasingly anxious. In her room he found her phone on the floor. That disturbed him. She always took great care of her phone.

He checked the basement last, knowing by now she must be down there. The door was jammed shut. The obstructing chair fell away when he wiggled the handle. He flicked on the light and found her huddled behind Jesse's drum kit. He knelt down and she clung to him.

"I heard you," she whispered, shaking badly. "My legs wouldn't work. My voice wouldn't work."

"It's okay. I found you."

"Something's wrong with Joy. That woman made her say things. Are they gonna take me back to the Light?"

"They've gone. You're safe now."

"I didn't mean for you to leave early. You should go back."

"Come upstairs."

He helped her to her feet. She wobbled against him, but managed to climb the stairs by herself, leaning on the rail.

"The chair was supposed to stop anyone getting in. I didn't do it right."

"I'll show you how to do it right. Later."

She was shivering uncontrollably. He sat her on the couch. Then he did something he probably shouldn't do, and in his mind's eye he saw Indio's eyes rolling in bemusement and Jesse's jaw dropping — he poured her a shot of whiskey.

"It smells weird." The glass shook in her hand.

"Just to calm your nerves, the physical reaction," he said. "Knock it back fast, get it over with."

She drank it because she trusted him, and gasped at the heat in her throat.

"Ooh, I can feel it here," she said, her hand on her stomach.

He grinned. "Don't get to liking it *too* much. I'm gonna call Indio and tell them to take a taxi home when they're ready."

"No, you should go back. I didn't mean to interrupt your life."

"You're part of my life."

He'd almost said *You are my life* — because, really, what else did he have? Jesse didn't need him. Indio didn't want him. Joy was impervious to him. Beatrice was gone and Harry never cared much one way or the other. In two years he could quit the Coast Guard, or not — it didn't seem important.

In a few weeks Wynter would become his full-time responsibility and interrupt his life completely, and he couldn't wait.

Magic

Wynter's attempt to feign near-ignorance of the rules for Texas Hold'em didn't work for long. She'd had two additional lessons with Caleb since Thanksgiving, and he'd told her not to reveal she could play — not a secret, he said, but a surprise.

For a full hour that evening she managed to fool Jesse, until her growing pile of "beginner's luck" chips revealed the ploy. She had not fooled Indio for a second. She could tell by the way he looked at her each time she made a bet or "accidentally" bluffed her way to victory. He didn't say anything, and nor did he show mercy. By the end of the night all her chips were stacked in front of him.

After she went to bed, she could hear her brothers' voices coming from the living room. They talked for a long time, though she couldn't hear the words, and sometimes laughter rippled down the hallway. She fought the urge to open her door a crack and eavesdrop. When she was with them, she felt their focus was constantly on her. She wanted to know what they were like when she wasn't around, especially when they were getting along well. She'd figured out last Christmas had been tense. Caleb had lost his temper over something Indio did, and Indio had left a day early, and Jesse hadn't spoken to Caleb for two days afterward. She couldn't even imagine Caleb and Jesse not speaking.

And only one week after that, she'd knocked on their door, not knowing what she'd find but trusting Joy's assurances that Caleb would help her. That she'd be safe at last.

She didn't trust Joy anymore. Today's strange visit with that woman and that van were fresh in her mind, but things had gone wrong a long time ago. Was it Joy's evasiveness about a stupid teddy bear and her violent outburst? The secret about Xay she'd made Wynter promise to keep? Or was it simply because Joy had fallen back into the Light? Wynter didn't blame her for that, but it was unthinkable she'd rejected the love Wynter had accepted from the moment Jesse opened his front door and wrapped a blanket around her.

She didn't even know for sure why Joy had escaped the ashram with her on that particular night, almost one year ago.

Her brothers were still talking when she fell asleep. Their voices merged with her dreams and turned to music, and the music turned to singing. The singing turned to screaming. The screaming became the wind whistling past her ears as she flew, higher and higher, above the clouds and into the freezing stratosphere. Higher and higher, into the blackness of space. There was no air here. She couldn't breathe.

She awoke with a gasp, pain shooting through her feet and exploding through her body to drive nails into her skull.

It was gone in an instant. There was nothing wrong with her.

She wiped the sweat off her face and checked the time — two in the morning. Her top was soaked through. She fumbled in the closet for a clean one and went to the bathroom to wash her face. The night was still, the house cold. Down the hall, the living room light was on — not the main light, but the glow of the corner lamp. She ignored the pain of pins and needles in her feet and went to investigate.

Indio was propped up lengthwise on the couch, reading a book. He looked up and smiled.

"Aren't you tired?" she said.

"I'm a night owl."

"What're you reading?"

"A science fiction novel from Jesse's bookshelf." He showed her the cover: *Fahrenheit 451*. "They burn all the books, and everyone watches giant TVs instead. You having a rough night?"

He knew that? As she'd learned earlier in the poker game, she should never underestimate Indio.

"I'm okay now." She went to the sliding door and looked out at the yard. "Are we gonna have a white Christmas?"

"We'd have to go to Montana for that."

"Do you want to move back to Montana?"

"Not especially. Might be fun to visit. Well, not fun — nostalgic."

"What did you used to do at Christmas?"

Indio closed the book and sat up. "Uh, same stuff as most kids, I guess. Mom was getting more and more into the Light, but she couldn't let go of Christmas. This grotty old plastic tree came out of its box every year and we covered it in tinsel to hide the fact it was falling apart. Went out to see the Christmas lights and throw snowballs. Mom made us these big red stockings from an old quilt. Our grandma — Harry's mother — she baked huge sugar cookies, bigger than your hand, and iced them elaborately. We were allowed to eat two each, every day, until they were all gone."

"Is that why Jesse and me made sugar cookies?"

"He wouldn't remember that. A lot of people bake sugar cookies for Christmas. We'd get one gift each under the tree, and then something big for all of us. One year it was a swing set. Mom bought it second-hand from a neighbor. Bits of it were always falling off. This was after Harry left. Another year, it was a tent. Those are the only ones I remember. She made pancakes — that powdered stuff in a bottle, not from scratch like Caleb does. They were still good. We had them with ice cream and fake maple syrup for breakfast."

"Ice cream for breakfast? That's outrageous."

"Yeah."

"You called her *Mom*, instead of Miriam."

Indio's frown said he didn't appreciate her pointing it out. "The perils of nostalgia. *Miriam* made us stay up as late as we could stand on Christmas Eve, which we thought was a treat. Pretty sure it was so she'd get to sleep in on Christmas Day. We watched those weird stop-motion movies from the 'sixties and 'seventies to try and stay awake."

"I don't know what those are."

He chuckled. "Oh god, you have to watch those. They're freaky. There are a dozen Christmas movies you need to see. Ask Jesse about it."

"Why not you?"

"Christmas is Jesse's thing."

A moment ago it had really seemed like Indio's thing, too.

"Can we watch one now?"

"Sure. Go fetch a blanket and I'll find something." He reached for the remote.

Wynter went to her room and put on socks and a robe, pulled the quilt off her bed and bundled it in her arms to carry back. She closed the hallway door behind her, so as not to disturb the others.

Indio was flicking through the channels. "Can't find any animated movies. Here we go — *Die Hard*. Love this one. We've only missed the first few minutes. The bad guys have taken some party-goers hostage in an office tower."

Wynter dumped the quilt on the couch. "I don't know much about Christmas, but that doesn't sound very Christmassy."

"It takes place on Christmas Eve. Good enough."

They sat under the quilt with their feet propped up on the coffee table.

"Where's it set?"

"Los Angeles — no snow, sorry. Oh — hang on, I'm gonna have to be Caleb."

"Hey!"

He'd put his hand across her eyes in the middle of a tense scene with a middle-aged businessman. Two seconds later she heard a gunshot. Indio laughed and moved his hand away and she realized the man had been killed.

"Jesse would never have done that to me," she said. "I've watched him play Mortal Kombat."

"Jesse has no clue about what's appropriate for fifteen-year-olds."

"He was fifteen once."

"Nope. He skipped twelve through fifteen. He always hung around with older kids — with my friends, or playing in bands with seniors at high school. He wants to show you *everything — now*." His smile turned sympathetic. "Seriously, though, no one needs to see the back of someone's head getting blown off. I won't do it again. There's a lot of dying in this movie. That was the worst one."

Indio sat back on the couch, the warmth of his shoulder pressing against hers. He pushed his long hair off his face.

"You're supposed to cut your hair at Christmas, remember?" she said.

"I remember."

"Let's do it now." Wynter jumped up before he could object, and found scissors in the kitchen drawer. "Do we need a comb or anything?"

"Nope. The scrappier, the better."

"A towel?"

"We'll sweep it off the tiles when we're done."

"Just like a real salon." Wynter had only been to a salon once, when she first moved in with Rosa. She held out the scissors. "Okay, show me. I've been waiting ages to see this."

Indio leaned all the way forward on the couch, and gathered up his hair into a ponytail at the top of his head.

"It's at least twelve inches long," Wynter said. "I bet I could make a friendship bracelet out of it."

"Gross."

"Why not? The Victorians, when their loved ones died, made jewelry and lockets out of their hair. I learned about it at school."

"I'm not dead, although Jesse might kill me in the morning."

"Why?"

"Never mind." He slid his hand forward on the ponytail, leaving about four inches hanging out. "Okay, go ahead."

"What, me? I can't do it."

"Sure you can. Hack away. Everything hanging out the end there." He waggled the ponytail.

Wynter moved closer and snipped a tiny bit of hair, close to Indio's fist.

"Be bold, baby. The blood's rushing to my head."

She took a deep breath and cut off the ponytail in three snips. Indio brushed the loose hair from his knees and sat back. Instinctively, she pressed her hands to her mouth — just because it looked so different. His hair was shorter even than that very first photo Caleb had shown her, on his phone. It sat just below his chin at the front, a little longer in the back, hanging in choppy long layers.

"Awesome. I love it," he said.

"You haven't seen it yet. It's..." She tilted her head, assessing him carefully. "It's pretty good. It's gone a bit more wavy." She looked at the mess of hair on the floor and was horrified all over again.

Indio grinned at her reaction and fetched a dustpan and brush.

"Seems like such a waste," Wynter said. "I can braid that, or maybe weave it."

"Absolutely not. It's going in the trash."

They settled under the quilt to finish watching the movie, with Indio explaining the things she didn't understand. He was relaxed compared to Thanksgiving, where they'd all been tense because of Caleb's moods and Joy's secrets, and even compared to the day they'd spent together in Enumclaw for his birthday, where they'd had some difficult moments. Was tonight's easygoing playfulness because he was feeling nostalgic? Because he enjoyed sharing a favorite movie with her? Because he was happy to be getting along with Caleb?

Must be the magic of Christmas.

Her First Christmas

Jesse rolled out of bed and stumbled over the lump on the floor.

"Sorry, bro..." He made it to his closet to rummage around for clothes.

The lump shifted slightly. "What time is it?" Indio mumbled.

"Nine-thirty. Can't you smell those pancakes?"

Indio groaned and rolled over.

Jesse toed him between the shoulder blades. "You watched *Die Hard* last night without me, didn't you. I heard it."

"Wynter wanted to watch a Christmas movie."

What the fuck?

"She was up until 5AM as well?" he yelled. "You wrecked her for Christmas! Her first Christmas!"

He kicked Indio in the head.

Indio grabbed his ankle and yanked him onto his butt. Jesse scrambled on top of him and they wrestled, crashing against the bookcase which promptly deposited a mechatronics textbook on Jesse's head.

Hardback, two inches thick, fucking heavy.

Jesse should have the advantage here – Indio was hampered by being inside a sleeping bag, after all. But wrestling with Indio never ended well for Jesse. Shouldn't have provoked the sleeping bear. Indio swept him onto his side and had him in a headlock within seconds.

"Which one of us has the black belt again?" Indio mocked him. "Last time I checked, wasn't me."

Jesse struggled ineffectually, refusing to give, so Indio didn't let up. Now the sleeping bag was hampering Jesse because he couldn't get his foot between Indio's legs.

"Caleb!" Wynter cried from down the hallway, her footsteps receding. "Caleb! They're killing each other!" She sounded terrified.

From the kitchen, Caleb's voice was barely audible. "They're not killing each other."

Nevertheless, two sets of footsteps approached Jesse's closed door. Caleb knocked once and swung the door open.

"Merry Christmas, boys. Jesse, your schedule says you have six things to do before we leave for the cabin. Indio, put your bike in the garage." He walked off.

Wynter, in her PJs, stared wide-eyed through the doorway at them. Indio loosened his grip and Jesse wriggled free, aiming a final frustrated punch at Indio's ribs, which his brother deftly blocked. Indio plumped his pillow and flopped his head back onto it.

"I'm gonna take a shower." Jesse grabbed his clothes. "Find some Christmas cartoons to watch on TV, Wyn. You were supposed to start with those."

Her eyes widened as he sidled past her. "Are you mad?"

"He's fake mad," Indio responded. Jesse stormed down the hallway. "Just be sure not to yawn today."

Jesse wasn't too mad. He did want everything to be perfect today. Eating breakfast together as a family would've been a good start, but Indio didn't emerge for another twenty minutes and the three of them weren't going to let the pancakes go cold. By then, Caleb and Wynter were loading up the truck and Jesse was cleaning the griddle.

Indio started into the remaining pancakes. He looked different...

"Dude, your hair," Jesse said at last.

"Yeah."

"Very rock n' roll. So was it worth it?"

"The haircut?"

"The movie! Wrecking her first Christmas for that movie."

"It's a great movie. Perhaps the greatest."

"It wasn't on the schedule!" Jesse gave an exaggerated huff and added, "So, did she like it? Did she even understand it?"

"Not all of it. I had to explain negotiable bearer bonds to her."

"Do you know what they are?"

"Nope."

"If she yawns, even once, it's no stocking for you."

"Yip—"

"Don't say it." That bloody *Die Hard* line was Indio's standard way of saying he didn't give a shit. At Christmas, everyone was *required* to give a shit about their stockings.

"Yippee—"

"Don't you dare!" Jesse grabbed a butter knife and assumed a threatening posture.

"Yippee-kai-yay, mother—"

"Don't you fucking dare say it!"

"Jesse, language!" Caleb barked, coming inside at that moment with Wynter on his heels.

Indio dissolved into laughter with his own foul language safely averted, at Jesse's expense. Wynter stared at Indio like he was a total stranger.

In fact, Indio and belly-laughing were a rare and precious combination, so, in the spirit of Christmas, Jesse silently forgave him everything.

Jesse grabbed a huge box of groceries out of the back of the truck and carried it up the path to the cabin. Indio stood at the front door, the key in his hand, staring at a note that had been pushed into a crack above the handle.

Indio yanked out the tri-folded piece of paper. "Wanna take bets? I bet this is Joy saying she's not coming."

No point betting against that. Hadn't they already figured out she wouldn't show? Especially after her little stunt yesterday.

"Open the door," Jesse said. "This weighs a ton and it's freezing out here."

Indio unlocked the door and Jesse walked into a large kitchen — basic, clean and tidy. Patricia had probably been up here to do some housekeeping earlier in the week. Jesse put the box on the table in the middle of the kitchen.

Behind him, Indio said, "*Fuck.*"

Jesse turned to see his brother glance from the unfolded note through the open doorway, where Caleb and Wynter were at the far end of the driveway, unloading supplies from the truck.

Indio slapped the note on the table. "She's gone back to the ashram."

Jesse took the note. It was three paragraphs of closely handwritten sentences and he didn't care to read it all. He glanced over the cult-speak and the *I love you*'s and found the important bit.

...move away from this darkness and toward the light...

"I guess, technically, you still win your bet," Jesse said. Easier to make a joke than imagine what Wynter was going to suffer in about ten seconds.

She came inside with a grocery bag in one arm and her backpack in the other, Caleb two steps behind her. Caleb set down his toolbox inside the door. Jesse went to take the grocery bag from Wynter, and handed Caleb the note.

"Is that from Joy?" Wynter said quietly. "She's not coming? That's okay. She's upset with me after yesterday."

"She's not upset with you," Caleb said as he finished reading it. "This is addressed to us all. She feels she made a mistake coming to Seattle. She calls the temple at the ashram her home, and she's returned to live there."

Wynter didn't react, except for a little twitch of her shoulders, like she'd been pinched. "Forever?"

"Sounds that way. This isn't because of you, Wynter. I think she'd already decided — maybe she already knew at Thanksgiving. I don't know why she came over yesterday. Maybe to explain it to you. Maybe to convince you to go with her."

"I would never do that."

"I know, hun. And maybe she knew, too. She said she wanted to give you one more chance."

"One more chance to save my dark heart."

"You don't have a dark heart!" Jesse cried, shattering the calm, surreal conversation.

Wynter came over and hugged him, like he was the one needing comfort. Caleb had his phone out, no doubt calling Joy, his brow drawn low as he went into *fix-it* mode. Indio was a shadow in the corner and he looked kind of angry. That couldn't be right. No, he was figuring out how to hide his relief while remaining outwardly sympathetic to Wynter's pain.

"Disconnected," Caleb said. "I'll call the office."

"Don't do that," Wynter said. "Can we enjoy our vacation, please? I have to go back to Deb and Brian's next week. I have to go back to that school the week after that. I have to go back to waiting, waiting, waiting, until I can come home forever. Joy waited a year and she went back home. Why shouldn't she go home? She needs to feel safe... like I do."

She could hardly speak for sobbing by the end, her breath misting the air. Caleb put his arm around her but she shrugged him off, shaking her head as she struggled to control herself.

"It's gonna snow," she said in a slightly more normal voice. "I checked the forecast. We have to build an igloo tomorrow, so I can see if it's warm inside."

Into the silence that followed, Caleb's phone pinged. Three pairs of eyes turned on him.

"Patricia. She's coming over to go through the things she wants me to do while we're here. Wynter, Jesse, go pick out your rooms and move your stuff in."

"Can I take the master?" Jesse said, not because he wanted it or thought he'd get it. He thought he *wouldn't* be allowed to have it, and then he could make a joke about it.

"Sure," Caleb said, deflating him.

"You're not gonna try and contact her, are you?" Wynter asked him.

"I don't have any other way to do that."

Wynter didn't look entirely satisfied with the answer. She picked up her backpack and followed Jesse through the large living room with a fireplace and a piano and a round dining table and couches, and into the hallway at the back.

"Wow, this sleeps a lot of people," Wynter said, putting her head around each door.

Two of the rooms had two bunk beds apiece, and there were two additional bedrooms with queen beds and adjoining baths. At the far end of the hall was a larger bathroom.

"*Two* masters!" Jesse said. "You know what that means?"

"I don't think we should."

"He *told* us to pick out our rooms. He *said* I could have the master, so by extension, he's okay with you having this second master."

"Doesn't seem right." Wynter sat on the bed. "Let's be nice to them. I know you didn't remember Joy, but they were raised with her, for a while anyway. They got her back, and now she's gone again. I think they're hurting, too."

"Caleb, maybe. I think Indio gave up a while ago."

"I think I did, too."

"Is this the secret Joy told you? That she was going back?"

Wynter shook her head.

"If she's gone, really gone for good, you don't have to keep her secret. I know it's upsetting you to keep it."

"You don't understand."

"You said it was nothing to do with you, so you shouldn't have to keep it. Please tell someone. Tell Caleb."

Wynter stood, her expression brightening as if they'd been talking about something else entirely. "I'm taking that last room with the bunks. They can fight over this room." She left to head in that direction.

"If you think that'll shame me into giving up my room...!"

Wynter's reply drifted down the hallway. "You have no shame, so I wouldn't even try."

"Damn straight!" Jesse fetched his bag and unpacked a few things in the first master, to stake his claim.

Patricia showed up shortly after, on the way to her cousin's place for Christmas. She had a long list of jobs for Caleb to tackle over the next three days, and Jesse knew he and Indio would be roped in to help. That was only fair. While Caleb was almost back to full strength, it would make Wynter happy if the work was shared around.

Visions of a relaxing vacation, playing Settlers of Catan and watching movies and possibly sipping cocktails around a blazing fire in a snowbound cabin, dissolved.

When Patricia took Caleb out the back to look at the broken water heater in the lean-to, Jesse heard them talking through his bedroom window. Caleb told her about Joy leaving. Patricia had only met Joy once, back in March when they all went to the diner and he and his brothers had put together their impromptu show for Wynter's birthday surprise.

Hearing Patricia's gentle questions and evident compassion, Jesse was struck by how different all their lives would be right now if Harry had returned her interest in him when they first moved to Seattle. Given her unwavering kindness to this family, she was the closest thing to a mother figure Jesse had known.

While Jesse wouldn't wish Harry on anyone, maybe Patricia could've tamed him. She'd run her diner and Harry would fix things around the place. She could've been their stepmom and they wouldn't have had Harry's lame girlfriends inflicted on them instead, including the one who messed up Indio somehow — Jesse didn't know the details, but he knew it was significant.

Wynter and Joy could've joined a ready-made family with a sober dad and a loving mom who took an interest in them. Parents who were *there* for them.

Jesse sat on the bed and pressed his palms into his eye sockets. *Pointless, stupid fantasies.*

"Why didn't Wynter take the other big room?" Indio was leaning in his open doorway.

"Cuz she's not a selfish entitled prick like me."

Indio looked like he might have a return quip. He swallowed it. "This place is an icebox. Doesn't look like we'll have hot water until tomorrow, either. But Patricia brought beer, whiskey, *and* enough lemon meringue pie to put us all in a sugar coma."

"Are you... Wynter seems to think you should be as cut up about Joy as Caleb is. Are you?"

Indio's brow tightened in a flash of emotion. He looked so much like Caleb for a second. And like Caleb, he wasn't likely to reveal much.

"She's your twin. Doesn't that mean anything?" Jesse prompted.

"I guess it means something. I don't know what."

"You need to see a therapist."

"Hell, no. I'll write a song about it."

Nobody's Business

Preparing a four-course meal in someone else's kitchen was always going to be a challenge. Jesse loved a challenge, but not on Christmas Day when everything had to be perfect, and not when he knew Wynter was burying her pain to please him, which meant he couldn't hover and criticize when she did stupid things like using the big pot to boil the peas, which left only a small pot to boil three pounds of potatoes. Not to mention why the hell had she put the peas on before the potatoes in the first place?

She was not following the schedule. And he kept his mouth shut about it.

"Fortunately, our brothers are the least fussy eaters on the planet," he said as Wynter scowled at her overcooked peas, which had been simmering, forgotten, on the back of the stove for an hour.

"Should we skip the mint dressing? It'll just make them even mushier."

"No! We need to add flavor back in because you..." He stopped himself. *Must not criticize...*

"I what?"

"Well, you probably boiled out all the flavor."

"We could mash them into the potatoes."

"That sounds gross."

"Why? Caleb always sticks his peas onto his fork with mashed potatoes, so it all goes into his mouth at once. I bet he'd love mashed potatoes-and-peas. *Peatatoes*, we'll call them."

She dumped her disgusting peas into his beautiful, creamy, perfectly seasoned mashed potatoes before he could stop her.

"Are you mad yet?" she challenged him.

He was stunned rather than mad. "Wait, you did that just to make me mad?"

"No, I did it to solve a problem. But I am curious why you're not mad yet. I know this meal is important to you, and I know you're being deliberately nice to me. I screwed up the pork stuffing, too. Not on purpose. I wasn't going to tell you. I tripled the recipe, like you said, but I forgot to triple anything except the pork. So it's basically just insipidly flavored sausage meat. And now it's cooked, we can't fix it." She glanced at the wall clock. "*T* minus seven minutes. We don't have time to fix it, anyway."

Jesse counted to ten in his head. "Anything else?"

"The artichokes taste funny."

He dismissed that. "No one knows what the hell to do with artichokes." He stirred the *peatatoes* until they became a vile green slop. "I'm not mad, Wyn. This is our best Christmas banquet ever."

"It's our first. A superlative requires at least three—"

"Go fetch Caleb from outside."

"Outside? He wasn't supposed to be working on Christmas Day!" She dashed out the back of the cabin to find him.

Indio wandered in looking hungry. "The potatoes are green."

"Thanks for pointing that out. I would never have noticed."

"Has she yawned yet?"

"No, but she already fucked up the potatoes, the stuffing, and possibly the artichokes."

"The what?"

Jesse slapped Indio's hand away from the appetizers. "She's tired and on edge. Last time she was like this, she broke me up with my girlfriend and had a mini panic attack. So whatever happens this time, it's on you."

Jesse's stocking ritual, which Indio had endured only once before because he generally didn't come home for Christmas, was everything Jesse claimed it would be, at least according to Jesse. In Indio's stocking was a rhyming dictionary.

"Checked your bookcases and you don't have one."

"That's true, I don't." The reason he didn't was because he used the internet, like a normal person. He didn't want to say that in front of Wynter as it would diminish the value of the rhyming dictionary *he'd* given her a few months ago. Jesse thought the gift was hilarious for exactly that unspoken reason.

Caleb's gift was a silk pink-and-white gel eye mask with a unicorn horn sticking out the top.

"Because you take so many naps," Jesse said.

Wynter was horrified he'd make a joke of Caleb's illness and recuperation. Caleb, for her sake, swallowed his pride and wore the mask across his forehead for the rest of the ritual.

Wynter's stocking was twice as big as theirs, and stuffed into it was a pair of fluffy bootie slippers. Jesse explained he was tired of seeing her walking around the house barefoot. She loved them and thought they looked like something a Viking warrior woman might wear.

It started snowing just as the sun was setting, as they cleared up after supper and boiled the kettle for the dishes. Wynter bounced out of her seat at the sight of flakes swirling around outside and yanked open the door.

"Hun, don't go outside," Caleb said when she put one foot over the stoop. He was still at the table, writing a list for the hardware store visit tomorrow.

"Two minutes, please? I've never really seen snow. I've never been outside while it's actually falling." She turned to Indio, her expression begging for support. "*Please* may I go out?" she asked Caleb again with exaggerated politeness.

"You may not. We've got no heating, no hot water, so there's no warming up afterwards when you get frostbite. Indio, why don't you get that fire going and we'll—"

"I can warm up in front of the fire!"

"You can go out tomorrow. Let's play one of Jesse's board games."

Wynter glared at Indio like it was all his fault for not backing her up.

Indio tied off the trash bag and handed it to her. "Take that out, will you? I'll bring the recycling."

She glanced at Caleb for permission. Indio did regret putting her on the spot, but there wasn't one good reason why she couldn't go out for a bit, especially when there was a chore to do.

Caleb, to his credit, gave in without further argument, with a little chin-jut of approval.

Indio followed her outside and they stopped for a moment in the driveway. There was only one thing to do when standing under falling snow, and he wanted to see if she'd do it. Sure enough, she tipped back her face and let the snowflakes kiss her skin. He did the same.

No way would Caleb or Jesse understand.

"I don't know how to play those board games," she said as they walked around the other side of the cabin to the trash cans.

"Neither do I. We can lose together. But if you beat me, and if the snow settles, and if Caleb fixes the hot water heater, and if Jesse helps me, I'll build you an igloo tomorrow."

"That's a lot of *ifs*."

"Also, it might only be a snowman. Depends how much snow we get."

He opened the trash can lid for her, stopping her arm before she could throw in her bag because there was something already inside. He tipped the can forward and reached in to grab it. Another Christmas stocking.

"That's Joy's," Wynter said.

"You threw it out?"

"No. I guess Jesse did."

He emptied the contents onto the ground. A pair of driving gloves — very retro and feminine with tiny buttons on the cuffs — because she'd just gotten her license. And a decorated photo frame with a picture of Jesse and Wynter from Halloween, after they scrubbed off their makeup.

"Did you make this?" he asked her, and she nodded. The frame was wrapped with fine wire and intricate beadwork. It was beautiful. "Can I keep it?"

Wynter took it from him, opened up the back of the frame and took out the photo, which she gave him.

"I meant the—"

She threw the frame into the trash can, along with the gloves and the stocking. She dumped her trash bag on top and closed the lid. The symbolism of the act was unmistakable.

"I have a gift for you," she said, blinking snowflakes off her eyelashes. Her nose and cheeks and ears were already red.

"I thought Jesse was the only Santa in our family."

"That's why I waited until now, to not steal his thunder. He chose a string of Christmas lights as his gift, and I'm cooking a gift for Caleb later. This is for you."

She took something out of her sweater pocket and held it out on the palm of her hand — a neatly folded flat origami pouch made from sheet music.

"I tried making one of these ages ago. Didn't work. So, I kept trying, and I think I finally nailed it." As he took it, she added, "Not the envelope, obviously. The thing inside."

He lifted the flap and extracted a three-inch-long wire guitar, perfectly formed, complete with a sound hole, six strings, and tuning pegs the size of pinheads.

"Incredible. How did you do it?"

"It has a thing on the back so you can use it like a paper clip or a bookmark. Do you like it?"

"I love it."

He clipped it into the V-neck of his hoodie for safekeeping, and they walked slowly back to the front door.

"When Joy came with the van yesterday," she said, "I think she wanted to take me back to the ashram with her."

"Yeah, I think so." Thank god Wynter had realized in time something was wrong, and saved herself. Joy's plan, though, had been monumentally stupid given Wynter was in the custody of the state of Washington. Joy wouldn't have been able to hide her at the ashram for long.

"When Momma arranged for me to go to Thailand, I wanted to go. You told me you understood, that you'd have been tempted, too." She slipped her hand into his. "But I wanted you to know, this time I wasn't tempted to leave here. Not for one second."

And he understood that, too. He didn't know why he and Joy had found it so hard to reconnect, or why she'd disconnected herself so thoroughly from Wynter once they left the ashram. None of that mattered. Wynter was here to stay. The sister he grew up with, he could brush her off as easily as snowflakes on his shoulder. The sister he just met was the only person in his life who accepted him without reservation, and he would never take that for granted.

As comforting as that thought was, there was something dark behind it, something he refused to examine too closely. His sense of discomfort was growing with the fear she was the only one who would *ever* accept him so completely, and that wasn't right.

Indio built the fire and Jesse meticulously explained the board game rules. Caleb had played before. Indio was bewildered by it, and he could see Wynter was too. Once they started, they got the hang of it. When it wasn't her turn, Wynter kept getting up to look out the window. The snow was light but steady. It was going to look pretty even if there wasn't enough to roll snowballs.

"Wyn, you have to pay attention," Jesse said. "People want to trade with you. People such as *me*."

Wynter came back to her seat and participated half-heartedly. "This is like Xbox but with no excitement, no gruesome deaths, and no top score ranking."

"It's very exciting," Jesse retorted. "For example, I'm gonna win in three rounds unless one of you figures out how to stop me. Caleb *could* win in two. He'll never figure it out. It's a medieval setting, so all the peasants you can't see, living in these villages, are dying gruesomely all the time. And you'll get a score at the end, which you can try to beat next time."

"Next time?" Wynter groaned.

Caleb did figure it out, of course, and won. Wynter didn't want to play again so she moved to the other side of the room, to the couch, and switched on the TV. Probably a good idea because Jesse was still smarting from her disparaging comments. Caleb opened Patricia's whiskey and the three of them set up a rematch.

They were halfway through the game when Wynter woke with a start. The back of the couch hid her from view, but they heard and they knew why. Indio watched his brothers tense up, preparing to jump out of their chairs and go to her, both hesitating because they didn't want to embarrass her by making a scene.

Wynter sat up, found the remote and switched off the TV.

"You okay, hun?" Caleb called.

Wynter went to the kitchen for a drink of water. Indio watched Caleb struggling to react appropriately, and Jesse struggling to contain his outrage. He figured her nightmares were at least as distressing for his brothers as they were for her. Indio was disturbed too, of course, but unless Wynter wanted to talk about it, unless she wanted comfort, there was nothing they could do.

"I didn't mean to fall asleep," Wynter said, wandering back into the living room. "I got tired and it's so cold in the bedrooms."

"You can sleep on the couch tonight," Caleb said.

"I'm not tired anymore."

"Wanna help me out here, then?" He indicated his cards.

"You don't need help."

She stood between Indio and Jesse instead, ostensibly to help Indio. All she did was aimlessly rearrange his cards and counters.

"Sucks to have nightmares at Christmas," Jesse said, giving Wynter a strange look. "Do you have nightmares at Deb and Brian's house?"

"I don't think so." Wynter got an odd look in her eyes, daring him to continue.

"So you have *more* nightmares around us than around strangers. I know you do." Why on earth was he spoiling for an argument? Wynter didn't need this crap. "I know you have one almost every night you're at home. I've heard you crying out. I've heard you washing your face in the bathroom. And in the morning you're wearing a different top because the other one got soaked with sweat."

Caleb glared at Jesse in disbelief that he'd bring all this up.

Jesse was still looking at Wynter. "She has nightmares because she's keeping a secret. It's eating her up. Joy told her something and she won't—"

Wynter launched herself at Jesse, slamming her fists into his chest. Something cracked and Jesse's chair collapsed, tipping him backward.

"Hey!" Caleb yelled at her, more in shock than anger.

She would've gone down with Jesse if Indio hadn't instinctively followed her motion and caught her around the waist. Jesse did go all the way down, hitting his head on the tiled floor. Dazed, he lay motionless for a moment before rolling onto his side with a groan.

At the look Caleb gave her, Wynter shrank back against Indio. She ran out of the room.

"Wynter, get back here!" Caleb yelled.

A door slammed at the end of the hallway. Caleb crouched down next to Jesse, who pushed away his helping hand.

"Joy told her something." Jesse was near tears. "It's not her fault, it's Joy's fault."

"Hold still." Caleb ran his fingers through Jesse's mop of dark curls, feeling for blood.

"I'm okay."

"Go sit on the couch." Caleb pulled him to his feet and handed him his whiskey. Then he started for the hallway.

"I'll go," Indio said, moving past him. Before Caleb could object, he added, "You looked like you were gonna murder her just now."

"I wasn't expecting... *that*. She's never..." Caleb shook his head, running out of steam, but he did sit down.

Indio went to Wynter's room and knocked. "Can I come in?"

"Yes." She was hunched up on her bed, her face white and her eyes round. "I can't believe I did that. I did to him what Joy did to me."

Indio sat on the edge of the bed. "Joy did far worse to you, baby, every day of your life."

She looked at him, long and hard, finally accepting without a word that what he said was true.

"Is he okay?" she whispered.

"Yeah. No blood."

She held up her hand, showing a streak of blood on her finger. Indio took a tissue from the box on the nightstand and wiped away the blood to reveal a small cut on the side of her index finger.

"How d'you manage this?"

"I think I scratched it on the zipper of his hoodie." She looked miserable. "I love him so much. He's my best friend. Pretty much my only friend. Why did I do that? I could've just told him to shut up."

"Next time, you'll know what to do."

"He had no right to say that about Joy."

"Maybe not. He's worried about you."

"Now Caleb's gonna pressure me about it. It's nobody's business."

"What if Jesse's right? What if it's eating you up?"

"He *is* right. I told him, at Halloween, that Joy told me a secret. He says she shouldn't have told me because it's nothing to do with me. Now I don't know what to do. There's no way out because I made a promise."

"Joy's gone, baby. You don't have to keep her secrets. *But*," he added quickly, before she had time to complain *he* was pressuring her, "I have a possible solution. Will you hear it?"

She nodded in silence.

"What if you told someone else? Someone you trust, outside the family, who could help you decide what to do with the secret."

"Such as?"

"Well, Patricia."

"I hardly know her."

"We've known her for years, ever since we moved to Seattle. You can trust her. You can tell her, and she won't betray your trust. She's the most sensible, down-to-earth person I ever met. She'll know what to do. Maybe the thing to do is keep the secret, but at least you've eased the burden of carrying it alone. Maybe the thing to do is talk about it, or tell Caleb, and she'll help you do that."

Wynter thought on it, sucking on the tiny wound on her finger. "I guess that would be okay."

He should make plans, before she changed her mind. "We could drop you off at Patty's diner tomorrow, on our way to the hardware store."

"How do I fix what I did tonight?"

"I think you can figure that one out yourself. You and Jesse will be okay – he's already forgiven you. Caleb... What you did surprised him. He has so much self-control, he forgets we don't all have it."

"When he yelled at me, it felt like everything I am was sucked out of my body. There's nothing left if he doesn't love me anymore."

"He'll always love you, no matter what you do." When she didn't respond, he pulled her into his arms. "You believe that, don't you?"

She nodded into his shoulder. "The same is true for you. Why won't you believe it? Why won't you?"

So much harder to have faith when he'd done so much worse to disappoint Caleb than Wynter ever would. He didn't have an answer for her.

Wynter came out with him and sat with Jesse on the couch, where they exchanged apologies and hugs and that was the end of that. Indio spoke to Caleb in the kitchen, explaining the plan.

Caleb agreed to it, but he was skeptical. "You think she'll talk to Patricia?"

"Even if she doesn't talk about this, I think it'll do her some good to spend time with a woman who's not about to disappoint her, or betray her... or hurt her."

Snow

"Wynter! Wake up! Snow blanket!"

Jesse was calling through her door. Wynter pulled back the drape. Her window overlooked nothing but a wire fence, which had bits of snow stuck in the diamonds. Nothing to yell about.

She went out to the kitchen, where Caleb was making coffee. That window overlooked the front yard and driveway, and everything was perfectly white.

"Beautiful!" she breathed.

"Looks like you're gonna get your igloo."

Caleb sounded okay, but last night must be on his mind and somehow they had to find a way to talk about it. She and Jesse were good, even though what she'd done was awful and what he'd said felt like a betrayal. Because they both felt so bad about it, their mutual empathy had already healed the rift.

Caleb was another matter entirely. She hadn't hurt him. She'd disappointed him on some deep level that she couldn't fix with an apology.

"Where did Jesse go?"

"He's already out there, scouting locations," Caleb said. "Indio is — well, his biological clock is a mystery to me. He needs to get up soon so we can get to the hardware store."

Wynter sat at the table and poured cereal into a bowl, and then milk. She wasn't hungry and wondered how she was going to get even one spoonful down her throat, which tightened as soon as Caleb sat opposite her with his coffee. He steepled his fingers against his chin, elbows on the table, and watched her.

"That's gonna get soggy, hun."

Wynter put down her spoon and leaned back in the chair. No way she could swallow cornflakes under his scrutiny.

"I know non-violence is one of your house rules," she said.

"It's in the top three."

"I'm so sorry."

"Okay, but I don't want an apology. I want to know what happened, so we can figure out how to stop it happening again."

Wynter wasn't sure where to start. "I panicked. That's all. I didn't want you to know and Jesse just said it anyway. Joy told me something that day you took me to her house. If I don't tell you, nothing changes for you. If I tell you, it could wreck everything or... it could be wonderful. Jesse told me she should never have made me promise to keep her secret, and that now she's gone I don't have to keep it. I don't know what you would say. Isn't this about loyalty and integrity? I know those are important to you. I don't wanna betray Joy, even though she's left us."

"You said nothing changes for *me* if you keep the secret. What changes for *you*, if you keep it?"

"Now I know about it, *everything* changes. I want to tell you. I want to tell you so much, so you can help me... help me find..." She hiccupped through her sobs, shaking her head to stop herself saying more.

Caleb was at her side, his arm around her. "Hush. Don't stress about this now. You'll talk to Patricia, won't you?" She nodded. "Okay. Talk it over with her. She's expecting you — she'll help you figure it out."

Wynter pressed her face into the crook of his shoulder. It still amazed her that when she screwed up, though it led to shame, it no longer led to pain.

Even Caleb did *consequences*, though—

"When you get back, you can help Jesse fix that chair."

The lunchtime crowd hadn't yet arrived and Patty's was quiet. Patricia sat with Wynter in the near-empty restaurant for an hour while Caleb and Indio were at the hardware store with Patricia's cash.

Wynter didn't know how much Patricia knew about her past in Arizona or her complicated family. Indio was right, though — she was easy to talk to. Once Wynter got started, she was able to tell her everything Joy had said. Patricia asked a few relevant questions to clarify things, and didn't probe further than she had to. She had a way of breaking things down to simplify them, and after a while Wynter felt a lot less confused.

"Before you decide on anything," Patricia said, "we need to determine if it's true. We need to talk to Harry."

"I've never even met him. I don't think Caleb wants me to meet him."

"I'll come with you. I'll set up a meeting."

"His number's in the phone book."

She leaned forward conspiratorially. "I used to be sweet on Harry. Did your brothers tell you that?"

Wynter could hardly believe it. "You and Harry?"

"Why so shocked? He can be very charming. I'm not sure the feeling was ever mutual. He's not easy to figure out. Oh, but he was so good looking."

"Which one of them looks the most like him?"

"Caleb, definitely. Those eyes. And sometimes he'd laugh exactly like Jesse."

"Everyone seems to think Indio is the most like him."

"A bit wild, is that what you mean?"

"Yes." Wynter played with the straw in her drink. "I don't want Indio to end up like him."

Patricia offered no assurances.

When Caleb and Indio came to pick her up, she expected Caleb, at least, to want to talk privately to Patricia. But he didn't, and she was glad — it made her feel more in control of the situation.

"We have a plan of action," Patricia told them. "I'm going to spend an afternoon with Wynter in Seattle as soon as I can arrange it. Okay with you?"

Caleb shrugged his assent, clearly curious but letting it go.

"This isn't a secret," Wynter said on the ride home. "It's a privacy issue, at least until I find out what's going on. And after that, it might turn into a surprise."

"It's okay, hun. We won't ask you about it. We'll let you ladies deal with it."

The truck was full of supplies. Caleb got to work on the boiler pump so they'd have heat in the radiators. Jesse had spent the morning making dozens of igloo bricks by packing snow into a rectangular bucket. He'd laid out a circle of bricks for the base. Indio helped him, while Wynter put together sandwiches and mugs of soup for lunch.

She took food out to Caleb at the back of the cabin. What he was doing wasn't strenuous and he was coping well, as far as she could tell. She dreaded the harder tasks he might have to do, not just because they might be beyond his capability but because he was unlikely to recognize or admit the fact. If their brothers didn't help at that point, she'd have to get tough with them.

"Indio and Jesse want to keep building the igloo," she told him. "Jesse says we'll fix the chair when it's finished. They do feel guilty for not helping you."

"That's nice, that they feel guilty about it," Caleb said, shaking his head.

"I can help."

"D'you know how to replace floorboards?"

"No. Do they?"

"I taught Indio a lot of DIY tricks over the years. Jesse somehow managed to always be somewhere else. He tends to break things faster than he can fix them. Oh, there is something you can do."

He took her into the kitchen.

"Patricia wants all the cabinet handles replaced. Some are already missing. These new ones have the holes in the same place, so you just have to unscrew the old ones and screw the new ones in. Give the doors a good scrub, while you're at it."

She got to work, eager to contribute.

Some time later, Jesse wandered in looking for more food. "I can do that."

"No, this was my assignment. I'm almost done." She was pretty proud of herself.

"We're on the fifth layer of the igloo." He closed the kitchen blinds. "You're not allowed to peek again until it's done, okay? We're running out of snow. Might have to steal some from the neighbors' yards."

"How many people can sleep inside?"

"Nobody's sleeping in there, Wyn."

"Why not, if it's warm?"

He shook his head. "To answer your question — in theory, I guess two people could fit if they curled up. It's not huge. We won't be able to stand up. Not even you."

"You don't sound enthusiastic about it."

"It'll be great." Jesse looked thoughtfully at the blocked window for a moment. "Indio says his memory of the one in Montana is more awesome than he thinks this one's gonna be. Whatever." He grabbed a muffin, courtesy of Patricia, and went back outside.

Wynter finished her job just as Caleb came in from the back.

"All done. Come with me and we'll turn the radiators on. I'll show you how it works."

She went around the cabin with him, to each room in turn, checking the hot water radiator valves and turning them on. He explained the pipes in great detail and, fascinating though it was, she wondered when she would ever need to know. His house didn't have this old-fashioned system. But to listen to him talk about something he knew so much about, and to hear the care and pride in his voice because he was doing something useful and doing it well — it was worth it.

Outside, Indio and Jesse were yelling at each other.

"They're just messing around again," Caleb said. "Sounds like a snowball fight. D'you want to join them?"

"I'm not allowed to see the igloo yet."

"I think they're in the back collecting snow."

They went into the backyard, where snowballs were flying fast and furious. It looked like fun. It also looked violent and painful as frozen missiles *thwacked* into bodies at high velocity. Wynter watched the fight, her heart pounding.

"Come on, Wyn!" Jesse jogged over to hand her a readymade snowball. "I need back-up. Indio's got a killer aim."

Wynter couldn't imagine throwing the snowball. She gave it back to a disappointed Jesse, who suddenly jerked forward as a snowball hit him sharply in the back of the head and disintegrated in a puff of white.

Jesse raced after Indio and tackled him to the ground. He shoved the snowball down the neck of Indio's hoodie. Indio swore loudly as he threw Jesse off, but he was still laughing.

"Who wants snow down their back?" Wynter said, trying to puzzle out the interaction. "I would be so mad if someone did that to me."

Caleb had been watching, too — or rather, watching her watch them. "They're just playing."

"I don't know how to do that."

"Sure you do. You play cards and video games and, um..." He couldn't seem to come up with another example. Certainly not an example of a physically active game that to her resembled something violent.

"I play guitar?" She rolled her eyes at him because she knew it didn't count, and followed him to the shed to get the stepladder so he could repair the roof of the lean-to. "This is why I couldn't play with Bea's little girl. I don't remember playing with anything, really, when I was little. In the Light they believed we were reincarnated, so our souls were old. No need for childish things."

"I don't know what to tell you, hun. I'll build you a doll house if you like, but you don't seem the type."

"No, I don't want a doll house." She glanced at her brothers again. They were finally organizing themselves to make more snow bricks. "When I move home, will you teach me more karate? All the moves."

"Of course."

"Maybe learning to fight, learning to wrestle and..." She mentally shuddered at the idea of physical interaction with people she didn't know, even kids her age, even at Caleb's dojo. "Maybe that'll help me not to be afraid of those sorts of games."

"Sounds like a plan. When you move home, that's what we'll do." He set up the stepladder next to the lean-to. "Hold this steady for me. I need to sweep off the snow before we can get started." Halfway up, he added, "I promise not to put a snowball down your back."

She couldn't tell if he was joking. She spent the next ten minutes worried he would, and wondering whether she'd like it.

Indio and Jesse came inside an hour before sunset. They'd already shed most of their outer clothes — igloo-building worked up a sweat, apparently. The cabin was a lot warmer now. Caleb came in from fixing the roof, and Wynter made them all hot drinks.

"Anything we can do?" Jesse asked Caleb with a sheepish grin because he knew he should've asked hours ago, and because he was hoping to be let off the hook now.

"One of the bunks in Indio's room is 'wobbly', according to Patricia," Caleb said. "Why don't you take a look? Indio, the window in the main bathroom is stuck. She thinks it was painted closed last summer. Tomorrow you can fix the floorboards in the linen closet."

"Do we have hot water yet?" Jesse said.

"I've replaced the heating element. It'll take a few hours to warm up."

"What can I do?" Wynter asked.

"Thanks, I appreciate your enthusiasm," he said in all sincerity, glancing at his brothers who were decidedly unenthusiastic. "Once the hot water's working, you can flush the washer with vinegar on a hot rinse cycle. It smells kinda funky. For now, you can bring in the rest of the stuff from the truck. We'll need it tomorrow."

"I'm not allowed to go out the front."

"Oh, the igloo's finished," Indio said.

"Why didn't you tell me?" Wynter cried, and ran outside.

The igloo was set in the middle of the front yard — a beautiful white dome about five feet high with a three-foot doorway facing the street. She ducked under the arch and went in. It was a lot smaller inside, because the walls were so thick.

Indio's face appeared in the doorway as he bent to peer inside. "What d'you think?"

"I love it. But it's cold in here."

"The heating element is a bunch of warm bodies, silly," Jesse called from somewhere outside.

"We need an entrance tunnel, like a real igloo," Wynter said.

"That's another hour's work!"

"I'll do it. Show me how."

Jesse took her to the neighboring yard — it appeared to be a holiday rental, like the cabin.

"Are we allowed to steal snow?"

"Precipitation belongs to humanity. More of a concern is that we're technically trespassing, but it looks like no one's home."

He showed her how to shovel and pack the snow into the bucket, avoiding the dirt and stones. He dragged it back to their yard, set the first brick in place outside the doorway, and gave her his waterproof gloves so she could keep going.

"Stack the bricks to the side here, and I'll help you build the tunnel when I've finished my chores inside."

"I think I can build a tunnel, Jesse."

She did build it, a three-foot-long tunnel with a two-foot clearance inside. It was dark when she was done, and she still had to bring in the stuff from the truck. She pulled back the tarp on the truck bed and reached for a plank of wood, only to discover she couldn't close her fingers around it.

She went inside. Indio was at the kitchen sink, trying with little success to wash black grease off his hands in cold water.

"My fingers are frozen through."

Indio took off her gloves and felt her hands. "Jesus, baby, you should've stopped sooner."

He poured the remaining water from the kettle into a bowl, as it still had some heat in it. As soon as she put her hands in, pain shot through them and she yanked them out.

"Too hot!"

"It's barely tepid."

He added cold water to the basin until she could stand it, and set the kettle boiling so he could gradually heat up the water as her hands got used to it.

"Take care of your hands, okay?" he said as he rubbed them gently under the water until the feeling returned to her fingers. "These are precious." He curled his pinkie around her right pinkie. "This one right here, this is the only one you're allowed to break or chop off. And this one—" He clasped his fist around her left thumb. "—is the most important of all."

"Not my other fingers?"

"Nope. Without this thumb supporting the rest of your hand, you can't fret a single note."

"There are more important things in the world than playing guitar, y'know."

She was teasing, and he knew because he responded with a quick, scolding glance up. But his attention was on her hands. At first she thought he was looking at the tattoo on her wrist, which she never bothered to cover anymore except for school. But he lifted her hands from the water so they lay flat, her palms resting on his, and tapped her right little finger.

"*Did* you break this one?"

Unlike the left one, it didn't straighten properly. Almost unnoticeable. No one else had ever noticed.

"I guess I might've. Caleb broke his arm when he was little. Don't most kids break something when they're playing around? Stacey told me she fractured her ankle jumping down the stairs." Her voice sounded breathless as she rushed through the justifications. "The piano lid fell on it," she finished, drawing back her hands.

Indio handed her a towel with a faint, tense smile to show he wanted to know the truth and wasn't going to ask, because he'd promised not to.

"Snow isn't quite as much fun as I thought it would be," Wynter said for a clear change of subject. "I still have to bring in the stuff from the truck."

"I'll do it. You find us some food."

Wynter went to check the refrigerator while Indio tipped out the bowl of water.

"I love our igloo," she said. "What do we do with it now?"

"Sit around in it. Take a photo of it. I don't know. It was Jesse's project."

"It was your project! Your promise to me if the snow settled."

"Jesse took over."

"Well, he is the engineer."

"And that's why it's functional, yet boring." Indio's smile was back to normal. "My suggestion to incorporate horizontal stripes was overruled."

"Stripes of what?"

"Dirt. Twigs. Anything to add a bit of interest."

"To be honest," Wynter said, gazing at the igloo sitting in the yard, illuminated by the glow from the cabin lights, "a window would've been nice. Don't tell him I said that."

Hotbox

The cabin was warm and cozy, and the hot water was finally running so they could shower. After more of Patty's finest reheated leftovers, they played a board game and then some poker. Jesse was hoping Wynter was *really* tired because he and Indio had already decided what they were going to do in the igloo that evening, and they needed her out of the way.

Caleb turned in first. Wynter wanted another go at the board game. Despite his eagerness to get to that baggie of pre-rolled joints stashed in his room, Jesse couldn't bring himself to throw the game and end it faster. Indio's annoyed looks in his direction showed *he* wished Jesse would get on with losing. When at last it was over, with Jesse the victor, Wynter declared she would go to bed and beat him tomorrow, as she had a new strategy in mind. She wasn't half as disappointed by the game as she'd seemed yesterday.

Indio and Jesse pulled their jackets and boots back on, took a couple of camping lanterns and a tarpaulin from the truck, and crawled on elbows and knees through the tiny tunnel into the igloo.

"That tunnel is actually a good idea," Jesse said. "See, she twisted it slightly, to keep out the wind."

"Maybe it's accidentally twisted cuz she can't build straight," Indio pointed out. "We could've just hung a tarp to keep out the wind."

"You have no appreciation for good engineering. Next year I'll build one with a working fireplace. Okay, I'm gonna bring in one more bucket of snow to block off the hole and I reckon we can hotbox this igloo."

Jesse went ahead with his plan, scraping together a snow brick and fitting it against the inner doorway. They sat on the tarp and lit up.

"So what did you learn about this secret of hers?" Jesse said.

"Nothing. Patricia's dealing with it."

"You're not at all curious?"

"I didn't say that."

"She seems... stoic about Joy leaving, doesn't she?"

"She's stoic about a lot of things. Joy's put herself in Wynter's past, and Wynter doesn't think about the past."

Jesse pushed his hand into his hair. "I fucked up last night. What happened was my fault — I can't help being curious."

"Last night is also in the past. She told me you're her best and only friend, which is... weird. But it does mean you're off the hook."

"I'm her best friend? That's neat. You jealous?" Jesse snorted as the weed took effect.

"I already have a best friend, and he's a guy — you know, the way it's supposed to be."

"I have a guy best friend, too. I've known Marcus since fourth grade. Anyway, nothing about this is the way it's supposed to be. Caleb was supposed to be done parenting until he has his own kids, and now he has to see her through high school and college — that's six or seven years."

"He'll be done in two."

"Really?"

"I mean, *she'll* be done in two, or less. She's almost sixteen, and then she'll be grown up."

"How can you know that?"

"How can you not know that?" Indio said. "You remember what fifteen-year-old girls are like, right? She's miles ahead of them."

"Maybe, in some ways."

"When she throws a tantrum because she's not allowed to go to the mall or get her whatever pierced, I'll modify my prediction."

"You could be right. I take credit for most of it."

Indio spluttered out a cloud of smoke. "You're kidding me."

"I trained her brain to be rational and inquisitive."

"She was already both those things. Anyway, that's, like, twenty percent of what's important in life."

"Try ninety-nine percent."

Indio waved his hand, uninterested in arguing the point.

"I'm doing my best," Jesse said defensively. "I've never had a little sister before."

"Neither have I. I'm not sure any of us are doing it right. Including Joy, obviously."

"So if Caleb's her parent and I'm her best friend — what are you?"

Indio shrugged.

"I know what you are," Jesse said smugly. "Her Siamese twin."

"We're not that similar."

"But you fit together."

"Cute, Jesse." From the way Indio shifted uncomfortably, Jesse could tell he'd hit a nerve. "I wonder, can we talk for two minutes without mentioning Wynter?" He sounded bemused rather than annoyed.

Jesse wasn't done talking about her, not even close. "At your gig, in that setting where you turn into a rock god, she called you *Indio squared*. That's what she's like, only all the time. She's a human being to the power of *n*. I haven't calculated *n* yet. The point is, everything is condensed — her past all crumpled up and squeezed inside, except when it pops up unexpectedly, usually in awful ways, and her knowledge of the big wide world all crammed in, more and more every day because every little thing is new to her, and that comes back at you rapid-fire with her weird questions and perspectives. I'm always on my toes. And *you*, you're someone different around her."

"No idea what you're yakking on about."

Jesse stared at the joint between his fingers. He'd already forgotten every word he just said. He knew those words had been gloriously coherent. "Makes perfect sense to me."

They both snickered. They were high enough that they didn't notice the scuffling in the tunnel until the snowball moved as someone pushed from the other side. Wynter's head popped up into the igloo.

Jesse jammed the joint into the wall of snow behind him. "Shit, you can't be here."

"I *knew* you'd sneak in here to sleep."

"We're not sleeping, baby," Indio slurred. "Go back to bed."

Wynter ignored him, scooped the rest of the snowball out of her way, and crawled all the way in. She was wearing thick PJs and a robe and her fluffy slippers, which were not intended for outdoors.

"Ooh, it *is* warm."

Jesse closed his hand guiltily around the baggie near his feet, with its one remaining joint, and pushed it into his pocket.

"I'm not here to spoil your fun," she said, seeing what he'd done.

"You are spoiling it," Jesse said. "Go away."

Wynter settled against a free spot on the wall, next to him. It was cramped now. Three pairs of feet met in the middle.

"Do you have a bump on your head from yesterday?" she asked.

"Yeah. Thanks for that. Hurts like hell, so I'm self-medicating."

"Will I get high from second-hand smoke?"

"You might get a buzz if we were in, say, a tiny unventilated space."

"Maybe you could punch a hole in the ceiling, for a chimney."

"Maybe you could leave."

"I don't mind. It smells okay."

"You need to wash your hair tomorrow morning," Indio said, "before Caleb gets a whiff."

"What about your hair?"

"Caleb doesn't care what my hair smells like, or the reason why."

"Does he ever smoke with you?"

"He hasn't touched it since I was a kid," Jesse said.

Indio agreed. "Summer of 2009, I believe it was, right before I left for Ohio. Before that, a handful of times in high school."

"So, he didn't much like it?"

"Oh, I think he liked it," Indio said with a chuckle. "And it made him super nice to be around. But getting high was always low on his list of priorities."

"Where is it on your list?"

"It's my number three priority," Indio said, a touch smarmy.

"Wyn, seriously, go back inside," Jesse said.

"I helped build this. I have a right to be here. And I'm gonna sleep in here if it kills me." She pulled two nickels out of her robe pocket, along with a single playing card. "Do you know how to play two-up?"

"Never heard of it," Jesse said.

"You're always showing me new games, so I'll show you one. It's an illegal Australian gambling game."

"Illegal?"

"Yes. It's only legal for one day of the year."

Jesse and Indio exchanged a look that indicated they thought she might be crazy.

"So, I'll be the spinner to start. These are supposed to be those big old British pennies, but I don't have any. And the card should be a little wooden paddle, which is called a kip." She held up the card and placed the coins on it. "Start with one heads up, one tails up. I spin them until I lose. Two heads, I win. Two tails, I lose and I pass the kip. One of each is called 'odds', and I spin again. I bet on myself. Jesse, you cover it. I'll cover Indio on his turn, and he covers you. Got it?"

"I guess..." Jesse said slowly. He'd never heard of anything so silly.

"We start with twenty dollars each, and we bet in multiples of five. We'll keep score in our heads."

"Why not start with four bucks, and bet in whole dollars?" Jesse said.

Wynter was unimpressed. "This is how I was taught."

"Okay, but you do understand that what I just said amounts to the same thing when it's pretend money?"

"Yes, Einstein. So, we play until someone wins all sixty dollars. You're supposed to throw the coins ten feet in the air for it to count — we'll say they have to hit the roof of the igloo."

"That's like, two feet in the air."

"It'll have to do. I'm gonna bet five on two tails."

She flipped the coins up against the ceiling a few inches above their heads. The coins fell on the tarp.

"*Odds*. I spin again."

"Can I bet on odds?"

"No. You weren't listening. Odds means spin again. I bet five on two heads this time. Indio, if you had some buddies in here, you could make side bets with them." She rearranged the coins on the kip and threw them again. One fell in a dark spot near the doorway and she took a lantern to examine it. "Two heads. I win! Jesse, give me five dollars." She held out her hand.

Jesse handed her an imaginary bill, his expression twisted in disbelief. "And you say this is illegal Down Under?"

"Except on ANZAC Day, which is like Veterans' Day but in April."

"There is zero skill involved."

"So maybe I have a chance of winning something, finally."

"Don't say that. You're smart. But this game is the dumbest thing I've ever seen."

"You only say that because you're losing. I bet five on heads again."

She lost and handed the kip to Indio, and the invisible five dollars back to Jesse. Indio made an effort to look interested, and in the end it was a pretty fun way to enjoy a high, especially any time one of them got close to losing their last five dollars. Wynter lost all her money first, to her great annoyance, and she sat back to watch the two of them compete, hiding yawns behind her hand.

Two minutes later she was asleep, leaning against Jesse and hampering the movement of his right arm for spinning the coins, so they called it quits. Jesse lit the last joint, waiting for Indio to stop him. He didn't.

"You'd think," Jesse said softly, putting his arm around Wynter to settle her more comfortably against his shoulder, "with those Aussies being upside-down and all that blood rushing to their brains, they'd be smart enough to come up with a better game than two-up."

"They're pretty smart for making it illegal. Didn't they invent wifi? And their money's made from plastic, which seems sensible."

"She had an Aussie friend at the ashram."

"I know. He gave her that tattoo."

Jesse shuddered. "That creeps me out."

"Why? It doesn't creep *her* out. I'm glad someone was nice to her."

"Yeah... *How* nice, I wonder?"

"C'mon, they were little kids. Why don't you try seeing things through her eyes, instead of applying your formulas and algorithms..."

Indio's voice drifted off. He was staring at the back of Wynter's head, not paying attention to what he was saying. He knelt forward suddenly, handing Jesse the joint, and swept Wynter's hair to one side.

"She's got these weird lines on the back of her neck."

Jesse tried to twist his head to see.

"Hold still, you'll wake her." Indio grabbed a lantern and held it up, brushing more hair out of the way. "Four faint white lines right under the hairline, going all the way down."

"You mean scratches?"

"Scars from old scratches, or from..." Indio met his eyes and Jesse's heart stuttered. Indio gently pulled down the collar of her robe. "They just sort of stop suddenly, all in a row, about where a t-shirt neckline would be."

Indio sat back on his heels. He took the joint and sucked on it thoughtfully.

"If someone used, say, a belt, over her clothes, that would make sense. It would mostly land on her t-shirt or shorts, leaving no lasting mark. Sometimes it missed and hit bare skin."

Jesse couldn't believe Indio's equanimity as he discussed someone flogging their sister.

Indio sat forward again, eased one side of Wynter's robe open to get to the clothes underneath, and lifted up the hem of her pajama top. As he pushed it higher to expose her back, careful not to wake her, Jesse tightened his arm around her shoulders. This felt wrong, like Indio was molesting her, except he was actually checking to see if someone else had.

Indio moved the lantern closer and peered at Wynter's skin. Jesse couldn't see, so he just sat there feeling surreal – and not because he was high. He felt sick.

"I don't see anything here," Indio said. Her top was pushed all the way up to her shoulder blades.

"Maybe an animal scratched her neck, or she crawled through brambles or something," Jesse said.

"No, the lines are thicker than claws or thorns."

"She implied once they used a cane." Not that that made him feel better about it.

"A couple of the scars are curved, not straight. I think it was probably the tail end of a belt or something else flexible."

Jesse felt tears pricking his eyes. "Wouldn't it have to draw blood to make a scar?"

Indio didn't answer that. Now his fingers went to her waistband. He lowered one edge a couple of inches, exposing her hip.

"See that?"

Jesse looked down. A white line snaked over the back of Wynter's hipbone, barely visible on her pale skin. Another, right next to it, tapered to a point at the upper end, while the lower edge cut off sharply.

Indio pulled the fabric lower still, to quickly check down to the base of her spine, before straightening her clothes and tucking her robe around her again. Jesse put his other arm around her, tears spilling down his cheeks, and looked at Indio over the top of her head.

"Is this one of those things in her past we're supposed to just not think about?" Jesse said.

"Until she tells us about it — yes. It's possible she doesn't even know she has scars, given where they are." He gave Jesse a sympathetic look. "I'll tell Caleb, when I get the chance. Then we just leave it alone."

"Aren't you angry? You don't even look upset."

"I feel everything you feel right now, Jesse. *Everything*. But I don't want her to see that side of me. I'll try and forget about it for as long as she does, and I'll deal with it when she does. You go ahead and get angry on her behalf, plot your revenge — that's a best friend's job. I think my job is to follow her lead." Indio scratched around for the burnt-out joints, and the coins and the card. "Let's get inside."

Jesse wiped his face and woke Wynter up. "Hey, you slept in the igloo. Congrats. We're done here."

She had no complaints about that, and they crawled out, one after the other. Jesse found extra blankets for her bunk and made her put two pairs of socks on. She rolled over and went right back to sleep.

"I'll sleep in there with you, if that's okay," he told Indio, who was getting into one of the bunks in the room opposite. For all that he enjoyed the fancy queen-size bed with adjoining bath, he felt like sticking close to his brother tonight.

Indio was fine with it. After raiding the kitchen for cookies, Jesse lay on the narrow bed meant for a ten-year-old, hands behind his head, and stared at the slats of the bunk above. Indio was doing the same thing, three feet across the room.

"I will get revenge," Jesse said.

"Fine. You clear it with Caleb first, so he can show you how to not get caught."

Ghosts of Me

Jesse exited Indio's room in the morning and almost ran into Caleb in the hallway. He knew exactly what conclusion Caleb was going to draw, given Jesse had the option of a queen-size bed and a private bathroom.

Caleb raised an eyebrow.

"What?" Jesse said, all innocence.

"Please tell me you two weren't smoking pot in there last night."

"No." Jesse made to walk away, stopped himself, and came clean. "In the igloo."

"Keep it out of the house."

"Wynter was there for a bit." May as well own up to it. "We didn't let her have any." That was sort of true. He made a mental note to Google the THC content of second-hand marijuana smoke.

"Did she ask?"

"No."

Caleb seemed satisfied with the answer. Jesse thought it was all rather trivial compared to what Indio was going to tell him soon about Wynter.

"You can fix the hinges on the shed door today," Caleb told him, "and Patricia wants a bolt lock on that main bathroom door. Oh, and repair the chair leg, obviously. Wynter can help with that."

"What are you doing today?"

"Gutters." Caleb grimaced. "My favorite thing." He was good with fixing machines and building stuff, but he sure hated routine maintenance. Not that it had ever stopped him doing what needed to be done.

Jesse did the bathroom lock first, in the hope the weather would warm up a bit before he had to go outside. He was done just in time for Wynter to use the shower, when she finally got up.

He went outside and started on the shed door. Caleb worked nearby, and that was cool — just fixing things up, side by side, not needing to talk or anything.

When Indio got up late in the morning, he took Caleb down the back of the property and Jesse knew what he was saying, although he couldn't hear him, and he started feeling sick again. He watched Caleb fold his arms and stare at the snow-covered ground as he listened. He asked a couple of questions and squeezed Indio's arm in a sort of gesture of appreciation.

Thank you so much for telling me our little sister has permanent scars from being lashed with a belt while left in the care of witches by an unbearably selfish mother who fled the country. And let's not forget an older sister who put her fingers in her ears and said la-la-la...

Caleb came right back to work on the gutters.

Wynter called them inside for lunch.

"Patricia just phoned me," she told them. "I'm going out with her tomorrow morning before the diner opens. We're going into Seattle for a couple hours."

This was something to do with Joy's damn secret. Jesse felt his anxiety rising. When he was helping Wynter with her school work or playing music with her, or watching a movie or talking about the bizarre new world she was experiencing, everything felt good and right. Now everything was off-kilter and he was powerless to do anything about it. Caleb acted like nothing was wrong. But Caleb had always held it together. All those years, all those times when he must've been worrying about something – about Harry, Indio, money, something – and he didn't let on, so Jesse always felt his world was safe. And Indio had joked about Jesse's revenge plans, while Jesse had been perfectly serious.

Was he the only one in this family capable of normal feelings?

Caleb reminded Indio about the floorboards he was supposed to fix, and told him he could split wood afterward for tonight's fire. Jesse said he'd do that. He needed to work off his nervous energy. Caleb had taught him how to use an ax safely, three winters ago. There were a couple of thick stumps at the back of the yard that he set about splitting into segments, like a pie.

When Wynter came up behind him he accidentally yelled at her because she might've been hit by flying chips or even a flying blade. He dropped the ax and hugged her, which surprised her even more than the yelling. He'd taken off his jacket because chopping was hot work, while she was a bundle of layers — sweaters and jacket and scarf and gloves.

"Are you upset about me going out tomorrow?" she said. "The secret thing?"

"No. Sort of. Everything feels strange since Thanksgiving."

"It's because you ate that cookie from the Light."

He chuckled but it turned into a sob that he swallowed before she noticed. Did he have a secret now? She didn't know he knew about those scars and what they meant.

She pulled away and said, "I am so sorry about the bump on your head."

"You've been sentenced to help fix the chair."

"That's fair."

"If you wanted to appeal, I'll be your attorney."

"But you were the victim. There's a conflict of interest."

"I'll sign a waiver."

Wynter grinned and headed for the house. She called over her shoulder, "I'm gonna bake you a carrot cake with cream cheese frosting."

"Please don't! Your baking sucks."

Wynter had made lasagne for dinner, specifically for Caleb's Christmas present, and it was really, really, good.

"I followed the recipe on the back of the packet," she told Caleb. "All these years you've been waiting for lasagne, and you could've just done what I did."

Caleb did not cook anything but pancakes, and he was sure lasagne wasn't as easy as she made it sound.

"What about that carrot cake you promised me?" Jesse said.

"I baked it, and then I threw it out. Sorry."

"Hmm. I guess they don't put the recipe on the back of a bag of carrots."

Caleb felt the underlying tension at the table as they finished up the meal. Jesse rinsed the dishes and Indio sat drinking his beer, both in silence, and all of them not knowing what to say, and concerned about this thing, whatever it was, that Wynter was doing tomorrow with Patricia and wondering how it was related to Joy, and to them.

"Indio," he said, "great job on those floorboards. Next time you're in Seattle, you could fix the floor in our laundry."

"I *could*," Indio said with that sullenness of his teenage years, except that he was more or less joking. At least, Caleb hoped so. Indio hated being told what to do, but he was part of this family and Caleb knew that helping out strengthened his connection with the rest of them.

"Are we only staying one more night?" Wynter said.

"Yes, hun. We'll go home tomorrow evening. You have to go back to Enumclaw on Sunday. Jesse will drive you." He drew a steadying breath as he prepared to say what he needed to say. "One of us needs to drive to Arizona."

Wynter went very still. "If I wasn't enough to make her stay, why do you think you're enough to make her come back?"

"We have to try. None of us parted on good terms the last time we saw her." For him that was — what, three days ago? Felt like longer, because since then he'd been waiting endlessly for Wynter to process it and react appropriately.

"You could write her a letter," Wynter said. "Please don't go there. I don't want to think of you in that place. Any of you."

She looked at each of them in turn. Indio turned his beer bottle around between his fingers. Jesse had his head in his hand, turned away to hide his expression.

"We can't give up that easily," Caleb said. "She's our sister. She sent you to me because she knew it was the right thing to do. I'll always be grateful for that, even if she failed you afterward. I'm not giving up on her."

Wynter's eyes flashed with defiance. He'd seen that look a hundred times in the eyes of her brother seated a few feet away – the same hard look in hazel eyes that were otherwise gentle, the same furrowed brow. There was fear there, too, and that was also Indio all over again. The fear she would do or say something she'd regret, and which would hurt them both with a wound that took a second to inflict and years to heal.

To stop her from doing so, he leaned forward and said, "I'm not used to failure, Wynter. I raised two brothers. It was tough and sometimes we caused each other pain. There was a time I thought I'd lost Indio. Can you imagine how that felt?"

She nodded mutely.

"So I can't give up on Joy." He turned to Indio. "I just got sent a heap of medical assessments and physical therapy appointments through next week as part of my transition back to regular duties. I can't get out of it. We need to do this now, before she... I don't know, before she settles in. So, you need to drive down on Monday. You need to demand to see her, and then... just talk to her."

"No," Indio said.

Caleb clenched his fist on the table. "Even if she won't come back with you, at least we've made contact, made the effort—"

"No."

Caleb sat back. "Jesse will go with you."

Jesse looked his way at last, and shook his head.

"Christ, what's wrong with you both?"

"There's nothing wrong with us," Jesse said. "There's something wrong with her." He glanced at Wynter before pressing on, his voice shaking with emotion. "She attacked Wynter, that weekend we all got together at home."

"What does that mean — *attacked?*"

"Tried to strangle her and gave her a black eye."

Caleb was speechless. For all of two seconds he'd assumed *attacked* meant she'd said something hurtful. Just words. Words didn't matter. Only actions.

And now... after both girls' earlier assurances that Joy had not been abusive at the ashram... Now what was he supposed to think?

What the hell happened to *no secrets?*

"I asked them not to tell you," Wynter said nervously. "I didn't want you to hate her."

"What happened?" He didn't recognize his own voice.

"She got mad because... I don't know why. She was scared. She wanted to leave early."

"She got mad about that teddy bear," Jesse said.

Had he heard right? "*What?*"

"She got mad about a fucking teddy bear!" Jesse yelled. "She's nuts. She belongs in that place with all the other brainwashed nutters. I never want to see her again."

Even Wynter looked shocked by his outburst. Indio hadn't reacted at all.

"I tried to give her a chance," Jesse said, his eyes glistening with unshed tears as he tried to calm himself. "So many chances. I tried because that's what Wynter wanted, and what you wanted. But after what *he* told you..."

He was referring to the scars on Wynter's skin, which they'd agreed not to talk about. A flash of confusion crossed her face.

"Her last chance just expired," Jesse finished. "I will never lift a finger to help her again, or to help you help her."

The impassive look on Indio's face said he agreed with every word.

Caleb was stunned. He was used to Jesse just... doing what he was told. Caleb was never unreasonable, so Jesse obeyed. Was this request unreasonable?

He'd spent a year avoiding blaming Joy for her behavior, although on principle he always held people accountable for their actions. Even Wynter. He'd made Wynter apologize, he'd made her fix her mistakes, or helped her fix them, but he had never allowed her to use the excuse, *The Light made me do it.*

Here he was, letting Joy off the hook because the Light made her do it.

Somehow, to him, Joy was still that girl with butterfly wings demanding piggyback rides in the yard, laughing with him as they jumped on the bed until the slats broke, crying on stage at the kindergarten concert because her mother didn't show while Caleb sat in the back with the other third graders listening to them snigger at the crybaby.

"I think..." He didn't know what he thought or which way to go. The only sure thing in his life was his sense of duty, to country and to family and to himself. "I'll apply for leave and drive down the week after next."

Wynter moaned a protest. "Don't go. You don't belong there. I don't want you to ever see that place."

Her voice shook and she clutched the edge of the table, white-knuckled, and suddenly he knew there was something much deeper, something more than just the notion he'd be wasting his time.

"Please don't go. I'll do anything. I'll tell you anything. Just don't go."

I'll tell you anything. Well, that was a deal worth considering. Jesse was watching her carefully — Jesse would take up the offer in a heartbeat, so eager was he for another one of those dark pieces, despite the pain it would cause.

But doing so would chip away at their trust. Caleb had to keep the big picture in focus.

"You don't need to tell me anything. I have to go to the ashram. I have to try."

"I will tell you something," she said in a flat, hard voice that made the temperature plummet. "I'll ask you a question, and then you'll see. Would you lock me in a dark room for four days and nights?"

"What...?"

"Can you imagine me in that room? *Her* — that other part of me. She's six years old and someone put her there. She doesn't remember who, but her mother — your mother — knows she's there."

She was going to make him see, and he didn't want to see.

"Would you stop feeding her for four days? Can you see her now? On the first day, she's pleading through the door until her voice is hoarse. Vomiting up every sip of water on the second day, until it's just bile. Too weak to move on the third, except to scrape her shins against a broken tile until they bleed because that takes away the pain in her stomach. Mostly sleeping through the fourth. Just floating away and wondering if anyone remembers she's there, if there's anyone left to bring her safely down."

Caleb pressed a hand over his eyes as his heart and his mind ground to a halt.

"She was supposed to find a better path to God," Wynter said, "because she refused to say the prayers and she stole food and answered back and I don't remember what else. Someone did open the door and got most of her out. It wasn't her mother or her sister. So part of her is still locked in that room, still floating away. I guess that's the part that still loves Joy and needs to hope Joy still loves her. The rest of her... The rest of me, my mechanical body and all the things I've become since I left that place — that part of me doesn't want Joy back."

Wynter reached across the table and took his hand. His focus narrowed to just that sensation, her hand on his. Jesse and Indio were here, somewhere, suffering just as he was. All he knew was the feeling of her fingers tangled up in his.

She said, "I know you'd never do those things, but you can imagine them now. I've put that picture in your head, and it's there forever. I don't want a picture in *my* head of you at the ashram, or anywhere near it. Joy belongs there, with those dark pieces floating around, those ghosts of me. You don't belong in that picture."

He couldn't imagine six-year-old Wynter because there were no photos of her at that age, or any age before fourteen, other than one baby picture. He could see this Wynter, *his* Wynter, in that dark room on broken tiles. And Indio had put another picture in his head earlier, of beatings so severe she still wore the scars on her skin, a year or more later.

"I'm sorry for hurting you like that," she said, "but there's nothing else I can do to make you understand. You can't fix everything. You can't fix Joy. I've decided to stop loving her."

That was his fault. He'd put the idea in her head — that you could decide to love, and decide to stop loving. Now she was using it against him and he had no defense.

"Okay. I won't go."

Wynter nodded and slowly pulled back her hand. "Tomorrow I'll tell you something else. Patricia and me, we'll figure out the details first — but I'm pretty sure it's something good. How many guitars did we bring? We should play something."

And just like that, she brushed it all away.

They had two guitars, and there was a piano in the living room that no one had yet touched. Caleb hadn't had five years of lessons from the age of nine for nothing, so he took the bench and did his best. Indio, who was entirely self-taught, eventually threw him off and took over, and after that things sounded a lot better.

San Diego

Patricia's face fell as she and Wynter pulled up in front of Harry's ramshackle clapboard house in Everett. On the opposite side of the busy street were warehouses and parking lots full of trucks. This was nothing like the suburban street where Caleb's house was — *Harry's* house, Wynter reminded herself. Her brothers had grown up in that house after moving from Montana. Harry was the one who'd left, and now he lived in this miserable place.

Wynter knew Caleb had told Harry about her, when she first arrived in Seattle a year ago. Harry had known nothing of her existence either, until then, and neither of them had shown an interest in meeting each other. She wasn't here for Harry.

"I only told him you wanted to talk about Joy," Patricia said, and that was halfway to the truth. Joy had never visited Harry. Wynter didn't know how he felt about that and it didn't matter — she wasn't here for Joy, either.

She was here for the truth about Xay.

Patricia squeezed her hand as they walked to the front door, which wasn't even a real door. It was a piece of drywall with a round hole where the handle should be. The siding and window sills badly needed painting. Why hadn't Caleb offered to do it? Or, if he had, why had Harry refused his help?

Patricia knocked. Instantly, a dog barked inside the house.

"Caleb once told me he has a dog called Lexie," Wynter whispered, standing behind her. Hiding. "He said she's very sweet and loves baby carrots dipped in peanut butter."

"Ah, I knew we should've brought snacks," Patricia said, throwing a smile over her shoulder.

In truth, Wynter wasn't sure Harry would be here when they came. He was probably like Joy, who broke commitments as fast as she made them.

Half a minute later, the door opened and there stood Harry. "Well. I wasn't sure you'd come."

He gave Patricia an awkward hug. He was tall like Caleb, slightly stooped, with a short spiky beard and weather-worn skin. Wynter recognized those dark blue eyes, and the crease between his brows, and even the way his hair grew in waves from his hairline, although his needed a cut and there was a lot of gray mixed in with the brown.

"This is Wynter," Patricia said.

Harry's lips quirked in a nervous, curious way, because he had no idea why she was here. "Miriam's girl. My boys can't stop talking about you. Come in, come in."

It hadn't occurred to Wynter that her brothers would talk to Harry about her. They didn't see him that often, and she didn't believe Caleb or Indio would say much. Jesse probably wouldn't know when to shut up.

They went inside, into a small, crowded living room with worn wooden floors. It smelled like cigarette smoke and household cleaner. Books and grocery bags and unopened mail littered every surface, including the couch and chairs. A black-and-white dog circled around them excitedly until Harry shooed her out the back door.

"I'll make us coffee, shall I? Or tea? Too early for a beer, Pat? I might have a bottle of wine around here..."

"Tea would be lovely, thanks, Harry," Patricia said, surveying the room with the look of a hawk calculating how to swoop on its prey.

Harry went to put the kettle on. Patricia flitted around the room, picking up every single thing that wasn't supposed to be there, stacking the books and mail on a table in the corner, and lining up the grocery bags next to it. Wynter watched in awe. It took her less than two minutes, and now the room looked much better. Patricia opened the drapes to let in the weak morning sunlight. She gave Wynter an encouraging look and they sat together on the couch.

A few minutes later, Harry brought them mugs of strong tea.

"Look at this, Pat. I should tip you." He moved a magazine and a grocery bag back where they had been before, as a sort of protest. He waved around an unopened official-looking letter. "I've got that big developer sending me offers and knocking on my door every other week, trying to buy me out to build a warehouse or a parking lot or something."

"They'll pay a good price if they're that desperate," Patricia said.

"Why would I move?" He settled into an armchair. "I've got the big yard out there. Lexie loves it."

Patricia looked past him, out the back where a huge shed occupied half of the yard. "You've still got that boat, then?" she said.

"Eh, I'll fix 'er up one of these days and sail down the coast." He assessed Wynter with that curious look again. "How are you finding Seattle?"

Wynter was as nervous as him. She pressed her hands between her knees. "I love Seattle. I'm living in Enumclaw right now."

"Oh, that's right. Caleb did say." He didn't seem to want to get into that. "Patricia, how's the restaurant business? Still doing your dad proud? I should get over there more often. Haven't seen you since the... uh, the wedding." A little chuckle covered for his embarrassment about the marriage-that-wasn't.

"You're always welcome at Patty's. Are you still working at the marina?"

"Three or four shifts a week, nights mostly. You were lucky to catch me at home this weekend."

Patricia set her mug on the coffee table. "Harry, I mentioned on the phone that Joy's gone back to Arizona. I'm so sorry you didn't get the chance to meet her. I only met her once myself."

"Well. I expect she doesn't remember me. Never mind." He gave Wynter a broad but forced smile, and she recognized something in his eyes — because they were Caleb's eyes — a pain he wouldn't acknowledge.

"Wynter wanted to talk to you about something Joy told her. Wynter, did you want to ask your questions, or do you want me to start?"

"I will." Wynter had already decided, on Patricia's advice, that she was going to tell her brothers about Xay — whether he was simply her friend at the ashram, or their half-brother. Either way, Joy was gone and she wasn't going to keep the secret any longer. That decision made it easier to face Harry now, and some of her nervousness left her.

"Can't think what this is all about," Harry said, overly casual.

"It's about Miriam and you. Your marriage, and why it ended, and what happened afterward."

Harry looked to Patricia like he thought this might all be a joke. "That's a lot of old history."

Wynter persisted. "Joy told me you met an Australian woman, Ember, in California, and that she had a baby — your son — in February '95. I wanted to know if that story is true."

Harry sobered. He set his fingers against his chin and narrowed his eyes. His gestures were so much like Caleb — except that he was ill at ease, and that made Wynter afraid he wouldn't talk. She wanted to yell at him, *No secrets, no lies!*

Harry said at last, "Did Joy tell the boys about this?"

"They don't know anything about it. Joy only found out about a year-and-a-half ago."

"Miriam told her?"

Wynter nodded. "Please, it's important for me to know if that boy was yours. I think I met him in Arizona, and I want to find him again."

Something got through to him, because his expression softened as he looked at her. He sat back in the chair.

"Yes, Ember did have a son. Our little... dalliance is the reason Miriam threw me out. Well, that's not quite true. We could've weathered it. We were getting through it. But then she found out Ember was pregnant. Miriam was pregnant too, y'see, with Jesse. It was too much for her. And Ember wanted nothing more to do with me. I never saw the baby. She took him back to Australia. And Miriam wouldn't take me back."

Wynter relaxed against the couch cushions, relief flooding through her. She'd promised to tell her brothers *something good*, and this was what she'd hoped for.

"He's the boys' half-brother, then," Patricia said. "They should know about it, Harry."

"I don't really..." Harry's defensive posture crumpled. "I'm ashamed of myself, Pat, even after all this time. What good will it do?"

Wynter got the feeling such a moment of honesty was a rare thing for him, that he'd surprised even himself by it.

"What's Ember's second name?" Wynter said, determined to get back on track. "I need to find them."

"She was already in the Light by then. You know how it is. They give themselves those fancy mystical-sounding names. I don't know her real name."

"Has she ever contacted you?" Patricia asked.

"Yes, actually, she did, about ten years ago. Called me from Australia and said she wanted her son to meet his father. She wanted me to send her two airfares. I didn't have that kind of money. And I thought... to be honest, I thought it might be a con. I didn't see the point. It was right about the time I was planning the move to Seattle with the boys, and I didn't want to know."

"They did come to America eventually," Wynter said. "They lived at the ashram in Arizona for about a year, until Miriam found out. She had them sent away."

Harry gave a bitter laugh. "Well, I don't entirely blame Miriam for doing that." He scrutinized Wynter. "And you plan to tell the boys about this? About him?"

"Yes, I'll tell them today. And I'm gonna find Xay."

"Zay?"

"Xavier."

"His name's Xavier? Huh. She never told me his name."

Wynter waited for Harry to ask about Xay. He didn't have any questions. Didn't matter. She'd tell Caleb and Indio and Jesse. She'd find Xay and *show* them who he was, and what he'd meant to her.

They didn't stay much longer. Harry's house was sad and his presence was depressing. It was like being around Joy, but Joy had the Light and it seemed Harry had nothing.

"I would love to be there when you tell them," Patricia told her when they stopped for a quick lunch on the way back to the cabin, "but I think you should have this moment all to yourself."

Wynter couldn't wait. Joy had worried how their brothers would react. Wynter didn't share those doubts any longer. Soon they would know, and soon after that she'd find Xay.

Xay

Indio was pretty much out of patience. Building the igloo had been pointless and fun. Working under Caleb's supervision was useful, no doubt... and no fun at all. He didn't mind doing the work for Patricia but when Caleb played boss man, every order grated on him.

They were fixing the seven-foot wooden fence down the side of the property, which had long sections broken or leaning. So not only was he working *for* Caleb, he was working *with* him. He did what he was told, because Caleb knew how to fix a fence, but he had a headache from clenching his jaw.

"I'll bet Jesse can help me finish this," he said after Caleb told him for the umpteenth time how to swing a wrecking bar.

Caleb didn't take the hint. "Jesse's gonna start another snowball fight if I give him an outside job."

"So tell him not to."

Caleb gave him a *look*, that look that said *I'm in charge so shut up*. "He has a list of things to do inside, which is the best use of his skills. Can't ask him to do more than he's capable of."

"He can't learn to fix a fence?"

"He'd have gotten bored about twenty yards ago. I don't have the energy to keep him in line today."

Indio turned away so Caleb wouldn't see his exasperation. Jesse was borderline ADHD but he wasn't a baby. Indio grabbed a new paling and set it against the rails, jamming his foot at the base to hold it in place for nailing.

"Check it's straight, please," Caleb said, without looking up from where he was working a few feet farther down.

Indio gritted his teeth, stuck the hammer into his belt, and found the spirit level.

"We're having a tough few days, huh?" Caleb said.

"*We?* We're the same as ever. Wynter and Jesse are having a tough time. Let's see, she gets a creepy visit from the Light and loses her sister, and she's having nightmares and anger issues. Jesse almost gets his head split open and then gets to cry over her scars." His throat closed up on the last word. "You've had it pretty good. You get to boss me around for a bit. You even got lasagne."

"We all lost a sister, Indio. We all suffer when Wynter has a nightmare or reveals some godawful thing from the past. We all feel it when Jesse's hurting so bad he cries."

Indio said nothing and hammered in nails.

Jesse walked up from the back of the house. "Need help moving the refrigerator, if you want me to clean the coils."

Caleb went inside with him, and Indio worked alone, his resentment simmering. He wanted to skip all the drama and just play music with Caleb. That was really the only time they could stand each other's company. Even yesterday, when he told him about those scars, Caleb hadn't *said* anything much about it. Indio could relay the facts, and Caleb could thank him for noticing, but they didn't know how to comfort each other afterward.

Next time he looked up from the fence, Wynter was walking over. She was biting her lip and didn't stop chewing on it until she was standing right next to him.

"I just met Harry," she said.

Of all the things he thought she was going to say, that didn't even make the list.

"Must've been a treat. Do they know?" He nodded toward the cabin.

"Not yet. Caleb is so much like him."

Indio shook his head. "Don't let the blue eyes fool you. They're nothing alike."

"Are *you* more like Harry, then?"

"I hope not."

"Aren't you gonna ask why I visited him?"

He was dying to know, of course, and anxious about it because, generally speaking, nothing good came from visiting Harry. "I figure you'll tell me soon enough."

"*Very* soon. I told Caleb and Jesse I'd fetch you inside. They're in the middle of something, so there's no rush." She looked at the pile of palings. "Can I help you with this?"

He showed her how to pry the old boards free and how to hold the spirit level, and pretty soon he felt just like Caleb must feel showing *him* what to do, passing along knowledge and making sure the job was done right. He looked down the length of fence and had to admit it was satisfying to see it standing up straight, with the new boards pale and fresh against the darker old ones, showing exactly how much work they'd put into it.

Wynter followed his instructions carefully, and every so often she grinned at him for no reason.

Finally, he said, "Your little secret is wearing out its welcome."

"It's not a secret. It's a surprise."

She put down the hammer and nails she was holding for him and wrapped her arms around his neck, and he returned the hug even though he had no idea what was going on.

"What's this for?"

"I don't get the chance very often."

She'd never hugged him quite like *this* either, with the full length of her body pressed against him, and making it last just because it felt good. He tightened his arms around her as a tsunami of emotion flooded through him — the things he'd been pushing down ever since he saw that note wedged into the door of the cabin and watched her non-reaction to being discarded by Joy, and then watched her anger at Jesse boil over, and her self-recriminations after, and seen those lines on her neck and hip and understood what they meant, and listened to her story of being locked up and starved.

And everything magnified through the stress of living in close quarters with Caleb — who was right, because he was always right. This had been a tough few days for Caleb, and Indio felt every one of these emotions just as keenly.

She stood on tiptoe to reach his ear. "You're shaking."

"It's freakin' cold."

They released each other and she said, "Let's go inside. Caleb wants us to bring in firewood."

Indio loaded up her arms with the wood Jesse had split, and grabbed an armful himself, and they went inside via the back door to stack it in the corner of the living room. Wynter took off her coat and sat on the floor with him, and he showed her how to build a fire.

"That's cheating," Jesse said, coming in from the kitchen just as Indio pushed a fire starter into the base of the pile of wood.

"It's a valid shortcut," Indio said. "I'll tell you one thing Harry's good for — he knows how to build a campfire with one match and a few damp sticks."

Jesse's ears visibly pricked up. "What's Harry got to do with anything?" Wynter gave him a look that told him to be patient. "You met with *Harry?*"

She lit the match and Indio carried on, leaving poor Jesse hanging. "We went camping pretty much every summer with Harry, and we always had a great fire every night."

"We should've built a bonfire out back today," Jesse said, pretending like he didn't care what was going on. "We got all that old wood from the fence and the floors, and those cabinets Caleb replaced in the laundry."

Caleb was right behind him. "Another time. We have to drive back this evening, after Patricia feeds us at Patty's."

"Free food — awesome!" Jesse said. "I'm gonna have the bacon triple cheeseburger."

"Sit down," Wynter said, pointing at the couch, "and I'll tell you something even more awesome than free food."

Jesse and Caleb sat on the couch, and Indio stayed where he was, cross-legged on the floor with Wynter as the fire took hold.

She took a deep breath, a smile tugging at the corners of her mouth.

"I have a story to tell... I'll start at the most important part. Harry has another son."

She didn't give them a chance to react. She kept going.

"He's a few months younger than you, Jesse. Patricia took me to meet Harry this morning so I could check it's true, because I only found out when Joy told me a couple months ago. Harry had an affair with a woman named Ember during a Light retreat in San Diego. That's the reason Miriam and Harry's marriage ended. He's your half-brother and his name is Xavier. He only answers to Xay. That's what I called him."

Silence pressed down as they absorbed it. Indio felt the excitement bubbling off her, the thrill of sharing the information that she assumed they would welcome. Indio wasn't sure what to think.

Caleb leaned forward on the couch. "You know him?"

"*Knew* him. He and Ember lived at the ashram for a year. Miriam found out and she made them leave. That was about six months before me and Joy left. I don't know where he is now. I want to find him."

"What's he like?" Jesse said, stunned but curious as ever.

Wynter sat up, eager to share. "He's amazing, Jesse. He was my friend. He was... I don't know if you'd call him musical but he loved music and he loved to sing. Roman was his best friend — they grew up together in Australia. They lived on the farm and I wasn't supposed to talk to them. But I used to sneak through a hole in the fence and meet them in this old storage shed. It was Xay's radio I'd listen to. We'd fight their little wind-up toys in the dirt, or they would play cards. Sometimes they'd clear space for a stage and pretend to be rockstars."

"But you never told us about him?" Jesse glanced at his brothers. "Something good in that place, and you never told us?" He wasn't accusing her of anything, but he was deeply confused.

"Joy didn't want you to know what Harry had done," she said, begging him to understand. "But even before that I didn't tell you because I had to leave everything behind. The good with the bad. And when I did try to find him, it led to danger. But now I'm safe again, and happy, I need you to know and I need to find him."

Indio found himself reassessing everything. He took her left hand, turning her inner wrist up to look at the little cog wheel with the cross in the center.

"He gave you this tattoo. X for Xay."

"Yes." She looked at him with uncertainty, sensing his doubts. "He called me his mechanical doll."

What the hell...?

Before he could put together a coherent response, Caleb said, "How would we find him?" Already in fix-it mode.

"I don't know his second name," Wynter said. "He and Ember may have left the Light or gone back to Australia. Harry never met his son, didn't even know his name. He spoke to Ember once in the last ten years. He doesn't know anything."

"I'll talk to him about it anyway. Jesse, you're the social media wiz — maybe you can track them down, just based on what Wynter already knows. Those aren't common names."

"I'll give it a shot," Jesse said. He asked Wynter, "Did he know about us?"

"No. He told me he didn't know who his father was. All the time he was there, he was Joy's half-brother and neither of them knew it. Maybe he still doesn't know. And Harry... he's ashamed of what he did, which is why he never told you."

"Why didn't Joy want you to tell us?" Caleb asked.

"She didn't want anything to do with Harry, but she didn't want to damage your relationship with him. She thought you'd resent him for the affair. She thought you'd resent Xay for... being born, I guess."

Indio was putting the washed sheets back on his bunk, in preparation for leaving, when Wynter found him.

"You were quiet all afternoon," she said. "Aren't you even a bit excited about Xay?"

"Sure, why not? I'm getting used to new siblings popping up out of the woodwork." He smiled, but it felt strained. This felt all kinds of wrong and he couldn't articulate why.

Wynter sat on the other bunk, watching him. He wasn't off the hook. He sat, too, facing her.

"Was Roman the same age as Xay?" he asked.

"Yes."

"See, this is the part I don't get. I assumed Roman was one of the kids from your classroom. I assumed that tattoo was drawn by one of those kids. Someone your own age. Xay and Roman were — how old? Sixteen, when you met them? And you were—?"

"Thirteen."

"That's like a seventh grader making friends with high school juniors. Sneaking out at night to hang with them? That's... odd."

"I lived in an odd place."

"True," he conceded. He was finding it hard, very hard, to think of this boy as a brother. He was someone important from Wynter's past, and for that reason Indio needed to make the effort to accept him.

"It didn't feel odd to me," she said. "Xay was always kind to me. He couldn't protect me from the teachers — he didn't know what was going on with them anyway. But he tried to comfort me. He protected me from Roman."

"Why did you need protection from Roman?"

"He could be a bit mean."

Indio had promised not to ask questions. This one he had to ask. "Did Roman ever hurt you?"

She hesitated, a brief intake of breath. "He said things sometimes. He was confused and angry and had some strange ideas. They said he had a dark heart, that the Light couldn't get in. They treated him harshly because of it, and sometimes he lashed out. Xay could calm him down, just by being his friend. And Xay was always there to defend me when Roman said the wrong thing. I felt safe with Xay. You have no idea how important it was, in that place, to have someone who made me feel safe."

"I do understand." Indio took her hand and rubbed it between his, consumed by his doubts. "I'm glad you had someone. But if Xay didn't know he shared four half-siblings with you, if he didn't know of that connection — why did he want to be *your* friend?"

From the way her expression darkened, and the way she withdrew her hand from his, he knew she understood now what he was getting at.

"It wasn't like what you're imagining. At first, I stole batteries for his radio. So, he was grateful, I guess. After that, he liked telling me all about the music we listened to, and about his life in Australia because he hated the ashram so much. He liked telling me what the outside world was like. Same as Jesse telling me about physics or bacon or Instagram. Same as you teaching me the hexatonic blues scale, and Caleb teaching me karate."

"You're saying he was like a big brother."

She touched her tattoo. "Would you do this to me?"

"Brand you?" She winced at that. "Of course not."

"Then he wasn't like a big brother. He was something else, and it was something good." She was massaging her little finger as she spoke. "I need you to understand... I need to explain. I did break this finger. Someone slammed the piano lid down. I pulled away just in time, so she grabbed my hand and forced it back on the keys, and slammed the lid again to make sure I learned my lesson. My finger swelled up and the nail went black. Xay bandaged it with a stick for a splint, and Roman went into a tirade about how he was doing it wrong, how it had to be strapped to the next finger."

A deep breath shuddered from her lungs. He reached across and took her hand again, enclosing it between his hands, just holding on, and she calmed down.

"We were kids," she said, "fumbling around with no one to help us. Roman was hard to love, but I loved Xay. I didn't know what to call it, but it was love. I loved him because he sat there for ten minutes arguing with Roman about the best way to bandage my finger. Like it was important. Like *I* was important. For weeks, I made him re-wrap the bandage every time I saw him, even after it stopped hurting."

She loosened her hand from his and examined the finger.

"Doesn't bend right, so he probably did do it wrong. But he put his time and his love into trying to fix things. Trying to fix my world. When you meet him, you'll see. He helped me survive — by *not* hurting me, by not holding me down so someone else could hurt me, by not filling me with fear with a look. He was just *there*, in that shed. Our safe place. He noticed me and that meant I existed. He was someone I could run to."

"Who does he look like?" Jesse said on the drive to Patty's. "I bet he has my amazing hair."

"His hair is nothing like yours," Wynter said. "It's Indio's color but sort of muddier. Or maybe that was dirt — all of us were pretty dirty. It *is* curly. Much messier and a bit wooly, which might also have been because of the dirt."

"Is he as smart as me?"

"Would that be a problem if he was?"

"My ego is gonna take a hit if my *baby* brother is smarter than me."

"He knew a lot about the world, that's all I can say. Of course, I knew nothing so he seemed smart to me. He was fun and easy going at first. The ashram made him resentful and bored, and he'd get this intense brow like the one Caleb wears most of the time—"

"What did she say about my brow?" Caleb said in the driver's seat.

"—and that Indio gets when he's on stage."

"I can be intense," Jesse said defensively. "What sort of music does he like?"

"Exactly the same as what I liked when you first met me, because he taught me everything I knew."

"Does he have an Aussie accent?"

"Of course. He taught me two-up and he tried, and failed, to explain the rules of cricket. He taught me all sorts of slang."

"Such as?"

"He and Roman would say things like *this arvo*, for afternoon, and *dunny* for toilet. They'd say they were *buggered* from working all day — that means tired. And they called each other *mate* instead of dude or bro or whatever you say."

"I don't say dude."

"Yeah, you do."

"Pretty sure I only say dude when I'm high."

"I wouldn't know about that, would I." Indio caught her giving the back of Caleb's head a meaningful look to acknowledge their sesh in the igloo that she'd interrupted. "You've actually called *me* dude a couple times, when you're in the middle of explaining something and you forget who you're talking to."

"No way," Jesse said. "Sorry about that."

"So, are you eager to meet him?"

Indio couldn't help feeling she wanted Jesse to express his eagerness only to punish Indio for his lack of enthusiasm.

"Absolutely! I'm dying to meet him. Although... now I have two younger siblings, that means I'm well and truly the middle child. I think that's supposed to be bad. Indio, as a long-time middle child, is that bad?"

"Yes," Indio said bluntly.

"Indio isn't as happy, for some reason," Wynter said.

"I'm happy, baby. Yesterday I thought I was living in a horror movie. Today it's turned into a soap opera. It's all good."

Caleb gave him a sharp look. Indio decided not to attempt another joke on the subject.

Royal Flush

Jesse spent the last few days of the year trying to find his new half-brother on the internet. In the past he'd tracked down buddies from grade school in Montana, and his old soccer coach, and even a random guy from South Africa he once met at a gig — but he couldn't find any trace of Xay.

"Xay is a place in Laos in southeast Asia," he told Caleb. "It's creating a lot of noise when I do any kind of search on that word. I've tried Xavier, too, pairing it with Ember and Arizona and Light, all sorts of things. I can't find anything relevant."

"Maybe he changed his name completely."

"Can we get a private investigator?"

"Sure. We'll do that next week after we win the lottery."

"I'm just throwing ideas out there. I do have another idea. Wynter won't like it."

Jesse drove down to Enumclaw on New Year's Eve to fetch Wynter. She was quiet in the car and he wondered if she was going to tell him what was wrong, or if he should ask first, or if she intended to tell Caleb when they got home. There was a time, not too long ago, when he'd have told her to spit it out. Now he was never quite sure what he should say. The more he found out about her past, the harder it got.

"Did you ever see those lines on Madeline's arms?" she said suddenly.

"Yeah. It's called cutting."

"Why does she do that?"

"I don't know why *she* does it, specifically."

"She wasn't there when I got back after Christmas."

"Where is she?"

"She went to visit her mom — she told me it was for two days. Debra and Brian told me she was still there, and then they admitted she was in the hospital. And now she's been moved to another foster home. A group home. Debra packed up all her stuff and a social worker came to collect it."

"Why was she in the hospital?" Jesse was pretty sure he could guess.

"They wouldn't tell me. Do you think she tried to kill herself?"

"I don't know. How would I know?"

"Because if she was sick or broke her leg or something, they would've told me that. She used to cut herself at night. She'd light a candle like it was some sort of ritual, and she used a razor blade. She never cared if I was asleep or not. She said she didn't know why she did it. I thought it was like having a tattoo — I mean, she did it really carefully, really neatly. I thought she liked the way it looked. But now I think it was something awful."

"She's pretty messed up, Wyn. I think you're probably right about why she was in the hospital. Deb and Brian didn't tell you because they didn't want to upset you. And the cutting... That's something kids do when they don't know how to express emotional pain."

He was terrified of saying the wrong thing. Wynter didn't express her emotional pain very well, either. *Only her mechanical body walked out* — that was how she'd once described it to Indio. And Xay called her a mechanical doll — what was that all about? She'd emptied herself out, pretended like it never happened so she could fill herself up with new experiences in this world. But it *had* happened, and pieces of it kept resurfacing.

"They won't tell me where she is," Wynter said. "I feel so badly for her. She told people at school we were sisters. Not foster sisters — real sisters. Everyone knew it was a lie, and she knew they knew, and she kept embellishing the story anyway. I should've made more effort to bring her home with me at Christmas, just for a day or two. She could've seen what a proper family is like."

"She'd get a pretty distorted view of a proper family if she stayed with us."

"What's wrong with our family?"

"Our family is awesome, most of it, most of the time. But it's not typical."

"She'd have seen people who like and love each other. Her mom isn't interested in her, like ours isn't, but at least we have each other. She has that horrible druggie brother, and there's a baby she's not allowed to be alone with. Her mom's boyfriend won't even let her hold it."

"She's out of your life now. Please don't stress about it."

"I can't stop thinking about her."

Jesse pulled up in the driveway, switched off the engine, and turned to her. "Madeline got dealt a horrible hand, and that's too bad. You were her friend for a while. You did what you could, and that helped her whether or not you can see how. But you're not responsible for anyone else's happiness or healing."

"You act like you're responsible for mine."

Did he? That would have to change before she became too dependent.

Not just yet. Maybe when she was sixteen. Or after high school.

"Well, I'm not responsible," he said emphatically. "In the end you get to decide what to do with the horrible hand *you* were dealt."

She smiled and spontaneously threw herself across the car for a hug. "My hand is looking pretty nice right now. A straight, maybe even a flush. When Indio moves home it'll be a full house. Literally! And when we find Xay... that's a royal flush."

"A royal flush never happens."

She pulled back and her face fell. "Is that your way of saying we won't find him?"

"No. Statistically, a royal flush almost never happens, except in the movies. I mean, it *could* happen. The odds are tiny."

"What are the odds?"

"In Texas Hold'em, it's 1 in 23,000."

"Did you just work that out?"

"Nope. I'm brilliant but I'm not a computer. I looked it up. I know all the odds, and I still can't beat Indio." He swung open his door. Before he got out, he said, "How many years do we have to play poker in order to see a royal flush if we play one game a week, twenty hands per game?"

"I don't know. How many?"

"I'm asking you to work it out. If you can tell me the answer before we get inside the house, I'll tell you my surefire plan to find Xay."

"Can I round off a bit?"

"Just a bit."

They got out and walked up the path, Wynter doing the mental arithmetic aloud.

"So... twenty hands per week is about 1000 hands per year. One thousand into 23,000... That's twenty-three years. Wow."

"But we got four people playing — four times as many chances per hand."

"That's only five years and nine months, then. And if we include Xay, once we find him, we have five people playing. Now it's only four-and-a-half years. That's gonna happen, for sure. Several times in our lifetimes, in fact."

"We were assuming the hands are independent, which they're not because your cards depend to some extent on what other people already have in their—"

"Jesse, shut up and tell me about your surefire plan to find Xay."

They went into the kitchen, where he made her sit and take out her phone while he sorted out lunch.

"Listen up. I can't find him online, but what if he's looking for *you*? He would never find you because you keep refusing to get on social media. We have to use what he already knows about you, in case he's been trying to look you up."

"He doesn't know anything. Not my full name, because even I didn't know it. Not anything about you or Harry. He wouldn't know to look for me in Seattle. He probably thinks I'm still in Arizona, and he'll never get any information out of the ashram."

"We'll get you accounts on a couple of different platforms."

"I'm not loving the idea, Jesse. I don't want my life on the internet. You told me it's easy to put information onto the web, but hard to erase it if you change your mind."

"You don't have to maintain the accounts or put anything too personal. We add some photos and enough info so he'd know it's you. He could contact you via the message systems on those sites."

"Can't I just join your account?"

"That's not how it works. Everyone has their own account."

Wynter agreed to the bare minimum, and Jesse made her sign up there and then while he dished out reheated leftovers. They sorted through photos — the Halloween picture, one of her and Caleb playing guitars in the jamroom, and her middle school graduation photo — and uploaded those. Jesse wrote her a profile to include a list of bands she and Xay liked, and important keywords — *Arizona, light, joy.*

"So we just wait?" she said, when it was done.

"Yes, we wait, and we get on with life."

"Are you going to the party tonight with Delia?"

"Yes, with *Delilah*."

"Can I come?"

"Yes, if it was up to me, but... no. Caleb's home at six, and I got grape soda so the two of you can chink glasses at midnight."

"I don't think he should stay up late. Doesn't he have to work tomorrow? And all those appointments?"

"It's your first New Year's Eve! You have to stay up. Caleb's fine. He survived the cabin, didn't he? He worked hard and he survived."

Wynter didn't look so sure about that. She'd been overly cautious about Caleb since he came home after the accident. "I'm gonna pretend to be too tired to stay up. He'll go to bed early if I do."

Jesse groaned. "You're all so boring. I'm the only interesting person in this family."

"Xay is interesting. I keep thinking he's like Caleb, because he looked after me, or like Indio, because he felt things so deeply. Now, I think, it's you he's gonna get along with the best."

"I could've told you that, because I get along with everybody. Even people I vehemently disagree with. I can't wait to learn about cricket."

She narrowed her eyes, checking to see if he was being sarcastic. He kept his expression neutral.

"Can we jam this afternoon?" she said.

"We'll do that tomorrow. Today, we'll make gaming videos for my channel."

"That's your thing, not mine."

"I'm gonna make videos of you playing Dishonored and Mass Effect 3 while I narrate how badly you're doing it. It'll make you a more interesting person, and it'll be funny as hell."

"Funny for you, maybe."

"We'll follow your progress over the next few months. The series will be called *Wyn for the Win*. I've already designed a crappy logo, which Indio is gonna spruce up when you ask him nicely. You get fifty percent of whatever we earn from it."

"I'll do it for one hundred percent."

"Why would I agree to that? What do I get out of it?"

"You get to laugh at me. And I'm only doing this if we also make videos of me teaching you the guitar, so I can laugh at you."

"I'll do that, if we also make videos of me teaching you drums, so *everyone* can laugh at you."

"Deal."

Thread

"New house rule," Jesse announced. "January third shall hereafter be known as Hot Chocolate Day. In honor of the anniversary of your arrival in Seattle, Wyn."

"More of a proclamation than a rule," Indio said. He was home for two days, his last visit before college started on Monday. He had a pretty relaxed schedule for the coming semester, and then he was done with college forever.

"The *rule* is that everyone drinks hot chocolate on January third. I bought marshmallows specially for the occasion."

Jesse came in from the kitchen bearing a tray of mugs and handed them out. They were watching one of his 'sixties sci-fi movies, or rather *enduring* it, waiting for Caleb to come home so they could drive to Patty's to eat.

"I'll take those marshmallows on the side, thanks," Indio said.

"Too late, I already put them in."

"Gross."

Wynter took a sip, leaving a line of powdered sugar from the marshmallows on her top lip. "Don't you like marshmallows?"

"I'm not a fan, and even less so in hot chocolate." He fished out the slimy lumps and dropped them on the tray.

"When you move to Seattle, you can control how the hot chocolate is served," she said sweetly.

"*When?*"

"You told me you'll finish all your credits by March. You should be looking for a job in Seattle already."

"I have a job in Portland. I've been doing work for a design company since November, and they've offered me a big fat contract starting the end of March."

"Dude, that's great!" Jesse said.

"It's *not* great," Wynter admonished him. "Seattle has design companies."

"Not one that's offered me a big fat contract," Indio shot back.

"You haven't *looked* in Seattle!"

"Wyn, once you move home, there's no room for Indio in this house anyway," Jesse said. He'd be just as happy as Wynter if Indio moved home, but at least he wasn't being impossible about it.

Wynter had the solution. "He can share with you."

"I shared with him for fifteen years. I served my time."

"We could turn the jamroom into a bedroom."

"Then where will we jam?"

"We could turn the dining room into the jamroom."

"Then where will we eat?"

"You told me you never used that room to eat until I arrived. We'll eat at the kitchen counter."

"No, we eat in the dining room now because we're civilized people."

"Can we build another room?"

"I'm not moving to Seattle," Indio said, to shut it down. Wynter gave him a long, thoughtful look. He glared back, wondering what was brewing in that brain of hers. She returned her attention to the movie.

As soon as Caleb walked in the door, she became nervous, psyching herself up to tell him something. As they pulled on jackets and hats, preparing to head out, she finally got there.

"Tomorrow, I'm taking the bus downtown."

Caleb frowned. "By yourself?"

"Yes. I have the money you gave me at Christmas so I might go shopping. Girlie things. You'd be bored silly."

"Since when do you buy girlie things?" Jesse said.

"Since I'm almost sixteen," she replied snootily, and Jesse suppressed a chortle.

"I'll drop you off and pick you up after," Caleb said. "I can find something to do around town."

"I'm taking the bus. I want to be independent."

Caleb's protective instincts were at war with his rational acknowledgment that Wynter did need a chance now and then to become more independent — Indio knew this because he was having exactly the same reaction. He kept quiet about it.

"Let's talk about this again tomorrow," Caleb said, no doubt to avoid an argument on their evening out.

Indio woke up Saturday morning to find Caleb, Jesse and Wynter all doing her tai chi, or whatever it was, on the patio. Somehow they'd all managed to get outside without him waking up on the couch. He took advantage of the vacant shower and then went to find food. On the breakfast bar was a public transportation timetable printed off the computer, with a map of downtown Seattle on the back. Was this Caleb's way of saying Wynter had won?

Indio got out the largest pan he could find and cooked bacon. The smell brought everyone inside, and he forked the bacon onto a plate.

While waiting for the coffee, Caleb slid the timetable across the counter to Wynter. "We'll take the bus together, as this is your first time."

"I can manage a thirty-minute bus ride!" Wynter blurted out. "I take a bus to school every day, all by my little self."

"You mean the safe bus on a familiar route, full of school kids?" Caleb said.

Jesse did a double-take. "Was that... was that an attempt at *sarcasm*? If Caleb ever masters sarcasm the universe will explode."

Wynter was the one who looked like she was going to explode. "Are all the weekend buses in Seattle full of perverts or something? You sound like Rosa."

Caleb gave her a look that made her flush in shame.

Indio put slices of bread to fry in the bacon grease, which made Caleb wince in horror and Jesse suck his lips in anticipation. Wynter couldn't win against Caleb, but maybe Indio could soften the blow.

"I was gonna drop by Frankie's," he said. "You remember E Sharp, the music store, Wynter? I can take you all the way in on the bike, and you could take the bus back when you're done."

Caleb took a few seconds to get with the program — not that he would call it a compromise. He'd call it a sensible plan to keep Wynter safe while allowing her age-appropriate freedom. "That's a great idea. I'll meet you at the bus stop after, and walk you home."

"The stop is four minutes away!" Wynter said. "And you don't like me riding on the back of his bike."

"Not true. I just prefer you on the back of mine, when there's a choice."

The way Wynter was assessing Indio convinced him she was hiding something. Shopping for girlie things was nowhere near the forefront of her mind. He flipped the sizzling bread as she tried to come up with an excuse for why the new plan was unacceptable. She failed.

"Once Indio drops you off," Caleb said, "you need to text me every half hour until you're back on the bus."

"I'll never remember to do that."

"Okay, I'll text *you* every half hour and you need to respond. Just a smiley or something."

Wynter huffed. "How about a kissy face, because I'll be *so* very happy to know you're keeping tabs on me?"

Jesse was finding the entire conversation hilarious. "Wow, you've suddenly become a smart-mouthed teenager. I skipped this stage altogether, by the way. If you want any tips, let me know."

Wynter glowered at him.

"So, we're clear on the rules of this little excursion?" Caleb said.

"Yes," she muttered. "But you only text me every hour."

"Every half hour."

Wynter growled in frustration, which made Jesse laugh out loud, which made her punch his arm.

After their greasy, delicious breakfast, Indio went downstairs so Jesse could play him the rhythm tracks for the songs he and Wynter had recorded over the New Year, after Indio had gone back to Portland.

"This one, *When the Sky Falls*, this is gonna make us famous," Jesse said. "As long as you don't screw up the vocals."

"You mean like you screwed up the outro?"

"I didn't screw up. Wynter told me to do it double-time."

"I'll have a word with her."

"She kind of took over the whole recording session. I'm not complaining or anything. She has an instinctive feel for the overall sound."

"Doesn't surprise me. How's your search for our long-lost brother going?"

"Hit a wall. He's vanished. Caleb's been on the phone to Harry a couple times and got nothing useful."

"Maybe he was a figment of her imagination all along," Indio joked.

"Ah, but then who drew the tatt?"

"Did she tell you why she's going downtown?"

"Nope. She's being mysterious and very... teenagery today."

Indio decided not to tell Jesse his suspicions. Wynter got on the bike and they rode into town. She seemed happy enough to visit E Sharp with him. Frankie wasn't in, so it would be a quick trip. Indio grabbed what he needed. Wynter had no reason to be there — she didn't even browse the guitars.

"Where d'you want me to drop you off?" he said, getting back on the bike.

"I can walk from here." She didn't take the helmet he offered, or hop on.

"Walk where? Come on, I'll take you."

"Um, Walmart?" She'd clearly named the first store that popped into her head.

Her phone pinged and she rolled her eyes before tapping a reply to Caleb.

"What's going on, Wynter?"

"I have an appointment and it's private."

"Like, a doctor's appointment?"

"No. Someone I know."

He grinned. "A boy?"

"No."

"A girl?"

"No."

"Are you really gonna walk there from here?"

"I'm calling a taxi, just as soon as you leave."

"How can you afford a taxi?"

"Caleb gave me fifty dollars for Christmas."

"You got free transport right here." He slapped the seat behind him. Part of him was enjoying watching her squirm, and part of him was anxious about the secrecy.

"There's something I need to do. Can you leave me alone, please?"

"No, baby, I'm not leaving you alone." He kept his tone playful, but he was worried as hell now. "Get on the bike and tell me where you wanna go."

Her mouth was a thin, flat line, her eyes hard. If he was Jesse, he'd make fun of her expression right now — it was both cute and perplexing. But then Jesse would probably throw his hands up and ride off, annoyed he couldn't persuade her but happy enough to let her win. Caleb would just force her to go home unless she gave up her secret.

Indio wasn't going to leave her or force her into doing anything. He waited for her to come to the right decision.

She said, "I'm going to visit Harry."

"Is he home?" Harry worked security and his hours were all over the place.

"Yes. I looked up his number in the directory and I texted him to arrange it."

"Okay. We can visit Harry. I haven't seen him since Christmas—"

"I need you to not be there. I need Caleb to not find out."

"Is this about Xay?"

"No, nothing to do with Xay. Nothing to do with anyone. I haven't even told Harry why, yet."

What on earth could it be? He couldn't think of a single point of commonality between the two of them. Except for Miriam. Surely it couldn't be Miriam.

"Look, I'll take you to Harry's. I'll wait outside if you want."

She considered this. He knew she'd agree to it. It took her a while longer.

"Okay. You can't tell Caleb."

"I won't. He's gonna wonder why you came home without buying anything."

"I'll tell him we went for a long ride instead. That's the truth, too." God forbid she lie to Caleb. "We need to stop at the store for baby carrots and peanut butter."

She got on the bike and he took her to Everett.

Harry wanted Indio to come inside. Wynter told him to wait outside, so he did. She was in there for a good thirty minutes, and then she said he could come in. He visited with Harry while she sat on the back stoop feeding Lexie the carrots and peanut butter. She'd spent a long time choosing that peanut butter at the store — it had to be raw, sugar free, and salt free. She must've Googled *peanut butter suitable for dogs* before she came here today.

Indio had been to Harry's place only a couple of times, and this visit went like the others. Harry tried to get him to take a beer, he refused because he didn't want to sit around getting comfortable, and then they talked about his band and his studies and Harry pretended like he was interested. It may have been genuine interest — it was always hard to tell and Indio never gave his father the benefit of the doubt.

As with any encounter with Harry, certain things weren't spoken of. Joy's return to Arizona. Jesse's split lip. And Xay. There was nothing to say about Xay that wouldn't require talking about Miriam. And the last thing either of them wanted to talk about was Miriam.

Indio used Wynter as his excuse to leave, saying he had to get her home because Jesse had a study session planned. By now the dog was delirious, having been spoiled with treats and tummy rubs. Harry and Wynter parted on cool, formal terms, just as you'd expect given this was only the second time they'd met. Neither gave any indication of what they'd talked about.

Indio took her down to the marina and they found a farmer's market to stroll around. He bought kettle corn for a snack, and she made him buy horribly expensive shrimp for Caleb, who loved seafood, and a big bag of purplish "heirloom tomatoes" for Jesse's next cooking adventure, although neither of them knew what they were.

They walked along the jetty and he showed her how to skim stones. She was not a fan of large bodies of water, perhaps because she couldn't swim.

"Caleb will make you take swimming lessons when you move home," he warned her. "I'll bet he already has your schedule lined up. Swimming, defensive driving, karate, shooting range."

"Would he teach me to ride a motorcycle?"

"I doubt it."

"He can't stop me when I'm eighteen."

"He'll find a way."

Her face screwed up because she couldn't make the stones skip more than twice.

"Seems like *you* found a way, today," he said. "What was your plan? Hop off the bus after a couple stops and call a taxi from there?"

"Yes. You wrecked everything. No one was supposed to know."

"I'm learning your tells."

"What does that mean?"

"I saw the signs that what you were saying aloud to Caleb was the opposite of what you were thinking."

"What signs?"

"I'm not saying. You might stop doing it and I'd lose the advantage. Caleb should've guessed you were lying about going downtown to 'shop'." He put air quotes around the word, because Wynter wasn't much of a shopper at the best of times.

"I said I *might* go shopping. I didn't lie."

"Well, I'm glad I saved you a taxi fare."

"I didn't ask you to."

"This is the only time I've ever interfered, baby. Gimme a break."

She smiled to show she was okay with it, after all.

"So," he said, "any hints on what this is all about?"

"I set a plan in motion. Now I'll sit back and see what happens." She glanced sideways at him. "Don't worry, it's nothing bad. If it doesn't work out, you'll never even know."

"So, this is Wynter at *almost* sixteen."

"Yes. I'm getting stronger. In my business class I learned something about how the world works, and I'm using it."

"Glad to hear school's useful for something."

"You better watch out, Indio. You're next on my list."

He held out his arms. "I'm right here. Do your worst."

"You're moving back to Seattle in March, so you need to start looking for a job now."

"Already have a job, like I told you guys yesterday."

"No, that's no good. You're moving here."

Wow, she was serious.

"Baby, we talked about this."

"I know you have a reason not to. You have *two* reasons to do so. Me and Jesse. Maybe Harry, too. I think you're his favorite."

"Unlikely."

"I'm just going by one thirty-minute conversation, so, as Jesse would say, the sample size is small. You're the one he's most proud of."

"Even if that's true, what difference does it make?" Indio squatted to pick up more stones, an excuse to avoid meeting her eye. "He spent my childhood beating me up and tearing me down."

"I know you wish you weren't like him. In some ways you are. Even what you said just then — *What difference does it make?* That's what he would say, because he doesn't know how to connect with his family. The difference is, he's all alone with no idea how to reach out. You've got us and you *have* reached out. You can reach a little bit further, can't you?"

"I'm not like him." Indio picked up and discarded stones at random. "If I had kids, I'd take care of them. If I had a family, I wouldn't throw it all away over some starry-eyed teenager in a cult."

"I'm sure Harry thought the same way when he was twenty-two."

Now she was just irritating him. Not deliberately. Only because of his own reluctance to talk about his father.

"Why are you doing this?" he said, straightening to cast one last stone across the water. "You think you can rescue me?"

"I *am* going to rescue you. I know how to, because we started out in the same place — that place where she left us because we weren't enough for her. We became nothing but shame and fear because of the things we did, and the things that were done to us." She had become still and intense, gazing at the water, and somehow that stilled him, too. He found himself utterly unable to speak or move as he watched her. "I walked out of that place. You can walk out, too. You can cut that part out and look for people who love you, and take what they're offering. It's so easy, Indio, because when they love you, they give it to you for free." She looked over at him, eyes narrowing as she assessed him. "Took me about two days to figure it out. It's taking you a lot longer, but you can do it."

The challenge in her tone revealed she truly did have expectations of him. A flicker of irritation returned, breaking the spell.

"It's a bit more complicated than—"

"It's not. It's simple. It really is."

He turned to the water, hiding from her. She did make it sound simple, seductively so. As soon as he considered the logistics, it felt impossible. He'd never intended to move back to Seattle and her heartfelt analysis wasn't going to change his mind this afternoon.

It changed *something*, though. He felt it in the pit of his stomach — the newly spun thread that had started as little more than instinct, it was becoming a visceral connection that bound them closer. She knew how to stir his darkest fears and wasn't afraid of doing so. Fears he'd never before articulated. It was unsettling, that she could see so clearly.

And reassuring, as well, to realize he was loved by someone who understood the darkest parts of his soul because she'd suffered the same.

This wasn't right, this thread that connected them. He had no right to it. To her. He shook his head to clear it, though his heart remained heavy.

He faced her again. "So, what's next on this list of yours?"

"Caleb. I need to find him a girlfriend."

Scolded

"Are you gonna tell him or shall I?" Jesse said as he and Wynter joined Caleb in the truck outside her foster home.

Wynter opened her mouth to speak.

"She aced the Geometry final," Jesse said, unable to contain himself. "Not the real one. A practice one. Ninety-four percent. You know what that means?"

"That she's worked real hard and deserves ice cream?" Caleb said, setting out for downtown Enumclaw to find a restaurant for lunch. It was Sunday afternoon, and his twenty-sixth birthday. Jesse had ridden his bike down the day before for an overnight visit.

"It means Jesse's the best teacher in the world," Wynter said, pleased with herself nonetheless.

"It *means*," Jesse said, "assuming she aces the *actual* test next week, she can start Algebra II this semester. She's supposed to be in tenth grade anyway. She'll finish by June, and with summer school combined with my unparalleled tuition she can complete Pre-calculus, too."

"There's more to high school than math, Jess."

"I've written an intensive study schedule across all subjects. It all works out. She can take her SATs this October."

"At sixteen?"

"Why not? I did."

"Is that what you want to do, hun?" Caleb said over his shoulder, concerned that Wynter didn't understand what she was getting herself into.

"It's fine by me. I got nothing else to do."

"There's also more to high school than the academics."

"Teenagers spend four hours a day on their phones, texting and using social media," Jesse said. "Wynter doesn't do that, so that's three-and-a-half thousand hours until graduation for her to get ahead."

"She might not use her phone *now*. That could change. Hun, you need to do what's best for you."

"I don't mind doing extra study." Wynter leaned forward from the back seat to poke Jesse in the ribs. "If it means I can spend *three-and-a-half thousand hours* with my unparalleled tutor."

"I'm gonna pretend you're expressing your genuine feelings," Jesse grumbled.

At the restaurant, she turned the topic to the thing she actually *did* care about, taking a seat beside Caleb and asking, "When will you get your foster license?"

"I finished my last parenting class this week. Svetlana's on board with it. She doesn't see a problem placing you with me, once the license is granted. I still have to do an interview at the agency's office, and yesterday was the first home visit."

"Did we pass?" Jesse asked sarcastically, still smarting a year after Tina had found their home wanting.

"We have a few things to fix up. I have to lock up the alcohol, the paint thinner and gasoline and power tools. And your weed, Jesse. You can't leave it lying around or smoke it when Wynter's home. You two can go through the first aid kit to see what's missing — I have a checklist. We need a fire escape diagram and we have to do a quarterly fire drill."

Jesse had his head in his hands, laughing under his breath. "Power tools?"

"I thought you'd be more upset about the weed," Wynter said.

"That's, like, a once-a-month thing. I'll survive. But they think you're gonna cut your arm off with a power tool? That's insane."

"That's only the start of it," Caleb said. "Wynter, you'll still meet once a month with Svetlana, like you've been doing. She can do unannounced visits, too. She needs to approve vacations longer than three days, and out-of-state trips. She needs to approve a haircut."

"Uh... what?" Jesse said. "I think Wynter can manage her own hair."

"Haircuts and piercings need approval. For the record, so do blood tests, surgery, contraception and major medical treatment. You're not allowed to do high risk activities like skiing or trampolining."

"Trampolines are high risk now?"

"I don't intend to get on a trampoline," Wynter said. "These rules are just silly. Why can't you approve those things?"

"The state will still have custody of you, hun, even though I'm your brother."

"Two more years of their rules?" She already looked like she was planning a rebellion. "I don't mind *your* rules. The rest isn't fair."

Life ain't fair. Caleb resisted the urge to give her that useless platitude. He had never used the line on his brothers, and he wouldn't use it now.

"Focus on the good parts," he said. "You'll be home. You can redecorate that bedroom, finally. Make it your own."

"My bedroom is perfect just as it is. This is gonna be a good year, I just know it. You'll meet Xay. Indio will move to Seattle. You'll find a wonderful girlfriend. And Jesse... well, nothing ever goes wrong in your life."

"Delilah dumped me. That was pretty traumatic."

"Why?"

"I told her *The Matrix* was ethically deficient."

"Is that a movie? Can I watch it?"

"When we reach the 'nineties. We haven't even started on the 'seventies yet."

"Will you dump me unless I agree it's ethically deficient?"

"But you *will* agree, because I'm right."

Wynter made a dismissive sound in her throat and turned to Caleb. "When d'you think Xay will find me?"

"It's been two weeks," Caleb said. "Give it some time."

Out of the blue, Indio got a text from Caleb saying he was driving to Portland on Friday night, and wanted to meet up before Indio's gig.

Someone was in trouble. Indio was fairly sure *he* hadn't done anything that required a face-to-face conversation, and Jesse was never a problem, so that meant either Harry had screwed up or Wynter was being... well, *almost*-sixteen again.

They met at a pub to eat, after soundcheck. Indio couldn't recall the last time he and Caleb had had a meal out together, just the two of them. Quite possibly, it had never happened. They both felt the awkwardness of the situation, the forced intimacy of sitting opposite each other with only two feet of table between them.

Indio let Caleb talk about their siblings, looking for clues that one of them was the reason for the visit. He didn't have much to say in return. He could ask how Caleb was coping with returning to full-time work. What was the point? Caleb wasn't going to admit to any reservations when it came to his physical fitness.

"How's Wynter finding that Talman?" he asked instead.

"She loves it. She still asks me before she plays it, like she needs permission."

"I'll buy something just for her. Something special, but not yet. Maybe in another year. Still figuring out the perfect instrument."

"She's teaching Jesse to play, and he's teaching her drums. It's a disaster on both counts, at least to my ear. The two of them are somehow four times louder than Jesse alone. They stir each other up. Have you seen those gaming videos he makes her do?"

"I have. They're hilarious."

"Well, maybe they are. Not sure they're... you know, respectful."

"Is she having fun with it?"

"I guess."

"Then leave them to it," Indio said. "He told me he wants to do a cooking series using his patented scheduling method — she can make fun of his chopping skills and his pedantry."

He watched his brother turning his beer bottle around and around. Caleb was not a fidgeter, and clearly he didn't come here just to complain about Jesse's YouTube channel.

Indio waited him out.

Caleb pushed the beer aside and folded his arms on the table. "There's something else. Something kind of weird. Harry called me. He says he'll give me fifty thousand dollars for a down payment on a new house."

Now, that was a surprise.

"Not a *new* house, of course. A bigger house. Maybe something a little farther out, a fixer-upper."

"Is he serious?" Nothing ever came of Harry's good intentions.

"He's just sold his place to a developer, with a ten-day settlement. They've been chomping at the bit to get his property. He says he'll rent something cheap, or maybe live on that damn sieve of a sailboat. It's just sitting there in his shed right now."

"Did you tell him you wanted to move?"

"No. But thirteen hundred square feet is feeling kinda cramped. It was fine for me and Jesse, but we need more space. I have almost no equity in the house, so his money is the only way I can do it."

"Wynter loves that house."

"It was the first house she ever saw. I could find something else she'll love. She still has this notion you're moving home after graduation." He held up a hand to stop Indio's protest. "I know that's not gonna happen. Still, we need a room for when you visit, and a bit more privacy for Jesse. We could find something with a bigger basement. Maybe a bit of land."

"That's some grand plans you got. What d'you think prompted Harry's generos..." Indio swallowed the sentence as the answer came to him. He smiled to himself, shaking his head.

"What?" Caleb said.

"No, nothing. I was wondering why Harry decided all of a sudden to act like a decent father."

"Maybe his mid-life crisis involves fantasies about living on a boat. I don't know."

Indio knew. He didn't know *how* she'd done it, but he knew she'd done it.

"Anyway, I'll wait until I have his money in my bank account before I tell the other two," Caleb was saying. "Knowing him, he'll forget what he promised." He sat back, still troubled.

"You staying for the gig tonight?" Indio said, to fill the silence.

"Sure. Haven't seen Blunderbelly in a year."

"I'll put Neil Young on the setlist, just for you. I'm thinking *Heart of Gold.* We do a sort of rocked-up reggae version of it."

"Nice."

"Yeah. Someone told me I should reach out more."

"I got big plans, son, big plans."

Harry handed Caleb a beer and settled into a deck chair on the driveway. They'd spent the day patching the fiberglass hull of Harry's thirty-foot sailboat. Harry, always looking for the quick fix, would've been happy to slap some resin on the damaged areas. Caleb insisted they cut out and patch the problems. After that, they'd prepared the boat for transport twenty-five miles down the road, to the Shilshole Bay Marina — securing the gear and starting the process of boxing up Harry's possessions.

"I'll do a test run down to San Francisco," Harry said. "Should be ready to go by August. What d'you think?"

"Sounds ambitious. You don't even have sails."

"I'll get there. We'll get there, won't we, Lexie?" The dog lolled about on a patch of dirt in the sun. Her ears pricked up at the sound of her name. She went right back to lolling. "The deck needs a lick of paint, too. I'm gonna rename her. When I think of a name. *Rosemary*'s fine but, y'know, doesn't mean anything to me."

Caleb had spent four years on cutters and knew little about sails. However, he knew a good deal about boats in general and was dismayed at the state of Harry's Catalina, purchased a decade ago on a whim. While Harry had some experience sailing in his youth, he'd never taken this boat out. He insisted it only required routine maintenance and a few repairs. Caleb could see it wasn't anywhere near seaworthy — and Harry didn't have the money to change that situation.

"You did a fine job on those repairs," Harry admitted. Caleb waited for more because Harry could never let an unforced compliment stand. "'Course, now she's got those ugly patches all over her svelte curves. I'll have to paint the entire hull."

"The fish won't care. She'll float just fine with patches."

"But she's not beautiful, is she. You never did care how a thing looked as long as it was functional." He lit a cigarette and puffed thoughtfully. "Beauty matters. You're right, though. She'll float."

"Are you gonna be okay?" Caleb refused to feel guilty about his father's situation, but it was hard not to be worried.

"Looking forward to it! What a life, eh? There's a nice community down there at the marina and they already know me. Very dog friendly, too. I'll sell the old pickup and use the motorcycle to get around. I'll be glad to get out of this place."

"Don't sell the pickup. How're you gonna haul your gear around? You'll be spending half your life at the hardware store for the next few months."

"Nah, I'll manage."

Harry had big dreams, for sure, and zero plans. No surprises there. As soon as he moved that boat to Shilshole, he'd buy a bag of ice and a crate of beer and stick a chair on the unpainted deck, and Caleb was pretty sure that was the *only* plan of his that would ever come to fruition.

Caleb sighed and moved on. "You told me you had some junk to throw out. I'll take that today."

"Sure thing. I put everything I'm keeping in the front room. You can take pretty much everything else. Put it on Craigslist or whatever. Twenty percent commission — how does that sound?"

"I don't want a commission. I want to help you out."

"Well, that's up to you. Don't say I never offered. Now, that antique in the bedroom — wedding present from my parents, that dresser was. You can get three hundred for the mirror alone."

"Harry... You gotta bring down your expectations."

"I'm just sayin', that's a fine piece of furniture. Nineteen-thirties classic, solid mahogany. One of you kids gouged a long scratch into the side, but overall it's not in bad shape."

"Quickest thing is if I take the furniture and tools to an antique store."

Harry waved away that suggestion. "They won't give you shit for it."

"I'll talk to Jesse, then. He knows his way around Craigslist and eBay. We'll figure it out. We can take some of it to a flea market."

"Whatever you think's best. How's Jesse doing?"

"Waiting to hear if he got a scholarship for next year."

"Smart kid." Harry shifted in his chair, like the idea of Jesse's brains made him uncomfortable. "I'm telling you, it's those magnetic letters his mom gave him when he was three. When she bought them I told her it was a waste of time — he can't read when he's three, I said. But what did I know?"

Caleb's turn to wince. Jesse's third birthday was the one Miriam bailed on, instead taking Joy to Arizona, never to return, and leaving Harry with three boys on his hands and hardly a clue what to do with them. And Jesse already knew his letters well before he was three. Miriam hadn't noticed. She'd never noticed much of anything.

"He's gonna be — how old this year? Twenty?" Harry drained his beer, stubbed out the smoke, and got himself busy organizing another one of each. "I was already in the Army at that age. You were in the Coast Guard — Antarctica, right? He's had it too easy, that kid."

"He turned out just fine."

Harry grunted out a belch. "When's Indio's graduation? I'd like to go." His eyes narrowed as a thought occurred to him. "He will graduate, won't he?"

"Yes. Probably could work a little harder on his GPA. Always insisted his portfolio was more important. Maybe he's right. He's got a full-time contract lined up in Portland."

"First Fairn to get a degree — did you know that?" Caleb did know that, and wished Indio was prouder of himself. "He'll do alright, that one. I was a bit tough on him cuz he always seemed kinda lazy, always sitting around with a sketchbook or a guitar or a joint. That's not gonna pay for a wife and a mortgage, is it? I guess I knocked some sense into him, in the end."

Caleb wasn't prepared to credit Harry for Indio's successes, so he kept quiet.

Harry gave him a sly look. "There was a time I only had to ask after the three of you. Now there's three more, eh?"

"We haven't heard from Joy since she went back to the ashram. And we can't trace Xay."

"Can't help you there, son, and I'm truly sorry about that. What about the little one?"

"Her grades are excellent. Not much into the social scene. Jesse's pushing her to graduate early. Says she's almost as smart as him."

"Miriam was a smart one, that's for sure. Or maybe the girl's mystery dad was a genius." He chuckled to himself.

"She works hard at the things that matter to her."

Harry's brow went up, briefly, like he knew something he wasn't saying. "No doubt."

Caleb had no idea what he meant. Harry had only met Wynter that one time, when Patricia brought her here to ask about Xay.

"So, you started house-hunting yet?"

Caleb hadn't wanted to bring that up, because it was tied to Harry's fifty thousand that may or may not happen. "Not yet. I'll sell our house first."

"I'll have that money to you in three days. You can count on it."

Caleb gave a quick, cautious smile — a conditional *thank you*.

"Don't think I won't come through. I've been scolded into it, y'know. My conscience has been pricked."

"Scolded by who?"

"Ah, that's a secret. Works out for everyone. You can get a bigger place and I downsize to a life of leisure on the water. I know I'll never win Father of the Year, son, but I'll make it up to you."

With money. *Great*.

Safe

"I heard you tell Jesse that Harry offered you twenty percent commission." Wynter fussed with the photo frames and dishes and paperbacks on the table, straightening everything into perfect rows. "How come I get fifty percent?"

Caleb unzipped his jacket and leaned back in the folding chair, stretching out his legs. "No reason. I'm just happy you came along with me today. This isn't gonna be as much fun as you think."

They were at a flea market, selling off Harry's tools and trinkets along with a few items Caleb and Jesse contributed. Caleb had promised her half the money from anything of his own they sold. He'd already taken the furniture and larger items to an antique store for cash, and dumped a couple of trailer loads at the transfer station.

Wynter was radiant with excitement. "But it is fun! We should do this every month."

"You get back to me in six hours."

Four hours later, they'd sold Caleb's old tool box, a filing cabinet, several vinyl LPs, and miscellaneous books and clothes, along with some of Harry's stuff. He handed her the money to count.

"Two hundred and seventy dollars, and change," she announced. "This is amazing! Isn't it?"

"Not too bad. It'll taper off now, though." He handed her fifty, an approximate half-share of his sold items. "Take a look around, see if there's anything worth getting."

She wandered off for half an hour, and came back with only one purchase.

"I saw a thousand things I wanted — nothing really worth having," she admitted, handing back the change. "Jesse told me to get him something. He likes old things, and he pretends to like beer, so I bought this." She showed him an antique pewter tankard, with the maker's stamp near the top of the handle.

"Nice. We can polish it up."

"The man said the pewter has lead in it, so he can't drink from it — it'll make him dumb."

"Eh, Jesse has brains to spare. D'you know why it has this glass bottom?"

"No."

"A couple hundred years ago, in England, they used to pay a shilling to recruit you into the Royal Navy. The press gangs would buy you a pint of ale and drop a shilling into the tankard. If you drank the ale, you were accepting the shilling and were signed up whether you liked it or not. So, the glass bottom meant you could check for the shilling before drinking."

"Is that true?"

Caleb shrugged. "So goes the legend."

"Even if you took the shilling, how could they force you to serve?"

"By hanging you if you refused."

She pulled a face. "Sometimes the world is too complicated and cruel to understand." She sat on the chair beside his and fiddled with the leftover bits of string they'd used to tie bundles of tent pegs and silverware together. "My life is good at the moment. Almost everything's perfect."

"Glad to hear it."

"How's your life going?"

"Better and better."

"Really?"

"I feel strong again." This was mostly true, and he figured his health was the reason she'd asked the question. His health and... probably Beatrice. To avoid talking about her, he added, "Since I was nine years old, I've lived in a house full of guys. I love having you around and I can't wait until you move home."

"Jesse said the same thing, except he doesn't like having to pull long hair out of the shower drain again."

"Maybe, if you took over that chore, his life would be almost perfect, too."

"I guess I never knew it was something that had to be done. Rosa had a cleaning woman so everything was always spotless. And Debra does the bathrooms in her house. At the ashram, we didn't have drains. We stood in the dirt under a pressure shower once a week."

"Didn't that leave you with muddy feet?"

"Yes. We mostly didn't wear shoes."

"Jesse has a hair-in-the-drain phobia. He was always nagging Indio about it."

As they talked, she was twisting and braiding the string absent-mindedly, occasionally dipping her fingers into the jar of assorted nuts and bolts and tiny gears to weave in bits of metal. It unnerved him, to see her doing something she'd spent her childhood doing in the Light, like someone had switched her fingers into automatic mode. But she seemed relaxed, and the movement of her hands mesmerized him.

"Did Indio care that Jesse nagged him?"

"Not in the slightest. He ignored him."

"But it bugged Indio when you did it."

"I wouldn't call what I did *nagging*. I had rules and Indio knew what they were. I don't like repeating myself. So, if he broke the rules I would tell him to fix the situation."

"What if he wouldn't? I mean, what if he just wouldn't do what you told him?"

"Well, his bad decisions had their own natural consequences. I'll give you an example, if you want to know how that brother of yours sabotaged himself with his stubbornness. Indio used to ditch classes. I would find out about it when the school called Harry about detentions. Detentions meant he missed basketball practice, and eventually he was dropped from the team. He suffered the consequences and I never had to lift a finger."

"It's so much easier to just follow the rules in the first place." She grinned at him.

"Absolutely." That twinge of discomfort resurfaced. Given her experiences at the ashram, he didn't want to be teaching her blind obedience to authority. "Listen, if you ever think my rules are unfair, you can tell me. We'll discuss it and make sure they're working for everyone."

"So far, I like your rules." She took another length of string and worked it meticulously into the complicated weave. "Jesse once told me Harry would hit you sometimes."

"Sometimes, when I was little. By thirteen, I was too big for him." He winced at old memories. "Most of the time."

"What about Indio and Jesse?"

"Jesse was usually too quick. He would run and hide under his bed when Harry came home drunk. He'd fall asleep under there sometimes and we'd just leave him all night. Indio was... Well, he and Harry rubbed each other the wrong way. I feel like I spent Indio's early teenage years refereeing fights between the two of them. When I wasn't around, they'd come to blows. I took him to karate with me, thinking it'd give him some coping mechanisms. And I think it helped — he started focusing better at school. He was committed to the bands he played with. Can't say it improved his behavior at home much."

"Was that Harry's fault, or his?"

Caleb sighed. "I don't know what to tell you, hun. Harry was hard to live with. I found a way to deal with it, and I guess so did Jesse. Indio never stopped struggling and all that anger against Harry was redirected against me."

"He was angry at Momma, too."

"Maybe. He was very young when she left, though. I'm not sure—"

"It's true. That's where it started, for him."

She was right, of course, and his attempt to deflect the topic from their mother failed.

"Like, when you make a mistake in the braid, somewhere at the start," she said, running her fingers along the braid she was making, examining it thoughtfully. "You cross the threads the wrong way, and you don't even notice it until later. You get to the end, and there's no way to fix the mistake without undoing the entire braid. But you can't undo a life. You have to live with the crossed threads that spoil the whole pattern. I don't know what the answer is. I think I could help him. I told him that, and he knows it's true. He keeps resisting. I can't fix those threads, but I could make them not matter — if only he'd come home."

"That's not your responsibility."

"It is, though. Only his family can do it, the ones who love him no matter what. Jesse understands. He told me a long time ago we just have to be there for Indio and he'll be okay. That's why he has to move to Seattle."

"I'm sorry, hun. He's twenty-three years old — he has to figure this out on his own."

"You still don't get it. Your life fell into place the day you grew big enough to fight back against Harry. You became a man and Jesse gained a protector. Indio's still a little kid whose mom left him in a bad place and never came back."

"What does that make you?"

"The same." She extracted the braid from the heavy can of nails that anchored it. "But I cut out that entire section with the crossed threads. Everything unraveled and I threw it away. Started again. So, she doesn't matter to me anymore. He still loves her. His six-year-old self still loves her, and needs to be loved."

"He's not six anymore."

"I know. He's mixed up about love. Except with Jesse. I love watching them together, even when they're fighting, because I know they'll always be okay. I think he loves Jesse exactly right. Like Xay and Roman, who grew up as brothers." She gave a wistful sigh as she knelt at the side of his chair and tied the finished bracelet around his wrist. "I hope they found each other again. Everyone should have someone like that."

"We've got that, haven't we? You and me — we'll always be okay?"

"I hope so." Seeing his dissatisfaction with that answer, she tried again. "You said love is an action, and I agree. But I know there's more to it. I love you and Jesse and Indio. It wasn't a decision. It just happened. I emptied myself out, and your love was the first thing to fill me up again. I don't know what comes next."

"It's okay, hun. I think every child in a healthy family feels that way, because that's the limit of their experience. Your experience is widening every day, and eventually you'll find friends to love, and then someone special, and then your own children."

What he'd hoped were reassuring words put a look of terror in her eyes. "I don't want to love anyone else. It's not safe. Do you like it?" She snapped the braid against his wrist, deliberately shutting down the discussion.

Caleb made a show of examining the bracelet. The subtle natural colors and different thicknesses of string, and the patterns she'd woven into the band along with the tiny bolts threaded on at intervals, made for an interesting piece.

"I think you just invented a new style of accessory," he said. "Industrial shabby chic?"

"Nothing chic about it. Do you like it? You never wear jewelry."

"I love it. I don't wear jewelry because no one ever gave me any before. Certainly not handmade."

He watched her tidy up the bits of string and straighten a few things on the table. Whatever problems he and Indio had developed over the years, he completely sympathized with Wynter's desire — her need — to bring the family together. And despite his frustrations at being unable to help Joy, he'd never felt so grateful to her for sending Wynter to his door.

And today he had reason to be grateful to Harry, too, because that fifty grand was sitting in his bank account, as promised.

"Hun, I've been thinking about moving us to a bigger house. Someplace I can fix up, to make it our own. For you and me, and Jesse for as long as he wants to stay."

Her mouth made an "O" of surprise. "I think that's an excellent idea."

"Then that's what we'll do." He had Harry's fifty grand. He would soon have Wynter in his care for as long as she needed him. He'd survived a nightmare illness and he was learning to live without Bea. His life was almost perfect, too.

A young woman came to browse through the stack of paperbacks.

"Oh, I love that bracelet," she said, reaching over to take Caleb's wrist. "Did you buy that here? Which stall?"

"My sister made it."

"Can I buy it off you? I have a friend it'd be perfect for."

"Not for sale, sorry."

The woman's face fell.

"I'll make you one," Wynter said.

"Today? How long will it take? I'll come back and pick it up."

"Half an hour or so."

"How much?"

"You can just have it. It doesn't cost anything to make."

"How sweet of you." She bought a stack of paperbacks for three dollars and left with the promise to return later.

"You know, Jesse would've put a twenty-dollar ticket on the bracelet," Caleb said.

"That's stupid. I only offered cuz I've got nothing else to do. It's made out of junk."

"It's made out of skill, time, and love," he corrected her.

She gave him a shy smile and selected scraps of string to start another bracelet.

"You okay with us moving?" he said. "I know you love our house."

"I do love it. We need something that works better for our family. A bigger rehearsal space, a second bathroom. Something quirky for Jesse, and a bedroom for him that fits a king-sized bed." At Caleb's bewildered expression, she added, "Yeah, he wants a king-sized bed. I would get lost in a big bed. And we need space for Indio, when he moves to Seattle." Her sidelong glance dared him to dispute it.

"Indio's not moving home, hun. And Jesse won't be living at home for much longer."

"We'll find a place so amazing, they'll never want to leave."

Caleb went outside when he heard Debra's car drive up. She'd been kind enough to bring Wynter to Seattle this weekend, a long weekend for Wynter because her school was on mid-winter break. Two weeks had passed since her previous visit, and things were moving fast.

Jesse was outside painting the fence, and already complaining about it as soon as Wynter got out the car.

"See that?" he said, pointing his drippy paint brush at the SOLD sign in the yard. "He wants the house prettied up, even though we already sold it. What's the point of..." He trailed off when he noticed Caleb.

"It does look pretty, Jesse," Wynter assured him, coming to Caleb for a hug because Jesse had forgotten all about the required greeting. "Are we house-hunting today?"

"We have a few open houses lined up," Caleb told her. "And tomorrow my realtor's driving us a little farther out to look at some properties nearer the mountains."

"Closer to Patty's? We could eat there every day!"

Caleb grunted a reply, thanked Debra, and told Wynter to take her bag inside.

"She texted me fifteen minutes ago," Jesse said when they were alone. "She wanted to know if you had a date last night."

"Why would I?"

"Valentine's Day! She got her hopes up."

Hard to believe that one year ago he'd been about to ask Bea to marry him. Now he'd been without her for six months and the idea of starting all over again with someone else still filled him with dread. His attention was primarily on his foster care license, which was on track to be approved within the next few weeks.

Way too much else on his mind right now.

His realtor had told him outright that if he waited three more years he'd get another $150 thousand for his house. He didn't love this house, didn't feel anything at all for it despite all the work he'd put in over the years, but sitting tight on a thousand-dollar-a-week investment was a wise move.

Buying a bigger place to keep Wynter happy, and to put behind him and Jesse the bad memories — *that* was a wiser move.

He'd had an offer within days — a retired couple from California wanting to move closer to their grandkids. He had Harry's money and pre-approval on a loan. So, he'd set Jesse the task of narrowing down locations for their new home, something close enough to both the university and the base to keep it convenient, and preferably close to their old high school, which Jesse was still determined Wynter would attend.

With Wynter tagging along and providing a unique perspective, they spent Saturday looking at suburban houses not too different from their own other than being more attractive. Less work for him — all good in theory. In practice he knew the urge would arise to start changing, expanding, fixing up.

On Sunday, his realtor Meghan drove the three of them out to a couple of houses in Issaquah, twenty miles east of Seattle. A little farther out than he'd intended, in a beautiful part of the state. They could afford a bigger house out here, especially if it needed a little work. Meghan drove them home via what she called the "scenic route" along the edge of Tiger Mountain State Forest.

"Stop, back up!" Wynter cried. "There was a *For Sale* board back there."

"That's not what you want," Meghan said. "It's pretty much fallen down."

"I thought we wanted a fallen down house?"

"I have my limits," Caleb said. Nevertheless, he asked the realtor to make a U-turn.

The board was on the main road, advertising a property three miles further along a winding road cut through thick forest.

"This reminds me of the forest we rode through, to go to that carnival," Wynter said, enchanted. "My ears are popping."

They were climbing over a thousand feet in elevation. At the end of the road, a high stone wall marked the front of the property, which had a duplicate board attached. Wynter jumped out to examine it, and the others followed.

Caleb wasn't prepared for what he saw. This wasn't a house so much as...

"Looks like someone high on crack smashed together a bunch of different buildings," Jesse said.

Caleb frowned at him but, well, he was right.

"It has a tower!" Wynter said, thumping the photo on the board. "This is what caught my eye. How can you not love a Rapunzel tower?"

The rest of the house, from the front, looked like a typical old farmhouse. The octagonal tower, attached to the right, with its narrow windows, conical roof, and Tudor-style facing, was entirely mismatched. And another photo showed an uninspired single-story extension sticking out the back.

"It's really ugly," Jesse said.

"I don't know, hun. Needs a lot of work," Caleb added, looking at the interior photos.

Seeing the eagerness on Wynter's face, and Jesse's frankly curious expression, he asked Meghan if they could see inside, and she called for the lock box number.

The double gates in the wall opened onto a long private driveway — more of a lane, with a huge patch of mature trees on the left hiding the house from view until they rounded a curve in the driveway.

"It's on five acres, and backs onto the State forest," Meghan said as she unlocked the door. "It's got privacy, but it has a lot of problems. To be honest, I wouldn't recommend it for your needs. I do have a cute place in Newcastle I'd love to show you..."

Wynter had run on ahead, dragging Jesse by the hand through the startlingly yellow kitchen, which hadn't been renovated since the fifties. Caleb saw a month's work and ten thousand dollars right there.

He walked through as Meghan hung back, presumably waiting for him to walk out in disgust. The kitchen led to a dining area overlooking an open plan living room with moldy carpet and old-fashioned flocked wallpaper. Beyond that was an archway leading into the tower.

"This is awesome. It's perfect!" Wynter walked around the empty tower room, about twenty feet in diameter with a rickety spiral staircase in the center.

"This is a dump," Jesse said. "I mean, it could be amazing, but..."

"Caleb wants a fixer-upper. Right?" She waited for Caleb to agree. Caleb held his tongue for now. "Indio will love this house."

"*Indio?*" Jesse said. "What's he got to do with—"

"We could put in a real log fire and this could be the family room."

"There's no chimney."

"The music room, then," Wynter called, racing up the stairs so fast they shook. "For the grand piano."

The second floor of the tower was similar to the first, an open room with peeling plaster and uneven floorboards. Several narrow arched windows graced the walls, and a door led through to the second floor of the main house. The staircase to the third floor was cordoned off with rope.

"It's probably not safe to go up there," Meghan said, catching up with them. "I can tell you, the top floor is in even worse shape, and the roof needs replacing."

"Does it have an open ceiling?" Jesse said, peering up the staircase, cautious excitement in his eyes.

Caleb poked around the windows with his finger and toed the rotting floorboards. "I think this should probably be condemned. Let's look at the rest of the house."

The original farmhouse rooms downstairs included a guest half-bath and utilities room, and upstairs, off a landing area, two bedrooms, one with an adjoining bath, a family bathroom, and a tiny third bedroom. Out the back, a large deck ran the length of the newer extension, which had two additional bedrooms, a bathroom, and a family room. From the family room was a view of the overgrown backyard and fields, and the forest in the distance.

"There's a basement!" Wynter shrieked, having found the door at the end of the corridor. She ran down the steps to the semi-finished basement. It extended under the entire new area of the house.

The others followed her down.

"This is where we'll make music," she said. "I want this house."

Caleb had warned her not to set her heart on any house until they bought it — this must be a practical decision, not an emotional one. And Jesse had agreed with him. But they went upstairs and outside, and now Jesse was wandering around the backyard, his face tilted up to examine the tower from every angle, and Caleb could tell he loved it, too.

"It's got four big bedrooms," Wynter went on, "and three more rooms in the tower. It's got the basement for our rehearsal space and all kinds of sheds and barns outside for the bikes and workshop and gym equipment. It's got land. You wanted land!"

Meghan was getting her hopes up because of all the questions Caleb had been asking. "What do you think?" she said. "We can arrange a termite and roof inspection before you make an offer."

Wynter sucked in her cheeks as she tried to keep quiet.

"I'll give you a few minutes to look around again," Meghan said, fading into the background.

The three of them leaned on the railing and looked out across the property to the forest.

"This is way more land, and more work, than I had in mind," Caleb said. "It must be twenty-five miles from your school, hun, and further still to the university."

"I'll drive her to school," Jesse said, catching Wynter's excitement. "Or there'll be a bus from Issaquah. Can you imagine the parties we could have here? Feels like we're miles from anywhere."

"That's because we *are* miles from anywhere."

"I love it," Wynter said. "I love it *so much*. We could have chickens. We could have cows!"

"No cows," Caleb said.

"Goats? Dogs?"

Caleb gave a *maybe* shrug.

"It feels so safe," Wynter said. "We're right at the end of the road — no one will come up here."

"Didn't you once abandon a car on Tiger Mountain?" Jesse asked Caleb.

"Yep. Far as I know, Grandpa Fairn's old Cavalier is still out there somewhere."

"What are you talking about?" Wynter said.

"That's a story for another time, hun."

"No, now. It'll help you emotionally bond to this house, which will help you make the decision to buy it."

Jesse chuckled. "Wyn, don't tell him your devious plan before it's been executed."

Wynter looked expectantly at Caleb. He kept the story for now.

But he did buy the house.

Milk & Juice

"Would you like an M&M?"

Nathan had appeared at Wynter's elbow as she did homework at the kitchen table. On his hot grubby palm was a red M&M. She resisted screwing up her nose and took the candy.

"I'll save it for later," she said, placing it on a notebook.

"You should eat it now."

"Why?"

"It makes your blood taste yucky, so the zombies won't bite you."

"That's okay, zombies stay away from me anyway."

"How d'you know?"

"I've literally never had any trouble with zombies. Never even seen one."

"Ohhh, you must have type O blood. Dad's type O, and they stay away from him, too."

"Yep, that must be it," she said tolerantly. "Lucky me."

Nathan didn't leave. "Still, you should eat it."

Wynter's eyes flicked to the sticky M&M, which had already made a red mark on the paper.

"It's really good. Chocolatey." His eyes were wide with hope and... something else.

"Did you break something in my room?"

Nathan nodded mutely.

Wynter jumped up and ran to her room. Nothing seemed amiss...

"I'm sorry."

She spun around to see Nathan in the doorway, holding her guitar. Not the Fender, which she'd long ago sent home, but a two-hundred-dollar acoustic with a great feel and a pretty nice tone.

Slowly, Nathan turned it around. The body was smashed in, right through the front leaving the sound hole a ragged mess. Blood shot to Wynter's head in a heated rush. She'd written seven songs with that guitar.

"I thought I could fix it. My paste doesn't work. Maybe Dad—"

"What the hell were you doing in my room?" she yelled. "Why were you messing with this?" She grabbed the guitar as Nathan froze, terrified, still gripping it. The neck was loose, barely attached to the body, and when she yanked on it, it broke free.

Nathan took off down the hallway.

Wynter ran after him, holding the guitar neck like a weapon. How could this happen? Why now, after months and months of those boys being nothing more than annoying noisemakers? They'd hardly ever touched her stuff before, despite Madeline's warnings, other than stealing pillows for their blanket forts and, once, a bracelet and two tampons to pay a bounty hunter.

She was supposed to be leaving this place in a few days. Or a few weeks. Soon, anyway. Soon Caleb would take her in and they'd move to their glorious new home. She'd been on edge for days, and *now* Nathan had decided to be a destructive brat?

He darted into the playroom and slammed the door on her.

"What happened? Is she mad?" she heard Aiden say.

Wynter opened the door, easily pushing Nathan out of the way as he tried to hold it closed.

"Which one of you monsters did this?" she demanded, ready to beat a confession out of them.

The boys scurried to the corner. Nathan was staring at the raised guitar neck in her hand, with its dangling strings and shards of wood hanging off the end. Aiden crouched with his arms over his head.

Wynter's knees gave way and she dropped to the floor. Her stomach clenched. She fought to keep from throwing up as a wave of terror washed over her. She braced herself on hands and knees until it passed, leaving her in a cold sweat.

"Are you mad?" Nathan said quietly, and Aiden peeked out from under his arm.

She shook her head as tears ran down her cheeks, one hand pressed over her mouth to hold the sobs in. The boys sat dumbfounded a few feet away, staring at her.

"It's okay if you're a little bit mad," Nathan said at last. "We needed a zombie shield. There's a new breed of them, with lasers for eyes. It's pretty scary."

"I'm not mad," Wynter said between sobs, unable to believe what she'd almost done. She'd almost hurt them. "I won't hurt you. I just want to go home."

"You mean your forever home?" Aiden said. That was the term the kids used all the time through the adoption process. Their forever home, their forever family.

Wynter nodded, crying freely now.

Aiden crept over. "This is gonna become my forever home in eleven days." He touched her arm tentatively. "We're going to the courthouse and then we'll have a party, like we had with Nathan. And Nathan will become my forever brother. You'll get your forever home soon."

Wynter hugged him tightly, though her limbs felt weak and shaky.

"We're sorry about your guitar," Nathan said. "It did save our lives, though, before it broke."

Wynter wiped her face. "I'm glad of that."

"We'll have to find something else now."

"I'll help you."

She unwound the guitar strings and they watched, fascinated, as she braided four protection cuffs for them, one for each little wrist. Guaranteed to deflect zombie eye-lasers.

Later, as she lumbered after them, zombie-like, shooting lasers so they could test the cuffs, her phone rang from the kitchen. She left the boys and went to answer it.

Caleb said, "My foster care license came today in the mail."

Wynter made a strangled, incomprehensible sound.

"You're coming home, hun."

"Come get me. Come get me now!" Wynter managed to say, rushing to her room to pack. She'd almost hit a little boy in blind anger. She needed to get out of this house before something worse happened.

"Not today," Caleb said. "You haven't been put in my care yet. There's paperwork to do."

"Today. I need to come home today." She opened a drawer, scooped up an armful of clothes, dumped them on the bed. She pulled Indio's old duffle bag out of the closet.

"It'll take twenty-four hours," Caleb was saying. "Then it's official. Jesse's running around the house with a broom. You should see him—"

"Send Jesse to pick me up. Please, I need to come home. My forever home." Her throat closed up and more tears stung her eyes, and she couldn't catch her breath. "I could come for an overnight stay, couldn't I? And then just stay while they do the paperwork. Please let Jesse fetch me."

"Let's do this by the book, okay? One more day. And it has to be Svetlana who brings you."

"What? Why?"

"That's just the rule, hun. The social worker has to transport you between homes."

Wynter sat heavily on her bed amid a tangle of clothes. "Okay," she choked out. "Okay. I'll wait."

After she hung up, she took out the things she'd need tomorrow, stacked them neatly on Madeline's bed, and proceeded to pack the rest.

She spared a thought for Madeline, who didn't have a forever home waiting for her one day, who would soon be eighteen and responsible for making her own. Wynter had waited a long time, but she had Caleb to provide her forever home. She was grateful beyond words to him, and to Deb and Brian for giving those boys a forever home.

Not everyone got their happy ending, but Wynter's was one day away.

On Tuesday afternoon, Wynter waited in the bedroom of her foster home for Svetlana, who wasn't available for the official transport until 4PM. Her stomach was in knots but her heart was light.

That morning, Debra had driven her to school to clear out her locker and say goodbye to her teachers. Debra left for work, offering a friendly goodbye hug, and now Wynter was alone in the house.

Wynter watched the clock on her phone tick past four. Every passing minute wound her gut tighter. Six minutes later, Svetlana's car pulled up on the street and Wynter gasped with relief and ran outside laden with her school backpack and the duffle bag of clothes, a pair of boots in her free hand and a coat across her arm. She dumped everything on the driveway and went back for a box of books and her phone and wallet. And the empty guitar case. Svetlana helped her load everything up.

As soon as they set out, she texted Caleb to say she'd be home in an hour. He planned to leave work early to be there.

At the small Columbia City house with the SOLD sign, Wynter jumped out of the car and ran to ring the bell. Jesse opened the door.

"Don't you have classes today?" she said.

"Nice to see you, too. Welcome home."

She flung herself on him. "You were the first person to open this door for me."

"I haven't forgotten. I didn't get a hug then, though, and I had to pay ten bucks to get rid of your taxi driver."

He grabbed the bags from today's "driver", who had stepped onto the porch.

"What's up, Svetlana? Can I get you a coffee or something?" he asked, the perfect host.

"You're so kind. Thank you, Jesse."

Jesse's face fell. He wanted her gone, and so did Wynter.

"Actually, we're all out of milk."

"I take it black."

"We're all out of coffee."

Svetlana gave him a long-suffering smile, getting the hint. "Why don't you grab the rest of Wynter's things, and I'll be on my way just as soon as I've talked to Caleb."

"He'll be home in about three minutes."

"I'm gonna sit on the porch and wait for him," Wynter said.

Jesse laughed. "Okay. You want hot chocolate?"

"Not this time."

They finished bringing everything in, and Svetlana moved her car to the street, then went inside to do whatever it was social workers did after bringing a foster child into a new home. She had an ominous checklist in her hand.

Wynter sat on the porch, her stomach still knotted up, her pulse racing. Jesse stood exactly where he'd stood almost fourteen months ago, leaning against the pillar to wait with her.

"Seriously, are you skipping classes?" Wynter said.

"I wasn't gonna miss your homecoming." He pointed to the balloons attached to the gate. "Did you even see those?"

"Sorry. Wasn't paying attention. You told me up-balloons are unethical because of a world shortage of helium, which is needed for important scientific work."

"Screw science today."

She gaped at him, then grinned. "I love you, Jesse. When can I start at your high school?" She'd spent an hour on the phone with him yesterday evening while he'd explained at length how he'd convinced Caleb she had to go to their old school, even though it was in another district from the new house, and how Caleb had sweet-talked the relevant people into finding a place for her.

"Suddenly you *want* to go to school? We found out your grade is away at camp this week, so we'll wait until next week."

"I get the whole week off?"

"You get *me* for the whole week. We'll go through their curriculum and get up to speed. For the first couple of weeks, until we move next month, you'll take the same bus I used to take when I didn't ride my bike. Twenty-seven minutes, door-to-door, including the walk at each end."

"Wow, that's precise. Did the bike take longer?"

"It was four minutes faster. On the days I planned to skip and go to the skateboard park, I always rode my bike."

"Wait — you skipped school? You never told me that."

"Only when there was nothing important going on. Once we've moved, me or Caleb will drive you in. On the days I can't pick you up there's a bus to Issaquah — twenty minutes straight down the highway. You can work in the library until one of us picks you up from there."

"You have everything planned!"

"Down to the minute. Caleb's gonna sign you up for swimming lessons and send you to driver ed. This summer we'll go camping. And now we have a bunch of songs recorded on Soundfish, and fifty downloads a day, maybe it's time to think about playing live."

"Not unless Indio moves to Seattle."

"We'll find another guitarist."

Wynter wrinkled her nose, not liking the sound of that.

"I have to learn all the house rules," she said. "Is there a written list? If I break one accidentally, you'll be my advocate, won't you?"

"There's no written list, and of course I'll be your advocate — even if you break one deliberately."

"I would never do that."

The Silverado pulled into the driveway. No headlights this time — sunset wasn't for another hour. Wynter stood up as Caleb walked toward her, and fell into his open arms.

"Welcome home," he said, his voice muffled against the top of her head.

They weren't even going to be in *this* home for much longer. Didn't matter. Caleb was her home. He felt and smelled exactly right, and the knots in her stomach unraveled as a wave of contentment washed over her. She cried uncontrollably.

Eventually, they went into the house and Caleb talked to Svetlana. Wynter was very embarrassed about the crying, especially because it had made Jesse cry, too. She went to her room and calmed herself down. Jesse had cleared Indio's old stuff out of the closet, so it really was *her* room now. She unpacked a few things before going to the kitchen, where Jesse told her what they were cooking for dinner.

She opened the pantry and stared in disbelief.

"Why is there so much food in here?"

"We have to keep a two-week supply of non-perishables and one week of perishables in the house at all times. And we're never allowed to run out of milk or juice, or they'll take you away."

"You just told Svetlana we're out of milk."

"Yeah, I realized my mistake as soon as I said it." Jesse opened the refrigerator. "She can check — we do have half a gallon in here."

On her way out, Svetlana said she'd be back in a week and after that there would be monthly visits.

"She can also drop in unannounced," Jesse said after she'd left, "so stay off the trampoline, in case she catches you on it."

"We have a trampoline now?"

"No, silly." He took a tray of meat from the fridge. "Okay, stir fry pork with snow peas and jasmine rice, followed by a 'seventies sci-fi movie marathon. Let's begin."

Defeated

Jesse lay in bed listening to Caleb coughing from the next room.

For the past three days, Caleb had woken up coughing, and Jesse had Googled enough websites about "life after sepsis" to know what it probably meant. And yet, he hadn't said anything. He didn't want to believe it. He was waiting for Caleb to do something about it — and Caleb refused to acknowledge the slightest weakness ever since he was approved for a return to full-time duties.

The United States Government said he was fit to serve. Therefore, he was fit to serve.

This morning, the first morning of Wynter's homecoming, Jesse knew he was going to have to do something because neither of them would forgive themselves if Wynter got sick.

He went to knock on his brother's door. Caleb sat on the edge of his bed, bent over double, breathing hard as he recovered from the coughing fit.

Caleb looked up, his face pale, his eyes sunken. "It's just a cough, Jess. I have a head cold."

He'd been suppressing that head cold with pills for a week. The cough, though, was not normal.

"You have pneumonia." Jesse held up his phone. "I'm calling your EO right now. I have his number."

"Is that some kind of threat?"

"No. I'm telling you what I'm gonna be doing in about thirty seconds. I'm calling to tell him that I'm taking you to the hospital. I know it's been five months now, but you're immunocompromised because of the sepsis. If you have pneumonia, Wynter could get sick, too."

Surprisingly, Caleb was nodding his head. "Okay, you're right. I was gonna turn myself in for a check-up today anyway. I just wanted..." He sagged forward again. "It's not pneumonia. It's just a cough and a cold. But I wanted her to come home. I figured, if this was something bad, if they put me in the hospital, they would've left her with Deb and Brian until I was well again."

"So this way, she goes to Patricia instead of staying in Enumclaw. Good thinking, except that you put your health at risk — and hers."

"I'll be fine, Jess. I don't even feel too bad. It's not pneumonia."

It *was* pneumonia.

One hour, one x-ray, and one distraught little sister later, Caleb was admitted to the hospital. Jesse didn't know whether to be furious with him or thankful his plan worked. He'd stayed on his feet long enough to have Wynter placed in his care, except that now he wasn't home to take care of her.

"Why is this happening?" Wynter moaned on the drive to Cougar Mountain. "Everything was finally perfect. Even your movies last night were pretty good."

"*The Omega Man* was 'pretty good'? *Silent Running*? What's the matter with you? Those are classics."

"I'm just saying, sometimes your movies are weird and kinda boring. When do we get to *Star Wars*? That's supposed to be good."

"I'll drive up to see you tomorrow night and we'll watch *Star Wars*."

"How long will he be in the hospital?"

"It's walking pneumonia, a bacterial infection, and right now it's not serious except that he was already weak, not that he'll admit to it. He'll be home in a few days but we both agree you should stay at Patricia's for the week, just to keep you safe. Svetlana is fine with the plan."

"What about keeping *you* safe?"

"I never get sick."

"Please come live with me at Patricia's."

"You're only twenty-five minutes away, and it's only for a week. I'll visit tomorrow and as often as I can next week."

"Will you at least visit over the weekend?"

"I'm going to Whidbey Island for the weekend with a bunch of friends."

"Why?"

"What kind of question is that? We rented a huge cabin and we're gonna party like it's our last party before buckling down for finals week, which it is."

"Are you going with these so-called friends because there's a girl you like?"

He glowered at her. "There's a... One of them is... There's this bio major from Seville, if you must know."

"Seville in Spain?"

Jesse pulled up in front of Patty's diner, where the parking lot was starting to fill up with the lunchtime crowd, and his mind flashed to Isabella's long lashes, generous curves, those strappy tops she wore even in the middle of winter, and the way she slipped her hand under his t-shirt as she talked to him about enzyme inhibition. Jesse was keen to determine the limit of this girl's inhibitions.

"She has the most incredible accent," he said.

"Is that a good reason to chase her?"

"It's a starting point."

Wynter rolled her eyes. "I don't know why you even bother. They never last."

"Don't knock it 'til you've tried it," he said carelessly.

Wynter thumped his arm and got out of the car.

He didn't mean to be flippant about it. He was worried about Caleb and he was kind of regretting that he was tied up this weekend. He should be here for Wynter.

Patricia was, as always, telepathically aware of their arrival and came out to give them both a warm welcome that made Wynter smile in a beautiful, genuine way that Jesse couldn't remember seeing before.

"Your room is all set up. Come along." Patricia wrapped an arm around Wynter's shoulders and led her toward the diner while Jesse fetched her bag from the back seat of the car.

"Patricia?" he called, and she turned. "Any chance you have a second guest room or a comfortable couch?"

❧

"You did the right thing." Caleb moved his bishop on the board. "I'm proud of you. I feel a lot better knowing you're there with her."

Jesse had given up Isabella's gorgeous accent and promising curves, and never mind Caleb being proud of him — he was proud of himself.

"When do you get out?"

"They're saying Sunday." Caleb had a controlled uneasiness in his manner that Jesse did not like. It meant he was shouldering some huge burden he didn't want to worry Jesse with. "Hey, we'll go camping for her birthday next week. She keeps asking about it. Indio says he can come."

"Indio and me are supposed to be studying for finals week."

"Bring your books with you. Just a couple of days, okay?"

"You think you should be camping in March after a bout of pneumonia?"

"A mild bout. I'll be fine. So, we have a ten-day window to deal with, between the Seattle house closing next week and taking possession of the new house. Patricia will let us stay with her. You could stay with a friend if you want. It'll be pretty cramped."

"I'll stay with you guys. Wyn and me plan to observe her chef for gourmet tips."

"No, the two of you will stay out of everyone's way."

Jesse grunted, studied the chess board, made his move. He had a question to ask, and while it was the last question he *wanted* to ask, it had to be asked. And fast, before Wynter came back from her vending machine search.

"That house... It needs so much work. Are you gonna be able to cope?"

He waited for Caleb's firm reassurances. What he got was a heavy sigh. Caleb didn't raise his eyes from the board. The hospital air-con whirred and outside a truck trundled past.

"Let's see how I'm doing a week from now," Caleb said at last. "The sale doesn't close until the seventeenth so until then I can always back out." He glanced at the open door. "God, I can't do that. How can I do that to her?"

"Why does a week from now matter? It's gonna take you a year to recover from the initial illness. Maybe more. That's just the way it is, and you'll set yourself back if you overdo it. Why can't you accept that?"

Caleb gave him a look that said he didn't appreciate the brutal facts. Jesse had been in denial, too, a completely irrational denial that went against everything he'd read about sepsis, simply because he couldn't bear for it to be true. His oldest brother had been his rock for as long as he could remember. Physical weakness was unthinkable. Yet here he was, physically defeated, and Jesse *had* finally accepted it.

"I need a week, Jess. The logistics if I do back out... that's a nightmare. I can't impose on Patricia while we look for something else. We'd have to rent a motel room or something. I don't know if Svetlana would approve of that."

Wynter returned with granola bars and a coffee.

"A motel room?" she said brightly, having overheard only the last part. "Are we going on another vacation?"

"Camping," Jesse said, pulling a face to show what he thought of it, which failed to dampen Wynter's excitement in the slightest. "Only insane survivalist-types go camping out of season."

"I *love* camping."

"You've never been."

"Nevertheless, I love it," she said firmly, handing Caleb his coffee.

"Get Jesse to pay you for this."

"The coffee was free. A nurse out the front there made it for me."

"How did you manage that?"

Wynter shrugged. "I said it was for you and she just did it."

"Was it that tall curly redhead?" Jesse asked.

"Yes."

"What is it with you and the nurses?" he asked his brother. "That Danish one was flirting like crazy earlier."

"She wasn't flirting," Caleb said.

"Well, you wouldn't notice," Jesse muttered.

"Maybe it was you she was flirting with," Wynter said unhelpfully.

"No, Wyn, thirty-year-old women don't flirt with me." Jesse kicked Caleb's knight off the board with his pawn. "They ruffle my hair and pinch my cheeks. Bloody annoying."

Caleb's uneasiness wasn't the only thing stressing Jesse today. The chess board was stressing him. Inexplicably, he had never in his life beaten Caleb. Losing at chess to Caleb was like losing at wrestling to Indio. In theory, he was smarter than Caleb and better trained than Indio, yet he couldn't beat either of them. But today something felt different. Something was off. Caleb wasn't playing *badly*, but where were the flashy sacrifices he was famous for? The two of them relished those vicious little skirmishes all over the board, pieces flying, and somehow Caleb always came out on top. Today, Caleb was overthinking his moves, and in response Jesse found himself not taking the bait quite so often, and now as he assessed the board he found himself in a stronger overall position than he'd thought.

Wynter perched on the edge of the bed to watch the game.

Caleb said, "Hun, I had an odd call earlier today. You remember Joy's roommate in Magnolia?"

"I didn't meet her. Joy said she was Australian."

"I didn't really meet her, either. Her name's Rain. She called me because she's left the Light."

Wynter was silent for several seconds. Then, "Why would she think you care? How does she even have your number?"

"When Joy went back to Arizona, she left pretty much everything behind, including her phone, and Rain found my number in there. She left the Light because of a conversation Joy and I had, that day I took you to see her in September."

"When you asked about the teachers?"

"Yes. She overheard us and it disturbed her, so she did some research on her own and I guess she became disillusioned. Being involved was wearing her down, she said. Every time she went on a retreat or a course she ended up feeling worse about herself, to the point where she was even considering going to the temple in Arizona, in the hope that becoming more devout would fix things. Fix her."

"There's always something wrong with the person, never with the Light." Wynter picked at the blanket. "You have to do whatever it takes to get on a better path to God, even if in the process you get... pulled apart, or stripped away. Why would she tell *you* all of this?"

"I think she wanted me to know... wanted *you* to know that despite what happened to you, something good came of it. She sounded sincere."

"Okay," Wynter whispered. "I hope she finds the thing that makes her happy."

Caleb expression tightened and Jesse's heart sank. That big farmhouse in the forest would make Wynter happy. Was it too much for Caleb right now?

"You really wanna do that?" Jesse said sharply as Caleb made his next move.

"You have a better idea?"

Jesse looked through the options. Caleb's move was perfectly fine. The best possible move, in fact. Jesse read a stark realization on his older brother's face. Caleb had never taken it easy on Jesse on the chess board, and he wasn't doing so now. He was the better player. And yet, Jesse was going to win.

"I think I'll save myself the humiliation," Caleb said, tipping over his king, his brow drawn low in confusion.

"Why did you do that?" Wynter cried. "It's not even in check."

"I'm resigning," Caleb said.

"But you still have six pieces."

"He can't win," Jesse explained, in shock.

He shook Caleb's proffered hand and put the pieces away and folded the board. He'd won a thousand chess games against others and never felt anything but glee. This time, he felt utterly awful.

"Don't take it so hard," Caleb told him with a quirk in his lips. "Had to happen, sooner or later. Beat me when I *don't* have pneumonia and it'll be worth celebrating. Also—" He tapped Jesse's hand and pointed to the hand sanitizer dispenser near the door.

"You're not contagious anymore."

"Let's not take chances."

Seeds

"I overheard the nurses talking about Caleb's medical discharge," Wynter said on the drive back to Patty's. "Does that mean he's coming home Sunday like we hoped?"

Jesse's head was still wrapped up in his chess victory. "Yep, he's doing great."

"I saw on his chart that a 'Dr Liu' is coming to see him later today. That's a new one."

Wynter knew all Caleb's doctors' names and appointment schedules, so she was probably right.

He backtracked over what Wynter had said.

"Wait... his *medical* discharge?"

"Yes. On Sunday."

"No, no. Wyn, think carefully. Did they use that exact term? Or did they say his discharge from the hospital?"

"They said the doctor from the base is coming to assess him for a medical discharge."

"Shit!" Jesse felt like the air had been sucked out of his body.

Wynter was panicking at his reaction. "What's the matter? Is something else wrong with him? What's going on?"

"A medical discharge means he's being thrown out of the Coast Guard."

"But... that's his job. That's his life. Why would they throw him out?"

"Because this pneumonia thing could be just the start. Probably not," he reassured her as she paled. "But there's a fair chance he's more susceptible to getting sick. The Coast Guard must've decided it's better to just let him go. He only has two years left on his contract anyway."

"He was going to renew that!"

"Damn, why didn't he say anything to me? He must know it's in the works. How did he think he was gonna pay for..." Jesse stopped himself and gave Wynter a sidelong glance.

"Pay for the mortgage," she finished.

"He'll find another job. He's extremely employable."

Wynter turned to stare out the side window and said, shakily, "And he never fails."

In the deserted restaurant on Saturday morning, Wynter sat at a booth and turned the page of her biology textbook. She sighed at the long list of questions. She needed to get through this work by April to stay on track. Jesse's ambitious plan was for her to not only test out of tenth grade, but take online summer school so she could start her junior year in September with some credits already under her belt.

While she stuffed her brain with convergent and divergent evolution, and tried not to think about Caleb and the mortgage and the amazing home they'd found and might not be able to have, Jesse was still asleep on Patricia's couch upstairs. His finals were in two weeks and he should be studying. After the hospital visit yesterday, they'd stayed up late watching movies and she couldn't bring herself to wake him.

Patricia brought her a cup of tea, a hot buttered date scone, and an encouraging squeeze of her shoulder, before walking over to the main door to welcome the first customer of the day for brunch.

The next time Wynter looked up from her books, a couple of families had come in, and the first customer was looking at her from his small table across the restaurant, stirring his coffee. A nondescript man in his sixties, with thinning dark hair, still wearing his wool coat and scarf like he expected to be thrown out on short notice.

He gave her a thoughtful look. Did she know him?

He was coming over with a determined stride and a black leather folder tucked under his arm. Wynter buried her nose in her books.

"Hello. Wynter?"

Wynter felt herself flushing in fear. She was certain she didn't know him from the outside world, which meant he must be someone from the ashram. He didn't *look* like he belonged in the Light, with his traditional clothes and his patronage at Patty's Western Diner...

"Charlie Bryant," he said. "I'm a journalist. I wonder, could I have a few minutes of your time?"

Wynter gripped her pen, unable to look up. A *journalist*. She'd never met a journalist but she knew he was going to ask about the Light. A dozen thoughts whirled through her mind. She'd promised Joy she wouldn't talk about the Light, and certainly not to say anything negative, but Joy was gone. Did she *have* to talk to him? Would he force her? What would Caleb say if he knew? Or was this all a trick? Was he from the Light after all, here to lure her back?

He sat, tentatively, on the edge of the opposite bench and set down his folder. She dared to look at him. He had keen bright eyes in a lined face, and an expectant hopeful look on his face. Wasn't he supposed to have a...

"Where's your tape recorder?"

"Oh, I use my phone." He took a phone from his coat pocket. "May I record you? I'm writing an article about the Light."

"I know."

His thick eyebrows went up. "Oh, you know?"

"I mean, I knew it must be about the Light." Wynter cast a hasty look around the diner, searching for Patricia.

"A young lady named Rain Legates contacted me a few weeks ago. I believe she knew your sister? I'm looking for more people like her, people who were involved in the Light and left. And when she told me about you, I realized that we've met before."

"Wynter?" Patricia was suddenly there, her hand on the back of Wynter's seat in an unmistakably protective stance. "Do you know this gentleman?"

"No... but..."

"Sir, do you mind?" Patricia held out a hand, politely inviting him to leave.

"He says he's a journalist."

Charlie flicked a card under Patricia's nose, and she took it.

"I think I want to talk to him," Wynter said.

Patricia gave her a searching look. "Are you sure?"

Wynter nodded, and Patricia left — heading not for the kitchen, but for the staff door that led to the stairs. Wynter knew where she was going.

"She's gone to fetch my brother. He might throw you out."

"I'll be quick, then." Charlie didn't look overly concerned. "I wrote an article about twelve years ago on the ashram in Arizona. The leadership gave me limited access to the devotees in the temple. I took some pictures, spoke to a few people, and that was it. And now, I want to write another article about how things have changed. May I ask you some questions?"

His finger hovered over the *record* button on his phone screen.

Wynter shook her head. "Please don't record me." What if Joy found out? What if Momma found out, and heard her voice on tape accusing the teachers of terrible things? Not that she was going to tell Charlie Bryant any of that stuff. She'd barely managed to tell her brothers and there was still so much she couldn't say.

Charlie slid his hand away from his phone. "Okay. I'll do it the old-fashioned way." He took a small notebook and pen from his inner pocket. His voice was soothing and he seemed like a nice man. Wynter had no idea what to do.

"Rain says your brother accused your sister, Joy, of—"

"No, wait. You said we met before. How?"

"At the ashram, when you were little. Four years old, maybe? I saw a group of children outside. A little blonde girl snuck away and asked me if I came by car. She asked if I would take her for a ride outside in my car. I heard an older girl call for her by name. *Wynter*. A very distinctive n—"

"Did I have a teddy bear?"

He looked taken aback. "No, I don't think so. Can you tell me what life was like for a child at the ashram? Did you feel safe?"

Wynter's throat closed up. She willed that staff door to open. How long had Patricia been gone? Thirty seconds? Where was Jesse? How long did it take to get up and get dressed and race down the stairs to rescue her? Was he taking a shower first?

Oh god, Jesse took fifteen-minute showers sometimes...

Charlie looked over his shoulder to follow her gaze. "If you'd prefer to have your brother present while we chat, that's perfectly okay."

Wynter found her voice. "Like I said, he'll probably just throw you out. He has a black belt in karate."

Charlie still didn't look perturbed. "You don't have to answer any questions you don't like. I'd like to get a general..."

His words faded out as Wynter drew in a sharp breath of relief because the door had opened. Jesse strode out in his sweatpants, bare feet, bare chest. He was pulling a hoodie over his head as he advanced. He dropped onto the seat beside Wynter and looked the journalist over.

"Charlie Bryant," Charlie said, offering his hand. To her surprise, Jesse shook it. "Can I give you my card?"

He handed another card to Jesse, who shoved it into his pocket without looking at it.

"You're early," Jesse said.

Wynter's jaw dropped. "You know him?"

"Rain gave me Jesse's number, as well as Caleb's," Charlie said. "And yours."

"She had no right to do that," Wynter said.

"Perhaps not."

"He texted me last night," Jesse told her. "You don't have to talk to him, Wyn, but this could be your chance to get back at them."

"Them?"

"The Light. The teachers."

"Jesse told me about the teachers," Charlie said, "but I can't print a story about what they did unless you give me a first-hand—"

"What else did he tell you?" Wynter turned to Jesse. "Was this why you were on your phone half the night? You told me you were texting that girl from Seville!"

"I was. I was texting them both. Pretty tricky, juggling the two. I think I only messed up that one time, right, Charlie?"

Charlie said, "I confess, no one has ever described my hips in such... *dramatic* terms before."

"So," Jesse said to Wynter, unembarrassed by his slip-up because nothing embarrassed Jesse, "I didn't lie."

"It was a lie of omission."

"It was a privacy issue."

Wynter harrumphed and shoved Jesse in the chest. "Does Caleb know he's here?"

"No way would Caleb allow this without being present."

"Why did you arrange it if Caleb would disapprove?"

Charlie cleared his throat to get their attention, a smile playing on his lips. "Wynter, why don't you go ahead and tell me whatever you're comfortable telling me. Rain never went to the ashram, and it's impossible to get an interview with the leadership these days. So, short of buying a two-thousand-dollar spa package at the retreat, you're my only window into that world."

"Are you going to put my name in your article?"

"Not if you don't want me to."

"But they'll know it was me. They'll figure it out."

"Well, I'll be as careful as I can."

"No, they'll know. I don't want to talk about the teachers."

Jesse muffled a groan of irritation.

"Okay. What would you like to talk about?" Charlie said.

"What was your first article about? Can I see it?"

"Sure." Charlie unzipped his black folder and took out a few photocopied pages, stapled together. "I wrote about the history of the ashram from the late 'seventies to the turn of the millennium. How it evolved. Back then, in 2002, the warehouse didn't exist. There were no retail stores or meditation retreats. It was a group of people living off the grid. By formalizing the Light as a religion and calling it a temple, they could get religious visas for people from all over the world."

Wynter was looking through the black-and-white pages. She pointed to a photograph, jabbing her finger against the sheet to stop her hand shaking.

"That's Miss Althea."

Jesse drew the page closer and examined the picture of the woman in her thirties with long thick hair, wearing a shapeless dress and holding a basket of vegetables, which the caption said came from the ashram's farm. She smiled for the camera but there was something wrong with her eyes. Wynter knew that look.

"A little strange, that one," Charlie said, watching Wynter carefully.

"Who's Miss Althea?" Jesse said.

Wynter swallowed the lump in her throat. "The disease started with her."

She quickly flipped to the next page.

"So, things have changed a bit since then," Charlie said, "and you were there, right when all those changes happened."

"I don't know anything about it." Wynter breathed deep to keep the dark pieces under. "I don't remember *before* there was a warehouse. I don't know when the regional offices were set up. I just... I just sat in the classroom and did chores and made things in the warehouse and packed orders."

"I see. Were you happy there?"

She shook her head sharply.

"If you could tell the world one thing about the Light, what would it be?"

Wynter turned another page, to a photo of two children crouched in the dirt, heads bowed, dirty hair flopping forward. Poking holes with their fingers. Planting seeds. In the background were a couple more children in smocks, turned away from the camera.

Four children, no faces.

Wynter said, "It makes you disappear."

"Wyn, is that you?" Jesse said in an odd voice, tapping the blonde child on the right.

"It is," Charlie said. "I wasn't given permission to print their faces or names. Wynter, do you know who those other children are? I'd like to track them down."

Wynter's ears were buzzing. Her breath shuddered as a wave of dizziness hit. Vaguely, she was aware of Jesse's arm going around her shoulder, of him sliding closer and saying something from far away...

"It's okay. It's okay."

It wasn't okay.

She forced herself to look at the picture again. Forced her finger to touch the dark-haired child next to her four-year-old self. Forced herself to speak his name, to bring him back into existence.

"Deedee."

Jesse wanted revenge on the Light. Was that worth Wynter having a mini-breakdown in front of him?

She had her hands pressed over her mouth as she shrunk back into the corner of the booth, her gaze still fixed on the photo.

"I'm not allowed to say it," she mumbled, and her hands went from her mouth to her ears, and she squeezed her eyes closed. "I'm not allowed to say his name."

As Jesse reached for Wynter, she started to slide under the table. Just like that day Joy had throttled her and she'd tried to escape. He caught her when she was halfway under, gripping her arms to pull her back to the seat.

"Joy's not here," Jesse said, in case that helped. He had no idea what to do and Charlie wasn't helping. The journalist looked startled — an odd expression on a guy who had surely seen it all. "Wyn, it's okay. You *are* allowed to say his name."

She collapsed against him, clinging to his arms.

"Deedee. I used to play with him. He left and they gave me... they gave me a teddy bear." The words tumbled out. "They told me *that* was Deedee but it wasn't. He was a real boy."

"Any idea who that kid is?" Jesse asked Charlie.

Charlie was scrolling through his phone. "I've got no information on any of them. There were families moving in and out of that place all the time. I have the original photo right here. A clearer picture, in case it helps her identify the others."

Jesse took the phone. To his surprise, Wynter grabbed at it like it might save her life, and together they looked at the photo. It was in color, and uncropped. In the foreground, the part that was cropped out of the magazine article, was twelve-year-old Joy looking solemnly at the camera. Wynter wasn't interested in that. She was zooming in on the boy.

"The children always left." Her voice was little more than a whisper. "They never stayed. After a while I stopped caring about them, and none of them cared about me, or about each other. Nobody cared who got hurt or why. I was the only one who was there forever."

"Maybe, when Deedee left, you did care," Jesse said. "You were so upset, they gave you the bear as a substitute, to make you feel better."

"It made me feel *worse*. His eyes were supposed to be blue."

"Like Deedee's eyes?"

She nodded, her tears falling on the phone. Jesse carefully extracted it from her hand and gave it back to Charlie.

"Send me that photo," Jesse told him.

"Of course. I still have questions, if—"

"I'll contact you if she wants to talk again."

Charlie looked like he wanted to say more. Patricia was coming over and he got the message it was time for him to go. He dropped a twenty-dollar bill on the table for his breakfast, took his black folder, and left.

Jesse managed to coax Wynter out of the seat and with Patricia's help got her through the kitchen and out the back, away from the curious stares of customers, and into the bracing morning air.

"What do you need?" Patricia said, as he settled with her on a bench the staff used on their smoke breaks. "Should I call Caleb?"

"No, I'll do that." Jesse didn't want his brother getting a half-informed garbled account, which it would be despite Patricia's best intentions. Also, this was all kind of Jesse's fault and he needed to get himself together before dealing with Caleb.

"Don't stay out here too long," she said, and went back inside.

Jesse held Wynter close, looking out across the mountain, jiggling his bare feet on the freezing concrete to stop them going numb. His only thought, when Charlie contacted him yesterday before jumping on a midnight flight from Phoenix, had been getting Wynter's story out there. Charlie had tried calling Caleb first, with no answer — unsurprisingly, as Caleb's routine was all over the place while he was in the hospital. Fortunately, he'd skipped Indio and called Jesse next. Indio would've given the guy a firm *no*. Maybe Caleb would've, too, which was why Jesse had organized the whole thing himself.

He knew it would be tough for Wynter, but if she wasn't going to tell the authorities what had happened to her, a journalist was surely the next best option. Jesse just wanted those people held accountable in some way.

He hadn't counted on Deedee coming up in the conversation. At least the mystery of her teddy bear phobia was solved.

"What was his real name?" he asked her now, rubbing her shoulder to keep her warm. To keep her pressed against him, which was the only thing keeping *him* warm. "Something starting with D?"

"His name was *Deedee*. We sat together on the mat doing... something..." Her fingers fluttered and she pinched her right finger and thumb. "Sewing buttons. We snapped beans. He painted my hair with mud to make it match his. Then they gave me a teddy bear with dead eyes. *This is Deedee*, they said. What happened, Jesse? I *did* stop talking about him. I forgot about him. How could I do that? He stopped existing."

All those times Wynter had spoken about feeling like she didn't exist at the ashram... It made sense now, even aside from their mother leaving her and the teachers abusing her.

He held her tighter, to keep her from floating away.

"I feel badly for Joy," she said after a while.

"Whatever you're about to say, just know that I *don't* feel badly for her and nothing you say will change that."

"She looked so... *empty* in that photo. She took care of me and watched over the other kids for her entire childhood. That was her job. And just when she was old enough to be treated as an adult, Momma left the ashram. Maybe Joy felt like I did, like she didn't exist."

Nope, not feeling it. Jesse kept the thought to himself. His initial reaction to the teddy-substitute scheme had been sympathetic. It was, after all, an attempt to make Wynter feel better even if it backfired. But now it just seemed weird. Joy knew Deedee had been real, yet she'd denied it right up until she returned to the ashram.

Much as he tried not to, he couldn't help feeling there was a malicious reason behind it all.

Jackpot

Two days before Wynter's sixteenth birthday, which Jesse said was a significant one, Caleb told her what she'd feared, that he didn't think they could move into that eccentric old farmhouse with the tower after all.

They'd spent the four days since his release from the hospital packing up their Seattle home. Or, rather, she and Jesse did the packing while Caleb sat next to a humidifier in the living room being told to rest. Wynter did allow him to sort through old paperwork and photos and clothes, deciding what to toss, and after that she let him wrap the breakables in the kitchen.

Tomorrow they were going on their weekend camping trip, and on Monday she would be starting at the new high school.

Indio rode up on Thursday afternoon, and he and Jesse moved the furniture into a rented truck. Patricia was going to let them store the boxes and furniture in her shed because tomorrow they were handing over the keys to the couple who had bought the house.

In a little over a week, they were supposed to be getting the keys to *their* new home.

Wynter walked slowly down the hallway of the little Columbia City house, looking into each room to bid a silent farewell to the first home she'd ever known. At the top of the steps to the basement, Caleb caught up with her. Officially, he was on sick leave. But in fact he was in the process of being separated from the Coast Guard "by reason of physical disability."

He was out of a job.

"I can't take on a thirty-year mortgage," he explained. "If I don't find steady employment before the seventeenth of this month, the bank will cancel the loan."

"Where will we live?"

"I have some money from the VA. We'll rent somewhere, sort ourselves out, and eventually we will buy the perfect home."

She stopped herself saying, *The house on Tiger Mountain is the perfect home.* Because she knew some part of Caleb was relieved about not going through with the purchase. Those crumbling walls and broken fences, that leaking roof and peeling paint, those five acres... It was too much for him. He would never admit it aloud, but since his rehospitalization he'd lost confidence in himself. He wasn't feeling strong, and he wouldn't show it because he knew how much she and Jesse needed him to be strong.

So, she didn't make a fuss about it. She didn't tell him how disappointed she was, because he already knew. She nodded bravely and prepared herself for a very different homecoming than the one she'd imagined. They'd lost the Seattle house, which meant a lot to her even if her brothers were happy to leave it. But they'd find another home, one day.

And she was in Caleb's care, which had always been the most important thing by far.

"I have to say goodbye to the jamroom," she said.

He followed her down the steps into the now-empty basement, leaving the door wide open to let in the late-afternoon light because the power had been turned off. Until yesterday there had been rugs and posters hung on the walls. They were all taken down. There had been cables taped to the floor. Nothing left but stained, well-worn carpet, which Caleb had made Jesse vacuum. He was insistent that they leave the house clean and tidy.

"What d'you think the new owners will use this room for?" she asked him.

"I think he plans to brew beer."

"What about upstairs? The two extra bedrooms?"

"Well, they have grandkids here in Seattle, so I expect those rooms will become children's bedrooms."

"Do children do that? Sleep at their grandparents' house?"

"Yes, hun, that's normal."

"I guess I like that idea. Children running through the house. As long as they're happy children."

"The Robinsons seem like nice folk. I'm sure they have happy grandchildren."

"When Mr Robinson is brewing his beer down here, I think if he listens carefully he'll hear echoes of our jam sessions. The ghosts of us."

"Hope he likes 'seventies rock and extended drum solos."

Caleb held out his arm and she went to him for a warm hug. Looking up at his familiar face, his jaw shadowed with an uncharacteristic week-old beard, she thought about everything he'd lost. His job, through which he defined himself. The woman he loved and the tiny girl who was supposed to call him *Daddy*. His health and his physical strength. And now, the home he'd planned to rebuild for her and for Jesse.

"We'll find our perfect home," she said, pressing her cheek to his chest. "I know it'll take a little longer, and that's okay. I can wait."

"You've waited so long already." He stroked her hair and sighed. "I feel like... everything is ending, and that's okay because I wanted to make a fresh start..."

So strange to hear Caleb use that phrase. *I feel...*

She wrapped her arms around him and squeezed tight.

"But now we're in limbo," he said. "I'm so sorry it didn't work out."

"Everything is perfect," she said, and she meant it.

Even that journalist... Perfect timing, in a way. She was leaving her first true home, closing that door so the next one could be opened, and Charlie had unwittingly helped her close another. People *did* disappear into the Light. It swallowed everything. Their mother's love. Their sister's sanity. Miss Althea's decency. The kindness of every teacher. Her little blue-eyed playmate. For years she'd been made to believe he never existed, which stoked her own fears of fading away.

Time to leave that fear behind. Deedee was real, living a life out there somewhere, hopefully a life as perfect as hers. Time to open the next door, wherever it led.

"You got mad at Jesse about the journalist, didn't you," Wynter said, not breaking the hug because Caleb surely couldn't get upset again if she was hugging him.

"Strong words were spoken," Caleb admitted. "He was unrepentant."

"That's because I forgave him. It wasn't anything to do with you."

"You may be turning sixteen, but I'm still the boss around here. I told him to lose the guy's number."

"I'm sure he memorized it. Just in case."

Caleb grunted.

From upstairs, Jesse called out that they were ready to leave. He and Caleb were going to drive the car and the Silverado, and Indio was driving the big moving truck.

Caleb released her and they reluctantly walked to the door. His toe kicked at something on the carpet. He bent down, and when he straightened he had a guitar pick between his fingers. One of the Clockwork Toys picks Indio had made for Wynter's eighth-grade band. Hunter had refused to take one, so she had two — she kept one in a safe place and used the other for practice.

Caleb turned it over in his palm, examining the cogwheel design.

"Your sign from the universe," he said, because her cogwheel tattoo matched his Coast Guard machinery tech symbol.

"That I belong to you."

He smiled and took her hand. "And here you are."

"Ride with me?" Indio said as they assembled outside the house.

Wynter was going to ride in the Silverado to keep Caleb company. Something in Indio's tone made her reconsider, and she shrugged assent. It was only a fifteen-mile trip and it would be fun to ride in the cab of the big moving truck.

"I need to drop the keys off with the realtor," Caleb said. "I'll see you guys there."

As his truck and Jesse's car departed, Wynter gave the house one last look. The sun was setting and it was almost as dark as that January evening more than one year ago when she arrived by taxi and checked the number on the gate to make sure she was at the right place before knocking on the door. The door now had a fresh coat of white paint. Didn't look right.

"What did you think you were gonna find when you showed up here?" Indio asked behind her, his thoughts apparently mirroring hers.

"I had no idea what to expect. But I thought... Joy is my sister and she got me out of that place. Caleb is my brother and that means something, too. He was just a name on a list but I thought there was a chance he'd understand the connection, and let me in. I didn't realize he had this whole other thing that made him act — his sense of duty."

"You hit the jackpot."

"Yeah. I feel bad for him, though, because he's upset about not being able to buy the house."

Indio jangled the keys and beckoned her over to the moving truck. She had to haul herself into it because the cab was so high off the ground. Indio paused, and instead of closing the door he leaned in the door frame.

"There's still a way you and Caleb and Jesse can get your dream home on the mountain."

For a second she thought he was joking. "Not you?"

His eyes flashed with that same annoyance she'd seen on the jetty, two months ago, right after she'd set this whole thing in motion.

"Wanna hear the plan, or not?"

"Will we have to lie or cheat? Caleb won't like that."

"Caleb won't like this, either. He doesn't have to find out. Kind of like that down payment that miraculously appeared in his bank account last month."

He raised a knowing eyebrow and she chewed her lip. *Busted.*

Warily, she said, "Tell me the plan."

"So there's a job opening, a long-term contract position that's perfect for Caleb."

"How do you know about it?"

"I did a little research."

"You're supposed to be studying for your finals."

"I'll ask you again — do you want to hear the plan, or not?"

She mimed zipping her lips.

"It's a consultancy job for a company downtown that does a lot of contract work for the Coast Guard. Right up Caleb's alley. On Monday morning, when we get back from our camping trip and he starts thinking about looking for a job, he'll find the ad and he'll probably apply."

"Will he get it?"

"I don't know. But maybe we could tilt the odds in his favor."

"How?"

"Mateo works for that company. Remember him?"

"The Fourth of July barbecue dad? He hates me."

"He doesn't hate you. He was a completely unsuitable guardian for you, but he was willing to do the right thing and take you in. His wife had reservations. She's irrelevant today. So, we tilt the odds. I have his number from Jesse. If you—"

"Wait, Jesse's involved with this?"

"Of course. We decided I should be the one to talk to you about it, after what he did setting up that journalist guy—"

"He told you about that?"

"After the fact, yeah."

"Charlie might be able to find Xay."

Indio shook his head at the change in subject, but indulged it. "Not likely."

"Don't you want to find him?"

"I'm just saying, a freelance journalist doesn't have cash lying around to spend on a full-blown missing persons investigation."

"You didn't answer my question."

He gave her a long look, and she knew he was choosing his words carefully. "If finding Xay helps you, then yes. If it hurts you... then, no."

"Why would it hurt me?"

He was suddenly too interested in studying his own boots, and Wynter's stomach dropped.

"How could you think he'd hurt me?" she whispered. "He was my only friend in there."

Indio raised his gaze and she'd never seen him look so pained and uncertain. "I get that. I don't mean he'd hurt you deliberately. But his reappearance in your life could hurt you. Stir up the past."

"You're wrong."

"Maybe."

Even if Indio was right, and she was sure he wasn't, what about the chance for Xay to meet his brothers, and for them to meet him? Did that mean nothing?

Indio had set his jaw. "We're talking about Mateo, remember? Jesse was concerned you'd refuse to call Mateo out of sheer stubbornness, if he asked you."

"You want *me* to call Mateo?"

He shut the door and came around to the driver's side. He wouldn't tell her more until they were well underway, heading east on I-90.

"Ask him to put in a good word for Caleb. That's how this works. Word of mouth. Clearly Mateo felt a sense of duty last year to help Caleb out, even though they barely knew each other. I think he'll do the right thing again, and get Caleb that job."

"Why me?"

"In case you hadn't noticed, Mateo has a weakness for pretty little girls in frilly dresses."

"I'm not a—"

"And *you* seem to have the talent for making intractable men do what you want. Caleb. Harry. Let's see if it works on Mateo."

"I don't know what to say to him."

"Caleb said he was a good guy, and I'm willing to trust his assessment. Maybe he doesn't know about Caleb's accident and the medical discharge. So, call him and explain the situation."

"Right now?"

"He'll be home for dinner."

Indio took a scrap of paper from his pocket and handed it over — a phone number. Wynter tapped in the digits, her heart in her throat. She put the phone on speaker. Mateo answered with a distracted monosyllable. In the background she heard the kids talking and the clink of dishes.

"It's Wynter, Caleb's sister. I'm sorry to disturb you at dinner."

"What can I do for you, Wynter?"

He was a good guy. *What can I do for you?* He wanted to be of service.

"Caleb had a bad accident a few months ago. Did you hear?"

"I did hear. How's he doing?"

"He's doing better. He was just discharged from the Coast Guard. He's devastated about it, actually."

"That's a damn shame. He did his country proud."

"The thing is... he needs a job because he found a home for me. The perfect home. My forever home."

Her eyes pricked and tears spilled over. She turned away quickly, not wanting Indio to see. And, almost at once, she turned back to him because he was the one person she felt comfortable hiding nothing from. Indio gave her a smile of encouragement before putting his eyes back on the road.

"I see," Mateo was saying. "Actually, there's an opening at my company. He should apply."

"I know about that. It's why I'm calling. Is there... is there anything you can do?"

Mateo was silent for a long time. Wynter held her breath.

"I'll see what I can do," he said.

What did that mean?

"*What* can you do?" she asked, seeking clarification.

Mateo chuckled deep in his chest. "Wynter, I'll see what I can do. I'll have my boss call him tomorrow morning. I don't think it'll be a problem."

"Thank you." Wynter swiped at her wet cheeks. "And I'm so sorry about that barbecue. I screwed everything up and I was so rude to your wife. And Jesse was... well, he was being Jesse. I'm sorry about him, too."

"That's quite alright. Don't you worry, now. We look out for our own."

As she ended the call, she realized Indio had pulled over on the freeway. Maybe because he thought she wanted comfort. She didn't want that. She needed to understand what was going on. She sat for a moment, staring at her phone.

"What does that mean," she said, "*We look out for our own?*"

"That's what Caleb would call duty."

"I think he'd also call it love."

Indio gave a little shrug. "Maybe. I mean, that's how he defines it." A frown flickered on his brow. "*Love* is a strong word, though. People shouldn't throw it around."

"Do you know what it means?"

"Not really." And now he turned away from her, wiping his hand across his lower face as he watched the traffic whizzing past, elbow propped on the window.

"Do you think Caleb loves you?"

She felt his entire body still, and she knew why. He'd expected her to ask *Do you love Caleb?* But that question was surely meaningless if he didn't know what love was.

"Has he given you the whole *acts of love* speech?" he said at last.

"Yes."

"Then, by his definition, I guess he loves me."

"I *know* he does. I know he feels more deeply than any of us can imagine. Not just love, but everything. He knows how to express love — through acts of duty — but he doesn't know how to express the rest. Or he doesn't think it's important to express it." Wynter's heart stuttered again because getting Caleb that job, that mortgage, might actually harm him more than help him. "He's terrified he can't manage that property. He needs help."

Indio's expression turned brittle as he looked over. "Don't start up with that again, baby. I told you, I can't live near him."

Wynter silently berated herself for harping on it, and she backed down. He hadn't pushed her, and she shouldn't push him. She unbuckled her seatbelt and climbed over the gearshift in the huge cab to hug him.

She said, "I won't ask you again. Even when you're old and gray, I won't ask again."

Indio rubbed her back briefly before setting her on her seat about half a minute before she was ready for the hug to be over.

One problem at a time, that's what Caleb would say. He had a job now, almost guaranteed. Which meant they had the house on Tiger Mountain. Indio moving home... she'd have to leave that in someone else's hands.

Everybody Wins

"So, Wynter," Indio said, at the wheel for the three-hour drive to the Gifford Pinchot National Forest. "You're a big fan of Caleb's house rules. He has a million more rules that apply to camping. Have you learned those?"

Caleb, in the back seat with Wynter, was determined not to let him dull her enthusiasm. "Wynter's a fast learner."

"I asked Jesse for the list," Wynter said, "and he said the only rule he cares about is he can't smoke weed on federal land."

Jesse twisted in his seat to frown at her for tattling, before giving Caleb a guilty sidelong look. *Had* he brought weed with him?

Caleb cleared the suspicion from his mind. He had other things to think about. That morning, his former colleague Mateo had called with a job opportunity. The two of them weren't in any kind of regular contact but he'd heard on the grapevine about Caleb's accident and medical discharge. Caleb had agreed to an interview next week to see what it was all about, with the distinct feeling the job was his if he wanted it.

He didn't plan on telling his siblings anything until it was in the bag. No reason to get hopes up. A job meant he could take on a mortgage, but given his physical state right now he still hadn't decided if he was going through with buying that rundown house. He'd even asked Indio to drive today, just in case his concentration or his back couldn't take it.

If he could survive a couple of freezing nights in a tent, on the other hand, he couldn't be doing too badly.

The last few miles of the journey, east of Mt St Helens, were on an unmarked rough road that took them deep into the forest. They had camped here as teenagers — first with Harry, and later without — and Caleb's favorite spot was a clearing set back thirty yards from the river bank, rather than right on the water where other campers tended to hang out. Not that it was busy at this time of year.

They pitched the tents, with Caleb ensuring Wynter did her share and learned along the way. There were no utilities provided, so they'd brought along a tank of drinking water. While Indio got their camp kitchen sorted, the other three walked down to the river with buckets to fetch washing water. The forest opened onto the rocky bank to reveal a stunning vista across the wide river. At the river's edge, the flow was slowed by smooth boulders, and they made their way out to fill the buckets.

"Can we fish in there?" Wynter asked.

"Didn't bring the gear this time," Caleb said. "This water's not great for fishing — it can get quite muddy. We're here to enjoy the view and the solitude."

"Where's the toilet?"

"There's a little shovel in the truck," Jesse said.

"And?"

"And, that's your toilet. Do you need a demonstration?"

She shoved him playfully in retaliation, and he stumbled down a rock into the ankle-deep water.

"Fuck! I don't have any spare sneakers."

"Watch it," Caleb said, meaning his language. He grabbed Jesse's arm and helped him out. To Wynter, he said, "No messing around near the water, hun."

"Sorry," she said with a sheepish look. "I didn't know about the toilet, though. Didn't realize it would be *quite* so... primitive."

"Memorable way to spend your sixteenth birthday, huh?" Jesse said. "Looks like rain, too, which will be awesome."

Wynter studied him for a full second before deciding he was being facetious.

"This camping trip *will* be awesome," she proclaimed as they headed back, collecting firewood along the way. "Every single thing that happens will be a new experience for me."

"Well, that's great for *you*," Jesse said. In Caleb's experience, Jesse always started a camping trip in a sour mood, mostly because of the *no phones* rule. He'd soon get used to resting his brain and by the end he'd be the one who didn't want to go home.

Indio had the camp stove out, but what was the point of camping without open fire cooking? Caleb showed Wynter how to build the fire, and once it was going he staked a swivel grill over it. They'd brought food for two days. Tonight, chicken legs on the grill. And Jesse's sneakers on a nearby rock, to dry out.

Caleb relaxed on the low fold-out chair that Wynter had insisted they bring along — just the one, just for him — and watched Jesse gently berate her on how she'd wrapped the potatoes in foil before showing her *his* way, and they pushed them into the edge of the fire to bake. He watched Indio open the beers and fetch plates, and was so grateful his wayward brother had stayed at Patricia's last night and come with them today when he had every excuse to go back to Portland, with one week left before his finals. Being outside always made Indio happy, though he may not realize it. It was going to drop to near-freezing tonight, and Indio still had a grin on his face as he turned the chicken and overruled Jesse, with Wynter's assistance, on the choice of music for their evening meal.

"This is the best chicken I've ever tasted," Wynter said as they ate, giving Indio a nod of thanks. "And the potatoes are perfect, Jesse, no doubt because of your well-engineered foil wrapping."

Jesse's turn to check if *she* was being facetious. The food was, of course, delicious.

"Indio," Caleb said, "have you picked up those tickets for your commencement in June? Jesse and Wynter both want to come, and I've got a yes from Harry, if that means anything."

"God, I'm not putting you guys through that," Indio said, licking grease off his fingers. "I'll skip it and just go to the party afterward."

Caleb forced himself not to rise to the bait, the challenge in Indio's eyes that dared him to make a scene about it. Or perhaps he was imagining it. Surely Indio didn't want a scene tonight, on a family vacation, Wynter's first night in a tent, and the eve of her sixteenth birthday.

They cleared up and stoked the fire as the temperature fell. Caleb had been told, quite specifically, to steer away from smoke given his recent lung infection. For now, though, the wind had dropped and he was comfortable enough sitting a little way from the fire.

Jesse, flat on his back observing the twilight sky, said, "Normal people would be checking the forecast on their phones when they're camping under cloudy skies."

"No internet," Caleb growled. They had the phones for emergencies. Otherwise the family was strictly offline for the duration.

"Fine." Jesse sat up and reached for the box of food. "Wyn, here's something all normal people do around campfires."

He found the ingredients for s'mores and showed Wynter how to make them, sticking the marshmallows on the end of twigs. Other than ice cream, which she was quite passionate about, she didn't really eat sweets and didn't think much of the s'mores.

Indio handed her his beer — bitter to wash away the sweet — and then she demanded water to wash away the taste of the beer. As Indio took back his beer, he flicked Caleb a look that spoke volumes. Caleb should be the one deciding whether or not she drank alcohol, even one sip. Indio hadn't bothered to check with him first. Jesse would've checked. The small act of defiance raised Caleb's hackles yet again.

"How do you make the guitar do that?" Wynter asked suddenly. The song playing was a blues number.

"That's a slide," Indio said. "Don't have one with me — I'll show you when we get home."

"Also known as bottleneck guitar," Jesse said, holding up his beer bottle. "Let's innovate!"

Indio scoffed. "In an emergency you can smash the neck off a bottle. I'm not gonna sacrifice fingers to the cause."

Jesse turned to Caleb. "Give me three minutes on my phone and I'll find out how to make one properly. I know there's a few different ways—"

"From a bottle? I don't believe you," Wynter said.

"You don't even know what a slide is," Jesse said dismissively.

Caleb was already reaching for the lighter fluid, stashed behind a rock for safety while the fire was burning. "I know how to do it. Get me some twine from the toolbox, and fill that can with cold water."

Jesse and Wynter did as instructed and sat close by to watch, while Indio lounged back like he'd seen it all before. Caleb felt like a boy scout leader as he wrapped the cotton twine around the neck of his empty beer bottle and dripped lighter fluid onto it, careful not to let it run.

"Lighter?"

Jesse slapped it into his palm. Caleb lit the string and rotated the bottle so it burned evenly. When the flame had burned out, he plunged the heated glass into the cold water for a satisfying *crack*. He fished out the bottle neck and held it up.

"You could've just scored it with a file from the toolbox and snapped it off," Indio said, unimpressed.

"Uh-huh. But this was way cooler." Caleb snatched it away from Wynter as she reached for it. "Gotta smooth it down a bit."

He sanded off the glass tube on a rock while Indio fetched his guitar from the cab of the truck. Indio sat on a rock and re-tuned the guitar to open G. He played some slide licks with Wynter at his feet watching everything, and then she had a go.

"Don't press too hard. You just wanna touch the strings with it," Indio said. "Jesse, find some Bonnie Raitt and Beck for her, and some newer stuff. Sonny Landreth, Derek Trucks—"

"Can't use my phone," Jesse said with an air of tragedy.

"Caleb, this is for educational purposes," Wynter pleaded.

Caleb shrugged, unmoved. "You can wait two days."

Her eyes narrowed in accusation. "You've been using your phone all evening to play music."

"Well…" He made up a justification on the spot. "That's down-loaded, not online."

"Speaking of which, I have surprising news," Jesse said. "Those songs we put on Soundfish after Thanksgiving? We earned fourteen dollars from streaming last month."

"Is that a lot?" Wynter said.

"You're seriously asking me if fourteen dollars is a lot?"

"I meant, is it a good amount to make from music?"

"It's up from $2.91 in January and seventy cents in December. Looks like our success is increasing logarithmically, at the rate of about five-fold per month. You can extrapolate from that and see if we're gonna be millionaires by the end of the year."

Jesse raised an eyebrow, waiting for her to extrapolate.

"If nothing else," he went on, "you can afford new strings. Congrats!"

"Don't we have to split it four ways?"

"We do," Caleb said.

Jesse balked. "You want to split fourteen dollars?"

"Every cent, and split again by song. Fifty percent to the songwriters, fifty percent to the artists. That's industry standard."

Jesse looked to his siblings for support, and got none. "I guess I'll make a spreadsheet," he grumbled. "Wyn, you can help me. You got an A in Tech last semester, right?"

Wynter's eyes were rolled heavenward as she concentrated on her calculations. "So… we'll be earning almost 150 million dollars by December. You can't tell me *that's* not a good amount to make from music."

"That's not too shabby. Caleb, you can quit your new job and buy three hundred farmhouses with that."

"What new job?" Caleb said.

Jesse sucked in his lips. Caleb looked from him to Indio to Wynter, and all three of them looked guilty as hell.

"Didn't Mateo call you?" Wynter said tentatively. "I thought I heard you on the phone this morning talking about a… a job?"

He'd gone outside the diner to take that call. No way had they heard a word of it, let alone any specifics.

"What's going on?"

Wynter glanced at Indio, like she was asking for permission to speak. Indio responded with his usual impassivity, and Jesse wouldn't look up. She was on her own.

"I called him yesterday to let him know about your recuperation, and he said he would put in a good word for you about that job. Or, well, I sort of asked him to."

Caleb sank back in the chair and closed his eyes as his gut clenched with anger. Not just at her. Clearly, they'd all plotted this. What right did they have to involve themselves in his career? And after that disastrous barbecue last year.

Mateo's call, which had filled him with hope and relief, was now an embarrassment. His little sister had begged for that job.

When he opened his eyes, she was kneeling in front of him, to bring their eyes level.

"I need to tell you more. More things that will upset you."

"Jesus, don't make him *angrier*," Jesse muttered.

"The first thing," she said, "is about your wooden sword."

Caleb wasn't expecting anything quite so random. "The bokken?"

"The what?"

"It's called a bokken. Or, it was. Jesse said he left it out and ran over it with the truck."

Wynter glanced at Jesse, confused.

Caleb sighed. "What's *your* story about how it broke?" Her quiet earnestness and his curiosity did, at least, dispel the anger.

"I was fooling around with it and the punching bag. Was it expensive?"

"If it was expensive, it wouldn't have broken."

"How much, exactly? I'll replace it."

"They're twenty bucks and up, depending on the wood and the craftsmanship."

"Which wood would you like?"

"I'll take African ebony, thanks."

"That's a thousand bucks, Wyn," Jesse warned her.

"Listen." Caleb put a hand on her shoulder. "You could've hurt yourself. Don't mess around with my stuff, okay? Let's leave it at that."

She smiled with a little exhalation of relief, before drawing a deep breath. She said, "Secondly, and I convinced myself this was a surprise but it's not, it's a secret because I was never gonna tell you even though you'd have found out eventually."

Caleb braced himself.

"When Patricia took me to visit Harry, he said something about a developer wanting to buy his property. So I went back to see him a week or so later, and I made him sell his house and give you the money."

"You... what?" Caleb and Jesse made the exclamation at the same time.

Indio, for some reason, didn't look shocked in the slightest.

"At Christmas," Wynter said, "he'd talked about being ashamed of his affair, ashamed of Xay's existence. I hated that. Xay's his son, and Harry needs to love him. He might never have the chance if we can't find Xay. I told him this makes it even more important to love the sons he has. I told him — love is what you do, not what you feel. I told him it would be an act of love to help you buy a bigger house."

"Oh, hun..." Caleb dragged a hand through his overgrown hair. "You shouldn't have done that."

"I'm glad I did it. Here's something I didn't understand until I talked to Indio afterward. When you do those acts of love, it helps that person, but it also makes you a better person. You'll get a new home, my forever home, and Harry becomes a better person. Everybody wins."

Caleb looked around her, to Indio on the other side of the fire. "You knew about this?"

"I took her to Everett," Indio said, "but I only figured out what she'd done when you told me about the money a couple weeks later."

"How the hell did you get fifty grand out of Harry?" Jesse said, still stunned.

"I just told you how," Wynter said impatiently.

Regardless of Mateo's job, Caleb was still undecided about buying the house, and that made it so hard, now, to look into Wynter's hopeful eyes and shatter her dreams. So, he said nothing.

She put her hand on his arm. "I know he's not a good person, but I found the part of him that wants to be a better father."

The Wet Season

"Why don't they make tents with skylights?" Wynter asked sleepily, curled up in her sleeping bag. "The stars — isn't that the whole point of camping?"

Caleb stashed his boots in the annex of the tent and lay back on his mat. "No stars tonight. That's a good idea, though. On warm nights we used to sleep out in the open."

"What were you all like, as boys?"

"Well... let's see," Caleb mused, grateful to find something safe to talk about after the night's earlier confessions. "Jesse was exactly the same, of course. Bouncing off the walls, talking a mile a minute when the conversation interested him, otherwise just sort of sitting back, taking it all in, then making some hilarious observation. Best thing Harry ever did for Jesse was buy him a drum kit when he was eight."

"What about Indio?"

"The opposite — quiet most of the time. He and Jesse were great friends, despite the age difference."

"Indio's less than three years younger than you — were you never close?"

"When we were very young. Until Joy left, he was pretty tight with her from what I remember, although he wants to deny that now."

"She remembers it differently, too."

"No, they were close. And he and I did play together a lot, too. Afterward... I didn't have time to be his buddy. Those last few years in Montana, Harry was a wreck. He's what I'd call a functioning alcoholic now. Back then he was much worse."

"What does that mean, *functioning*?"

"It means he still drinks too much, but he controls it better. Hides it better, too. It's not as destructive but it's stopping him from progressing, from having good relationships — with us, with friends and colleagues, with women."

"Is he gonna be okay living on that boat?"

"He used to talk all the time about doing it, so I guess it's what he wants."

"Are you okay about the money?"

Caleb turned to look at her, two feet away in the dark. "I need to sleep on it."

The rain woke him up. Damn, rain on a camping trip made everything just a little tougher. And Wynter was not in her sleeping bag. Caleb put his head out of the tent. She was over on the far side of the campfire ashes, just standing there with her face upturned.

Across the way, the flap of the other tent was open and Indio was watching her. Why the fuck wasn't he telling her to get out of the rain?

"Wynter!" Caleb yelled.

"I love it!" she called back, holding out her arms to welcome the raindrops. It was hammering down, and freezing cold. "We used to run around in the monsoons."

"Get in here."

"I'm going for a walk." She was wearing the sweatpants and t-shirt she'd gone to bed in, and her feet were bare.

"Come back here!" He was angry now as he reached for his boots.

She headed off through the trees, toward the river bank along the track they'd walked earlier in the day.

Caleb pulled on his boots and grabbed a flashlight. He indicated Indio should stay in his tent — no point in both of them getting wet — and went after her. She wasn't walking fast and he caught up as she reached the river.

He grabbed her arm. "What are you doing?"

"I want to watch the raindrops bounce on the river," she said, like it was the most normal thing in the world.

"Come back. This is crazy."

"It's just rain. I love it."

"I don't care. You don't wander off in the night."

He hated the harshness in his tone, and the alarm it put in her eyes, but he was scared for her. He pulled her back toward the campsite, and he was out of breath as they entered the clearing. His lungs felt clogged. He knew that feeling. Must've breathed in some smoke after all.

Wynter dug in her heels just outside the boys' tent.

"What the hell's the matter?" he yelled at her.

"I don't like the tent."

She tried to pull away. He coughed, his chest rattling with the effort.

"Christ, Wynter, the tent is all we've got."

"Your anger won't fit in that tiny space."

"*What?*"

He let her go and she hugged her arms around herself, a drowned rat with hair plastered to her face, wet skin gleaming. He tried to see it from her perspective. He *was* angry. He was angry because he didn't understand what was going on and because after two minutes out in this freezing rain he needed to sleep for a week.

"Deedee loved the rain. I went to fetch him so we could run around outside but he was..." She gave him a stark look.

"You can tell me about this inside."

"I have to go back to the river."

She backed away, turned, and ran off again. He took two paces and had to stop because he couldn't draw breath.

He fell to his knees in the mud. What the hell was wrong with him?

From the corner of his eye he saw Indio stride past, barefoot, into the forest. Caleb dragged himself up and staggered after him. He found them a little farther down the path. Indio was hugging her tightly against him, so tightly she couldn't escape this time, though she was still agitated.

"They put Deedee in a box," she gasped. "That's what Joy said. You heard her say it."

"Joy was talking about a teddy bear," Indio said, as confused as Caleb was.

"He was a real boy." She managed to pull away from him but he caught her wrists just in time. "They made me forget. Like he never existed."

Indio wrapped his arms around her again and said, "He does exist. He's in that photo—"

"No." She shook her head fiercely against his chest. "Not any more. He wouldn't get up. He's dead. You heard her say it! *We put him in a box, and we put the box away.*"

"Oh, god..." Indio said, and caught Caleb's eye. "That's why Joy freaked out. They covered up his death."

Caleb didn't know what the hell was going on, except that he was going to pass out if he didn't sit down and warm up soon.

"We need to get back." Another coughing fit took over.

This time, Wynter didn't resist as Indio guided her through the rain, an arm around her shoulder. Caleb made her get in the back of the truck, fetched a bag of clothes from his tent, and got in the front. He turned on the engine, and then the heater full-blast. As always, she seemed unconcerned about being cold and he couldn't tell how cold she was anyway, because he was even colder. Indio brought their blankets from their tent, and then went back to his tent to dry off.

No sign of Jesse, who always slept like a log.

"I'm okay now. I'm okay," Wynter said, over and over through chattering teeth. "You're gonna get sick again. I'm sorry. I had a dream it was raining, and the next thing I knew, I was out in the rain."

Caleb leaned between the seats to reach her, and tried rubbing her arms with a blanket. His breathing was labored, his own arms leaden, and so he stopped to deal with himself first. As the windows misted, he dried off in the confined space and pulled dry clothes out of the bag for both of them.

"What you did was dangerous," he said. "You could've slipped and fallen in the river, or gotten lost in the woods."

"I'm sorry. Please don't get sick again."

He twisted around to face her, stroked her hair by way of forgiveness.

"Deedee was real," she said, sounding more like herself now. "We played together all the time. He was always right there, and then suddenly he was gone and they kept telling me the teddy bear was Deedee. They hit my hand with a ruler every time I asked for the real Deedee. He wasn't a bear with dead eyes. He was a real boy with blue eyes and he died."

"Okay. I believe you." Caleb pulled a fresh windbreaker over his head. Wynter wasn't making any effort to change. "What was his full name?"

"I don't know. He was just Deedee."

"Was he born at the ashram? Who were his parents?"

"I don't know. I don't know when he arrived. I didn't know who anyone's parents were because the kids were in a separate place. Charlie said people passed through the ashram all the time. How will we ever find out where he came from?"

"If his parents were in the Light when he was born, and didn't register his birth, and his death was covered up, then there's no record of him."

"Charlie has that one photo but you can't even see his face."

"He's alive in your memory, hun. Proof he existed. And there are at least a few people out there who know the truth. His parents, for starters. The adults who lived there at the time, the leadership. And Joy. Can you tell me how he died?"

"He was sick for a while and they wouldn't let me near him."

"They weren't keen on vaccinations at the ashram, so it could've been any common childhood illness."

"It started to rain so I went to find him. He wouldn't wake up. I lifted his eyelids but he wouldn't open his eyes. And he was so cold." Her breath caught in a sob and she pressed her face in her hands. "He vanished and his clothes vanished and I wasn't allowed to ask why. I kept asking. I kept saying his name. So they gave me a teddy bear and told me there was never a boy called Deedee. Only the bear."

She was shivering all over, but calm now, fully in the present. She accepted the bundle of dry clothes from him, and he turned away while she changed.

"Are you still angry?" she said, her teeth chattering.

He drew a deep breath and spoke quietly. "No. Not with you."

He switched off the engine, which had been masking the sound of the rain on the roof. They listened in silence for a while. Wynter kneeled forward from the back and put her head on his shoulder, and wrapped one arm across his upper chest. Water cascaded down the windshield.

"It reminded me of the monsoon," Wynter said, "but it's not warm."

"Huh, you noticed that."

"It rained, like, twice a year in Arizona."

"That can't be true."

"Well, I'm talking about the wet season. I loved it. All the adults running around like geckos without their tails because they were never ready for it. Every time it happened, it was like they'd never seen it before. Chaos!"

"You like chaos, huh?"

"I liked *that* chaos."

"When we're camping, I'm not a fan of chaos. Let's get back to the tent." He balled up their wet things. "Indio's gonna be grouchy as a bear tomorrow morning.

❧

Indio got up at first light to walk in the woods, to warm himself up. There was a bluff overlooking the river he used to climb, as a kid, and he was pleased to find it again. When he returned, he crossed paths with Wynter on her way to the river with an armful of muddy clothes. The result of last night's escapade. She was wearing nothing but a too-big t-shirt — his t-shirt — over her panties, and her boots. He shivered just to see her dressed like that.

"Happy birthday," he said, wondering if she was going to want to talk about her 2AM stroll in the rain. Caleb would've made sure she was okay. No reason to bring it up again, today of all days. "How's sixteen treating you?"

She grinned, in a good mood despite everything. "So far, so good. I'm going to the river to rinse this."

After last night, he probably shouldn't let her go anywhere alone. "I'll come with you."

They walked toward the river. They could ignore her rainstorm revelations, but he was curious about what had happened before that.

"What was with all those confessions around the campfire?"

"Clearing the air," she said. "In the Light, they had this thing called Reflections and Intentions. You had to confess before the group, or you were made to confess, and then you stated your intent to get back on the right path. They did it all the time. The biggest one was on New Year's Eve."

"You're telling me you confessed to Caleb, on the eve of your birthday, as a nod to some old Light ritual?"

"I know it's hard for you to understand. I know you'd rather be skinned alive than confess anything to him."

They reached the river, which was a torrent after last night's rain, and walked along a little way to find a safe place to approach the bank. She dumped the clothes on a rock.

"You didn't tell him everything, though," Indio said. "You're holding back a lot. Almost everything, in fact."

As she sorted through the clothes, she gave him a sidelong look that said she didn't like him pointing that out. "I already told him about Xay," she said archly, "and that time they locked me up for days. I already told you about the teachers. Did I leave something out?"

"How would I know?"

A flash of irritation lit her eyes before she turned away. Damn, he hadn't meant to do that.

She knelt to dunk the cuffs of Caleb's sweatpants in the water.

"Sometimes," she said, "I think you know a lot more than you say. Maybe you've already guessed things. I don't know. I don't want to talk about it."

The breeze blew her loose, still-damp hair aside and, because the t-shirt was too big and the neckline too low at the back, he saw those white lines on her skin as he stood over her.

"How about you?" she said conversationally, without looking up. "What do you need to confess?"

"You have scars on the back of your neck and hips."

Immediately, her hand went to rub her neck. The other one dangled in the freezing water and she remained hunched over.

"You said you would never ask me to tell you anything else," she said.

"I'm not asking you anything. I'm confessing that I've seen your scars. From a belt or something."

She straightened and faced him, tense with an unfathomable anger that stretched back through the years, and a good measure of it was directed at him for knowing too much. The hardness in her eyes shocked him. Not the eyes of a girl. She was a woman with stories to tell, and scars to prove it, but he had no right to goad her into sharing anything.

"I'll tell you one more thing, Indio."

He waited, his breath cold in his chest.

"Did Jesse show you that old article by Charlie Bryant?" she said.

"Yes. He told me and Caleb everything."

"The woman in the first photo, that's Miss Althea. She made the scars. I didn't know I had scars, but... it was her. She had an office with a lock. If you were sent to her office, you knew it was gonna be bad."

"Is she still there?"

"She left a few months before we ran away. She did something to me... something worse than before. I don't remember what happened, or why. She did something that broke me, and they sent her away."

Her choice of words sent a wave of nausea through him. He tried to concentrate on the facts. "That was only... what, two years ago? But you don't remember it?"

She shook her head. "I was sick afterward. Not sick in my stomach or anything, just... sick. I couldn't get up. It's all a jumble in my head. I remember going to the shed to find Xay, a long time later. He was distraught that night because I hadn't been back in so long. And because that was his last night at the ashram, although I didn't know it until I got there. He and his mom were sent to Nevada, and all the other families were reassigned, and a while later Roman ran away, and I was the only child left."

She turned to watch the river, drawing in a lungful of air. Her breath misted as she exhaled the darkness, the pain and the memories, and when she looked back at him he hardly recognized her.

"I feel happier than fifteen, much stronger, and more alive." She gifted him a slow, thoughtful smile that warmed him through. "I guess this is what sixteen feels like?"

"I wouldn't know, baby," he said lightly. "I'm gonna say it's different for everyone. I spent my sixteenth birthday hitchhiking through Idaho, wasted."

"*What?*" She crouched again to wring out the clothes, throwing a look over her shoulder. "Why don't I know that story?"

"Uh, that wasn't a good summer for me." Caleb had been about to leave for bootcamp and somehow, even though Indio couldn't wait to see the back of him, the prospect was terrifying.

"The entire summer?"

He shrugged and she went back to washing the mud off her arms and splashing water on her face. For some reason, he felt he should look away — and couldn't. He backed up a few paces, confident she wasn't going to do something silly and fall in. She was squatting between bent legs, shifting her feet further apart so she could reach into the water, like a baby giraffe.

No, like a wild forest dryad with knotted hair and green eyes set in porcelain skin...

She stood and raised the edge of the t-shirt to wipe her face dry, revealing more of her body than he was supposed to see — her hip and then her stomach and ribs and the curve of her breast.

He felt a deep tug in his groin, a response so natural and automatic that for a moment he could kid himself it was okay.

Definitely *not* okay.

He turned away and stared blindly into the forest, disgusted with himself. He started back for camp, striding ahead of her.

"Wait up! Indi—"

He heard a squelchy thud, and turned to see her sprawled in the mud amid the pile of clothes. She swore — that must be another *sixteen* thing, because he'd never heard her cuss before — and held up her muddy hands to him, grinning again.

He walked back and pulled her up by the elbow. She had mud all the way down one side of her leg — hip to ankle.

"I hate camping!" she cried, but good-naturedly, and deliberately wiped her hands on his sweatshirt.

"Hey!" He held her at arm's length while she chuckled. He was more than a little annoyed at her for being careless, which broke the earlier tension, so that was a relief.

"I'm gonna wade in to wash this off," she said.

"You are not. The current's too fast today. Wash your hands."

He could sound remarkably like Caleb when he wanted to. She responded accordingly, returning to the water's edge but with an insolent twist of her mouth. She dipped her hands in the water. Indio grabbed Caleb's sweatshirt out of the muddy heap of clothes, rinsed it, and handed it to her. She stood to wipe her leg down, and then he finished off the bits around the back of her thigh with deft swipes to get it over with fast. She had yet more of those narrow scars high up on her legs, cutting off where her shorts cuffs would be if she was wearing them, and his dismay at seeing that washed away the last of his bizarrely inappropriate reaction.

Then something else came to mind, a memory of doing this to Jesse when he was a fat toddler with long dark curls falling in his eyes. Jesse was standing in the tub, giggling and squirming as Indio wiped shit off his legs with a towel — actual shit, after a toilet training accident. Indio remembered being furious that Caleb had put *him* on clean-up duty.

Something was wrong with that memory — there was an edge to it. Why wasn't Mom doing this? Why was Caleb already in charge at nine years old?

"Come on," he said sharply, and set off again.

They returned to camp and stuffed the muddy clothes into plastic bags. Indio nudged Jesse until he stirred. Wynter said she was supposed to boil water for oatmeal and coffee, so he helped her set up the stove. She listened attentively to his instructions while he tried not to think about the inexplicable thing that had just happened. Her fingers were too cold to work the stove's knobs. He could've offered to warm them up in his hands, but he didn't need to be touching any part of her right now. He lit it himself and set water to boil.

Jesse came out of the tent. "Hey, Wynter, did you have fun last night? What was that all about?"

She ducked her head. Indio glared at Jesse, who opened his arms and mouthed *What?* He'd find out soon enough.

"Fetch the bacon," Indio told him, indicating the ice box under the truck on the other side of the site. "And a pan."

Jesse headed to the truck — not before his eyes flicked over Wynter's bare legs and he gave Indio an appreciative smirk. She was facing away and didn't see. Now *there* was something he should feel ashamed about, his brother's behavior. Would that be hypocritical? The difference was that Jesse's reaction was in jest because it was so fucking hilarious to leer at your sister when she wasn't looking, while Indio's reaction had been painfully real.

Caleb emerged from the other tent, went straight to the truck bed, and lifted the tarp. He brought over Wynter's bag and gave it to her.

"Happy birthday."

Her eyes lit up. "Did you put a gift in here?"

"Uh, no, hun. Those are your things." He pointed at their tent. "Go get dressed."

Caleb headed into the woods, toward their makeshift bathroom. While Jesse started the bacon, Indio followed his older brother.

"Is she okay?"

"I think so. Isn't she always?" Caleb leaned against a tree, curling his fingers into a fist. "She once told me she felt like she was shrinking away into nothing at the ashram. That she didn't exist."

"Turns out, her fears were literal."

"I have to report that boy's death. If they covered it up, someone needs to find out what happened."

"It'll get Miriam in trouble. She must've known about it. Joy clearly knew about it."

"She was twelve years old!"

"She's known for ten years and never reported it."

"What do we do?"

"We let it go, Caleb. He died of measles or the flu or something, and they probably panicked, probably thought they'd be accused of neglect. No one's going to jail over it. Don't go digging that up, because it's Wynter who's going to suffer. She has her answer — the boy existed. He lived and died, and she forgot him, and now she remembers. She's okay with it, so we need to be okay with it."

Caleb pressed his forehead to his fist for a moment, and Indio had no idea what he was planning to do.

"I need to think it through," he said at last. "I feel like I'm living in a dream. Every decision is like wading through mud. Nothing feels real anymore since... This body doesn't feel like me. My own *mind* doesn't feel like me."

Weird as hell to hear Caleb baring his soul like this. Indio struggled to come up with something helpful to say.

"Your doctors told you that's a common long-term effect of serious sepsis. Jesse's told you that. None of us expects you to be Superman again just yet."

Eventually, though, and sooner rather than later, Caleb would regain that role in the eyes of their younger siblings. For them, he couldn't put a foot wrong, and his ego was healthy enough to recover from a few months of physical weakness.

After his own misstep this morning, Indio wanted to crawl into a hole and hibernate for fifty years.

He walked reluctantly back to camp.

This family hadn't sung *Happy Birthday* in many years, and they weren't about to start now. At breakfast, Jesse produced a little cake with sixteen candles, only four of which would light because the rest had gotten damp. Indio was glad to see his brother make the effort, though.

Wynter blew the candles out. Jesse insisted she take the piece cut from the center.

"Sheet cake for breakfast," Caleb said, scraping the excessive frosting off his corner piece. "I wonder how long this tradition will last."

"I'll save mine until lunchtime," Wynter said.

Jesse wouldn't hear of it. "You have to eat it now. One bite. One really big bite."

She gave him a suspicious look. "Is there something wrong with it? Is it super-sour or something? Are you gonna video me eating it for YouTube?"

"I would, if phones weren't outlawed. Eat."

She took a cautious bite, chewed, and screwed up her face as she lowered the cake to reveal a chain hanging from her mouth. She spat the mouthful into her hand.

"Why'd you make me do that? You got into trouble with Caleb for spitting out food, and you made me do it?"

"It's your birthday, so he's not allowed to get mad." Jesse grabbed a water bottle to wash off her hand and extracted a silver necklace chain.

"Do you love it?"

"It's covered in goo."

"You didn't even put it in a baggie?" Indio said.

"I admit, I didn't think it through properly."

Jesse rinsed the chain clean and gave it back to her. The pendant was a simple retro-style rocketship, in honor of the sci-fi movies they'd been watching together.

"I do love it," she said, and gave him a hug.

Caleb handed her an envelope, without ceremony. "That's cash."

"Way to ruin the surprise," Jesse said.

"It's the exact amount needed for your learner's permit and driver ed course."

Caleb got his hug, and Jesse looked over at Indio.

"Bro, you're up."

Indio's breath hitched as he sought an excuse. His gift had just become wildly inappropriate.

"I saw it in the tent," Jesse said, clueless. He was the nearest to their tent, and went to get it.

Wynter gave Indio an expectant smile as Jesse handed the wrapped gift to him, and he had no choice but to pass it along to Wynter.

"It's a book," Jesse said helpfully.

"I can tell, thank you, Jesse," she said.

"What is it — a thesaurus like she wanted?" Jesse said, as a joke.

"Way to ruin the surprise," Indio muttered.

Jesse feigned contrition while Wynter unwrapped the thesaurus.

"Perfect! It's a matched set with my rhyming dictionary."

She opened it to the half-title where, days ago, days before this *thing* happened, Indio had drawn an elaborately ornate book plate and inscribed it — stupidly, as it turned out — with three words:

What is love?

Surrounding that he'd designed a word cloud of twenty or so synonyms from the thesaurus itself: affection, amity, amour, devotion, partiality, like, lust...

He'd actually written the word *lust* in a gift to his sister. What was the matter with him? It was supposed to be nostalgic and sweet because of the text message she'd sent all of them on Valentine's Day last year.

And this was a thesaurus, so it all made sense... except that now it was creepy and awkward.

Creepy and awkward for him, anyway. Wynter and the others had no idea what was going through his head or what had happened that morning, and they thought it was cute and clever. They admired the artistry, the layout, the fonts. He was a graphic designer, for fuck's sake, and it looked amazing.

She'd wanted a thesaurus and now she had one. But he'd given her something else today, something dark and painful and terrifying, although she'd never know it. Something so shameful he couldn't meet her eye as she thanked him.

He got up abruptly, volunteering to fetch water to wash the plates, thereby avoiding the hug she was about to give him.

Happy birthday, baby.

Double Trouble

They locked up their stuff, packed snacks and water, and spent most of the day hiking through the woods and along the river. Wynter wanted to identify the species of every fern and insect that caught her attention, and after about the fifth request Caleb relented and let her look up the information on his phone, struggling through the patchy reception. They all knew she was only doing it as an excuse to make frequent stops, to make sure Caleb didn't wear himself out after all that coughing in the night. Caleb, to his credit, played along.

Back at camp by mid-afternoon, they brought out a couple of guitars. Despite his rough night, Caleb seemed happy and relaxed, and that made him bearable. He hadn't ordered anyone to do anything for several hours. The hike had done him some good.

It left Indio wound tight as a spring.

He went through some slide techniques with Wynter and that was okay, that was safe. Then, while he and Jesse discussed the best way to make bread in the campfire, Wynter practiced a riff over and over until he snapped at her.

"Give it a rest."

She looked up, confused, and he instantly regretted his tone.

"Why don't you play some of *our* music?" he said with a tense smile.

Caleb tried to hand him the other guitar — they'd only brought along two — but he shook his head and went to the truck to get flour and maple syrup and other things for the bread. Jesse assessed the firewood situation, and Caleb played and sang with Wynter.

"That sounds lovely."

A couple of college-aged girls had appeared from the trees. The blonde who'd spoken had a European accent. Backpacking tourists seemed the likely story.

"Good afternoon, ladies." Jesse jumped up, casually running his hand through his hair in an attempt to calm the curls.

"We heard your music from our camp just down there," the girl said. Her friend hung back shyly. "I'm Idette and this is Anke."

Jesse introduced everyone and engaged them in a conversation about their trip so far. They were from Hamburg and were halfway through their tour, having already backpacked up the west coast. They'd hiked into the forest three nights ago.

"We haven't been able to start a campfire," Idette lamented. "Is the weather always this miserable in Washington?"

It was actually a pleasant day, after last night's rainstorm and a cold start. Damp, but the temperature had risen to the sixties. Jesse and Caleb commiserated with them, and Indio minded his own business. He realized he was sulking, which set off another wave of self-disgust. The girls were nice-looking, in that healthy freckly outdoorsy way, and even the shy one managed to start talking after Jesse made her laugh. Had his mood been better, he'd have competed with Jesse for their attention.

Wynter had closed down, which was her normal reaction to strangers. She set aside the guitar and came over to help him mix the bread. The girls eventually left, saying something about dropping by again or perhaps hiking with them tomorrow morning or some other vague invitation. Indio wasn't really listening.

Jesse came to check on the breadmaking. "You made it too sticky."

"We like it sticky," Wynter said defensively.

Jesse edged her out of the way and took over, adding more flour before turning the dough out to knead. He left it to rise, and enlisted Wynter's help with the rest of the food. Indio watched how Jesse put an arm over her shoulder as he explained the fermentation process in excruciating detail. They touched each other a lot, those two, from the way they would sit shoulder-to-shoulder to play a video game, or thump each other playfully when they were annoyed, or hug after an argument. Why did all that seem perfectly innocent, while Indio dreaded the idea of ever touching her again?

He convinced himself he was having a wild overreaction and for a few minutes it worked. Then he recalled that flash of pale skin and the physical pull of emotion that had sucked the breath from his chest, and he felt like a pervert all over again. Like that man who'd lured her to Oregon.

No, he wasn't like that man. He would never trick Wynter, or hurt her. And unlike *that* pervert, Indio could hardly breathe from the shame.

While he was at the truck fetching drinking water, Jesse came over.

"Bumped into those girls at the river. They invited us to their place after sunset to help with their fire. I said we'd go."

Indio couldn't imagine why the girls would want *him* there, as he hadn't spoken a word earlier. "Which brother are they expecting you to bring with you?"

"They didn't specify."

"Pretty sure they're expecting Caleb."

"*He's* not gonna come."

"Then you get double trouble. Knock yourself out."

"They have weed!" Jesse hissed.

"Wasn't there a rule about weed and national parks?"

"Strictly speaking, and federal law notwithstanding, Caleb said I couldn't bring it in, not that I couldn't *smoke* it."

Perhaps the company of women unrelated to him was a good idea. He agreed to go. Jesse had the decency to wait until Wynter went to bed, which was mercifully soon after darkness fell.

"Our neighbors asked me to visit and build them a fire," Jesse told Caleb, and then he just stood there like he was waiting for permission.

Caleb looked mildly surprised before nodding assent. Jesse grabbed the lighter fluid, and Indio jumped up and walked off with him. He sure as hell wasn't going to wait for permission.

Indio built the girls the perfect campfire while Jesse rolled their herb into perfect joints and asked them to speak in German. This progressed to asking them to say dirty things in German, and they obliged, although Jesse and Indio wouldn't have known the difference. It all sounded harsh and unsexy to Indio.

By the end of the first joint, Idette was pressed up against Jesse and playing with his curls. By the end of the second, they were kissing and tickling each other like they were very old friends. The other girl, Anke, was much harder work. She sat just close enough to Indio to reach the joint when it was passed, and just far enough away to project "hands off" signals. Or it might be shyness. Indio was debating how much work he should put into finding out.

"Your sister's voice is lovely," Anke said. "Do you sing or play?"

"No." He didn't want to give her the idea she could ask for a demonstration. "She got all the musical talent in this family."

Jesse came up for air, grinning, and didn't contradict him.

"What are your talents?" Anke said.

Indio took another look at her and figured maybe she wasn't as shy as she seemed. Yet her expression was open and innocent. Her mixed signals infuriated him, or would have, if he weren't high.

Jesse and Idette had their hands inside each other's clothes. It was time to establish one way or the other how this was going to end. If nothing else, it looked like the other couple wanted some privacy.

"You wanna go in, and we'll find out?" Indio asked Anke, jerking his thumb at the tent.

She shrugged like she could go either way. But she did go in, and he crawled after her. She became rather eager, and before long he realized it mattered that he'd come unprepared.

"Condom?" he said.

She pulled her backpack in from the annex and proceeded to unpack it, every single piece of clothing and food, a tangle of photographic equipment and maps, until she reached the bottom. It was all a bit comical. Despite the wait, that at least put him in a better mood.

She finally found a strip of condoms scrunched up inside a cosmetics pouch and handed one to him, as well as a travel-sized tube of lube. Indio didn't know they made those. She spent a few seconds yanking off his clothes, while leaving most of hers on. Given the choice Indio would've preferred it the other way around, but he was happy to let her take the lead. He just needed to lose himself in some other girl right now.

He remembered he hadn't showered in two days, and then realized she probably hadn't showered in three so it didn't matter. He'd managed to work open her shirt, so at least he had some flesh to amuse himself with.

With her friend and his brother only a few yards away, they made a valiant effort to keep the noises to a minimum. Meanwhile, from Jesse's side of camp came the sound of stoned laughter punctuated by stoned chortling.

When they were done, Indio waited until the other couple had calmed down a bit, got dressed, and went out. Jesse and Idette didn't seem to have progressed beyond necking and feeling each other up, although clearly they were having a great time of it.

"I'm heading back," Indio said.

Anke came out, her clothes all neatly straightened, and sat by the fire with a bottle of water. Jesse kissed Idette on the side of the neck, on that tendon under the ear where girls love it, and she giggled and let him go. Anke politely thanked Indio for building their fire.

"You didn't have to come back with me," Indio said when they were out of earshot. "I thought you'd want to use the tent."

"I don't have to screw every girl I meet, y'know. What's the point of sleeping with a girl you're never gonna see again?"

Indio said, dry as dust, "Can't think of one good reason."

Caleb was still up, tidying the campsite. They'd been gone a couple of hours. Jesse got the fire blazing again and they settled around it with the rest of the bread to snack on. It tasted even better than it had a few hours ago, when it had been pretty good.

Caleb would know they'd been smoking weed, of course. Indio couldn't tell if he was resigned to it, or annoyed, or didn't care in the slightest. Would Caleb have visited those girls if Wynter wasn't with them? Or if there had been three girls? He couldn't guess the answer. Caleb was Mr Super-Mature but he wasn't a puritan about sex. He hadn't gotten stoned in years, but he drank whiskey and beer for the buzz. In those ways he was like Indio, but everything tempered by self-control for the sake of his self-respect and his family.

As always, when he thought on his older brother, Indio admired everything about him in theory while hating the specific ways it had made his own life miserable.

"God, I need a hot shower," Jesse said.

"You sure do," Caleb said.

Indio was thinking of the riverbank, though his feelings were mercifully subdued now, because of the weed. He pushed it all aside and concentrated on the memory that had come back to him. "Was there a clawfoot bathtub in Harry's house in Anaconda?" he asked.

Caleb shook his head. "You're thinking of the house before that, in Missoula — the last house we lived in with Miriam. That bathroom had brass fittings and this beautiful black-and-white tiled floor. Other than that, the place was a dirt-cheap decrepit rental."

"I had this flashback earlier, of Jesse running around without diapers. I had to clean him up in that clawfoot bathtub."

"Gross," Jesse said, wiping breadcrumbs off his chin. "Do we have to talk about this?"

Indio ignored him. "Why was I cleaning him up? Helping out with Jesse was never my job."

"You don't remember that time Mom disappeared for a few days to go on a Light retreat?" Caleb said.

Indio shrugged.

"She was completely hooked on the Light by then. This was spring break, when I'd just turned nine, so you were six-and-a-half. She announced she was going away for three days, and I had to take care of the three of you. She must've spent half an hour showing Joy how to change Jesse's diapers."

"She left us all alone?" Jesse said.

"Not all alone," Caleb said. "You had me. Mom put two half-gallons of milk in the fridge and three boxes of mac n' cheese up on the counter, and some bananas and cookies and a box of cereal. Then she left."

Caleb leaned forward to poke at the fire. "I was terrified and excited all at once. I was the man of the house. I had no idea how to cook mac n' cheese. Read the box and figured it out. I did burn it a little on the first day. Joy changed those diapers about twice and gave up, so after that we let you run around in a t-shirt and whenever you looked like you were gonna go, we'd whisk you off to the bathroom. We watched TV and played outside, and I learned how to well-and-truly boss you guys around."

He gave Indio a sly look, as if to acknowledge that episode in their lives had been the start of it all.

"Then the fourth day rocked up, and Mom wasn't back. I remember looking at the empty counter, feeling this panic roll over me. Hoping another box of mac n' cheese would magically appear. We'd eaten everything. But I figured it out. We ate crackers and peanut butter for lunch. I boiled potatoes for dinner and we ate them with butter and salt. They were great. The next day, I shook cocoa powder into the last of the milk, put it in the blender to make it bubble up, and we had chocolate shakes for breakfast. You guys thought I was the best. I found a tin of soup and watered it down for lunch. She never kept a stock of food in the pantry because we moved around so much. That's all there was."

Now Caleb was frowning into the fire. Parts of what he said brought back more memories for Indio. He remembered those salted potatoes, and they *were* great.

"The rest of that day you kept coming up to me, each of you in turn, again and again, to tell me you were hungry. Like I was gonna wave a wand and fix it. You didn't ask where Mom was, or when she was coming home, or why she stayed away so long. You just looked at me and said, *I'm hungry.* And it sank in, then. These three little people relied on me. Five days earlier, I'd wanted that responsibility. Now I started to think she might never come back, so I had to fix the problem. That made me feel better – having made that decision. *Just fix the problem.* I put Joy in charge, and I went across to our neighbors' backyard. I knew they came home at 6:30. I knew I had twenty minutes. They had this huge doggie door but no dog. I squeezed through and raided their pantry, and we ate like kings.

"Next morning, Mom was home, asleep in her bed. She got up, went to the store, came back and made breakfast. And none of you had a single complaint about her absence, or about how I took care of you. Everything back to normal. When I told her she only left three boxes of mac n' cheese, she never asked me how I fed you. She said, *No, Caleb, I left five boxes.*"

Caleb's expression turned somber as he watched the fire.

"That's when I knew I couldn't trust her. I loved her, but I didn't trust her. Whenever she would go grocery shopping, I'd sneak into the pantry after she unpacked. I'd take a can of soup or a couple of granola bars, and hide them until I had quite a stash. Just in case she left us alone again. I hated that I stole from our neighbors — and I don't think they ever found out — but I didn't feel bad taking food from Mom. I didn't feel bad for not trusting her. I knew what I had to do, and I did it."

"Did she ever do that again?" Jesse said.

"Well, that was just a few months before she took us to Harry's and left us for good."

"But we got Harry instead, which was *awesome*," Indio said with a forced laugh. Caleb's story cut deep and he wasn't ready to admit it.

Caleb ignored his jibe and said, "Best thing about that week, Jess, is you were toilet trained by the end of it. You weren't even three years old."

"On that note," Jesse said, "I'm going to bed."

He stuck in his earbuds and went into the tent. Indio was trying to recall more memories from that house. As with all his childhood memories it was a painful, exhausting task. Caleb watched him from the other side of the fire and for a moment he felt completely exposed, like Caleb knew, somehow.

Which was impossible. It was his guilty conscience, and probably the weed, making him paranoid. Caleb didn't notice that sort of thing. He didn't care what you *felt* about anything, unless you made a big deal of it.

Wynter being the exception, of course. He'd been concerned about her feelings from day one.

"I need to give that money back to Harry," Caleb said suddenly.

So, *that* was the reason for his thoughtful expression.

"No fucking way," Indio said.

"I'll rent a place until I sort myself out. I'll take that job and save up a down payment by my own damn self."

"No. Whether you buy a derelict house on an unmanageable property, that's your decision. But you're keeping Harry's money. Jesus, he owes you *something* after all these years."

"He already gave me the house in Seattle."

"You took over the mortgage. Not the same thing."

"I *kicked him out* and took over the mortgage."

"Not one of us ever shed a tear over that." Was Caleb's pride going to screw everything up? Indio softened his tone, in the hope Caleb would acknowledge the emotional factors for once. "Give her the home she's fallen in love with. You've got the rest of your life to fix it up and make it pretty. Right now, whatever condition it's in, that's the home she needs."

"The home she *wants* includes you."

He shook his head and Caleb let it drop. No way could Indio live in the same house as Wynter. Not after the way his body had betrayed him this morning.

Looking back over the past year, he realized his heart had betrayed him well before that.

He said, "You know something? In that diner in Portland, after she ran away, she told me the same thing she told you. They made her feel like she didn't exist. She told me *you* made her feel like she existed. You're the center of her world, so make it count."

Trespassing

On the drive home, Jesse leaned forward from the back seat.

"Indio, turn off at Auburn. We'll show you the house. It's only half an hour east of here."

Jesse was well aware of Caleb's reluctance to proceed with the purchase. Getting Indio on-side might tip the balance — that eclectic house was an artist's dream.

"Please! Can we?" Wynter said, coming to the same conclusion. "Indio, you'll love it. It's like a gothic castle and a fairytale cottage had a baby."

"And then someone's grandma came in and wallpapered it," Jesse added.

Caleb had been quiet all morning, and silent on the drive, too. He glanced at Indio. "You're the driver. You're in charge of the vehicle and the route."

"Yesssss!" Wynter whisper-shouted.

"He won't get to see much more than a gate in a wall," Caleb pointed out.

Indio turned off and they traveled twenty miles along the tree-lined highway, climbing steadily to twelve hundred feet up Tiger Mountain.

"Take my picture!" Wynter handed Jesse her phone and he took a photo of her standing beside the board with the SOLD banner. He couldn't remember ever seeing her so excited.

"Nice wall," Indio said, bemused. There was nothing much to see.

Wynter raced over to the gate and rattled it in frustration — it was secured with a chain and padlock. "The house is empty, isn't it? Why can't we get in?"

"I don't get the keys for eight days," Caleb said. "It's not officially ours yet."

Jesse did a double-take. Caleb sure sounded like he was going ahead...

Wynter grinned at Caleb. "I knew it. I knew this was my forever home."

"You're buying it, then?" Jesse said, under his breath.

Caleb exchanged a quick look with Indio. "I was thinking last night about that house in Missoula. The last place we were all happy, I think. We played together. We pulled together when the mac n' cheese ran out. I took charge, but we *all* figured out how to cope. We can cope with this place, can't we?"

We, of course, didn't include Indio. He had his life in Portland, his great job, his band. And right now he was wandering off in the opposite direction, dragging his hand along the wall. Well, screw him. Jesse and Wynter and Caleb would make this place a home.

From the look on Caleb's face, he was thinking exactly the same thing. He said, "Thanks for putting up with me these last few months. I know it's been tough for you."

"For both of us," Jesse said, caught off-guard. "We coped."

It still made him nervous that Caleb was yet to regain his full health. And the smoke-induced cough played on Jesse's conscience because even though he'd told everyone what a dumb idea it was to go camping in March, he'd gone along with it in the end.

"This afternoon, when we get back, you're going to your doctor to get that cough checked out — right?"

Caleb nodded grimly. "I'll do that."

"Boost me over, Jesse," Wynter called out. "I'll open the side gate from the inside."

"It's probably padlocked, too."

Wynter pushed her face against the bars of the main gate to see. "I don't think so. I think it's just a bolt."

She started climbing the gate.

"Hey." Caleb rushed over to stop her. "You can't get over those spikes."

Wynter let go with a moan of frustration. "I'll go over the wall, then. Jesse!"

Jesse gave Caleb a helpless shrug and squatted so Wynter could climb on him. He stood, and she clambered up the wall, putting her feet on his shoulders to get the last few feet of height necessary. She sat on top of the wall and swung her legs over.

"That's a ten-foot drop," Caleb said, like he thought she wouldn't do it. Jesse thought she probably would — she wasn't the adventurous type, but today she was very determined.

"I climbed up here with a plan," she said.

Directly behind the wall, a thick tree branch extended at just the right height. She grabbed it and hitched herself off the wall. Once she was dangling from it, she was out of sight.

In the two seconds of silence that followed, Caleb muttered a curse. Then they heard her drop to the ground.

"You okay?" Caleb called.

She appeared at the gate. "Yes. There is a problem, though. The side gate is padlocked after all. I guess I'm stuck here."

"Help me over," Jesse said. "I'll send her back."

"Then you'll be stuck here," Wynter said.

"Throw over a sleeping bag and I'll camp out until you rescue me next week. I'd appreciate a roll of toilet paper, too, and the little shovel. Maybe some crackers."

Despite the jokes, they did have a bit of a problem on their hands.

Indio had returned to rattle the gates and examine the chain. "Wynter, see if the gate controls work."

Wynter found the control box and pressed a button. The gates swung open four inches until the chain stopped them. The motor whirred in protest. Indio worked the chain a little looser, and the gates opened a little more — enough that they could squeeze through.

"We did it!" Wynter grabbed Indio's hand and dragged him down the driveway.

"We're trespassing, hun," Caleb called after her, but Jesse could tell he was as pleased as the rest of them at finding a way in.

The driveway curved to the left around the trees, and the house came into view. Wynter had wanted this house because of the tower, and Jesse was already imagining what he was going to do with it. When they had that $150 million in December.

Indio loosened himself from Wynter's grip and stood facing the house with his arms folded, a few yards from the front door.

"You always said people shouldn't live in neat little boxes," Jesse said. "And *voilà*! Not one thing about this house is neat or boxy."

"Fixing up this place is gonna be a full-time gig," Indio told Caleb.

"That's why I got ten percent knocked off the asking price," Caleb said. "The builder's report lays out what needs to be done. I can do most of it myself." He shook his head. "Yeah, it's gonna take a few years."

"Come around the back," Wynter said.

She was already heading that way. The open area to the left of the house was an ugly concreted square with grass pushing up through the cracks. Judging by the oil spills and crooked carports, it had been used to park vehicles.

"Basketball court?" Indio suggested. He arched an eyebrow at Jesse to show what he thought of his own idea.

Beyond the concrete was the largest of the three sheds, this one in fairly good shape. They walked around the back of the house, Wynter explaining, for Indio's benefit, what room lay behind each window.

"There's two bedrooms here," she said, indicating the extension. "You and Jesse could have them."

"That's gonna be difficult because I live in Portland."

She pulled a face. "I'm gonna sleep in the main house, in the back room up there. And Caleb gets the master, although it doesn't have a tub."

"I don't take baths," Caleb said.

"Don't you want a bedroom in the tower?" Jesse asked her.

"No, Jesse, the tower will be our medieval castle. We can make those rooms into anything we want — a study, a library, a banquet room, a great hall for our hunting trophies, or fake trophies. We could put a pool table in there. The entire top floor could be a games room with a dungeon theme, full of torture devices like you wanted."

"Full of *what?*" Indio hissed at him.

Jesse *had* said something about a dungeon, and had perhaps laden it with sexual innuendo, but... "I think she misunderstood something," he said quickly.

Caleb was assessing the building and grounds with a careful eye, the massive scope of the project. "We won't have the money to do anything for a while."

"Wish I could show you the basement," Wynter told Indio, brushing off Caleb's hardcore practical considerations. "It's huge. We'll have a rehearsal space, a recording studio, and still have room for a den like that mansion on the lake. If we level this ground right here—" She spun on the spot in the backyard with her arms out. "—and tidy up the lawn, we could put in a mini-golf course."

"God, not mini-golf," Jesse said. Come June, if nothing else turned up, he was going to be working his *sixth* summer at the mini-golf.

"Okay, but a lawn would be nice. And there's a derelict trailer over there in the far field that we can renovate for camping."

They climbed onto the deck to look through the two French windows, one at each end.

"That's the family room," Wynter said, pointing to the rear set. "And this is the living room."

"What's the difference between a family room and a living room?" Indio asked.

"That one has a real fireplace, and this one has a pot-belly stove."

"I meant the functional difference."

"We sit around watching TV as a family in the family room," Jesse said, "and we... y'know, *live* in the living room. We drink our after-dinner coffee in there, and entertain guests before torturing them in the tower."

Jesse joined Indio sitting on the steps of the deck, and Caleb and Wynter leaned on the railings, and together they watched the sky darken over the distant forest.

"We could've driven into that forest and walked in from the back, couldn't we?" Indio said.

"I guess so," Caleb said. "We'd need GPS to make sure we ended up at the right house."

"Isn't Grandpa Fairn's Cavalier out there somewhere?"

"Yes!" Wynter cried. "Caleb, you have to tell me that story now."

Her enthusiasm encouraged him. "It was the year Harry moved us to Seattle — so, eleven years ago. Around Easter, he came here to find work and a place to live, and we stayed behind in Anaconda. I had to get your two brothers through the last few months of the semester."

"When you were only just fifteen?"

"Yup."

"He was used to being in charge by then," Jesse said. Caleb's campfire story had proven that, though Jesse didn't remember any part of that episode.

"Harry found a decent job — managing industrial cleaning crews — and bought the house at a time when banks would lend to anyone. In May, he calls and tells me to pack the rest of our stuff into the trunk of Grandpa's twenty-year-old Chevrolet Cavalier and join him. I didn't have a license yet, so I told him no way. I wasn't going to start my driving career with a misdemeanor on my record. Also, I was dating Suzanne Norris, my first girlfriend, so that was a huge incentive to delay leaving."

"I remember her," Jesse said. "Her braces made me want to have braces."

Indio said, "Her brother traded me his guitar for twenty bucks, a broken skateboard, and half a pack of Marlboro Reds stolen from Harry."

"So, Caleb, did you leave when Harry told you to?" Wynter asked.

"I did not. Harry was mad about it, but he was six hundred miles away. I'd been getting Grandpa out of the community home three times a week to supervise my driving. He slept through most of it, to be honest. Anyway, I had the hours, but I couldn't get my license until six months after my fifteenth birthday, the date I got my learner's permit. Next thing I know, our landlady's at the door telling me Harry called her to give notice, and we have to be out in two days. Harry thought that would force my hand. I gave her all the cash Harry had given me for groceries, and sold off the TV and stereo and most of our tools and furniture, to cover the rent until mid-July and to keep us going. Harry's plan was to abandon all that stuff, anything that didn't fit in the car."

"What a waste!"

"That's Harry for you. I put aside gas money for the trip, and spent the last of the cash on a beat-up trailer so we could bring our beds with us. I knew Harry would have us sleeping on the floor if I didn't bring those beds."

"You made a ramp so we could get the washer and dryer into the trailer, too," Indio said.

"We'd have been washing our clothes in the bathtub, otherwise."

"And we put my kick drum in there," Jesse said. "I had the rest of the kit on the back seat with me." Jesse had driven his brothers mad banging those drums in the back.

"The day arrived," Caleb continued. "I had Grandpa come to the testing station with me and got my license. That's also when I told him I was taking his car to Washington, which he wasn't happy about – not that he'd driven it much since he moved into the home. We never saw him again because he died a few months after we left Anaconda."

"What happened with the car?" Wynter asked.

"The damn car broke down about every hundred miles on the way to Seattle. Took us three days to make the trip. Somewhere near Tiger Mountain, I had to call Harry on a payphone to pick us up. He didn't want to pay for a tow truck, so I helped him push the car off the interstate, down a dirt road into the forest, and into a ditch. He took off the plates and we left it to rust."

Caleb contemplated the forest, shaking his head at the memory.

"That was an amazing trip," Indio said into the silence. "I got nothing but good memories of being on the road, sleeping under the stars, praying it didn't rain cuz we had no tarp on the trailer."

Jesse agreed. "We ate granola bars and frosted animal crackers and Hot Pockets the whole way."

The best part of the trip, though, was that the sense of adventure had eased the tension between his brothers, who at the time were barely speaking to each other.

"Glad you guys enjoyed it," Caleb muttered. "I was waiting to be pulled over and hauled off by Social Services. I wonder what became of Suzanne Norris. She was my first kiss. I wonder if her hair still smells like honey."

"Wherever she is," Wynter said, "she has nice straight teeth."

Caleb kissed the top of her head. "Come on, we should leave before a nosy neighbor calls the cops on us."

They started back, Wynter running on ahead and asking endless questions about the fences and trees and renovations, forcing Caleb to catch up so he could answer them.

"What d'you think?" Jesse asked Indio as they followed some distance behind. "Are you inspired to move onto the family estate?"

Indio pushed his hands into his pockets and glanced at Caleb and Wynter. "Don't keep asking. I can't be... this close right now."

"Why not? You and Caleb have been good since Christmas."

Indio winced, and Jesse's stomach sank. Something wasn't right — and Indio wasn't going to explain himself.

He left his brother to mope and caught up with the others on the driveway.

"So, Wyn, what will Xay think of this place?"

"We're more than a hundred miles from the ocean, so he'll probably hate it. But he loves snow, even though he's never seen it. We'll get snow up here, won't we?" she asked Caleb.

"Plenty of snow."

"Will you take responsibility for mowing that lawn?" Jesse asked her.

"With the ride-on in the shed? Yes!"

"Let's wait until you have your driver's license before you hop on a mower," Caleb said.

"Oh, yeah, and Svetlana might not approve. You said we could get goats to keep the grass down."

"I don't believe I did," Caleb said carefully.

She took his hand. "Thank you for my forever home. Today was the best day of my life."

"Really?" Caleb looked down at her. "We didn't do anything special."

"We didn't have to."

Jesse glanced over his shoulder, at Indio who was staring at his boots as he walked. He refused to let his brother's baffling mood bring him down.

"I do have some bad news," he said, flinging his arm over Wynter's shoulder. "New house — so we're gonna need a whole new set of house rules."

THE END

Wynter's story continues in *Lost Melodies*.

SONS OF THE GODS

Packed up tight in the old Cavalier
Brother at the wheel, crunching the gear
Shouting out orders like he owns the road
Trailer in tow, our whole life in that load
Little bro in back, banging on his drum
Leave him alone, he's just having fun
Six hundred miles to paradise – let's go!
That was never home anyway, y'know?

It's a long hard ride so take a seat
Fumes smell like freedom, the water is
    sweet
Running on hope as the miles creep by
Planning a clean slate under a new sky
When we grow up we'll get matching tat-
    toos
We are sons of the gods!
With nothing to lose

The kid is starving, top of every hour
Cute smile buys lunch, it's his super-
    power
Taking turns picking tunes on the radio
    dial
We'll be rockstars one day…
Could take a while
Big bro losing his cool under the hood
We're snapping legs off o' chairs for fire-
    wood
Sleeping under stars, guarded by trees
Look at that sunrise…
Hey, where are the keys?

It's a long hard ride so take a seat
Fumes smell like freedom, the water is
    sweet
Running on hope as the miles creep by
Planning a clean slate under a new sky
When we grow up we'll get matching tat-
    toos
We are sons of the gods!
With nothing to lose

I'll ride out the boss man
And the little one's beat
I'll write a fresh start
Where the crossroads meet
We're brothers by blood
We don't have to be friends
But let's hold on to this feeling
When the adventure ends

It's a long hard ride so take a seat
Fumes smell like freedom, the water is
    sweet
Running on hope as the miles creep by
Planning a clean slate under a new sky
When we grow up we'll get matching tat-
    toos
We are sons of the gods!
With nothing to lose

We are sons of the gods!
We'll get matching tattoos

Wondering what the songs sound like?
Visit the playlist on YouTube:
saracreasy.com/WWsongs

More about the Wynter Wild series

books2read.com/saracreasy

Sign up to my newsletter for updates
saracreasy.com

(Note: Mild spoilers in the following descriptions)

LITTLE SISTER SONG (Book 1)

She's about to turn their lives upside down...

On a freezing Seattle night, teenager Wynter shows up on Caleb's doorstep in shorts and sandals, seeking help. Seeking sanctuary. Claiming to be his sister.

Caleb — Coast Guard hero with the perfect girlfriend — practically raised his two younger brothers. He always plays by the rules. He always wins. His duty is clear: give his little sister a home.

Pancakes for breakfast, rock music in the basement... Wynter knows she belongs here.

But when the authorities step in, will Caleb realize he needs to bend the rules?

OUT OF TUNE (Book 2)

A family worth fighting for.

Struggling to find her place in the world, Wynter turns to the one thing she understands: the raw, rebellious power of music. Assembling a rock band of misfits teaches her more about life than any classroom.

Meanwhile, her brothers are dealing with her impossible foster mother, their father's wedding, and their troubled love lives.

When the world refuses to bend to Wynter's will, she takes drastic action to achieve the united family she longs for.

RHYTHM AND RHYME (Book 3)

Gone in a heartbeat...

After 8 months on the outside, Wynter is gaining confidence as she opens up to her brothers about her childhood, and even manipulates their useless father into stepping up at last.

Yet her sister Joy finds life away from the cult increasingly difficult. She reveals a secret about someone from Wynter's past, forever altering the family dynamics.

When a horrific accident threatens to tear everything apart, will Wynter's dreams of a happy family be destroyed?

LOST MELODIES (Book 4)

No secrets, no lies.

Wynter finally has the home she always dreamed of when Caleb buys a ramshackle farmhouse on the mountain. With Jesse to guide her at every step (even when she'd rather he didn't), she has her first boyfriend, her first job, and a new band at school.

But one of her brothers is hiding a shameful secret. Just when her hopes of a united family seem possible... he's gone. And one by one, her successes are falling apart.

Wynter feels strong enough to handle anything. So why is she retreating into fantasy?

DISTORTION (Book 5)

The past taints everything.

Wynter has a safe home with her family. Her music career is taking off with an overseas recording opportunity and a new all-girl rock band. Her brothers could use some help.

Indio returns from London and there's a room waiting for him if he'll take it, as well as an old flame in the wings. Caleb has a new chance at love, and Jesse continues his search for the perfect girl.

Out of the blue, their mother Miriam returns seeking reconciliation. Her years of neglect have distorted her children's chances for love and happiness.

Do they want closure on the past... or revenge?

NATURAL HARMONICS (Book 6)

When love makes sense...

Wynter and her brothers are ready to rock venues all over Seattle. No one can deny the natural chemistry Rule212 has on stage.

Behind the scenes there's tension brewing.

It's not easy to work, play, *and* live together. Family means everything to Wynter and she'll do whatever it takes to protect hers.

But something at the very heart of this family is ripping it apart.

No secrets or lies — it's one of Caleb's house rules. So why does everyone keep breaking it?

DUET (Book 7)

Two hearts yearning...

As Wynter and Jesse set out on an adventure-filled road trip to rescue Indio from drugs and despair, Caleb resolves to take control of his family as relationships deteriorate.

Meanwhile in Sacramento, Xay Morant lives with his ailing mother and a whole heap of bitterness over his year spent in the Light. He's doing okay, all things considered.

But he's never forgotten the girl from the ashram who used to climb through a hole in the fence in the dead of night to listen to rock songs on the radio with him...

MINOR KEY (Book 8)

A bittersweet tune...

Three years ago, Xay left Wynter to face the nightmare alone. She's been searching for him ever since — and now he's found her first.

Can he pick up the pieces of a past she's trying to forget?

As Wynter and her brothers prepare to head off on tour with their band Rule212, tragedy strikes this already wounded family.

Where will they find healing?

BROKEN STRINGS (Book 9)

Where does forgiveness begin?

A newcomer forces Wynter and her family to reassess their priorities. Meanwhile, her new bestie could be perfect for Jesse, and Xay has an opportunity to chase his rockstar dreams.

What could break the strings binding this family together?

Caleb, rock-solid, has never faltered... until now. To help him, Indio must find a way through his resentment. With Jesse hiding an impossible secret and Wynter forced into silent anguish, can they all pull together despite the pain?

THE BEAT GOES ON (Book 10)

Strong enough?

A mountain hideaway, an eccentric medieval tower, farm animals, homegrown veggies, and music all day long... Wynter's appearance in her brothers' lives rocked their world.

But something is holding them all back from the bright future they've worked so hard for.

The secret to unraveling the past lies in that off-the-grid commune in southern Arizona where, in her fourteenth year, Wynter met a free-spirited Aussie boy and his best friend who together changed her view of the world forever...

ECHOES (Book 11)

Sunshine and shadows

Wynter and her family have the chance of a lifetime to tour Australia. Every night they step on stage to make music, but offstage they're each dealing with their own challenges. As pressures build and nerves unravel, one of them suddenly vanishes without a trace.

As Wynter struggles to maintain faith in her family and in herself, a heartbreaking secret is sending echoes from the past...

TWELVE DAYS OF JESSEMAS (short story)

Christmas is Jesse's thing. Over the past four years it's become Wynter's thing, too. But these two siblings are growing up and growing apart. What happens when Jesse gets a better offer and decides not to come home for Christmas this year?

Short story sequel to the Wynter Wild series. Available at Amazon in Kindle Unlimited or ebook.

Wynter Wild Book Club Guide:
Q&As for discussion and analysis

A companion guide for fans of the series

Explore the Wynter Wild series like never before with 160 thought provoking questions — and all the answers! Dive into the themes, uncover the depths of the characters, and break down the twists and turns of Wynter's journey.

Perfect for sparking lively book club discussions or deepening your own understanding of her world, this guide offers fresh insights and new perspectives of the entire series.

Available at Amazon in Kindle Unlimited or ebook.
books2read.com/WWguide

Short stories

WAITING FOR HER (a Fairn boys story)

Caleb is 9 years old when Momma leaves him and his brothers at their estranged father's house for the summer. Navigating Dad's moods and covering for his neglect are more than any child should have to face, but Caleb knows it's his responsibility to step up and grow up.

With his mother gone, taking his twin sister with her, Indio is battling anger and grief as well as the nagging guilt it's all his fault. Resisting Caleb's newfound authority, struggling to keep little Jesse out of trouble, he never gives up hope. Momma will be home for his 7th birthday, won't she? All he has to do is wait for her.

FREE with newsletter sign-up.

THE FEAST THAT WASN'T (a Fairn boys story)

It's the Fairn boys' third Christmas alone with their father. The last two were miserable, but this year will be different — Harry's girlfriend has invited them to her family's Christmas Day feast! Jesse (5) anticipates gravy and pie, while Indio (9) is reluctant to get into the holiday spirit.

And Caleb (11) is learning that Harry's apathy could ruin everything. Can he inspire his brothers to make the most of the season and give them all a Christmas to remember?

SOUL SURVIVOR (a Fairn boys story)

For 12-year-old Caleb, structure is survival. Home life is ruled by his volatile father, Harry, whose drinking fuels unpredictable violence and bouts of emotional cruelty against his three sons. Amid the chaos, Caleb struggles to maintain his identity and integrity while keeping his brothers safe.

Harry's plans for a glorious Halloween bonfire could be the highlight of the year. But as the pyre rises, so does the threat to everything the brothers hold dear.

About the Author

Sara Creasy grew up in a tumbling-down Victorian house in the Midlands, UK, tapping out her first stories on a tiny blue typewriter. After moving to Melbourne as a teenager, her love of all things fantastical hooked her on escapist drama. Then she grew up—but she still plays with words.

Her debut novel *Song of Scarabaeus* (Harper Voyager, 2010) was nominated for the Philip K. Dick Award and the Aurealis Award. The sequel is *Children of Scarabaeus*.

The Wynter Wild series, starting with *Little Sister Song* (2019), is a contemporary drama featuring musical siblings from bad beginnings who are navigating together through unanticipated life changes, revived family secrets, and the many meanings of love.

Visit her website at saracreasy.com where you can sign up to her newsletter WildWord and stay informed about what she's writing next.

Follow Sara on Facebook:

facebook.com/saracreasywrites

Note from Sara: Honest reviews and word-of-mouth help indie authors like me get our books to readers who'll love our stories. If you'd like to leave a rating or review for my books on Amazon or Goodreads, scan these QR codes — and thank you!

Printed in Poland
by Amazon Fulfillment
Poland Sp. z o.o., Wrocław

62785918R00185